T0126464

The Other Irish Tradition

THE OTHER IRISH TRADITION

AN ANTHOLOGY

Edited by Rob Doyle

DALKEY ARCHIVE PRESS

Copyright © 2018 by Rob Doyle
First Dalkey Archive edition, 2018.

Library of Congress Cataloging-in-Publication Data
Identifiers: ISBN 978-1-94315-024-3
LC record available at https://catalog.loc.gov/

Please see the Rights and Permissions pages at the end of this volume
for individual credits.

www.dalkeyarchive.com
McLean, IL / Dublin

Printed on permanent/durable acid-free paper

Table of Contents

An Introduction

THE IMPORTANCE OF originality in art is not as self-evident as is sometimes assumed. Entire civilisations have risen and fallen for whom our modern insistence that artists must strive to innovate would have seemed bizarre. Ancient Egypt flourished for three thousand years during which the highest ambition of any painter was to imitate the style and techniques of his predecessors, iterating the glory of the Pharaohs and illustrating the soul's passage through the afterlife. Byzantium or ancient China likewise had no use for the notion that art must always be seeking new pathways, outdoing itself. Each of these eras had a style: rules were obeyed and techniques copied with the utmost fidelity so that painting and sculpture could reliably serve their religious, political, or magical functions (it was never *pure* art). Accomplishment lay in mastering these techniques, not in revolutionising them. The common factor among such eras is their stability: why indulge a mania to innovate when civilisation is ticking along just fine?

Here we are, however, in our twenty-first-century world where all is change. Rather than perpetuate itself over unvarying centuries, the scientific, capitalist West annihilates its belief systems and social modes with telescoping frequency. The familiar world becomes alien within a single lifespan. In such a world of relentless evolution, art is perpetually in danger of being outstripped, every 'realism' of describing a vanished reality. Just as capitalism erases difference to make way for a homogenous global culture, artistic traditions are swept aside, denounced as irrelevant almost as soon as they have established themselves. Today, Ezra Pound's modernist command to *Make it New!* sounds like nothing so much as a corporate slogan for

Apple or Huawei. Capitalism and the avant-garde check each other out from across the room, seeing much to admire.

While novelty for its own sake may in this sense be reactionary, the alternative—art that *doesn't* evolve, only reproduces the forms of the past—feels inadequate to the world we live in. The world keeps changing, and art and literature change with it. Some artists respond to our times with a countercultural insistence on difficulty and complexity; others mimic the distracted, neuronal velocity of contemporary life and achieve impact by striking on its own terms.

Artists generally don't view themselves as seeking to push their art forward, placing themselves on a progressive historical timeline. As Susan Sontag noted, the whole notion of the 'experimental artist' is misguided and philistine: it assumes a choice, whereas in reality each artist will simply create the work he or she is compelled to create, and either it will be original or it won't. Likewise, on the other side of the fence—that of the audience—the whole question of progressivism doesn't really come into it. We read Borges, say, and we are dazzled by the brilliant originality of expression, the ecstasy of invention, and the lightning-bolt realisation that *wow, writing can do that!* Such an author isn't 'experimenting'—he is simply being himself, fully and magnificently. Too vital and single-minded to be ghettoised by dreary labels—or by dull conventions—the best writers don't try to be original: they just figure out how to become what they are, and they *are* original.

These are uncertain times to be a writer, full of digital possibility on one hand and apocalyptic murmurings on the other. We consume and produce more text than ever, much of it the ephemera of 'content', but novels, short stories, and poetry collections are in a phase of existential doubt, questioning their relevance in an age of connectivity. Few would dispute that prose fiction, in particular, no longer occupies the prestigious, agenda-setting position at the centre of our culture that it once did.

The claim that the possibilities of the novel form have been used up is not much younger than the form itself. Back in 1880s Paris, the Goncourt brothers were already grumbling as much into their journal, declaring the death of the novel decades before the great leaps forward of modernism that marked the zenith of the form's artistic potency. In an essay titled 'An Introduction to a Variation', Milan Kundera writes:

> I often hear it said that the novel has exhausted all its possibilities. I have the opposite impression: during its 400-year history, the novel has missed many of its possibilities; it has left many great opportunities unexplored, many paths forgotten, calls unheard.

Some time after the dawn of the novel genre, and the exuberant, *avant-garde avant la lettre* inventions of Sterne, Rabelais, and Cervantes, the novel congealed—that is, what we believed and expected the novel to be congealed, with the result that it eventually became a rather staid, predictable genre. The Creative Writing MFAs proliferating across the Western world can seem like factories for these not-so-novel novels, with their narrative arcs, contraptions of plot, and dutiful focus on interpersonal relations. During the heyday of modernism the novel was still, as D. H. Lawrence had it, 'the one bright book of life'. Nowadays, perhaps it would be better to think of it as just one among a variety of imaginative long prose forms, discarding our assumption of its inherent primacy. Even if Kundera is right and the novel bears rich seams of untapped potential, it feels like a cultural *idée fixe*, an attitude in its afterlife, to maintain this belief in its centrality.

It is not only the books pages and publishers who uphold this increasingly suspect prejudice, but many writers too. There are those, for instance, who see their primary contribution as residing in their fiction, whereas no one else really sees it that way. Who now reads the novels that the aforementioned Susan Sontag considered the real meat of her work? It is her essays that have lasted. In our own time, Will Self makes frequent appearances in *The Guardian* to declaim the Death of the Novel, only to persist in writing novels that presumably not even he can be bothered to read. His true legacy may well turn out to be YouTube videos of his engaging public lectures. In the case of J. G. Ballard I would go one further: his novels and stories, I like to imagine, were the means by which Ballard established a platform to practise the art form at which he truly excelled: the interview. In Ballard's interviews, the startling ideas for which his fictions provide hulking vehicles are presented in their undiluted state. We needn't sit through hundreds of pages of gear-grinding plot development and shoddy characterisation to reach the point of fascination: the interviews are theory-fictions in which the climax runs right the way through.

A few years ago, David Shields chucked a Molotov cocktail into the stately parade of contemporary 'literary fiction' when he published his polemic *Reality Hunger*, attacking this zombie belief in the primacy of the novel and fiction itself. The wagon-circling that ensued seemed indicative of how forcefully his provocations had hit home. Never mind that Shields was essentially making the same case that Milan Kundera had made years earlier in *The Art of the Novel* and *Testaments Betrayed*, or that Geoff Dyer had in *Out of Sheer Rage*, or that Alain Robbe-Grillet had in *Towards a New Novel*—Shields's book felt timely and vital, an updating of the polemic for a device-cluttered, hyper-real age. Why drag out over three hundred plot-clogged pages what could be said in a brief, searing blast? Why assume people still mainly want to be *entertained* by books, when so much better entertainment exists elsewhere? Why the artifice, the time-wasting? Why pretend?

In the twenty-first century, Shields argued, we are so saturated with unreality and artifice that most prose fiction cannot muster the immediacy and force that would make it worth reading. Non-fiction, he pleaded, is no longer the deferential, lesser cousin to fiction and the novel. While the traditional novel of made-up characters and plot mechanics might once have been the best medium to convey ideas, nourish, and fascinate, that time is past.

Every decade has its David Shields. The novel has been declared dead so often that we should probably stop worrying and assume it is as invincible as James Bond. Some readers will always go back to novels for the kicks of narrative and atmosphere, and they will always find authors who excel in the genre. Nonetheless, Shields is probably right to suggest that the great era of fiction is behind us, and we inhabit the threshold of a period that will be defined by another kind of writing—a post-fictional New World awaiting its pioneers. Many of the most interesting books today are being written in the liminal territories beyond the novel's traditional heartland. These enticingly hard-to-categorise books dispense with the artifices of plot and character, and concern themselves more with lived experience than invented worlds. These are happy times for the mutant-novel, the book that doesn't fit in, the genre-bender. Or, to hijack a phrase from Captain Beefheart, the novel isn't dead—it just smells funny.

So where does Ireland stand in all of this? Irish writing, we are told, is currently enjoying a renaissance. It is certainly true that many notable writers have emerged in recent years. Strange, original talents are blossoming, wielding styles and perspectives as various as the inspirations they bring to bear on their work. Energetic independent presses have thrown down a challenge to the status quo, compelling mainstream publishers to up their game. Literary journals such as *The Dublin Review, Stinging Fly, Gorse, Penny Dreadful, Moth, Banshee, Tangerine* and others provide platforms both for emerging talents to cut their teeth, and better-known writers to road-test new material.

In short, things are looking up. Let's not forget that during the years of our economic boom, Ireland was something of a cultural wasteland, with few writers emerging from the aridity and a nostalgic conservatism in much of the fiction being published here. The result was that a generation of Irish readers felt alienated from the national literature, which seemed to speak to and from a different world than the one they knew. Not generally known for their high earnings, writers won little admiration amid the *nouvelle richesse* and property worship. In the decade that has elapsed since the economy crashed, however, there has been a recognition that it might after all be worthwhile to devote one's time and energy to the discipline of literature. Irish people are interested in their writers again.

The newer wave of Irish writers has helped to lift Irish writing from the parochialism and conservatism in which it was in danger of being submerged. There has long been a sense on this island that we know what a short story or a novel should look like and what rules it should obey; anything that deviates from the formula tends to be treated with suspicion. Certain conventions have persisted for so long and grown so pervasive that we can forget that conventions are all they are. Some examples: the automatic valorising of subtlety and understatement; a default tone of melancholy lyricism; a preference for fabulation over first-hand experience; a suspicion of work that traffics in ideas rather than interpersonal relations. Such modes are fine in and of themselves: indeed, they have produced some of our greatest writing, with many masters working within and renewing them.[1] A problem only arises for

---

1. Writing about the sixteenth-century German painter Matthias Grünewald, E. H. Gombrich reminds us that 'an artist can be very great indeed without being "progressive", because the greatness of art does not lie in new discoveries.'

readers of Irish literature who prefer something different, who are not especially moved by the art of understatement or the dissection of relationships and communities. The predominance of a certain type of fiction in Ireland (there are whole anthologies of work that doesn't veer from the formula) can leave such readers cold, inducing them to abandon Irish writing altogether in favour of freer, more daring international fare.

It is peculiar that Irish writing ever fell into the habit of stolid conventionalism. The writers to whom we pay the greatest amount of cultural lip service are those who were most flagrantly unconventional and inventive: James Joyce, Samuel Beckett, Flann O'Brien. As a nation we drop their names and celebrate our Bloomsdays and repeat how great they are, only to treat with suspicion contemporary writing that declines to play it safe, attempting to blaze new trails as O'Brien did with *At Swim-Two-Birds*, or Joyce with *Ulysses*. The exception proves the rule: Kevin Barry's 2015 novel, *Beatlebone*, included an intriguing, metafictional section in which the author airs his doubts around his material and the challenges it presents him with. The startlement with which this welcome if fairly modest deviation from the meat-and-two-veg, MFA-approved model was greeted, suggested how constrained we had grown in our expectations. What would ideally be a widespread, let's-try-it-and-see approach was in fact rare enough that even faint stirrings of it caused a sensation. (Three hundred years before Kevin Barry, Laurence Sterne was doing stuff like that in his sleep!) Meanwhile, writers are hailed as 'modernist' when they faithfully imitate the techniques that were modern a century ago. Mistaking a bygone generation's inventions for some perennial, Platonic form of originality, we applauded purveyors of a safely 'experimental' formula of the kind that Geoff Dyer has labelled 'secondhand avant-garde', while ignoring the new frontiers being staked out by writers unsatisfied with traditional fictive models.

Again, things are changing, and fast. In today's global, online culture, young Irish writers are as likely to be influenced by South American, Japanese, or Central European writers as they are by those who happen to have lived on the same rainy island as themselves. Among earlier generations, it was commonly said that James Joyce cast an inescapable shadow over the literary landscape. Today, it is as likely for Irish writers to feel similarly daunted by the legacies of, say, Roberto Bolaño or David Foster Wallace. Writers are no longer automatically influenced primarily by their national literature, because nationhood and nationality are no longer what they once were. Concomitantly, the Ireland of Frank O'Connor or Brian Friel probably looks as foreign as sub-Saharan Africa to today's younger Irish writers. An effect of living in the single-culture world, alienation from one's own history and race scrambles old assumptions and patterns of literary activity. On the plus side, a fecund internationalism nourishes the latest wave of Irish writing.

Rather than the priestly solemnity and social realism that gets so much of the airtime, it is arguably the playful, freewheeling inventiveness uniting Laurence Sterne and Flann O'Brien that represents the deeper identity of the Irish literary tradition. It is the modest aim of this anthology to provide a reminder that Irish writing has always had room for such playfulness and genre-rupturing freshness: for subversives, instinctual avant-gardists, and outsiders who strain at the leash of convention.

The Other Irish Tradition makes absolutely no claims to completeness. It should rather be seen as a sampler of work by authors celebrated or obscure who, at some point in their careers, or throughout them, were willing to try something new, roaming beyond the limits of convention to expand the territory of our literature. Presented chronologically, the selection places the colossal names of Irish experimental writing alongside work by lesser-known writers, and new talents that are striking out in strange, uncharted directions. Some pieces have been included not so much for their formal originality as for their subject matter, which strikes me as transgressive or unprecedented. There is an emphasis on satire, comedy, and what might accurately be called serious fun. I have also indulged an entirely personal preference for Ireland's tradition of writers in self-imposed exile, whose books are permeated by drift and expatriation, a cosmopolitanism rooted in an inescapably Irish sensibility.

I have tried to seek out as many female writers as possible who fit the aesthetic or set of aesthetics represented here: the male-heavy selection is due to the fact that Irish women writers weren't publishing as much formally daring work until quite recently. Undoubtedly this is due to the well-known historical factors of societal inequality. Any similar, hypothetical future volume covering the next fifty or hundred years will certainly allow for a neater split (*The Long Gaze Back* and *The Glass Shore*, two anthologies edited by Sinéad Gleeson, are a good starting point for anyone seeking out Irish women writers).

This anthology does not pretend to propose a new canon, but rather offers an alternative, refracted perspective on the canon that exists. The work collected in these pages will hopefully open up new ways of looking at Irish literature through the prism of its singular geniuses, obscure but startling talents, oddities, subversives, and transgressors. More than this, I hope that the anthology will simply provide plenty of rich and surprising reading. Combining familiar texts with lesser-known gems, a wander through its pages should enable readers to make exciting discoveries, reacquaint themselves with seminal works by master authors, and stimulate further reading from the deep and variegated pool of Irish literature.

The Other Irish Tradition

Jonathan Swift

A Modest Proposal for Preventing the Children of Poor People From Being a Burthen to Their Parents or Country, and for Making Them Beneficial to the Publick

WORLD-FAMOUS FOR HIS bitingly misanthropic novel *Gulliver's Travels*, the satirist and churchman Jonathan Swift was born in Dublin to an impoverished Anglo-Irish mother in 1667, his father having died two months earlier. Coming of age against a backdrop of political turmoil, Swift studied at Trinity College Dublin, completing a Master's degree before the college was closed as a consequence of the invasion of England by William of Orange. Swift moved to England for a decade, where he served as a trusted assistant to the statesman and essayist Sir William Temple. It was during his time in England, reading avidly from Temple's private library, that Swift began to write. His first major satirical work, *A Tale of a Tub*, was published in 1704. By then, Swift had trained for the priesthood and begun leading a small congregation in Dublin.

He returned to England to edit the Conservative government's newspaper, *The Examiner*. When it became clear that the Tories would soon lose power, he returned again to Ireland, where he became the dean of Saint Patrick's Cathedral in Dublin. Swift is buried in the grounds of the cathedral, next to his lifelong lover, Esther Johnson, whom he called 'Stella' and to whom the letters collected in *The Journal to Stella* are addressed.

Due to his prominence in public life, and the scathingly satirical nature of his work, Swift often wrote under pseudonyms. In his later years, his views on politics, society, and mankind itself grew increasingly black. His great work, *Gulliver's Travels*, was published in 1726 and has never been out of print since. As Swift wrote in a letter to his fellow satirist Alexander Pope, that work was meant 'to vex the world, not to divert it'. The short, notorious satirical work included here, 'A Modest Proposal for Preventing the Children of Poor People From Being a Burthen to Their Parents or Country, and for Making Them Beneficial to the Publick', was written and published anonymously in 1729. Following a stroke in 1742, and bereft after the death of his 'Stella' and numerous friends, Jonathan Swift died in 1745.

A Modest Proposal

For Preventing the Children of Poor People in Ireland from Being a Burthen to Their Parents or Country, and for Making Them Beneficial to the Publick

IT IS A MELANCHOLY object to those, who walk through this great town, or travel in the country, when they see the streets, the roads and the cabin-doors crowded with beggars of the female sex, followed by three, four, or six children, all in rags, and importuning every passenger for an alms. These mothers instead of being able to work for their honest livelihood, are forced to employ all their time in strolling to beg sustenance for their helpless infants who, as they grow up, either turn thieves for want of work, or leave their dear native country, to fight for the Pretender in Spain, or sell themselves to the Barbadoes.

I think it is agreed by all parties, that this prodigious number of children in the arms, or on the backs, or at the heels of their mothers, and frequently of their fathers, is, in the present deplorable state of the kingdom, a very great additional grievance; and therefore whoever could find out a fair, cheap and easy method of making these children sound and useful members of the common-wealth, would deserve so well of the publick, as to have his statue set up for a preserver of the nation.

But my intention is very far from being confined to provide only for the children of professed beggars: it is of a much greater extent, and shall take in the whole number of infants at a certain age, who are born of parents in effect as little able to support them, as those who demand our charity in the streets.

As to my own part, having turned my thoughts for many years, upon this important subject, and maturely weighed the several schemes of our projectors, I have always found them grossly mistaken in their computation. It is true, a child just dropt from its dam, may be supported by her milk, for a solar year, with little other nourishment: at most not above the value of two shillings, which the mother may certainly get, or the value in scraps, by her lawful occupation of begging; and it is exactly at one year old that I propose to provide for them in such a manner, as, instead of being a charge upon their parents, or the parish, or wanting food and raiment for the rest of their lives, they shall, on the contrary, contribute to the feeding, and partly to the cloathing of many thousands.

There is likewise another great advantage in my scheme, that it will prevent those voluntary abortions, and that horrid practice of women murdering their bastard children, alas! too frequent among us, sacrificing the poor innocent babes, I doubt, more to avoid the expence than the shame, which would move tears and pity in the most savage and inhuman breast.

The number of souls in this kingdom being usually reckoned one million and a half, of these I calculate there may be about two hundred thousand couple whose wives are breeders; from which number I subtract thirty thousand couple, who are able to maintain their own children, (although I apprehend there cannot be so many, under the present distresses of the kingdom) but this being granted, there will remain an hundred and seventy thousand breeders. I again subtract fifty thousand, for those women who miscarry, or whose children die by accident or disease within the year. There only remain an hundred and twenty thousand children of poor parents annually born. The question therefore is, How this number shall be reared, and provided for? which, as I have already said, under the present situation of affairs, is utterly impossible by all the methods hitherto proposed. For we can neither employ them in handicraft or agriculture; we neither build houses, (I mean in the country) nor cultivate land: they can very seldom pick up a livelihood by stealing till they arrive at six years old; except where they are of towardly parts, although I confess they learn the rudiments much earlier; during which time they can however be properly looked upon only as probationers: As I have been informed by a principal gentleman in the county of Cavan, who protested to me, that he never knew above one or two instances under the age of six, even in a part of the kingdom so renowned for the quickest proficiency in that art.

I am assured by our merchants, that a boy or a girl before twelve years old, is no saleable commodity, and even when they come to this age, they will not yield above three pounds, or three pounds and half a crown at most, on the exchange; which cannot turn to account either to the parents or kingdom, the charge of nutriments and rags having been at least four times that value.

I shall now therefore humbly propose my own thoughts, which I hope will not be liable to the least objection.

I have been assured by a very knowing American of my acquaintance in London, that a young healthy child well nursed, is, at a year old, a most delicious nourishing and wholesome food, whether stewed, roasted, baked, or boiled; and I make no doubt that it will equally serve in a fricasie, or a ragoust.

I do therefore humbly offer it to publick consideration that of the hundred and twenty thousand children, already computed, twenty thousand may be reserved for breed, whereof only one fourth part to be males; which is more than we allow to sheep, black cattle, or swine, and my reason is, that these children are seldom the fruits of marriage, a circumstance not much regarded by our savages, therefore, one male will be sufficient to serve four females. That the remaining hundred thousand may, at a year old, be offered in sale to the persons of quality and fortune, through the kingdom, always advising the mother to let them suck plentifully in the last month, so as to render them plump, and fat for a good table. A child will make two dishes at an entertainment for friends, and when the family dines alone, the fore or hind quarter will make a reasonable dish, and seasoned with a little pepper or salt, will be very good boiled on the fourth day, especially in winter.

I have reckoned upon a medium that a child just born will weigh twelve pounds and, in a solar year, if tolerably nursed, encreaseth to twenty-eight pounds.

I grant this food will be somewhat dear, and therefore very proper for landlords, who, as they have already devoured most of the parents, seem to have the best title to the children.

Infant's flesh will be in season throughout the year, but more plentiful in March, and a little before and after, for we are told by a grave author, an eminent French physician, that fish being a prolifick dyet, there are more children born in Roman Catholic countries about nine months after Lent, than at any other season: therefore, reckoning a year after Lent, the markets will be more glutted than usual, because the number of Popish infants is at least three to one in this kingdom, and therefore it will have one other collateral advantage, by lessening the number of Papists among us.

I have already computed the charge of nursing a beggar's child (in which list I reckon all cottagers, labourers, and four-fifths of the farmers) to be about two shillings per annum, rags included; and I believe no gentleman would repine to give ten shillings for the carcass of a good fat child, which, as I have said, will make four dishes of excellent nutritive meat, when he hath only some particular friend, or his own family to dine with him. Thus the esquire will learn to be a good landlord, and grow popular among his tenants, the mother will have eight shillings neat profit, and be fit for work till she produces another child.

Those who are more thrifty (as I must confess the times require) may flay the carcass; the skin of which, artificially dressed, will make admirable gloves for ladies and summer boots for fine gentlemen.

As to our city of Dublin, shambles may be appointed for this purpose, in the most convenient parts of it, and butchers we may be assured will not be wanting; although I rather recommend buying the children alive, and dressing them hot from the knife, as we do roasting-pigs.

A very worthy person, a true lover of his country, and whose virtues I highly esteem, was lately pleased in discoursing on this matter, to offer a refinement upon my scheme. He said, that many gentlemen of this kingdom having of late destroyed their deer, he conceived that the want of venison might be well supplied by the bodies of young lads and maidens, not exceeding fourteen years of age, nor under twelve; so great a number of both sexes in every country being now ready to starve for want of work and service: And these to be disposed of by their parents if alive, or otherwise by their nearest relations. But with due deference to so excellent a friend, and so deserving a patriot, I cannot be altogether in his sentiments: for as to the males, my American acquaintance assured me from frequent experience, that their flesh was generally tough and lean, like that of our school-boys, by continual exercise, and their taste disagreeable; and to fatten them, would not answer the charge. Then as to the females, it would, I think, with humble submission, be a loss to the publick, because they soon would become breeders themselves: And besides, it is not improbable that some scrupulous people might be apt to censure such a practice, (although indeed very unjustly) as a little bordering upon cruelty; which, I confess, hath always been with me, the strongest objection against any project, however well intended.

But in order to justify my friend, he confessed, that this expedient was put into his head by the famous Salmanaazor, a native of the island Formosa, who came from thence to London, above twenty years ago, and in conversation told my friend, that in his country when any young person happened to be put to death, the executioner sold the carcass to persons of quality as a prime dainty, and that, in his time, the body of a plump girl of fifteen, who was crucified for an attempt to poison the emperor, was sold to his Imperial Majesty's Prime Minister of the State, and other great mandarins of the court, in joints from the gibbet, at four hundred crowns. Neither indeed can I deny, that if the same use were made of several plump young girls in this town, who, without one single groat to their fortunes, cannot stir abroad without a chair, and appear at a play-house, and assemblies in foreign fineries, which they never will pay for; the kingdom would not be the worse.

Some persons of a desponding spirit are in great concern about that vast number of poor people, who are aged, diseased, or maimed; and I have been desired to employ my thoughts what course may be taken, to ease the nation of so grievous an incumbrance. But I am not in the least pain upon that matter, because it is very well known, that they are every day dying, and rotting, by cold, and famine, and filth, and vermin, as fast as can be reasonably expected. And as to the younger labourers, they are now in almost as hopeful a condition. They cannot get work, and consequently pine away for want of nourishment, to a degree, that if at any time they are accidentally hired to common labour, they have not strength to perform it, and thus the country and themselves are happily delivered from the evils to come.

I have too long digressed, and therefore shall return to my subject. I think the advantages by the proposal which I have made are obvious and many, as well as of the highest importance.

For first, as I have already observed, it would greatly lessen the number of Papists, with whom we are yearly overrun, being the principal breeders of the nation, as well as our most dangerous enemies, and who stay at home on purpose with a design to deliver the kingdom to the Pretender, hoping to take their advance by the absence of so many good Protestants, who have chosen rather to leave their country, than to stay at home, and pay tithes against their conscience, to an Episcopal curate.

Secondly, the poorer tenants will have something valuable of their own, which by law may be made liable to distress, and help to pay their landlord's rent, their corn and cattle being already seized, and money a thing unknown.

Thirdly, whereas the maintenance of an hundred thousand children, from two years old, and upwards, cannot be computed at less than ten shilling a piece per annum, the nation's stock will be thereby increased fifty thousand pounds per annum, besides the profit of a new dish, introduced to the tables of gentlemen of fortune in the kingdom, who have any refinement in taste, and the money will circulate among ourselves, the good being entirely of our own growth and manufacture.

Fourthly, the constant breeders, besides the gain of eight shillings sterling per annum, by the sale of their children, will be rid of the charge of maintaining them after the first year.

Fifthly, this food would likewise bring great customs to taverns, where the vintners will certainly be so prudent as to procure the best receipts for dressing it to perfection, and consequently have their houses frequented by all the fine gentlemen, who justly value themselves upon their knowledge in good eating, and a skilful cook, who understands how to oblige the guests, will contrive to make it as expensive as they please.

Sixthly, this would be a great inducement to marriage, which all wise nations have either encouraged by rewards, or enforced by laws and penalties. It would increase the care and tenderness of mothers towards their children, when they were sure of a settlement for life, to the poor babes, provided in some sort by the publick to their annual profit instead of expence; we should soon see an honest emulation among the married women, which of them could bring the fattest child to market; men would become as fond of their wives, during the time of their pregnancy, as they are now of their mares in foal, their cows in calf, or sows when they are ready to farrow, nor offer to beat or kick them (as it is too frequent a practice) for fear of a miscarriage.

Many other advantages might be enumerated: for instance, the addition of some thousand carcasses in our exportation of barreled beef: the propagation of swine's flesh, and improvement in the art of making good bacon, so much wanted among us by the great destruction of pigs, too frequent at our tables, which are no way comparable in taste, or magnificence, to a well-grown, fat yearling child, which roasted whole will make a considerable figure at a Lord Mayor's feast, or any other publick entertainment. But this, and many others, I omit, being studious of brevity.

Supposing that one thousand families in this city, would be constant customers for infants flesh, besides others who might have it at merry-meetings, particularly weddings and christenings; I compute that Dublin would take off annually about twenty thousand carcasses, and the rest of the kingdom (where probably they will be sold somewhat cheaper) the remaining eighty thousand.

I can think of no one objection that will possibly be raised against this proposal, unless it should be urged, that the number of people will thereby be much lessened in the kingdom. This I freely own, and 'twas indeed one principal design in offering it to the world. I desire the reader will observe, that I calculate my remedy for this one individual kingdom of Ireland, and for no other that ever was, is, or, I think, ever can be upon Earth. Therefore let no man talk to me of other expedients: of taxing our absentees at five shillings a pound; of using neither clothes nor household furniture, except what is of our own growth and manufacture; of utterly rejecting the materials and instruments that promote foreign luxury; of curing the expensiveness of pride, vanity, idleness and gaming in our women; of introducing a vein of parcimony, prudence and temperance; of learning to love our country, wherein we differ even from Laplanders, and the inhabitants of Topinamboo; of quitting our animosities and factions, nor act any longer like the Jews, who were murdering one another at the very moment their city was taken; of being a little cautious not to sell our country and consciences for nothing; of teaching landlords to have at least one degree of mercy towards their tenants. Lastly, of putting a spirit of honesty, industry and skill into our shop-keepers, who, if a resolution could now be taken to buy only our native goods, would immediately unite to cheat and exact upon us in the price, the measure, and the goodness, nor could ever yet be brought to make one fair proposal of just dealing, though often earnestly invited to it.

Therefore, I repeat, let no man talk to me of these and the like expedients, till he hath at least some glimpse of hope, that there will ever be some hearty and sincere attempt to put them in practice.

But as to my self, having been wearied out for many years with offering vain, idle, visionary thoughts, and at length utterly despairing of success, I fortunately fell upon this proposal, which, as it is wholly new, so it has something solid and real, of no expence and little trouble, full in our own power, and whereby we can incur no danger in disobliging England. For this kind of commodity will not bear exportation, the flesh being of too tender a consistence, to admit a long continuance in salt, although perhaps I could name a country, which would be glad to eat up our whole nation without it.

After all, I am not so violently bent upon my own opinion, as to reject any offer proposed by wise men, which shall be found equally innocent, cheap, easy and effectual. But before something of that kind shall be advanced in contradiction to my scheme, and offering a better, I desire the author or authors will be pleased maturely to consider two points. First, as things now stand, how they will be able to find food and raiment for one hundred thousand useless mouths and backs. And, secondly, there being a round million of creatures in human figure, throughout this kingdom, whose whole subsistence put into a common stock, would leave them in debt two million of pounds sterl. adding those, who are beggars by profession, to the bulk of farmers, cottagers and labourers, with their wives and children, who are beggars in effect; I desire those politicians who dislike my overture, and may perhaps be so bold to attempt an answer, that they will first ask the parents of these mortals, whether they would not at this day think it a great happiness to have been sold for food at a year old in the manner I prescribe, and thereby have avoided such a perpetual scene of misfortunes, as they have since gone thro', by the oppression of landlords, the impossibility of paying rent without money or trade, the want of common sustenance, with neither house nor clothes to cover them from inclemencies of weather, and the most inevitable prospect of entailing the like, or greater miseries upon their breed for ever.

I profess in the sincerity of my heart, that I have not the least personal interest in endeavouring to promote this necessary work, having no other motive than the publick good of my country, by advancing our trade, providing for infants, relieving the poor, and giving some pleasure to the rich. I have no children by which I can propose to get a single penny; the youngest being nine years old, and my wife past child-bearing.

Laurence Sterne

From *The Life & Opinions of Tristram Shandy, Gentleman*

TRISTRAM SHANDY, LAURENCE STERNE's madcap novel of errant genius, was not only written over the course of several years—1759 to 1767—it was read over as many years too: Sterne published the novel serially, in nine volumes across five instalments. *Tristram Shandy* has been called the 'undoubted progenitor of all avant-garde novels of our century' (by Italo Calvino), and 'the most put-down book in English literature' (by V. S. Pritchett, who also called Sterne a 'bore', and compared reading him to being 'cornered by some brilliant Irish drunk'). To the Czech author Milan Kundera, Sterne is a trailblazer to whom the novel 'means unlimited liberty of formal invention', and whose work represents one of literature's 'great lost opportunities', in that its key discovery—'the immense possibilities for playfulness inherent in the novel'—was generally not followed up.

Sterne was born in 1713 in Clonmel, County Tipperary, and spent much of his childhood travelling with his military father's regiment, gaining an affection for soldiers in the process. He was schooled in England and studied at Cambridge on a scholarship, thereafter becoming a vicar, the experience providing the material for Parson Yorick, a character in *Shandy*. Sterne married Elizabeth Lumley in 1741, and they had a daughter, Lydia. In 1759, he had his first taste of notoriety when his *chronique scandaleuse*, *A Political Romance*, was publicly burned due to its anticlerical flavour.

Following the death of his mother, and while his wife en-
dured a nervous breakdown, Sterne began work on *Tristram
Shandy*, claiming that every sentence of his buoyant novel
was 'written under the greatest heaviness of heart'. After self-
publishing the first two volumes to enormous success, Sterne
moved to 'Shandy Hall' in Coxwold, Yorkshire. In 1762 he
moved to France in search of respite from the lung ailment that
afflicted him for much of his life. His wife and child settled
there, but in 1767 Sterne returned to England, where he fell
for the much younger Eliza Draper. After his death, his body
was stolen by grave robbers and sold in Cambridge for use in
an anatomy lecture. When a medical student recognised the
corpse, it was returned to Coxwold. Sterne is buried there, near
to his 'Shandy Hall'.

Tristram Shandy is a novel in which the narrator, seeking to
tell the story of his life, never quite catches up with himself (he
only gets round to narrating his birth in the fourth volume).
Eventually he concedes that the telling of a life takes longer
than the living of it. The section presented here is from the first
volume.

From *The Life & Opinions of Tristram Shandy, Gentleman*

Chapter XI

YORICK WAS THIS PARSON'S name, and, what is very remarkable in it, (as appears from a most ancient account of the family, wrote upon strong vellum, and now in perfect preservation) it had been exactly so spelt for near—I was within an ace of saying nine hundred years;—but I would not shake my credit in telling an improbable truth, however indisputable in itself;—and therefore I shall content myself with only saying,—It had been exactly so spelt, without the least variation or transposition of a single letter, for I do not know how long; which is more than I would venture to say of one half of the best surnames in the kingdom; which, in a course of years, have generally undergone as many chops and changes as their owners.—Has this been owing to the pride, or to the shame of the respective proprietors?—In honest truth, I think, sometimes to the one, and sometimes to the other, just as the temptation has wrought. But a villainous affair it is, and will one day so blend and confound us all together, that no one shall be able to stand up and swear, 'That his own great grandfather was the man who did either this or that.'

    This evil had been sufficiently fenced against by the prudent care of the *Yorick's* family, and their religious preservation of these records I quote, which do farther inform us, That the family was originally of *Danish* extraction, and had been transplanted into *England* as early as in the reign of *Horwendillus*, king of *Denmark*, in whose court, it seems, an ancestor of this Mr. *Yorick's*, and from whom he was lineally descended, held a considerable post to the day of his death. Of what nature this considerable post was, this record saith not;—it only adds,

That, for near two centuries, it had been totally abolished, as altogether unnecessary, not only in that court, but in every other court of the Christian world.

It has often come into my head, that this post could be no other than that of the king's chief Jester;—and that *Hamlet's Yorick*, in our *Shakespeare*, many of whose plays, you know, are founded upon authenticated facts—was certainly the very man.

I have not the time to look into Saxo-Grammaticus's Danish history, to know the certainty of this;—but if you have leisure, and can easily get at the book, you may do it full as well yourself.

I had just time, in my travels through *Denmark* with *Mr. Noddy's* eldest son, whom, in the year 1741, I accompanied as governor, riding along with him at a prodigious rate thro' most parts of *Europe*, and of which original journey performed by us two, a most delectable narrative will be given in the progress of this work. I had just time, I say, and that was all, to prove the truth of an observation made by a long sojourner in that country;—namely, 'That nature was neither very lavish, nor was she very stingy in her gifts of genius and capacity to its inhabitants;—but, like a discreet parent, was moderately kind to them all; observing such an equal tenor in the distribution of her favours, as to bring them, in those points, pretty near to a level with each other; so that you will meet with few instances in that kingdom of refin'd parts; but a great deal of good plain houshold understanding amongst all ranks of people, of which every body has a share;' which is, I think, very right.

With us, you see, the case is quite different;—we are all ups and downs in this matter;—you are a great genius;—or 'tis fifty to one, Sir, you are a great dunce and a blockhead;—not that there is a total want of intermediate steps,—no,—we are not so irregular as that comes to;—but the two extremes are more common, and in a greater degree in this unsettled island, where nature, in her gifts and dispositions of this kind, is most whimsical and capricious; fortune herself not being more so in the bequest of her goods and chattels than she.

This is all that ever staggered my faith in regard to *Yorick's* extraction, who, by what I can remember of him, and by all the accounts I could ever get of him, seemed not to have had one single drop of *Danish* blood in his whole crasis; in nine hundred years, it might possibly have all run out:—I will not philosophize one moment with you about it; for happen how it would, the fact was this:—That instead of that cold phlegm and exact regularity of sense and humours, you would have look'd for, in one so extracted;—he was, on the contrary, as mercurial and sublimated a composition,—as heteroclite a creature in all his declensions;—with as much life and whim, and *gaieté de coeur* about him, as the kindliest climate could have engendered and put together. With all this sail, poor *Yorick* carried not one ounce of ballast; he was utterly unpractised in the world; and at the age of twenty-six, knew just about as well how to steer his course in it, as a romping, unsuspicious girl of thirteen: So that upon his first setting out, the brisk gale of his spirits, as you will imagine, ran him foul ten times in a day of somebody's tackling; and as the grave and more slow-paced were oftenest in his way,—you may likewise imagine, 'twas with such he had generally the ill luck to get the most entangled. For aught I know there might be some mixture of unlucky wit at the bottom of such *Fracas*:—For, to speak the truth, *Yorick* had an invincible dislike and opposition in his nature to gravity;—not to gravity as such;—for where gravity was wanted, he would be the most grave or serious of mortal men for days and weeks together;— but he was an enemy to the affectation of it, and declared open war against it, only as it appeared a cloak for ignorance, or for folly: and then, whenever it fell in his way, however sheltered and protected, he seldom gave it much quarter.

Sometimes, in his wild way of talking, he would say, That gravity was an errant scoundrel; and he would add,—of the most dangerous kind too,—because a sly one; and that, he verily believed, more honest, well-meaning people were bubbled out of their goods and money by it in one twelve-month, than by pocket-picking and shop-lifting in seven. In the naked temper which a merry heart discovered, he would say, there was no danger,—but to itself:—whereas the very essence of gravity was design, and consequently deceit;—'twas a taught trick to gain credit of the world for more sense and knowledge than a man was worth; and that, with all its pretensions,—it was no better, but often worse, than what a *French* wit had long ago defined it,—viz. '*A mysterious carriage of the body to cover the defects of the mind,*'—which definition of gravity, *Yorick*, with great imprudence, would say, deserved to be wrote in letters of gold.

But, in plain truth, he was a man unhackneyed and unpractised in the world, and was altogether as indiscreet and foolish on every other subject of discourse where policy is wont to impress restraint. *Yorick* had no impression but one, and that was what arose from the nature of the deed spoken of; which impression he would usually translate into plain *English* without any periphrasis,—and too oft without much distinction of either personage, time, or place;—so that when mention was made of a pitiful or an ungenerous proceeding,—he never gave himself a moment's time to reflect who was the Hero of the piece,—what his station,—or how far he had power to hurt him hereafter;—but if it was a dirty action,—without more ado,—The man was a dirty fellow,—and so on:—And as his comments had usually the ill fate to be terminated either in a *bon mot*, or to be enliven'd throughout with some drollery or humour of expression, it gave wings to *Yorick's* indiscretion. In a word, tho' he never sought, yet, at the same time, as he seldom shunn'd occasions of saying what came uppermost, and without much ceremony;—he had but too many temptations in life, of scattering his wit and his humour,—his gibes and his jests about him.—They were not lost for want of gathering.

What were the consequences, and what was *Yorick's* catastrophe thereupon, you will read in the next chapter.

Chapter XII

The *Mortgager* and *Mortgagée* differ the one from the other, not more in length of purse, than the *Jester* and *Jestée* do, in that of memory. But in this the comparison between them runs, as the scholiasts call it, upon all-four; which, by the bye, is upon one or two legs more, than some of the best of *Homer*'s can pretend to;—namely, That the one raises a sum, and the other a laugh at your expence, and thinks no more about it. Interest, however, still runs on in both cases;—the periodical or accidental payments of it, just serving to keep the memory of the affair alive; till, at length, in some evil hour—pop comes the creditor upon each, and by demanding principal upon the spot, together with full interest to the very day, makes them both feel the full extent of their obligations.

As the reader (for I hate your *ifs*) has a thorough knowledge of human nature, I need not say more to satisfy him, that my Hero could not go on at this rate without some slight experience of these incidental mementos. To speak the truth, he had wantonly involved himself in a multitude of small book-debts of this stamp, which, notwithstanding *Eugenius*'s frequent advice, he too much disregarded; thinking, that as not one of them was contracted thro' any malignancy;—but, on the contrary, from an honesty of mind, and a mere jocundity of humour, they would all of them be cross'd out in course.

Eugenius would never admit this; and would often tell him, that one day or other he would certainly be reckoned with; and he would often add, in an accent of sorrowful apprehension,—to the uttermost mite. To which *Yorick*, with his usual carelessness of heart, would as often answer with a pshaw!—and if the subject was started in the fields,—with a hop, skip, and a jump at the end of it; but if close pent up in the social chimney-corner, where the culprit was barricado'd in, with a table and a couple of arm-chairs, and could not so readily fly off in a tangent,—*Eugenius* would then go on with his lecture upon discretion in words to this purpose, though somewhat better put together.

Trust me, dear *Yorick*, this unwary pleasantry of thine will sooner or later bring thee into scrapes and difficulties, which no after-wit can extricate thee out of.—In these sallies, too oft, I see, it happens, that a person laugh'd at, considers himself in the light of a person injured, with all the rights of such a situation belonging to him; and when thou viewest him in that light too, and reckonest up his friends, his family, his kindred and allies,—and musterest up with them the many recruits which will list under him from a sense of common danger;—'tis no extravagant arithmetic to say, that for every ten jokes,—thou hast got an hundred enemies; and till thou hast gone on, and raised a swarm of wasps about thine ears, and art half stung to death by them, thou wilt never be convinced it is so.

I cannot suspect it in the man whom I esteem, that there is the least spur from spleen or malevolence of intent in these sallies.—I believe and know them to be truly honest and sportive:—But consider, my dear lad, that fools cannot distinguish this,—and that knaves will not; and thou knowest not what it is, either to provoke the one, or to make merry with the other,—whenever they associate for mutual defence, depend upon it, they will carry on the war in such a manner against thee, my dear friend, as to make thee heartily sick of it, and of thy life too.

REVENGE from some baneful corner shall level a tale of dishonour at thee, which no innocence of heart or integrity of conduct shall set right.—The fortunes of thy house shall totter,—thy character, which led the way to them, shall bleed on every side of it,—thy faith questioned,—thy works belied,—thy wit forgotten,—thy learning trampled on. To wind up the last scene of thy tragedy, CRUELTY and COWARDICE, twin ruffians, hired and set on by MALICE in the dark, shall strike together at all thy infirmities and mistakes:—The best of us, my dear lad, lye open there,—and trust me,—trust me, *Yorick*, *when to gratify a private appetite, it is once resolved upon, that an innocent and an helpless creature shall be sacrificed, 'tis an easy matter to pick up sticks enough from any thicket where it has strayed, to make a fire to offer it up with.*

Yorick scarce ever heard this sad vaticination of his destiny read over to him, but with a tear stealing from his eye, and a promissory look attending it, that he was resolved, for the time to come, to ride his tit with more sobriety.—But, alas, too late!—a grand confederacy with **** and **** at the head of it, was form'd before the first prediction of it.—The whole plan of the attack, just as *Eugenius* had foreboded, was put in execution all at once,—with so little mercy on the side of the allies,—and so little suspicion in *Yorick*, of what was carrying on against him,—that when he thought, good easy man! full surely preferment was o'ripening,—they had smote his root, and then he fell, as many a worthy man had fallen before him.

Yorick, however, fought it out with all imaginable gallantry for some time; till, over-power'd by numbers, and worn out at length by the calamities of the war,—but more so, by the ungenerous manner in which it was carried on,—he threw down the sword; and though he kept up his spirits in appearance to the last, he died, nevertheless, as was generally thought, quite broken-hearted.

What inclined *Eugenius* to the same opinion was as follows:

A few hours before *Yorick* breath'd his last, *Eugenius* stept in with an intent to take his last sight and last farewell of him: Upon his drawing *Yorick's* curtain, and asking how he felt himself, *Yorick* looking up in his face took hold of his hand, —and after thanking him for the many tokens of his friendship to him, for which, he said, if it was their fate to meet hereafter, —he would thank him again and again,—he told him, he was within a few hours of giving his enemies the slip for ever.—I hope not, answered *Eugenius*, with tears trickling down his cheeks, and with the tenderest tone that ever man spoke,—I hope not, *Yorick*, said he.—*Yorick* replied, with a look up, and a gentle squeeze of *Eugenius*'s hand, and that was all,—but it cut *Eugenius* to his heart.—Come,—come, *Yorick*, quoth *Eugenius*, wiping his eyes, and summoning up the man within him,—my dear lad, be comforted,—let not all thy spirits and fortitude forsake thee at this crisis when thou most wants them;—who knows what resources are in store, and what the power of God may yet do for thee?—*Yorick* laid his hand upon his heart, and gently shook his head;—For my part, continued *Eugenius*, crying bitterly as he uttered the words,—I declare I know not, *Yorick*, how to part with thee, and would gladly flatter my hopes, added *Eugenius*, cheering up his voice, that there is still enough left of thee to make a bishop—and that I may live to see it.—I beseech thee, *Eugenius*, quoth *Yorick*, taking off his night-cap as well as he could with his left hand,—his right being still grasped close in that of *Eugenius*,—I beseech thee to take a view of my head.—I see nothing that ails it, replied *Eugenius*. Then, alas! my friend, said *Yorick*, let me tell you, that 'tis so bruised and mis-shapen'd with the blows which **** and ****, and some others have so unhandsomely given me in the dark, that I might say with Sancho Pança, that should I recover, and 'Mitres thereupon be suffered to rain down from heaven as thick as hail, not one of them would fit it.'—*Yorick*'s last breath was hanging upon his trembling lips ready to depart as he uttered this;—yet still it was uttered with something of a *cervantick* tone;—and as he spoke it, *Eugenius* could perceive a stream of lambent fire lighted up for a moment in his eyes;—faint picture of those flashes of his spirit, which (as *Shakespeare* said of his ancestor) were wont to set the table in a roar!

Eugenius was convinced from this, that the heart of his friend was broke; he squeez'd his hand,—and then walk'd softly out of the room, weeping as he walk'd. *Yorick* followed *Eugenius* with his eyes to the door,—he then closed them—and never opened them more.

He lies buried in the corner of his church-yard, in the parish of ——, under a plain marble slab, which his friend Eugenius, by leave of his executors, laid upon his grave, with no more than these three words of inscription, serving both for his epitaph and elegy.

Alas, poor *YORICK*!

Ten times a day has *Yorick*'s ghost the consolation to hear his monumental inscription read over with such a variety of plaintive tones, as denote a general pity and esteem for him;—a foot-way crossing the church-yard close by the side of his grave,—not a passenger goes by without stopping to cast a look upon it,—and sighing as he walks on,

Alas, poor Yorick!

Chapter XIII

It is so long since the reader of this rhapsodical work has been parted from the midwife, that it is high time to mention her again to him, merely to put him in mind that there is such a body still in the world, and whom, upon the best judgment I can form upon my own plan at present, I am going to introduce to him for good and all: But as fresh matter may be started, and much unexpected business fall out betwixt the reader and myself, which may require immediate dispatch;—'twas right to take care that the poor woman should not be lost in the mean time;—because when she is wanted, we can no way do without her.

I think I told you that this good woman was a person of no small note and consequence throughout our whole village and township;—that her fame had spread itself to the very out-edge and circumference of that circle of importance, of which kind every soul living, whether he has a shirt to his back or no,—has one surrounding him;—which said circle, by the way, whenever 'tis said that such a one is of great weight and importance in the *world*,—I desire may be enlarged or contracted in your worship's fancy, in a compound-ratio of the station, profession, knowledge, abilities, height and depth (measuring both ways) of the personage brought before you.

In the present case, if I remember, I fixed it about four or five miles, which not only comprehended the whole parish, but extended itself to two or three of the adjacent hamlets in the skirts of the next parish; which made a considerable thing of it. I must add, That she was, moreover, very well looked on at one large grange-house, and some other odd houses and farms within two or three miles, as I said, from the smoke of her own chimney:—But I must here, once for all, inform you, that all this will be more exactly delineated and explain'd in a map, now in the hands of the engraver, which, with many other pieces and developements of this work, will be added to the end of the twentieth volume,—not to swell the work,—I detest the thought of such a thing;—but by way of commentary, scholium, illustration, and key to such passages, incidents, or inuendos as shall be thought to be either of private interpretation, or of dark or doubtful meaning, after my life and my opinions shall have been read over, (now don't forget the meaning of the word) by all the *world*;—which, betwixt you and me, and in spite of all the gentlemen-reviewers in *Great-Britain*, and of all that their worships shall undertake to write or say to the contrary,—I am determined shall be the case.—I need not tell your worship, that all this is spoke in confidence.

Chapter XIV

Upon looking into my mother's marriage-settlement, in order to satisfy myself and reader in a point necessary to be clear'd up, before we could proceed any farther in this history;—I had the good fortune to pop upon the very thing I wanted before I had read a day and a half straightforwards,—it might have taken me up a month;—which shews plainly, that when a man sits down to write a history,—tho' it be but the history of *Jack Hickathrift* or *Tom Thumb*, he knows no more than his heels what lets and confounded hindrances he is to meet with in his way,—or what a dance he may be led, by one excursion or another, before all is over. Could a historiographer drive on his history, as a muleteer drives on his mule,—straight forward;—for instance, from *Rome* all the way to *Loretto*, without ever once turning his head aside, either to the right hand or to the left,—he might venture to fore-tell you to an hour when he should get to his journey's end;—but the thing is, morally speaking, impossible: For, if he is a man of the least spirit, he will have fifty deviations from a straight line to make with this or that party as he goes along, which he can no ways avoid. He will have views and prospects to himself perpetu-ally soliciting his eye, which he can no more help standing still to look at than he can fly; he will moreover have various

Accounts to reconcile:

Anecdotes to pick up:

Inscriptions to make out:

Stories to weave in:

Traditions to sift:

Personages to call upon:

Panegyricks to paste up at this door:

Pasquinades at that:—All which both the man and his mule are quite exempt from. To sum up all; there are archives at every stage to be look'd into, and rolls, records, documents, and endless genealogies, which justice ever and anon calls him back to stay the reading of:—In short there is no end of it;—for my own part, I declare I have been at it these six weeks, making all the speed I possibly could,—and am not yet born:—I have just been able, and that's all, to tell you *when* it happen'd, but not *how*;—so that you see the thing is yet far from being accomplished.

These unforeseen stoppages, which I own I had no conception of when I first set out;—but which, I am convinced now, will rather increase than diminish as I advance,—have struck out a hint which I am resolved to follow;—and that is,—not to be in a hurry;—but to go on leisurely, writing and publishing two volumes of my life every year;—which, if I am suffered to go on quietly, and can make a tolerable bargain with my bookseller, I shall continue to do as long as I live.

Chapter XV

The article in my mother's marriage-settlement, which I told the reader I was at the pains to search for, and which, now that I have found it, I think proper to lay before him,—is so much more fully express'd in the deed itself, than ever I can pretend to do it, that it would be barbarity to take it out of the lawyer's hand:—It is as follows.

'And this Indenture further witnesseth, That the said *Walter Shandy*, merchant, in consideration of the said intended marriage to be had, and, by God's blessing, to be well and truly solemnized and consummated between the said *Walter Shandy* and *Elizabeth Mollineux* aforesaid, and divers other good and valuable causes and considerations him thereunto specially moving,—doth grant, covenant, condescend, consent, conclude, bargain, and fully agree to and with *John Dixon*, and *James Turner*, Esqrs. the above-named Trustees, &c. &c.—to wit,—That in case it should hereafter so fall out, chance, happen, or otherwise come to pass,—That the said *Walter Shandy*, merchant, shall have left off business before the time or times, that the said *Elizabeth Mollineux* shall, according to the course of nature, or otherwise, have left off bearing and bringing forth children;—and that, in consequence of the said *Walter Shandy* having so left off business, he shall in despight, and against the free-will, consent, and good-liking of the said *Elizabeth Mollineux*,—make a departure from the city of *London*, in order to retire to, and dwell upon, his estate at Shandy Hall, in the county of ——, or at any other country-seat, castle, hall, mansion-house, messuage or grainge-house, now purchased, or hereafter to be purchased, or upon any part or parcel thereof:—That then, and as often as the said *Elizabeth Mollineux* shall happen to be enceint with child or children severally and lawfully begot, or to be begotten, upon the body of the said *Elizabeth Mollineux* during her said coverture,—he the said *Walter Shandy* shall, at his own proper cost and charges, and out of his own proper monies, upon good and reasonable notice, which is hereby agreed to be within six weeks of her the said *Elizabeth Mollineux's* full reckoning, or time of supposed and computed delivery,—pay, or cause to be paid, the sum of one hundred and twenty pounds of good and lawful money, to *John Dixon*, and *James Turner*, Esqrs. or assigns,—upon TRUST and confidence, and for and unto the use and uses, intent, end, and purpose following:—𝕿𝖍𝖆𝖙 𝖎𝖘 𝖙𝖔 𝖘𝖆𝖞,—That the said sum of one hundred and twenty pounds shall be paid into the hands of the said *Elizabeth Mollineux*, or to be otherwise applied by them the said trustees, for the well and truly hiring of one coach, with able and sufficient horses, to carry and convey the body of the said *Elizabeth Mollineux*, and the child or children which she shall be then and there enceint and pregnant with,—unto the city of *London*; and for the further paying and defraying of all other incidental costs, charges, and expences whatsoever,—in and about, and for, and relating to, her said intended delivery and lying-in, in the said city or suburbs thereof. And that the said *Elizabeth Mollineux* shall and may, from time to time, and at all such time and times as are here covenanted and agreed upon,—peaceably and quietly hire the said coach and horses, and have free ingress, egress, and regress throughout her journey, in and from the said coach, according to the tenor, true intent, and meaning of these presents, without any let, suit, trouble, disturbance, molestation, discharge, hinderance, forfeiture, eviction, vexation, interruption, or incumbrance whatsoever.—And that it shall moreover be lawful to and for the said *Elizabeth Mollineux*, from time to time, and as oft or often as she shall well and truly be advanced in her said pregnancy, to the time heretofore stipulated and agreed upon,—to live and reside in such place or places, and in such family or families, and with such relations, friends, and other persons within the said city of *London*, as she, at her own will and pleasure, notwithstanding her present coverture, and as if she was a *femme sole* and unmarried,—shall think fit.—And this Indenture further witnesseth, That for the more effectually carrying of the said covenant into execution, the said *Walter Shandy*, merchant, doth hereby grant, bargain, sell, release, and confirm unto the said *John Dixon*, and *James Turner*, Esqrs. their heirs, executors, and assigns, in their actual possession now being, by virtue of an indenture of bargain and sale for a year to them the said *John Dixon*, and *James Turner*, Esqrs. by him the said *Walter Shandy*, merchant, thereof made; which said bargain and sale for a year, bears date the day next before the date of these presents, and by force and virtue of the statute for transferring of uses into possession,—All that the manor and lordship of *Shandy*, in the county of ——, with all the rights, members, and appurtenances thereof; and all and every the messuages, houses, buildings, barns, stables, orchards, gardens, backsides, tofts, crofts, garths, cottages, lands, meadows, feedings, pastures, marshes, commons, woods, underwoods, drains, fisheries, waters, and water-courses;—together with all rents, reversions, services, annuities, fee-farms, knights fees, views of frank-pledge, escheats, reliefs, mines, quarries, goods and chattels of felons and fugitives, felons of themselves, and put in exigent, deodands, free warrens, and all other royalties and seigniories, rights and jurisdictions, privileges and hereditaments whatsoever.—And also the advowson, donation, presentation, and free disposition of the rectory or parsonage of *Shandy* aforesaid, and all and every the tenths, tythes, glebe-lands.'—In three words,—'My mother was to lay in (if she chose it) in *London*.'

But in order to put a stop to the practice of any unfair play on the part of my mother, which a marriage-article of this nature too manifestly opened a door to, and which indeed had never been thought of at all, but for my uncle *Toby Shandy*;—a clause was added in security of my father which was this:—'That in case my mother hereafter should, at any time, put my father to the trouble and expence of a London journey, upon false cries and tokens;— that for every such instance, she should forfeit all the right and title which the covenant gave her to the next turn;—but to no more,—and so on, *toties quoties*, in as effectual a manner, as if such a covenant betwixt them had not been made.'—This, by the way, was no more than what was reasonable;—and yet, as reasonable as it was, I have ever thought it hard that the whole weight of the article should have fallen entirely, as it did, upon myself.

But I was begot and born to misfortunes;—for my poor mother, whether it was wind or water—or a compound of both,—or neither;—or whether it was simply the mere swell of imagination and fancy in her;—or how far a strong wish and desire to have it so, might mislead her judgment;—in short, whether she was deceived or deceiving in this matter, it no way becomes me to decide. The fact was this, That in the latter end of *September* 1717, which was the year before I was born, my mother having carried my father up to town much against the grain,—he peremptorily insisted upon the clause;—so that I was doom'd, by marriage articles, to have my nose squeez'd as flat to my face, as if the destinies had actually spun me without one.

How this event came about,—and what a train of vexatious disappointments, in one stage or other of my life, have pursued me from the mere loss, or rather compression, of this one single member,—shall be laid before the reader all in due time.

James Clarence Mangan

A Sixty-Drop Dose of Laudanum

A NOTABLE ECCENTRIC, and an anomaly of Irish literature, James Clarence Mangan's greatness was recognised by later colossi, including James Joyce (who was otherwise chary of acknowledging Irish influences), and William Butler Yeats, who claimed that, 'To the soul of Clarence Mangan was tied the burning ribbon of Genius'. The influence of Clarence Mangan's life and work has also been acknowledged by Shane MacGowan, singer and songwriter with The Pogues.

Born in 1803, Clarence Mangan lived a grim and relatively short life, dying of cholera in 1849 after a spiral into alcoholism, depression, and malnutrition. It is said that only two people attended his funeral. Unlike many other notable Irish writers, he was not Anglo-Irish, but a grocer's son, born in Dublin and educated by the Jesuits. Known primarily as a poet, Mangan published early work in the *Dublin University Magazine*. Later, growing increasingly patriotic after the outbreak of the Great Famine in 1845, he wrote for the nationalist publications *The Nation* and *The United Irishmen*. A mercurial, flamboyant, and somewhat camp figure, Mangan's literary output was complex and various, including well-known nationalist poems such as 'Dark Rosaleen', along with more enigmatic work that prefigured French symbolism and other modernist advances. Having taught himself German, Mangan began publishing translations of Goethe, and then translated poems from Irish, German, and various Eastern languages. His interpretations were so free, however, that many of these 'translations' are more accurately accredited to Mangan as original works. It is likely that he did not even know some of the languages he claimed to have translated from. A gleeful perpetrator of literary hoaxes who foreshadowed Fernando Pessoa, Jorge Luis Borges, and Roberto Bolaño, Clarence Mangan also published numerous 'translations' of which no original existed.

In addition to his alcoholism, Clarence Mangan was an opium addict, and his preferred brand of the drug appears in the title of his aphoristic, strikingly modern collection of prose fragments, *A Sixty-Drop Dose of Laudanum*. A self-mythologising *poète maudit*, he roamed Dublin wearing a blond wig, cloak, and green spectacles. Near the end of his life he wrote an unfinished autobiography that ends mid-sentence. A nationalist who wrote subversively in the language of the occupier, the Irish language having been suppressed under colonial rule, James Clarence Mangan's gravestone in Glasnevin Cemetery bears the inscription, 'Ireland's National Poet', along with lines from his most famous patriotic poem: 'O my dark Rosaleen, do not sigh, do not weep'.

A Sixty-Drop Dose of Laudanum

Laudanum: from *laudare*, to praise, this drug being one of the most praiseworthy in the *Materia Medica.*—*Cullen.*

You may exhibit thirty, fifty, eighty, or a hundred drops to produce sleep; every thing depends on the temperament; but where your object is to excite and enliven, I recommend you to stop short at sixty.—*Brown.*

"A dose to dose Society:" quoth the Trumpeter—"then it must be uncommon strong, comrade!"—*Adventures of a Half-crown.*

So saying, he shed sixty drops of the liquid in his black flask into a cup, muttering mysterious words all the while.—*The Rival Magicians.*

————*Count o'er*
————*threescore !*
Childe Harold, e. iii. st. xxxiv.

Drop One.

MANY LITERARY BEGINNINGS ARE difficult; many the reverse. Where there is much taste there is much hesitation: where energy predominates the novice enters on his career with a bold and joyous heart eager to scale "the steep where Fame's proud temple shines afar."

Thus poets in their youth begin in gladness,
Though thereof comes in the end despondency and madness.

Our first efforts, it is true, are not always our happiest. Neither are our first loves. Yet both are most dear to our recollections; for with all first things there is associated a certain mysterious magic. Who are they that can forget their first kiss—the first hand they pressed—the first fiddle they played (some few play this through life)—the first time they bade their friends farewell—

Lo di ch' han detto a dolci amici a Dio

or "the first dark day of nothingness" after the death of a relative? Byron has celebrated the old Athenians as

First in the race that led to God's goal,

and Moore deeply excites our sympathies by his song to the American damsel whom he met when a little girl, on the banks of the Schuylkill, all wool, furs, muffs and boas—

When first I met thee, warm and young

We have all heard the antiquarian ditty concerning the period at which yews were first seen in burying-grounds—

O do you remember the first time eye met yew?

We recall our "first grey hair" which brought us wisdom—the first day of April, which made fools of us again—the first day of the year, with its bells,

—and that sweet time
When first we heard their ding-dong chime.

And shall not *I* hereafter call to mind this first specimen of the genuine "Black Drop" that ever trickled from my pen with that mingling "of sweet and bitter fancies" inseparable from a review of whatever is interesting in the Past?

Drop Two.

It is impossible that a man can ever make a transcendent artist, that is, that he can excel in music, sculpture, painting, &c. unless he be endowed with a capacious understanding. Just principles with reference to the Fine Arts cannot, in my opinion, coexist with illiberal or erroneous notions upon general subjects. Persuade me who can that Nincompoop Higglethwaites, Esquire, who knows neither the world nor himself—who has studied neither books nor men—can possess a genius for music! A genius for eliciting sounds of all degrees of intonation through the medium of certain machinery I readily grant him—but how can he pretend to move the passions—he who has himself no passions—who knows nothing about them—who regards them as superfluities—and the sum total of whose ambition is to become a correct copyist of the rules of his art? A musician, forsooth! Bah! He has about as much title to the name of musician as an ape has to that of man.

Drop Three.

This earth may be characterised as the Great Emporium of the Possible, from whence contingencies are for ever issuing like exports from a warehouse. And Necessity is to the moral world what Fashion is to the social—the parent of perpetual fluctuations. The changes through which men and nations, and their feelings, manners, and destinies are passing and must pass, are not experimental merely; they are superinduced by irresistible, though to a philosophical eye obvious, agencies. When all the varieties of all those changes shall be exhausted, "then is the end nigh;" the Emporium will be thrown down as useless; and the Possible, taught a lesson by the Past, will thenceforth take refuge in spheres from which vicissitude and destruction shall be altogether excluded.

Drop Four.

Sir L. Bulwer's last portrait—that prefixed to his *Leila*—I take to be a total failure—in fact, a regular humbug. The look is precisely that of a man whom the apparition of a long-legged spider on the wall is about to send into strong hysterics. And such a look was called up for the nonce! Surely the author of Pelham must have lost all sympathy with the ludicrous when he suffered this to be thrust under the public eye. The affectation was the more supererogatory as Bulwer is really a well-favoured gentleman, the everyday expression of his physiognomy being of quite as stare-arresting an order as he need wish to see transferred either to canvas or foolscap.

Drop Five.

If you desire to padlock a punster's lips never tell him that you loathe puns: he would then perpetrate his atrocities for the sake of annoying you. Choose another course: always affect to misunderstand him. When an excruciator has been inflicted on you, open wide your eyes and mouth for a minute, and then, closing them again abruptly, shake your head, and exclaim, "Very mysterious!" This kills him.

Drop Six.

I should far and away prefer being a great necromancer to being a great writer or even a great fighter. My natural propensities lead me rather to seek out modes of astonishing mankind than of edifying them. Herein I and my propensities are clearly wrong; but somehow I find that almost every thing that is natural in me is wrong also.

Drop Seven.

The idea entertained by all girls under twenty of literary men is, that they are *very clever*. Distinctions between one order of intellect and another they can never be brought to comprehend. With them the sonneteer and the epic poet are on a common level as to talent; the sonnetteer, however, is usually the greater pet, as he has more small talk.

Drop Eight.

Apropos of sonnets, one of the choicest in our language is that addressed to Dr. Kitchener. I met with it many years ago in some obscure publication, which, I suppose, has since gone the way of all paper:

> Knight of the Kitchen—telescopic cook—
>   Beef-slicing proser—pudding-building bard—
>   Swallower of dripping—gulper-down of lard—
> Equally great in beaufet and in book!
> With a prophetic eye that seer did look
>   Into Fate's records who bestowed thy name,
>   By which thou floatest down the tide of fame
> As floats the jackstraw down the gurgling brook.
> He saw thee destined, by the boiler's side,
>   With veal and mutton endless war to wage:
> Had he looked further he perchance had spied
>   Thee ever scribbling, scribbling, page by page:
> Then to thy head his hand he'd have applied,
>   And said—"This child will be a Humbug of the Age."

Drop Nine.

The longing which men continually feel for *rest* while engaged in the struggles and stormy turmoils of Life, is an unconscious tending of the heart towards its natural goal, the Grave.

Drop Ten.

My impression is that the Irish were not originally so warlike a nation at all as is popularly supposed. The Danes unquestionably beat them hollow in military ardour, as well as prowess and skill. *Imprimis*, the Danes were always the invaders, the aggressors—the Irish standing only on the defensive, *pro aris et focis*. Secondly, the Irish bards usually designate the Danes as *an fionn-treabh sar-bhorb*,—"that fair-haired and most fierce tribe," manifestly leaving it to be implied that they (the bards) were not accustomed to consider the Irish as equally fierce. In the third place, the Danes first taught the Irish the use of many battle-weapons, and, among others, of the curt-axe, so formidable afterwards in the hands of the galloglass. If the Irish had been by nature a very martial people, instinct would have directed them to the inventing of those implements of destruction for themselves. Fourthly, the successful result of the Battle of Clontarf, instead of being spoken of by Irish writers as a thing of course, is for the most part made a theme for wonder and extraordinary exultation; as if the Irish had been habituated to such drubbings by their enemies that a solitary victory on their own side was to be celebrated as scarcely less than miraculous. Besides, all are agreed that the aborigines of Ireland, the Firbolgs, meddled very little with cold iron, except when they took the scythe or spade in hand; and there is no satisfactory evidence that the Battle of Moy-Tuire drove them out of the island, or did more than disperse the great bulk of them over it. The northern portions of the Irish tribes I do believe were fond enough of war, both in the way of business and pleasure; but the Hibernian Milesians appear to have thought that they had on occasions too much of a good thing. Upon native Irish valour no slur can ever be cast; but it certainly owes much of its renown nevertheless to the example set it by the Goths. It is remarkable in fact that the dark-haired races have ever been more prone to the cultivation of arts than arms. Three-fourths of all the eminent musicians and painters of Europe have been dark. On the other hand, disdain of the refinements of social life, impetuosity, and fierceness bordering on savageism appear to be the prominent natural characteristics of the light-haired. The happy—not the *golden*—medium is found in the auburn, who have more equanimity of disposition than either, as well as more genius for historical and metaphysical research, greater mental flexibility, and, generally speaking, superior capability of adapting themselves to any position that circumstances require them to occupy.

Drop Eleven.

Touching hair—I never cared what the colour of a woman's was. My love laughs at locks as well as locksmiths. Still I have made my observations, in an unobtrusive way, and with the eye of a simpleton. Red-haired women, I have discovered, are usually the liveliest of their sex, but also the most changeable-(never, however, *double*)-minded. There is an absolute passion for coquetry in them: you can no more steady them to one object, *i.e.* yourself, of course, than you can fix a ball of quicksilver. A very vain man, if he have more regard for his soul's weal than his heart's, will be particularly sweet on this class, for they never fail to teach him by many bitter lessons all the hollowness of the philosophy of self-love. The raven-black are not always, as people fancy, the most impassioned—unless they happen to be from Spain or Italy. Of the brown it is difficult to predict any thing in a general way, except that their perceptions are usually very acute;—their affections also are easily won and easily wounded; they are of the nervous temperament; and I apprehend that more broken hearts are found among these than among the others. I have noticed that as to both intellect and feeling much in all cases depends on the size of the brain, and more on its activity. I believe, but am not positive, that D'Israeli (the Younger) asserts that very great self-possession in women indicates want of heart. I disagree: in my opinion it merely shows a capacity for concentration of thought. But I perceive I am wandering from my text; and so, lest I lose myself altogether, I stop short without further apology.

Drop Twelve.

The most opaque of all the masques that people assume to conceal their real characters is enthusiasm. In the eyes of women enthusiasm appears so amiable that they believe no imposter *could* counterfeit it: to men it seems so ridiculous that they are satisfied nobody *would*.

Drop Thirteen.

It is a singular fact, that the great majority of French authors, whatever the nature of their subject, write as if they were haranguing.

Drop Fourteen.

Poets call women light-footed. I do not know upon what ground. Sauntering one day along, rather at my ease, I passed forty-seven of them in succession between Carlisle Bridge and Granby Row. As to their dancing, it never satisfied me. There always appeared to me some mysterious hugger-muggery about the movements: it was their drapery that danced—not they. Stage *danseuses* of course I make no account of here, as they are either "to the manner born," or trained to it, and people stare at them as monstrosities.

Drop Fifteen.

If every individual were to develop his inmost dispositions to the world in writing, publishers would undoubtedly realize large fortunes by the novelties wherewith we should see the press teeming. What can be stranger, *par exemple*, than the fact that I, who, with all my sins, am not, I hope, wickeder than my neighbours, should be haunted by a continual longing to become a captain of robbers? Not that I should care much about the plunder. It is the idea of exercising influence, of controlling and coercing, that captivates my fancy. But why should I not wish rather to exercise the same influence over the mild and the amiable? It is, that an involuntary though fallacious association connects in my mind mildness and amiability with weakness, and invests force of even the rudest kind with an air of majesty and grandeur? I cannot tell; but the fact is as I record it. Let the metaphysicians explain it in their own way.

Drop Sixteen.

The modern English and Irish fashion adopted by women of wearing the hair all in a clump at the west of the head is most detestably execrable. My blood curdles when I think of it.

Drop Seventeen.

There are some few women who will despise you for loving them, but none who will *hate* you without a much better reason.

Drop Eighteen.

All the blank-versifying in Europe to the contrary notwithstanding, revenge of personal wrongs is a mean passion. It is the
gratification of self-love in one of its most abominable forms.
I am convinced that none besides grovelling minds are capable
of harbouring it. Remark that hurricanes are most inclined to
prostrate mud hovels: they can only rage impotently around the
pyramid whose apex kisses heaven. So, the momentary sway of
the fiercer passions over elevated minds leaves no perceptible
trace behind: it is in base natures alone that it stimulates to
havoc and destruction.

Drop Nineteen.

From the moment that any man tells me that he cannot understand the humour of Rabelais, I never care to speak to him, or
to hear him speak to me, on literary topics.

Drop Twenty.

There is one phenomenon sometimes attendant on dreaming,
at least on *my* dreaming, which, as far as I can discover, no
writer, not even Macnish, has ever noticed. I allude to the
marvellous power which the mind possesses during sleep of
*re-creating the same images over and over with no exercise of
memory on the part of the dreamer.* To me this is a mystery
altogether inexplicable, nor have I ever met with any one
capable of clearing it up. As the meaning of my italics may
not be exactly divined, I will condescend to details. I dream,
for instance, that I am compelled to traverse four and twenty
chambers in succession—let me call them A, B, C, &c. Each
of these chambers is characterised by some architectural or
other peculiarity of its own—a pillar perhaps in the centre of

it—a strange picture on the wall—a sphinx on a marble table, or some other distinguishing feature. I journey through the entire number from A to Z; and by the time I have reached Z I have lost all remembrance of the preceding three and twenty chambers. *I am conscious of the loss of the remembrance.* Very well. On reaching Z, I am compelled to return through the chambers back again to A. And here we have the mystery. For now, as I open each door and entry, my memory, dormant up to the moment of my entrance, *revives*, and I recognise at once, *in the correct order of their succession*, the objects I saw as I passed along first. Having arrived at A, I again resume my journey to Z, and the same series of anomalies takes place. When I am in B, I have not the faintest recollection of C, yet, on re-entering C, I recall it again distinctly and vividly. I have no notion, however, what D may contain, till, upon opening the door, I recognise everything. And so I progress to Z; and then travel back a second time to A, only to re-commence my involuntary pilgrimage, which is repeated perhaps thirty times over. The grand puzzle here is, *How* the imagery of the chambers is created. *Primâ facie*, it would seem as though it existed altogether independent of *my* consent or that of any of my faculties. Of course it cannot so exist; but of one thing I am certain,—that what is called imagination has no share in creating it. Imagination is always conscious of exercising its own power. Moreover, unless there be a determinate effort for the purpose, the forms it produces are never twice the same. Now, in me, there is no such effort; there is no effort of any kind. My will is passive throughout. *I do not know what it is that I am about to see as I open the door.* Besides, what the will helps to fabricate the will can help to destroy; and I am painfully conscious that I cannot destroy the minutest portion of the scenery before me. The English Opium-Eater's dreams about the staircases of Piranesi will perhaps occur to the reader. Between those dreams and mine, however, there is scarcely one salient point of resemblance. I doubt even whether the Opium-Eater ever had such dreams as I have been endeavouring to describe: if he had, they would have appeared too remarkable to one of his metaphysical habits of thought to be passed over in silence. I may add, that I regret he should not have been visited by them; for I believe him to be one of the few men in England qualified to supply a theory in explanation of the phenomenon which they involve.

Drop Twenty-One.

People never pardon an *avowed* want of sympathy with themselves, because it is want of respect. Xanthus was one day beginning in my presence with a rapt air Mrs. Hemans' poem, "I dream of all things free," when I drily edged in, "Freestone among the rest, I presume." This *mauvaise plaisanterie* cost me an acquaintance. Xanthus was hurt, not so much because I did not participate in his enthusiasm, as because I took no trouble to disguise my want of participation in it. It is the way of the world. Most of us prefer the dissimulation that flatters us to the sincerity that wounds.

Drop Twenty-Two.

Not that I would insist that we are always to blame for our preference. False politeness may in no case be a virtue, but unnecessary cruelty is at all times a vice. I must hate it, in whatever shape it comes. Quarrelling with the truth and, quarrelling with the motive that dictates the utterance of the truth, are two distinct things. It is lawful for me to grieve over the *malus animus* that levels a shaft against my self-love. I contract an aversion towards the archer, because he is barbarous in the abstract, not because he wounds *me*. My feelings would not be a jot less bitter if he had victimized my enemy instead.

Drop Twenty-Three.

The most exquisite pleasure of which we are susceptible is the state of feeling that follows a cessation of intense pain. Reflection on this truth might make us melancholy, if we did not remember that our final agonies must be succeeded by repose.

Drop Twenty-Four.

Want of gratitude hardly deserves to be branded as *in*gratitude. A mere negation of all sentiment should not be mistaken for the blackest of vices. Favours are often slighted from constitutional insensibility; or they may be involuntarily forgotten. Where they are, wrongs are forgotten just as soon. He who serves others and is not thanked may find that he can injure them without being hated. Heaven forefend, however, that he should make the experiment for the sake of philosophising on the result!

Drop Twenty-Five.

I have noticed that those men who give bad characters of women have usually worse characters themselves.

Drop Twenty-Six.

L. E. L (poor L. E. L!) remarks in her *Romance and Reality* that memory is the least egotistical of all the faculties, forasmuch as it rather recalls to us the individual we have conversed with or the book we have read than the feelings we have experienced. I am inclined to differ. Wherever the memory of our feelings is vague it must be because the feelings themselves were equally vague. For my own part I have always a much better recollection of the emotions that were excited in my mind by hearing a certain air or perusing a particular story than I have of the music or the volume itself.

Drop Twenty-Seven.

None but exalted spirits, who can calmly look down upon human events and human frailties as from an eminence, are capable of unalterable friendship; for none but they can calculate beforehand the errors they shall have to pardon as well as the excellences they can prize. Even those persons, however, though they may feel friendship, can rarely inspire it—so much more difficult is it for mediocrity to appreciate nobleness than for nobleness to tolerate mediocrity!

Drop Twenty-Eight.

Distrust nine girls in ten who instead of talking to you on a first introduction listen with apparent deference to all that your foolish tongue utters to them. Depend upon it that they are making a study of your character for their own purposes. I except the tenth girl because she is a *niaise*, and has really nothing to say. It may be supposed that some of the sex remain silent on these occasions from bashfulness. I think the supposition a mistake. I have met proud girls and cold girls, and silent girls and silly girls. So have others. But when and where has any body ever met with a bashful girl? Never and nowhere.

Drop Twenty-Nine.

A friend once told me that Catiline was as great a man as Caesar, but not so fortunate. I contested his assertion and maintained that the failure of Catiline's enterprises proved his mind to have been of an inferior order. I think so still. In my opinion wisdom and circumspection are indispensable essentials of greatness. A great man must not only be able to foresee what *ought* to succeed, but what *will* succeed. He must conquer all adverse circumstances. Napoleon's greatness consisted not in *being* Emperor of France, but in having made himself so. Neither was his defeat by Russia half so fatal to his reputation in the eyes of Europe as the folly he had evinced in tempting it.

Drop Thirty.

While as yet we are young—while we are unhackneyed in the sodden ways of this world—our souls dwell in our eyes, and beauty is our only loadstar. Nothing has such charms for us as the society of a being who superadds grace and animation to her native loveliness. The sense of existence is deepened and quickened within us before her. A thousand newborn pulses of tremulous delight agitate our bosoms. We are tenants of a sphere apart. Fancy is intoxicated with the present and anticipates a future all triumph and transport. We stand spell-chained within the charmed circle of an enchantress. The depth of our devotion to beauty may be estimated by the aversion we feel at this time of life for its antipodes. Sex does not so much enter into our calculations as philosophers think. An ugly woman shocks us. She may be a De Stael; but what we care at eighteen for metaphysics, from the lips of man or woman? She is ugly; and disgust and weariness constitute our paramount feelings. We are spiritless, melancholy, *lonely*. Time lags on his long path, and the burden of life presses us down towards the clay we half wish to mingle with for ever. The folding-doors of the imagination are flung to with a sound, sullen and hope-destroying, which reverberates through the innermost hollows of the heart. The desire of signalizing ourselves languishes. Fame appears as valueless as its common type, a bubble on the water. The world is robed in gloom. How mighty are even momentary influences in early youth! Well! a few years and all this sensibility passes away. Beauty and ugliness can move us no more. All that is left to us is the ability to ponder on our former feelings—to laugh at or weep for our illusions, as our temperament inclines.

But if we laugh at any mortal thing
'Tis that we may not weep; and if we weep
'Tis that our nature cannot always bring
Itself to apathy.

Are we the happier for the change? Certainly we are not the quieter. We create less agitation in the drawing-room, but more every-where else. Alas! We are scarcely the happier either. While we can neither adore nor abhor as of yore we are compelled to praise and scold much louder than ever. We care nothing for any thing, yet are forced to seem interested in every thing. One only hour remains to us in which we are privileged to throw off the mask and be ourselves—and that is our death hour. Then, however, the world pays us little heed—and we—small blame to us—return the compliment.

Drop Thirty-One.

The African Magician in *Aladdin*, traversing Isfahan, and crying out for his own private purposes, *Who will exchange old lamps for new ones?* is an excellent vaticinatory hit at the *soi-disant* Illuminati of modern times.

Drop Thirty-Two.

Aladdin displayed infinite tact in leaving to the Sultan the honor of putting the finishing hand to the building of his palace. The Sultan was then in the position of a critic to whom a great poet submits an epic, and who adds a line to the end of it: the critic may boast that he has assisted in the composition of the work; and the Sultan might have said, I and Aladdin have constructed this palace. His vanity was tickled; and his son-in-law rose at least five stories high in his opinion. Aladdin, however, afterwards spoiled all by his impatience. The Sultan was too slow a coach for him; and he had recourse to the lamp. Here was a want of *savoir faire*, for which he suffered accordingly. It is thus that the cleverest men perpetually make asses of themselves in the long run—marring in a quarter of an hour by some piece of headstrong *gaucherie* all the advantages secured to them by previous years of prudence and industry.

Drop Thirty-Three.

This same palace of Aladdin, though reared in one night, had not its parallel for beauty—and would have remained the most durable of earthly edifices—a wonder for all after-ages—if the genii that had constructed it had not of their own accord removed it—they bore it away to an unknown land, and it returned no more. So, love at first sight, the birth of an instant, strikes nevertheless its roots far deeper in the heart than the affection which takes months in maturing,—and never could depart or die if they who excited it did not themselves contribute to abolish its existence. For they are fickle in their homage—or they were false from the beginning—or they betray a baseness of character long hidden—or time furrows their cheeks—and then the love vanishes for ever—going down, with no hope of resurrection, into the deepest of all moral graves—the grave of indifference.

Drop Thirty-Four.

Very crafty persons may be at once known by the great breadth between their eyes. I have remarked that persons with this peculiarity of feature are also better qualified than others to judge of physical beauty and the harmonies of external proportion.

Drop Thirty-Five.

When you pen a common-place you should always strain a point to redeem it by a *jeu-de-mot*. Yet perhaps I am unphilosophical

in my advice, for most great truths are essentially common-
place. So, for that matter, are all the dogmas and dictates of
reason—the reason of many, *c'est a dire*, not of all, for what is
high treason with the Old-clothesmen is high treason with the
Purple-and-Fine-lineners.

Drop Thirty-Six.

Life is a game which perversely varies its character according to
the age at which we play it; in youth, when much may be lost,
it is a game of chance; in manhood, when little remains to be
won, it is a game of skill.

Drop Thirty-Seven.

Gay people commit more follies than gloomy; but gloomy people commit greater follies.

Drop Thirty-Eight.

The intellect of poets feeds their vanity; that of philosophers
counteracts theirs.

Drop Thirty-Nine.

No neglect, no slight, no contumely from one of his own sex
can mortify a man who has been much flattered and courted by
women. No matter from what source it may emanate, he will
always and necessarily attribute it to envy.

Drop Forty.

Perseverance has enabled me to find my way to XL. Whether it
will ever enable me to find *the* way to excel, *reste á savoir*.

Drop Forty-One.

Many persons have experienced a strange sensation of uneasiness and apprehension, as it were, of undefined evil, at hearing the knolling of a deep bell in a great city at noon, amid the bustle of life and business. The source of this sensation I take to lie, not so much in the mere sound of the bell as in the knowledge that its monitions, of whatever character they may be, are wholly undictated by human feelings. We are more or less jealous of the interference of our fellow-beings in our concerns, even where their motives are purely disinterested, because, in spite of us, we associate with it the idea of ostentation and intrusiveness. But, a solemn voice from a mass of inanimate metal, especially when the hum and turmoil of the world are around us, is like the tremendous appeal of a dead man's aspect; and its power over us becomes the greater because of its own total unconsciousness of the existence of that power.

Drop Forty-Two.

It is seldom that any one who is ingenious at finding arguments is ingenuous in stating them. A clear-headed man, for all that, may be a very candid one; and a great misfortune it is for him to be so. Being always reasonable, he is of course, from the nature of society, always engaged in controverting some absurdity. Hence *tracasseries* with his friends, and all these other kinds of asseries before the world to which these usually lead.

Drop Forty-Three.

The world has less tolerance for novel theorists upon morals and metaphysics than for even *soi-disant* discoverers in the sciences. The reason is obvious. Almost every man confesses to himself his ignorance of all things relating to the mysteries of the external world; but it is difficult to persuade any man that he is not himself the best judge of what passes in his own mind.

Drop Forty-Four.

If a combination of the Sublime and the Sarcastic be possible, I fancy I find it in two lines by Gleim:

> *Und Friedrich weint?*
> *Gieb ihm die Herrschaft über dich, O, Welt,*
> *Weil er, ob auch ein König, weinen kann!*

> And Frederic weeps?
> Give him dominion over thee, O, Earth!
> For this, that he, albeit a king, can weep.

Drop Forty-Five.

Victories, after the lapse of some years, ruin a country even more certainly than defeats. The money which governments raise from speculators for carrying on successful wars must be repaid to them with interest; and as it is the nature of wealth to go on producing wealth an enormous accumulation of the circulating medium must take place in the coffers of the few to the detriment of the many. The larger party tending to pauperism in an inverse ratio with the augmenting prosperity of the smaller party, affairs daily grow more generally worse; until at last the very continuance of existence of the nation becomes a problem to be solved only by a revolution.

Drop Forty-Six.

Experience is a jewel picked up by a wrecked mariner on a desert coast—a picture-frame, purchased at a preposterous cost, when decay has done its duty on your finest Titian—a prosing lecturer who sermonises a sleeping congregation—a warden who alarms the citadel when the enemy has broken through the gates—a melancholy moon after a day of darkness and tempest—a sentinel who mounts guard over a pillaged house—a surveyor who takes the dimensions of the pit we have tumbled into—a monitor that, like Friar Bacon's Brazen Head, tells us that *Time is past*—a lantern brought to us after we have traversed a hundred morasses in the dark and are entering an illuminated village—a pinnace on the strand found when the tide has ebbed away—a morning lamp lighted in our saloon when our guests have departed, revealing rueful ruin—or any thing else equally pertinent and impertinent. Why then do we panegyrise it so constantly? Why do we take and make all opportunities to boast of our own? Because, wretched worms that we are! we are so proud of our despicable knowledge that we cannot afford to shroud from view even that portion of it which we have purchased at the price of our happiness. Parade and ostentation—ostentation and parade for ever!—"they are the air we breathe—without them we expire."

Drop Forty-Seven.

"How populous—how vital is the grave!" cried Young. He was in the right in the sense he contemplated. He was in the right, too, in a separate sense. The grave is vital to the renown of those great men who had none during life. "Silent as the grave," say some:—bah! the grave is your only betrayer of secrets. It is the *camera obscura* which the student of human nature must enter to behold sights unrevealable by "garish day," and "amid the hum, the crowd, and shock of men." Stagnant waters picture the sky better than stormy:

Nicht in truben Schlamm der Bache

Der von wilden Regenguszen schwillt,
Auf des stillen Baches eb'ner Flache
Spiegelt sich das Sonnenbild *

"The day of a man's death is better than the day of his birth," saith Solomon. To the man of genius at least it proves so. If his friends do not embalm him like the Egyptians, or give him money like the Greeks, to pay Charon his fare, they do more— they write recommendatory letters to Posterity in his behalf. Yes: fame, like Mrs. Shelley's Frankenstein, is a genuine production of the sepulchre. "The nightmare Life-in-Death is she." She springs up from the dust of him who seeks her no more, as the phoenix rises from its own ashes. "The grave-dews winnowing through the rotting clay" are distilled into an *elixir vitae* which, unlike St. Leon's, turns out no burden to its possessor. The season of requital is come, and the crowd cry out, *Le roi est mort, vive le roi!* What is the reason? How is the anomaly explained? Why all this hullaballoo, begotten on a sudden? Because the man *is* dead: because *he is out of the way.* He is "fallen from his high estate." He has ceased personally to excite the wonder and wrath and envy of others. His works are before the world, to be sure, and that is mortifying, but he, the worker, is behind the world, and that is fortifying. No fear of pleasing him now by flattery. He can no more "hear the voice of the charmer, charm he never so wisely." Walls have ears, quoth the proverb, but those of the tomb are an exception. "Can honor's voice provoke the silent dust" to smile a reply to a compliment? Low in the arms of the Mighty Mother he lies, no more the unconscious stirrer-up of heart-burnings among those whom he overlooked,

---

* Never in the bosom of the stream,
   Dulled and troubled by the flooding rains,
   Rather on the stilly lake the beam
   Of the mirrored sun remains.
            Friedrich Schiller.

but hated not, and who hated him because they could not over-look him. Therefore let the shell and lute now resound with his praises! Ah! after all, human nature has been libelled. "We are not stocks and stones." We are glad of all opportunities to effect a compromise between our jealousy and our justice. And is not this much? Let him who thinks it little re-model society upon a plan that shall enable men to possess passions "as though they possessed them not," for otherwise he is scarce likely to be satis-fied on this side of the Millennium.

Drop Forty-Eight.

Horace Smith's shop-board with "Going, Stay-maker," is very good, and better still if true; but I certainly once saw over a gateway the notification, "John Reilly, Carpenter *and Timberyard.*"

Drop Forty-Nine.

The Irish Annalists sustain the literary character of their country famously. I like samples of style such as those *que voici.* "Mac-Giolla-Ruadh plunged into the river and swam to the shore, but was drowned before he landed." "The Kinel-Owen defeated the Kinel-Connell with terrible slaughter *for* Niall Garbh O'Donnell lost one leg in the battle." "The Lord Lieutenant and Maurice Fitzgerald then returned to Ireland, both in good health, except that Maurice Fitzgerald caught a fever on the way, from which he did not recover." "Hugh Roe now sent word to the Italians to come and assist him, but this they were not then able to do, for they had all been killed some time before by," &c. Pope, it occurs to me, has an Irish line in his *Essay on Man.*

> Virtuous and vicious every man must be;
> *Few* in the *extreme*, but *all* in the *degree.*

And Schiller another in his *Robbers*:

Death's kingdom—*waked* from its *eternal* sleep!

And Milton another in his *Paradise Lost*:

And in the *lowest* deep a *lower* deep.

Drop Fifty.

Poets are the least sympathising of breathing beings. They have few or none of the softer feelings. One cause of their deficiency in these is that they have already vented them in verse. Pour the wine out of a flask and you leave the flask void. A second and better reason for their insensibility is this, that two master-sentiments cannot coexist in one bosom. The imagination refuses to share its sovereignty with the heart. "One fire tires out another's burning," says Shakespeare, who, I fancy, took a much deeper interest in the fate of his own dramas than in all the affairs of the world besides. The use of poetry to poets is that it preserves them from great crimes and gross vices. If it quenches every spark of sympathy in their breasts, on the other hand it absorbs them too much to allow them to seek a reputation by throat-cutting or city-burning. Negatively poetry is thus of use to mankind. With regard to its positive use to them, as this is an age of discoveries we may perhaps find it out by-and-bye.

Drop Fifty-One.

A translator from Spanish, French, High Dutch, &c. should always improve on his original if he can. Most continental writers are dull plodders, and require spurring and furbishing. I see no harm in now and then giving them a lift and a shove. If I receive two or three dozen of sherry for a dinner-party, and by some chemical process can convert the sherry into champagne, my friends are all the merrier, and nobody is a loser. As to translations from the Oriental tongues, no one should attempt them, unless for the purpose of adducing them as documentary evidences in support of some antiquarian theory, about which the world does not care three halfpence. By the way, I submissively insist that Mr. Lane's new version of the *Arabian Nights*, now coming out in numbers, is the most quackish jackassicality of latter days. Mr. Lane is a good writer and a shrewd observer, but he cannot—no man can—Europeanize Orientalism. One might as well think of introducing Harlequin's costume into the Court of Chancery.

Drop Fifty-Two.

Shelley was remarkable for very bright eyes; so was La Harpe; and so was Burns. Maturin's eyes were mild and meditative, but not particularly lustrous: when he raised them suddenly, however, the effect was startling. Byron's did not strike the observer as much as might have been expected, probably because of his ill health. As De Quincey correctly remarks, the state of the eyes greatly depends on that of the stomach. Carleton has a fine intelligent eye, filled with deep, speculative thought, "looking before and after." My idea, nevertheless, is, that in general too much stress is laid on the expression of the eyes. In many faces their supposed character is derived from the other features. What eye can be more beautiful and expressive than that of an infant, who has no passions, and whose mind is as yet a blank?

Drop Fifty-Three.

I disapprove of encouraging the working classes to read too much. One inevitable result of their knowledge must be, that their wants will become multiplied in a greater degree than their resources. For a successful and summary method, however, of enlightening the multitude by means of books, I refer readers to the history of the Caliph Omar and the Alexandrian library.

Drop Fifty-Four.

"Murder," says Shakespeare, "though it hath no tongue, will speak with most miraculous organ." Here is evidence that the existence of the organ of Destructiveness was not unknown to our ancestors. Or perhaps "will speak" points to the nineteenth century, and the passage is a prophecy. I neither know nor care.

Drop Fifty-Five.

Apropos of poetical prophecies, Shelley has recorded a remarkable prediction by Byron anent the mode of his (Shelley's) own death:—

> —'O, ho!
> You talk as in times past,' said Maddalo.
> ''Tis strange men change not: you were ever still
> Among Christ's flock a perilous infidel,—
> A wolf for the meek lambs: *if you can't swim,*
> *Beware of Providence!* I looked at him,
> But the gay smile had faded from his eye.
> —Shelley's *Julian and Maddalo*

Drop Fifty-Six.

One more word upon Craniology. Whence, I should like to learn, springs the propensity to general ridicule?—to scout most things and people as humbugs? Spurzheim's theory makes it a product of deficient Veneration and great Destructiveness and Congruity, *i.e.* Wit or Humour. I largely doubt. Rabelais lacked

Congruity; so did Swift. Curran's masque exhibits but a moderate share of it. In Godwin and Wordsworth it appears full; yet to both wit is an abhorrence. Voltaire had large Veneration. Sterne's head, it is true, answers to the required *laid ideal*, but making Sterne's head do duty for the head of every man who is the reverse of stern is something too bad. For myself I place faith in but four of the thirty-two organs: Self-esteem, Secretiveness, Firmness, and Hope; but this last I would call Castle-building; and I conceive that it and Ideality are the same faculty.

Drop Fifty-Seven.

One of the finest passages in modern fiction is the meeting between Watson and Welbeck in Brockden Brown's *Arthur Mervyn*. The stern concentrated rage of the avenger—the more awful from its calmness—and the wordless resignation and despair of the wretched seducer are portrayed with a terrible faithfulness to nature. The introductory words of Watson—"It is well. The hour my vengeance has long thirsted for is arrived. Welbeck! that my words could strike thee dead! They will so, if thou hast any claim to the name of man,"—prepare us for the harrowing disclosures that follow—the death of Watson's sister "from anguish and a broken heart," and the suicide of their lunatic father in consequence. And when Watson, having narrated the latter circumstance, draws a pistol from his breast, and, approaching Welbeck, places the muzzle against his forehead, saying with forced calmness—"This is the instrument with which the deed was performed," who, even of those that cannot *feel* the scene, but must acknowledge the graphic nature of the conception? The duel, also, across the table, with its unlooked for result in the death of Watson, and the whole of the subsequent narrative of the interment of the corpse in the cellar—how peculiarly, but how powerfully they are given! Our interest in the entire affair is heightened by the singular character of Welbeck, who, by the way, is not at all like the Falkland of

Caleb Williams, though Dunlop, Brown's biographer, fancies he perceives a marked resemblance between them. Let us hope that *Arthur Mervyn* will find a place among the Standard Novels. It deserves the honor fully as much as *Edgar Huntly.*

Drop Fifty-Eight.

Writing a poem for the sake of developing a metaphysical theory, is like kindling a fire for the sake of the smoke.

Drop Fifty-Nine.

Love, even fortunate love, never leaves the heart as it found it. An angel once dwelled in the palace of Zohir, and his presence was the sun and soul of that edifice. But, after years, there came a devil, stronger than the angel; and the devil drove the angel from the palace and took up his own abode therein. And a woeful day was that for the palace, for the devil brake up the costly furniture and put all things at sixes and sevens, and the mark of his hoof was every where visible on the carpets. But when some time had passed, he too, went away; and now the palace was left a lonely wreck, for the angel never more would return to a dwelling that had been desecrated by a devil. So it continued to wax older and crazier, till at last one night a high wind came and swept it to the earth where it lay ever after in ruins. Many say, however, that the angel might have remained in it to this day had he combated the intruder with might and main in the beginning, but that he chose rather to hold parley with him, and even invited him to come under the roof.

Drop Sixty.

Inscribed in the Chronicle of the Forty-four Mandarins is the record of the confessions of A-HA-HO-HUM, Man of Many

Sciences, Son of the Dogstar, and Cousin to the Turkey-cock; and thus it runneth: I, A-HA-HO-HUM, HAVE TRAVERSED THE EARTH, AND THE HEARTS OF MEN HAVE BEEN LAID BARE TO ME; AND LO! MY TESTIMONY CONCERNING ALL THINGS IS THIS:—

𝔑o 𝔚all is 𝔇ense, and no 𝔚ell is 𝔇eep, where a 𝔚ill is 𝔇aring.

                                        THE-OUT-AND-OUTER.

George Egerton

The Spell of the White Elf

Born in Melbourne in 1859, Mary Chavelita Dunne Bright—who would later adopt the pen name George Egerton—spent her childhood in Australia, New Zealand, and Chile, commencing a cosmopolitan lifestyle that would influence her progressive, outward-looking literary work. Born of a Welsh Protestant mother and an Irish Catholic father, Egerton claimed throughout her life that she felt 'intensely Irish'. She lived in Dublin during her formative years, as well as spending two years at school in Germany, and further periods of her young adulthood in New York (where she worked as a journalist) and Norway. She eloped to Norway with a married man, whom she then married herself. While living there she devoured the literature—Ibsen, Strindberg, Nietzsche—that would inspire her own writing. In Norway she also had a brief affair with the future Nobel Prize winner Knut Hamsun, and used the encounter as the basis for a short story, 'Now Spring Has Come'. Egerton's highly successful first collection of stories, *Keynotes*, is dedicated to Hamsun, and she was the first English translator of his modernist masterpiece *Hunger* (in 1899), introducing Hamsun to the English-speaking world.

After the collapse of her first marriage, Egerton married an impecunious novelist named Egerton Tertius Clairmonte (her *nom de plume* would combine his first name with that of her mother), moved to rural Ireland, and began writing in earnest. Published in 1893, *Keynotes* was to be by far Egerton's most successful book, propelling her into celebrity as a 'New Woman' and early advocate of feminist emancipation. Zestful and experimental, her writing anticipates the modernist twentieth-century focus on human beings' inner lives, while her insistence on the autonomous sexual lives of women, and her denunciation of feminine sexual 'purity' as a male-imposed ideology, put her ahead of her time. A further collection of stories, *Discords*, found some success, continuing Egerton's exploration of female desire, social oppression, and sexuality. However, her subsequent works—plays, a novel, and more story collections—failed to win much popularity.

Thomas Hardy acknowledged Egerton as an influence, particularly in his portrait of 'New Woman' characters in *Jude the Obscure* and other novels. The story included here, 'The Spell of the White Elf', is from *Keynotes*. Incidentally, the mention of Nietzsche in the story came three years before the philosopher had been translated into English, possibly making it the first reference to him in English literature.

George Egerton died in Sussex, England, in 1945.

The Spell of the White Elf

HAVE YOU EVER READ out a joke that seemed excruciatingly funny, or repeated a line of poetry that struck you as being inexpressibly tender, and found that your listener was not impressed as you were? I have; and so it may be that this will bore you, though it was momentous enough to me.

I had been up in Norway to receive a little legacy that fell to me; and though my summer visits were not infrequent, I had never been up there in mid-winter, at least not since I was a little child tobogganing with Hans Jörgen (Hans Jörgen Dahl is his full name), and that was long ago. We are connected. Hans Jörgen and I were both orphans, and a cousin (we called her aunt) was one of our guardians. He was her favourite; and when an uncle on my mother's side (she was Cornish born; my father, a ship captain, met her at Dartmouth) offered to take me, I think she was glad to let me go. I was a lanky girl of eleven, and Hans Jörgen and I were sweethearts. We were to be married some day—we had arranged all that—and he reminded me of it when I was going away, and gave me a silver perfume-box, with a gilt crown on top, that had belonged to his mother; and later when he was going to America he came to see me first. He was a long, freckled hobbledehoy, with just the same true eyes and shock head. I was, I thought, quite grown up. I had passed my 'intermediate,' and was condescending as girls are; but I don't think it impressed Hans Jörgen much, for he gave me a little ring, turquoise forget-me-nots with enamelled leaves and a motto inside (a quaint old thing that belonged to a sainted aunt, they keep things a long time in Norway), and said he would send for me; but of course I laughed at that. He has grown to be a great man out in Cincinnati and waits always. I wrote later and told him I thought marriage a vocation and

I hadn't one for it; but Hans Jörgen took no notice,—just said he'd wait. He understands waiting, I'll say that for Hans Jörgen.

I have been alone now for five years, working away, though I was left enough to keep me before. Somehow I have not the same gladness in my work of late years. Working for one's self seems a poor end even if one puts by money. But this has little or nothing to do with the white elf, has it?

Christiania is a singular city if one knows how to see under the surface, and I enjoyed my stay there greatly. The Hull boat was to at 4.30 and I had sent my things down early; for I was to dine at the Grand at two with a cousin, a typical Christiania man. It was a fine, clear day, and Karl Johann was thronged with folks. The band was playing in the park, and pretty girls and laughing students walked up and down. Every one who is anybody may generally be seen about that time. Henrik Ibsen— if you did not know him from his portrait, you would take him to be a prosperous merchant—was going home to dine; but Björnstjerne Björnson, in town just then, with his grand, leonine head, and the kind, keen eyes behind his glasses, was standing near the Storthing House with a group of politicians, probably discussing the vexed question of separate consulship. In no city does one see such characteristic odd faces and such queerly cut clothes. The streets are full of students. The farmers' sons amongst them are easily recognised by their homespun, sometimes home-made suits, their clever heads and intelligent faces; from them come the writers, and brain carriers of Norway. The Finns, too, have a distinctive type of head and a something elusive in the expression of their changeful eyes; but all, the town students too, of easier manners and slangier tongues— all alike are going, as finances permit, to dine in restaurant or steam-kitchen. I saw the *menu* for to-day posted up outside the door of the latter as I passed—'Rice porridge and salt meat soup, 6*d*.,'—and Hans Jörgen came back with a vivid picture of childhood days, when every family in the little coast-town where we lived had a fixed *menu* for every day in the week; and it was quite a distinction to have meat balls on pickled herring day, or ale soup when all the folks in town were cooking omelets with bacon. How he used to eat rice porridge in those days! I can see him now put his heels together and give his awkward bow as he said, 'Tak for Maden tante!' Well, we are sitting in the Grand Café after dinner, at a little table near the door, watching the people pass in and out. An ubiquitous 'sample-count' from Berlin is measuring his wits with a young Norwegian merchant; he is standing green chartreuse; it pays to be generous even for a German, when you can oust honest Leeds cloth with German shoddy: at least, so my cousin says. He knows every one by sight, and points out all the celebrities to me. Suddenly he bows profoundly. I look round: a tall woman with very square shoulders, and gold-rimmed spectacles is passing us with two gentlemen. She is English, by her tailor-made gown and little shirt-front, and noticeable anywhere.

'That lady,' says my cousin, 'is a compatriot of yours. She is a very fine person, a very learned lady; she has been looking up referats in the University Bibliothek. Professor Sturm—he is a good friend of me—did tell me. I forget her name; she is married. I suppose her husband he stay at home and keep the house!'

My cousin has just been refused by a young lady dentist, who says she is too comfortably off to change for a small house-keeping business, so I excuse his sarcasm. We leave as the time draws on, and sleigh down to the steamer. I like the jingle of the bells, and I feel a little sad; there is a witchery about the country that creeps into one and works like a love-philter, and if one has once lived up there, one never gets it out of one's blood again. I go on board and lean over and watch the people; there are a good many for winter-time. The bell rings. Two sleighs drive up, and my compatriot and her friends appear; she shakes hands with them and comes leisurely up the gang-way. The thought flits through me that she would cross it in just that cool way if she were facing death; it is foolish, but most of our passing thoughts are just as inconsequent. She calls down a remembrance to some one in such pretty Norwegian, much prettier than mine, and then we swing round. Handkerchiefs wave in every hand. Never have I seen such persistent hand-kerchief-waving as at the departure of a boat in Norway; it is a national characteristic. If you live at the mouth of a fjord, and go to the market town at the head of it for your weekly supply of coffee beans, the population give you a 'send off' with flutter-ing kerchiefs; it is as universal as the 'Thanks.' Hans Jörgen says I am Anglicized, and only see the ridiculous side, forgetting the kind feelings that prompt it.

I find a strange pleasure in watching the rocks peep out under the snow, the children dragging their hand-sleds along the ice. All the little bits of winter life of which I get flying glimpses as we pass, bring back scenes grown dim in the years between. There is a mist ahead; and when we pass Dröbak cud-dled like a dormouse for winter's sleep I go below. A bright coal fire burns in the open grate of the stove, and the "Rollo" saloon looks very cosy. My compatriot is stretched in a big arm-chair reading. She is sitting comfortably with one leg crossed over the other, in the manner called 'shockingly unladylike' of my early lessons in deportment. The flame flickers over the patent leather of her neat low-heeled boot, and strikes a spark from the pin in her tie. There is something manlike about her; I don't know where it lies, but it is there. Her hair curls in grey flecked rings about her head; it has not a cut look, seems rather to grow short naturally. She has a charming, tubbed look; of course every lady is alike clean, but some men and women have an individual look of sweet cleanness that is a beauty of itself. She feels my gaze, and looks up and smiles; she has a rare smile, it shows her white teeth and softens her features.

'The fire is cosy, isn't it? I hope we shall have an easy passage, so that it can be kept in.'

I answer something in English.

She has a trick of wrinkling her brows, she does it now as she says—

'A-ah, I should have said you were Norsk. Are you not really? Surely you have a typical head, or eyes and hair at the least?'

'Half of me is Norsk, but I have lived a long time in England.'

'Father of course; case of "there was a sailor loved a lass," was it not?'

I smile an assent and add: 'I lost them both when I was very young.'

A reflective look steals over her face. It is stern in repose; and as she seems lost in some train of thought of her own, I go to my cabin and lie down; the rattling noises and the smell of paint makes me feel ill. I do not go out again. I wake next morning with a sense of fear at the stillness; there is no sound but a lapping wash of water at the side of the steamer, but it is delicious to lie quietly after the vibration of the screw and the sickening swing. I look at my watch—seven o'clock. I cannot make out why there is such a silence, as we only stop at Christiansand long enough to take cargo and passengers. I dress and go out. The saloon is empty but the fire is burning brightly. I go to the pantry and ask the stewardess when we arrived? Early, she says; all the passengers for here are already gone on shore; and there is a thick fog outside; goodness knows how long we'll be kept. I go to the top of the stairs and look out; the prospect is uninviting and I come down again and turn over some books on the table, in Russian, I think. I feel sure they are hers.

'Good morning!' comes her pleasant voice.

How alert and bright-eyed she is! it is a pick-me-up to look at her.

'You did not appear last night; not given in already, I hope!'

She is kneeling on one knee before the fire, holding her palms to the glow, and with her figure hidden in her loose, fur-lined coat and the light showing up her strong face under the

little tweed cap, she seems so like a clever-faced slight man, that
I feel I am conventionally guilty in talking so freely to her. She
looks at me with a deliberate, critical air, and then springs up.

'Let me give you something for your head! Stewardess, a
wine-glass!'

I should not dream of remonstrance, not if she were to command me to drink sea-water; and I am not complaisant as a
rule.

When she comes back I swallow it bravely, but I leave some
powder in the glass; she shakes her head, and I finish this too.
We sat and talked, or at least she talked and I listened. I don't
remember what she said; I only know that she was making clear
to me most of the things that had puzzled me for a long time—
questions that arise in silent hours, that one speculates over, and
to which one finds no answers in text-books. How she knew
just the subjects that worked in me I knew not; some subtle
intuitive sympathy, I suppose, enabled her to find it out. It was
the same at breakfast; she talked down to the level of the men
present (of course they did not see that it might be possible for
a woman to do that), and made it a very pleasant meal.

It was in the evening—we had the saloon to ourselves—
when she told me about the white elf. I had been talking of
myself and of Hans Jörgen.

'I like your Mr. Hans Jörgen,' she said, 'he has a strong nature
and knows what he wants; there is reliability in him. They are
rarer qualities than one thinks in men; I have found through life
that the average man is weaker than we are. It must be a good
thing to have a stronger nature to lean to. I have never had that.'

There is a want in the tone of her voice as she ends, and I feel
inclined to put out my hand and stroke hers,—she has beautiful
long hands—but I am afraid to do so. I query shyly—'Have
you no little ones?'

'Children, you mean? No, I am one of the barren ones; they
are less rare than they used to be. But I have a white elf at home

and that makes up for it. Shall I tell you how the elf came? Well, its mother is a connection of mine, and she hates me with an honest hatred; it is the only honest feeling I ever discovered in her. It was about the time that she found the elf was to come that it broke out openly, but that was mere coincidence. How she detested me! Those narrow, poor natures are capable of an intensity of feeling concentrated on one object that larger natures can scarcely measure.

'Now I shall tell you something strange. I do not pretend to understand it; I may have my theory, but that is of no physiological value—I only tell it to you. Well, all the time she was carrying the elf she was full of simmering hatred and she wished me evil often enough; one feels those things in an odd way. Why did she? Oh, that—that was a family affair; with perhaps a thread of jealousy mixed up in the knot. Well, one day the climax came, and much was said, and I went away and married and got ill and the doctors said I would be childless. And in the meantime the little human soul—I thought about it so often—had fought its way out of the darkness. We childless women weave more fancies into the "mithering o'bairns" than the actual mothers themselves. The poetry of it is not spoiled by nettle-rash or chin-cough any more than our figures. I am a writer by profession—oh, you knew! No, hardly celebrated; but I put my little chips into the great mosaic as best I can. Positions are reversed; they often are now-a-days. My husband stays at home and grows good things to eat, and pretty things to look at, and I go out and win bread and butter. It is a matter not of who has most brains, but whose brains are most saleable. Fit in with the housekeeping? Oh yes. I have a treasure, too, in Belinda. She is one of those women who must have something to love. She used to love cats, birds, dogs, anything. She is one bump of philo-progenitiveness; but she hates men. She says: "If one could only have a child, ma'am, without a husband or the disgrace! ugh, the disgusting men!" Do you know I think that is not an uncommon feeling amongst a certain number of women. I have often drawn her out on the subject; it struck me, because I have often found it in other women. I have known many, particularly older women, who would give anything in God's world to have a child of "their own" if it could be got just as Belinda says, "without the horrid man or the shame." It seems congenital with some women to have deeply rooted in their innermost nature a smouldering enmity—ay, sometimes a physical disgust—to men. It is a kind of kin-feeling to the race dislike of white men to black. Perhaps it explains why woman, where her own feelings are not concerned, will always make common cause with woman against man. I have often thought about it. You should hear Belinda's "serve him right" when some fellow comes to grief! I have a little of it myself [meditatively], but in a broader way, you know. I like to cut them out in their own province.

'Well, the elf was born; and now comes the singular part of it. It was a wretched, frail little being with a startling likeness to me. It was as if the evil the mother had wished me had worked on the child, and the constant thought of me stamped my features on its little face. I was working then on a Finland saga, and I do not know why it was, but the thought of that little being kept disturbing my work. It was worst in the afternoon time when the house seemed quietest; there is always a lull then, outside and inside. Have you ever noticed that? The birds hush their singing, and the work is done. Belinda used to sit sewing in the kitchen, and the words of a hymn she used to lilt in half tones—something about joy bells ringing, children singing—floated in to me, and the very tick-tock of the old clock sounded like the rocking of wooden cradles. It made me think sometimes that it would be pleasant to hear small, pattering feet and the call of voices through the silent house; and I suppose it acted as an irritant on my imaginative faculty, for the whole room seemed filled with the spirits of little children. They seemed to dance round me with uncertain, lightsome steps, waving tiny, pink, dimpled hands, shaking sunny, flossy curls, and haunting me with their great innocent child-eyes, filled with the unconscious sadness and the infinite questioning that is oftenest seen in the gaze of children. I used to fancy something stirred in me, and the spirits of unborn little ones never to come to life in me troubled me. I was probably overworked at the time. How we women digress! I am telling you more about myself than my white elf.

'Well, trouble came to their home, and I went and offered to take it. It was an odd little thing, and when I looked at it I could see how like we were. My glasses dimmed somehow, and a lump kept rising in my throat, when it smiled up out of its great eyes and held out two bits of hands like shrivelled white rose leaves. Such a tiny scrap it was! it was not bigger, she said, than a baby of eleven months. I suppose they can tell that as I can the date of a dialect; but I am getting wiser,' with an emotional softening of her face and quite a proud look. 'A child is like one of those wonderful runic alphabets; the signs are simple but the lore they contain is marvellous. "She is very like you," said the mother, "hold her." She was only beginning to walk. I did. You never saw such elfin ears, with strands of silk floss ringing round them, and the quaintest, darlingest wrinkles in its forehead, two long, and one short, just as I have,'—putting her head forward for me to see. 'The other children were strong, and the one on the road she hoped would be healthy. So I took it there and then "clothes and baby, cradle and all." Yes, I have a collection of nursery rhymes from many nations; I was going to put them in a book, but I say them to the elf now.

'I wired to my husband. You should have seen me going home. I was so nervous,—I was not half as nervous when I read my paper (it was rather a celebrated paper, perhaps you heard of it) to the Royal Geographical Society; it was on Esquimaux marriage songs, and the analogy between them and the Song of

Solomon. She was so light, and so wrapped up, and my *pince-nez* kept dropping off when I stooped over her (I got spectacles after that) and I used to fancy I had dropped her out of the wrappings, and peep under the shawl to make sure (with a sick shiver), to find her sucking her thumb. And I nearly passed my station; and then a valuable book—indeed, it is really a case of Mss., and almost unique—I had borrowed for reference, with some trouble, could not be found, and my husband roared with laughter when it turned up in the cradle. Belinda was at the gate anxious to take her, and he said I did not know how to hold her,—that I was holding her like a book of notes at a lecture; and so I gave her to Belinda. I think the poor little thing found it all strange, and when she puckered up her face and thrust out her under lip, and two great tears jumped off her lashes, we all felt ready for hanging. But Belinda, though she doesn't know one language, not even her own, for she sows her *h*'s broadcast and picks them up at hazard—she *can* talk to a baby. I am so glad for that reason she is bigger now. I couldn't manage it: I could not reason out any system they go on in baby talk. I tried mixing up the tenses, but somehow it wasn't right. My husband says it is not more odd than salmon taking a fly that is certainly like nothing they ever see in nature. Anyway it answered splendidly. Belinda used to say (I made a note of some of them): "Didsum was denn? Oo did! Was ums de prettiest itta sweetums den? Oo was. An' did um put 'em in a nasty shawl an' joggle 'em in an old puff-puff? Um did; was a shame! Hitchy cum, hitchy cum, hitchy cum hi, Chinaman no likey me!" This always made her laugh, though in what connection the Chinaman came in I never *could* fathom. I was a little jealous of Belinda, but she knew how to undress her. George, that's my husband's name, said the bath water was too hot, and that the proper way to test it was to put one's elbow in. Belinda laughed; but I must confess it did feel too hot when I tried it that way; but how did he know? I got her such pretty clothes, I was going to buy a pragtbind of Nietzsche, but that must wait. George made her a cot with her name carved on the head of it; such a pretty one.'

'Did you find she made a change in your lives?' I asked.

'Oh, didn't she! Children are such funny things. I stole away to have a look at her later on, and did not hear him come after me. She looked so sweet, and she was smiling in her sleep. I believe the Irish peasantry say that an angel is whispering when a baby does that. I had given up all belief myself, except the belief in a Creator who is working out some system that is too infinite for our finite minds to grasp. If one looks round with seeing eyes, one can't help thinking that after a run of eighteen hundred and ninety-three years Christianity is not very consoling in its results. But at that moment, kneeling next the cradle, I felt a strange, solemn feeling stealing over me; one is conscious of the same effect in a grand cathedral filled with the peal of organ music and soaring voices. It was as if all the old, sweet, untroubled child-belief came back for a spell, and I wondered if far back in the Nazarene village Mary ever knelt and watched the Christ-child sleep; and the legend of how he was often seen to weep but never to smile came back to me, and I think the sorrow I felt as I thought was an act of contrition and faith. I could not teach a child scepticism; so I remembered my husband prayed, and I resolved to ask him to teach her. You see [half hesitatingly] I have more brains, or at least more intellectuality than my husband; and in that case one is apt to undervalue simpler, perhaps greater, qualities. That came home to me, and I began to cry, I don't know why; and he lifted me up, and I think I said something of the kind to him. We got nearer to one another someway. He said it was unlucky to cry over a child.

'It made such a difference in the evenings! I used to hurry home,—I was on the staff of the "World's Review" just then; and it was so jolly to see the quaint little phiz smile up when I went in.

'Belinda was quite jealous of George. She said "Master wor-
ritted in an out, an' interfered with everything; she never seen
a man as knew so much about babies, not for one as never 'ad
none of 'is own. Wot if he didn't go to Parkins hisself, an' say as
how she was to have the milk of one cow, an' mind not mix it."
I wish you could have seen the insinuating distrust on Belinda's
face. I laughed. I believe we were all getting too serious; I know
I felt years younger. I told George that it was really suspicious:
how did he acquire such a stock of baby lore? *I* hadn't any. It
was all very well to say "Aunt Mary's kids." I should never be
surprised if I saw a Zwazi woman appear with a lot of tawny
pickaninnies in tow. George was shocked! I often shock him.

'She began to walk as soon as she got stronger. I never saw
such an inquisitive mite. I had to rearrange all my bookshelves,
change "Le Nu de Rabelais" (after Garnier, you know), and several others from the lower shelves to the top ones. One can't be
so Bohemian when there is a little white soul like that playing
about, can one? When we are alone, she always comes in to say
her prayers, and good-night. Larry Moore of the "Vulture"—he
is one of the most wickedly amusing of men; prides himself
on being *fin de siècle* (don't you detest that word?) or nothing;
raves about Dégas, and is a worshipper of the decadent school
of verse; quotes Verlaine, you know—well, he came in one evening on his way to some music hall. She's a whimsical little
thing, not without incipient coquetry either,—well, she would
say them to him. If you can imagine a masher of the Jan van
Beer type bending his head to hear a child in the white "nighty"
lisping prayers, you have an idea of the picture. She kissed him
good-night too (she never would before), and he must have
forgotten his engagement, for he stayed with us to supper. She
rules us all with a touch of her little hands, and I fancy we are
all the better for it. Would you like to see her?'

She hands me a medallion, with a beautifully painted head
in it. I can't say she is a pretty child—a weird, elf-like thing,

with questioning, wistful eyes, and masses of dark hair—and yet as I look the little face draws me to it, and makes a kind of yearning in me, strikes me with a 'fairy blast,' perhaps.

The journey was all too short, and when we got to Hull she saw me to my train. It was odd to see the quiet way in which she got everything she wanted. She put me into the carriage, got me a foot-warmer and a magazine, kissed me and said as she held my hand—

'The world is small; we run in circles; perhaps we shall meet again; in any case I wish you a white elf.'

I was sorry to part with her; I felt richer than before I knew her. I fancy she goes about the world giving graciously from her richer nature to the poorer-endowed folks she meets on her way.

Often since that night I have rounded my arm and bowed down my face and fancied I had a little human elf cuddled to my breast.

***

I am very busy just now getting everything ready; I had so much to buy. I don't like confessing it even to myself, but down in the bottom of my deepest trunk I have laid a parcel of things—such pretty, tiny things. I saw them at a sale; I couldn't resist them, they were so cheap. Even if one doesn't want the things, it seems a sin to let them go. Besides, there may be some poor woman out in Cincinnati. I wrote to Hans Jörgen, you know, back in spring, and—Du störer Gud! There is Hans Jörgen coming across the street!

James Joyce

From *Ulysses*

IT IS A PITY that James Joyce's convention-smashing master-piece, *Ulysses*, has garnered a reputation for being forbiddingly difficult. Too many people have missed out on the pleasures of this rich, scandalous book as a result. Joyce himself—modern literature's subversive-in-chief—is commemorated in his native land primarily by 'Bloomsday', an annual festival we can be sure he would have mocked with relish. The citizens who don Edwardian garb and roam the city each year on 16 June may or may not know what exactly lies at the origin of their feast day: Bloomsday, like *Ulysses* itself, honours the date on which a young James Joyce first received a handjob from his new and lifelong love, the chambermaid Nora Barnacle. In a letter written years later, a winningly grateful Joyce reminisced with Nora about how she had slid her hand 'down inside my trousers and pulled my shirt softly aside and touched my prick with your long tickling fingers and gradually took it all, fat and stiff as it was, into your hand and frigged me slowly until I came off through your fingers, all the time bending over me and gazing at me out of your quiet saintlike eyes'.

Ending with the glamorous sign-off 'Trieste–Zurich–Paris', *Ulysses* is both a definitive dismissal of all parochialism and petty nationalism (with its richly allusive and cosmopolitan textures), and an impassioned effort at mining the hometown particular for the seam of the universal. Set in Dublin on one day in 1904, the novel is an exuberance of playfully juggled styles, ingenious structuring, human insight, and warm, bawdy humour. By turns poignant, barely comprehensible, zestfully witty, and downright filthy, *Ulysses* marked a modernist great-leap-forward in world literature, mirrored by the publication in the same year—1922—of T. S. Eliot's poem *The Waste Land.* Together with Joyce's other great works—the much-loved story collection *Dubliners, Portrait of the Artist as a Young Man,* and the daunting *Finnegans Wake—Ulysses* established its author as a colossus.

The eldest of ten siblings, James Joyce was born in 1882 in the south Dublin suburb of Rathgar. He was educated under the Jesuits, eventually studying modern languages at University College Dublin, where he wrote his first stories and articles. In 1904 he began writing the stories that would be published a decade later as *Dubliners.* Having met Nora Barnacle that same year, he persuaded her to leave Ireland with him, commencing a trans-European peripateticism that would last the rest of their lives. The couple lived in Trieste–Zurich–Paris, as well as Rome and what is now Poland, and raised two children, George and Lucia. Living on the continent, Joyce committed himself to his writing, first while earning a living as an English-language teacher, then with the ample patronage of Harriet Shaw Weaver, editor of *The Egoist* magazine. After a torturous process, *Ulysses* was finally published in 1922 in Paris, by Sylvia Beach, owner of the Shakespeare & Company bookshop. Afterwards, plagued by chronic eye troubles and haunted by the schizophrenia of his daughter, Joyce devoted himself to writing his final novel, *Finnegans Wake* (1939). The year after its publication, Joyce died in Zurich, to where he and his family had returned in flight from Occupied France. He is buried there, alongside Nora Barnacle.

The extract included here, the so-called 'Ithaca' section from *Ulysses*, is the novel's penultimate chapter, and shows Joyce at his most playful and formally inventive, as Leopold Bloom and the young Stephen Dedalus walk home after a boozy Dublin night.

From *Ulysses*

WHAT PARALLEL COURSES DID Bloom and Stephen follow returning?

Starting united both at normal walking pace from Beresford place they followed in the order named Lower and Middle Gardiner streets and Mountjoy square, west: then, at reduced pace, each bearing left, Gardiner's place by an inadvertence as far as the farther corner of Temple street, north: then, at reduced pace with interruptions of halt, bearing right, Temple street, north, as far as Hardwicke place. Approaching, disparate, at relaxed walking pace they crossed both the circus before George's church diametrically, the chord in any circle being less than the arc which it subtends.

Of what did the duumvirate deliberate during their itinerary?

Music, literature, Ireland, Dublin, Paris, friendship, woman, prostitution, diet, the influence of gaslight or the light of arc and glowlamps on the growth of adjoining paraheliotropic trees, exposed corporation emergency dustbuckets, the Roman catholic church, ecclesiastical celibacy, the Irish nation, jesuit education, careers, the study of medicine, the past day, the maleficent influence of the presabbath, Stephen's collapse.

Did Bloom discover common factors of similarity between their respective like and unlike reactions to experience?

Both were sensitive to artistic impressions, musical in preference to plastic or pictorial. Both preferred a continental to an insular manner of life, a cisatlantic to a transatlantic place of residence. Both indurated by early domestic training and an inherited tenacity of heterodox resistance professed their disbelief in many orthodox religious, national, social and ethical doctrines. Both admitted the alternately stimulating and obtunding influence of heterosexual magnetism.

Were their views on some points divergent?

Stephen dissented openly from Bloom's views on the importance of dietary and civic selfhelp while Bloom dissented tacitly from Stephen's views on the eternal affirmation of the spirit of man in literature. Bloom assented covertly to Stephen's rectification of the anachronism involved in assigning the date of the conversion of the Irish nation to christianity from druidism by Patrick son of Calpornus, son of Potitus, son of Odyssus, sent by pope Celestine I in the year 432 in the reign of Leary to the year 260 or thereabouts in the reign of Cormac MacArt († 266 A.D.), suffocated by imperfect deglutition of aliment at Sletty and interred at Rossnaree. The collapse which Bloom ascribed to gastric inanition and certain chemical compounds of varying degrees of adulteration and alcoholic strength, accelerated by mental exertion and the velocity of rapid circular motion in a relaxing atmosphere, Stephen attributed to the reapparition of a matutinal cloud (perceived by both from two different points of observation Sandycove and Dublin) at first no bigger than a woman's hand.

Was there one point on which their views were equal and negative?

The influence of gaslight or electric light on the growth of adjoining paraheliotropic trees.

Had Bloom discussed similar subjects during nocturnal perambulations in the past?

In 1884 with Owen Goldberg and Cecil Turnbull at night on public thoroughfares between Longwood avenue and Leonard's corner and Leonard's corner and Synge street and Synge street and Bloomfield avenue. In 1885 with Percy Apjohn in the evenings, reclined against the wall between Gibraltar villa and Bloomfield house in Crumlin, barony of Uppercross. In 1886 occasionally with casual acquaintances and prospective purchasers on doorsteps, in front parlours, in third class railway carriages of suburban lines. In 1888 frequently with major Brian Tweedy and his daughter Miss Marion Tweedy, together and separately on the lounge in Matthew Dillon's house in Roundtown. Once in 1892 and once in 1893 with Julius (Juda) Mastiansky, on both occasions in the parlour of his (Bloom's) house in Lombard street, west.

What reflection concerning the irregular sequence of dates 1884, 1885, 1886, 1888, 1892, 1893, 1904 did Bloom make before their arrival at their destination?

He reflected that the progressive extension of the field of individual development and experience was regressively accompanied by a restriction of the converse domain of interindividual relations.

As in what ways?

From inexistence to existence he came to many and was as one received: existence with existence he was with any as any with any: from existence to nonexistence gone he would be by all as none perceived.

What act did Bloom make on their arrival at their destination?

At the housesteps of the 4th of the equidifferent uneven numbers, number 7 Eccles street, he inserted his hand mechanically into the back pocket of his trousers to obtain his latchkey.

Was it there?

It was in the corresponding pocket of the trousers which he had worn on the day but one preceding.

Why was he doubly irritated?

Because he had forgotten and because he remembered that he had reminded himself twice not to forget.

What were then the alternatives before the, premeditatedly (respectively) and inadvertently, keyless couple?

To enter or not to enter. To knock or not to knock.

Bloom's decision?

A stratagem. Resting his feet on the dwarf wall, he climbed over the area railings, compressed his hat on his head, grasped two points at the lower union of rails and stiles, lowered his body gradually by its length of five feet nine inches and a half to within two feet ten inches of the area pavement, and allowed his body to move freely in space by separating himself from the railings and crouching in preparation for the impact of the fall.

Did he fall?

By his body's known weight of eleven stone and four pounds in avoirdupois measure, as certified by the graduated machine for periodical selfweighing in the premises of Francis Froedman, pharmaceutical chemist of 19 Frederick street, north, on the last feast of the Ascension, to wit, the twelfth day of May of the bissextile year one thousand nine hundred and four of the christian era (jewish era five thousand six hundred and sixtyfour, mohammadan era one thousand three hundred and twentytwo), golden number 5, epact 13, solar cycle 9, dominical letters C B, Roman indiction 2, Julian period 6617, MXMIV.

Did he rise uninjured by concussion?

Regaining new stable equilibrium he rose uninjured though concussed by the impact, raised the latch of the area door by the exertion of force at its freely moving flange and by leverage of the first kind applied at its fulcrum gained retarded access to the kitchen through the subadjacent scullery, ignited a lucifer match by friction, set free inflammable coal gas by turning on the ventcock, lit a high flame which, by regulating, he reduced to quiescent candescence and lit finally a portable candle.

What discrete succession of images did Stephen meanwhile perceive?

Reclined against the area railings he perceived through the transparent kitchen panes a man regulating a gasflame of 14 CP, a man lighting a candle, a man removing in turn each of his two boots, a man leaving the kitchen holding a candle of 1 CP.

Did the man reappear elsewhere?

After a lapse of four minutes the glimmer of his candle was discernible through the semitransparent semicircular glass fanlight over the halldoor. The halldoor turned gradually on its hinges. In the open space of the doorway the man reappeared without his hat, with his candle.

Did Stephen obey his sign?

Yes, entering softly, he helped to close and chain the door and followed softly along the hallway the man's back and listed feet and lighted candle past a lighted crevice of doorway on the left and carefully down a turning staircase of more than five steps into the kitchen of Bloom's house.

What did Bloom do?

He extinguished the candle by a sharp expiration of breath upon its flame, drew two spoonseat deal chairs to the hearthstone, one for Stephen with its back to the area window, the other for himself when necessary, knelt on one knee, composed in the grate a pyre of crosslaid resintipped sticks and various coloured papers and irregular polygons of best Abram coal at twentyone shillings a ton from the yard of Messrs Flower and M'Donald of 14 D'Olier street, kindled it at three projecting points of paper with one ignited lucifer match, thereby releasing the potential energy contained in the fuel by allowing its carbon and hydrogen elements to enter into free union with the oxygen of the air.

Of what similar apparitions did Stephen think?

Of others elsewhere in other times who, kneeling on one knee or on two, had kindled fires for him, of Brother Michael in the infirmary of the college of the Society of Jesus at Clongowes Wood, Sallins, in the county of Kildare: of his father, Simon Dedalus, in an unfurnished room of his first residence in Dublin, number thirteen Fitzgibbon street: of his godmother Miss Kate Morkan in the house of her dying sister Miss Julia Morkan at 15 Usher's Island: of his aunt Sara, wife of Richie (Richard) Goulding, in the kitchen of their lodgings at 62 Clanbrassil street: of his mother Mary, wife of Simon Dedalus, in the kitchen of number twelve North Richmond street on the morning of the feast of Saint Francis Xavier 1898: of the dean of studies, Father Butt, in the physics' theatre of university College, 16 Stephen's Green, north: of his sister Dilly (Delia) in his father's house in Cabra.

What did Stephen see on raising his gaze to the height of a yard from the fire towards the opposite wall?

Under a row of five coiled spring housebells a curvilinear rope, stretched between two holdfasts athwart across the recess beside the chimney pier, from which hung four smallsized square handkerchiefs folded unattached consecutively in adjacent rectangles and one pair of ladies' grey hose with lisle suspender tops and feet in their habitual position clamped by three erect wooden pegs two at their outer extremities and the third at their point of junction.

What did Bloom see on the range?

On the right (smaller) hob a blue enamelled saucepan: on the left (larger) hob a black iron kettle.

What did Bloom do at the range?

He removed the saucepan to the left hob, rose and carried the iron kettle to the sink in order to tap the current by turning the faucet to let it flow.

Did it flow?

Yes. From Roundwood reservoir in county Wicklow of a cubic capacity of 2400 million gallons, percolating through a subterranean aqueduct of filter mains of single and double pipeage constructed at an initial plant cost of £ 5 per linear yard by way of the Dargle, Rathdown, Glen of the Downs and Callowhill to the 26 acre reservoir at Stillorgan, a distance of 22 statute miles, and thence, through a system of relieving tanks, by a gradient of 250 feet to the city boundary at Eustace bridge, upper Leeson street, though from prolonged summer drouth and daily supply of 12 1/2 million gallons the water had fallen below the sill of the overflow weir for which reason the borough surveyor and waterworks engineer, Mr Spencer Harty, C. E., on the instructions of the waterworks committee had prohibited the use of municipal water for purposes other than those of consumption (envisaging the possibility of recourse being had to the impotable water of the Grand and Royal canals as in 1893) particularly as the South Dublin Guardians, notwithstanding their ration of 15 gallons per day per pauper supplied through a 6 inch meter, had been convicted of a wastage of 20,000 gallons per night by a reading of their meter on the affirmation of the law agent of the corporation, Mr Ignatius Rice, solicitor, thereby acting to the detriment of another section of the public, selfsupporting taxpayers, solvent, sound.

What in water did Bloom, waterlover, drawer of water, watercarrier, returning to the range, admire?

Its universality: its democratic equality and constancy to its nature in seeking its own level: its vastness in the ocean of Mercator's projection: its unplumbed profundity in the Sundam trench of the Pacific exceeding 8000 fathoms: the restlessness of its waves and surface particles visiting in turn all points of its seaboard: the independence of its units: the variability of states of sea: its hydrostatic quiescence in calm: its hydrokinetic turgidity in neap and spring tides: its subsidence after devastation: its sterility in the circumpolar icecaps, arctic and antarctic: its climatic and commercial significance: its preponderance of 3 to 1 over the dry land of the globe: its indisputable hegemony extending in square leagues over all the region below the subequatorial tropic of Capricorn: the multisecular stability of its primeval basin: its luteofulvous bed: its capacity to dissolve and hold in solution all soluble substances including millions of tons of the most precious metals: its slow erosions of peninsulas and islands, its persistent formation of homothetic islands, peninsulas and downwardtending promontories: its alluvial deposits: its weight and volume and density: its imperturbability in lagoons and highland tarns: its gradation of colours in the torrid and temperate and frigid zones: its vehicular ramifications in continental lakecontained streams and confluent oceanflowing rivers with their tributaries and transoceanic currents: gulfstream, north and south equatorial courses: its violence in seaquakes, waterspouts, artesian wells, eruptions, torrents, eddies, freshets, spates, groundswells, watersheds, waterpartings, geysers, cataracts, whirlpools, maelstroms, inundations, deluges, cloudbursts: its vast circumterrestrial ahorizontal curve: its secrecy in springs and latent humidity, revealed by rhabdomantic or hygrometric instruments and exemplified by the hole in the wall at Ashtown gate, saturation of air, distillation of dew: the simplicity of its composition, two constituent parts of hydrogen with one constituent part of oxygen: its healing virtues: its buoyancy in the waters of the Dead Sea: its persevering penetrativeness in runnels, gullies, inadequate dams, leaks on shipboard: its properties for cleansing, quenching thirst and fire, nourishing vegetation: its infallibility as paradigm and paragon: its metamorphoses as vapour, mist, cloud, rain, sleet, snow, hail: its strength in rigid hydrants: its variety of forms in loughs and bays and gulfs and bights and guts and lagoons and atolls and archipelagos and sounds and fjords and minches and tidal estuaries and arms of sea: its solidity in glaciers, icebergs, icefloes: its docility in working hydraulic millwheels, turbines, dynamos, electric power stations, bleachworks, tanneries, scutchmills: its utility in canals, rivers, if navigable, floating and graving docks: its potentiality derivable from harnessed tides or watercourses falling from level to level: its submarine fauna and flora (anacoustic, photophobe), numerically, if not literally, the inhabitants of the globe: its ubiquity as constituting 90 % of the human body: the noxiousness of its effluvia in lacustrine marshes, pestilential fens, faded flowerwater, stagnant pools in the waning moon.

Having set the halffilled kettle on the now burning coals, why did he return to the stillflowing tap?

To wash his soiled hands with a partially consumed tablet of Barrington's lemonflavoured soap, to which paper still adhered, (bought thirteen hours previously for fourpence and still unpaid for), in fresh cold neverchanging everchanging water and dry them, face and hands, in a long redbordered holland cloth passed over a wooden revolving roller.

What reason did Stephen give for declining Bloom's offer?

That he was hydrophobe, hating partial contact by immersion or total by submersion in cold water, (his last bath having taken place in the month of October of the preceding year), disliking the aqueous substances of glass and crystal, distrusting aquacities of thought and language.

What impeded Bloom from giving Stephen counsels of hygiene and prophylactic to which should be added suggestions concerning a preliminary wetting of the head and contraction of the muscles with rapid splashing of the face and neck and thoracic and epigastric region in case of sea or river bathing, the parts of the human anatomy most sensitive to cold being the nape, stomach and thenar or sole of foot?

The incompatibility of aquacity with the erratic originality of genius.

What additional didactic counsels did he similarly repress?

Dietary: concerning the respective percentage of protein and caloric energy in bacon, salt ling and butter, the absence of the former in the lastnamed and the abundance of the latter in the firstnamed.

Which seemed to the host to be the predominant qualities of his guest?

Confidence in himself, an equal and opposite power of abandonment and recuperation.

What concomitant phenomenon took place in the vessel of liquid by the agency of fire?

The phenomenon of ebullition. Fanned by a constant updraught of ventilation between the kitchen and the chimneyflue, ignition was communicated from the faggots of precombustible fuel to polyhedral masses of bituminous coal, containing in compressed mineral form the foliated fossilised decidua of primeval forests which had in turn derived their vegetative existence from the sun, primal source of heat (radiant), transmitted through omnipresent luminiferous diathermanous ether. Heat (convected), a mode of motion developed by such combustion, was constantly and increasingly conveyed from the source of calorification to the liquid contained in the vessel, being radiated through the uneven unpolished dark surface of the metal iron, in part reflected, in part absorbed, in part transmitted, gradually raising the temperature of the water from normal to boiling point, a rise in temperature expressible as the result of an expenditure of 72 thermal units needed to raise 1 pound of water from 50° to 212° Fahrenheit.

What announced the accomplishment of this rise in temperature?
A double falciform ejection of water vapour from under the kettlelid at both sides simultaneously.

For what personal purpose could Bloom have applied the water so boiled?
To shave himself.

What advantages attended shaving by night?
A softer beard: a softer brush if intentionally allowed to remain from shave to shave in its agglutinated lather: a softer skin if unexpectedly encountering female acquaintances in remote places at incustomary hours: quiet reflections upon the course of the day: a cleaner sensation when awaking after a fresher sleep since matutinal noises, premonitions and perturbations, a clattered milkcan, a postman's double knock, a paper read, reread while lathering, relathering the same spot, a shock, a shoot, with thought of aught he sought though fraught with nought might cause a faster rate of shaving and a nick on which incision plaster with precision cut and humected and applied adhered which was to be done.

Why did absence of light disturb him less than presence of noise?
Because of the surety of the sense of touch in his firm full masculine feminine passive active hand.

What quality did it (his hand) possess but with what counteracting influence?

The operative surgical quality but that he was reluctant to shed human blood even when the end justified the means, preferring, in their natural order, heliotherapy, psychophysicotherapeutics, osteopathic surgery.

What lay under exposure on the lower, middle and upper shelves of the kitchen dresser, opened by Bloom?

On the lower shelf five vertical breakfast plates, six horizontal breakfast saucers on which rested inverted breakfast cups, a moustachecup, uninverted, and saucer of Crown Derby, four white goldrimmed eggcups, an open shammy purse displaying coins, mostly copper, and a phial of aromatic violet comfits. On the middle shelf a chipped eggcup containing pepper, a drum of table salt, four conglomerated black olives in oleaginous paper, an empty pot of Plumtree's potted meat, an oval wicker basket bedded with fibre and containing one Jersey pear, a halfempty bottle of William Gilbey and Co's white invalid port, half disrobed of its swathe of coralpink tissue paper, a packet of Epps's soluble cocoa, five ounces of Anne Lynch's choice tea at 2/- per lb in a crinkled leadpaper bag, a cylindrical canister containing the best crystallised lump sugar, two onions, one, the larger, Spanish, entire, the other, smaller, Irish, bisected with augmented surface and more redolent, a jar of Irish Model Dairy's cream, a jug of brown crockery containing a naggin and a quarter of soured adulterated milk, converted by heat into water, acidulous serum and semisolidified curds, which added to the quantity subtracted for Mr Bloom's and Mrs Fleming's breakfasts, made one imperial pint, the total quantity originally delivered, two cloves, a halfpenny and a small dish containing a slice of fresh ribsteak. On the upper shelf a battery of jamjars (empty) of various sizes and proveniences.

What attracted his attention lying on the apron of the dresser?

Four polygonal fragments of two lacerated scarlet betting tickets, numbered 8 87, 8 86.

What reminiscences temporarily corrugated his brow?

Reminiscences of coincidences, truth stranger than fiction, preindicative of the result of the Gold Cup flat handicap, the official and definitive result of which he had read in the *Evening Telegraph*, late pink edition, in the cabman's shelter, at Butt bridge.

Where had previous intimations of the result, effected or projected, been received by him?

In Bernard Kiernan's licensed premises 8, 9 and 10 little Britain street: in David Byrne's licensed premises, 14 Duke street: in O'Connell street lower, outside Graham Lemon's when a dark man had placed in his hand a throwaway (subsequently thrown away), advertising Elijah, restorer of the church in Zion: in Lincoln place outside the premises of F. W. Sweny and Co (Limited), dispensing chemists, when, when Frederick M. (Bantam) Lyons had rapidly and successively requested, perused and restituted the copy of the current issue of the *Freeman's Journal* and *National Press* which he had been about to throw away (subsequently thrown away), he had proceeded towards the oriental edifice of the Turkish and Warm Baths, 11 Leinster street, with the light of inspiration shining in his countenance and bearing in his arms the secret of the race, graven in the language of prediction.

What qualifying considerations allayed his perturbations?

The difficulties of interpretation since the significance of any event followed its occurrence as variably as the acoustic report followed the electrical discharge and of counterestimating against an actual loss by failure to interpret the total sum of possible losses proceeding originally from a successful interpretation.

His mood?
He had not risked, he did not expect, he had not been disappointed, he was satisfied.

What satisfied him?
To have sustained no positive loss. To have brought a positive gain to others. Light to the gentiles.

How did Bloom prepare a collation for a gentile?
He poured into two teacups two level spoonfuls, four in all, of Epps's soluble cocoa and proceeded according to the directions for use printed on the label, to each adding after sufficient time for infusion the prescribed ingredients for diffusion in the manner and in the quantity prescribed.

What supererogatory marks of special hospitality did the host show his guest?
Relinquishing his symposiarchal right to the moustache cup of imitation Crown Derby presented to him by his only daughter, Millicent (Milly), he substituted a cup identical with that of his guest and served extraordinarily to his guest and, in reduced measure, to himself the viscous cream ordinarily reserved for the breakfast of his wife Marion (Molly).

Was the guest conscious of and did he acknowledge these marks of hospitality?
His attention was directed to them by his host jocosely, and he accepted them seriously as they drank in jocoserious silence Epps's massproduct, the creature cocoa.

Were there marks of hospitality which he contemplated

but suppressed, reserving them for another and for himself on future occasions to complete the act begun?

The reparation of a fissure of the length of 1 1/2 inches in the right side of his guest's jacket. A gift to his guest of one of the four lady's handkerchiefs, if and when ascertained to be in a presentable condition.

Who drank more quickly?

Bloom, having the advantage of ten seconds at the initiation and taking, from the concave surface of a spoon along the handle of which a steady flow of heat was conducted, three sips to his opponent's one, six to two, nine to three.

What cerebration accompanied his frequentative act?

Concluding by inspection but erroneously that his silent companion was engaged in mental composition he reflected on the pleasures derived from literature of instruction rather than of amusement as he himself had applied to the works of William Shakespeare more than once for the solution of difficult problems in imaginary or real life.

Had he found their solution?

In spite of careful and repeated reading of certain classical passages, aided by a glossary, he had derived imperfect conviction from the text, the answers not bearing in all points.

What lines concluded his first piece of original verse written by him, potential poet, at the age of 11 in 1877 on the occasion of the offering of three prizes of 10/-, 5/- and 2/6 respectively for competition by the *Shamrock*, a weekly newspaper?

An ambition to squint
At my verses in print
Makes me hope that for these you'll find room.
If you so condescend

Then please place at the end
The name of yours truly, L. Bloom.

Did he find four separating forces between his temporary
guest and him?
Name, age, race, creed.

What anagrams had he made on his name in youth?
Leopold Bloom
Ellpodbomool
Molldopeloob
Bollopedoom
Old Ollebo, M. P.

What acrostic upon the abbreviation of his first name had
he (kinetic poet) sent to Miss Marion (Molly) Tweedy on the
14 February 1888?

> *Poets oft have sung in rhyme*
> *Of music sweet their praise divine.*
> *Let them hymn it nine times nine.*
> *Dearer far than song or wine.*
> *You are mine. The world is mine.*

What had prevented him from completing a topical song
(music by R. G. Johnston) on the events of the past, or fixtures
for the actual years, entitled *If Brian Boru could but come back
and see old Dublin now*, commissioned by Michael Gunn, lessee
of the Gaiety Theatre, 46, 47, 48, 49 South King street, and
to be introduced into the sixth scene, the valley of diamonds,
of the second edition (30 January 1893) of the grand annual
Christmas pantomime *Sinbad the Sailor* (written by Greenleaf
Whittier, scenery by George A. Jackson and Cecil Hicks, costumes by Mrs and Miss Whelan, produced by R. Shelton 26
December 1892 under personal supervision of Mrs Michael

Gunn, ballets by Jessie Noir, harlequinade by Thomas Otto) and sung by Nelly Bouverist principal girl?

Firstly, oscillation between events of imperial and of local interest, the anticipated diamond jubilee of Queen Victoria (born 1820, acceded 1837) and the posticipated opening of the new municipal fish market: secondly, apprehension of opposition from extreme circles on the questions of the respective visits of Their Royal Highnesses, the duke and duchess of York (real) and, of His Majesty King Brian Boru (imaginary): thirdly, a conflict between professional etiquette and professional emulation concerning the recent erections of the Grand Lyric Hall on Burgh Quay and the Theatre Royal in Hawkins street: fourthly, distraction resultant from compassion for Nelly Bouverist's non-intellectual, non-political, non-topical expression of countenance and concupiscence caused by Nelly Bouverist's revelations of white articles of non-intellectual, non-political, non-topical underclothing while she (Nelly Bouverist) was in the articles: fifthly, the difficulties of the selection of appropriate music and humorous allusions from *Everybody's Book of Jokes* (1000 pages and a laugh in every one): sixthly, the rhymes, homophonous and cacophonous, associated with the names of the new lord mayor, Daniel Tallon, the new high sheriff, Thomas Pile and the new solicitorgeneral, Dunbar Plunket Barton.

What relation existed between their ages?

16 years before in 1888 when Bloom was of Stephen's present age Stephen was 6. 16 years after in 1920 when Stephen would be of Bloom's present age Bloom would be 54. In 1936 when Bloom would be 70 and Stephen 54 their ages initially in the ratio of 16 to 0 would be as 17 1/2 to 13 1/2, the proportion increasing and the disparity diminishing according as arbitrary future years were added, for if the proportion existing in 1883 had continued immutable, conceiving that to be possible, till then 1904 when Stephen was 22 Bloom would be 374 and in

1920 when Stephen would be 38, as Bloom then was, Bloom would be 646 while in 1952 when Stephen would have attained the maximum postdiluvian age of 70 Bloom, being 1190 years alive having been born in the year 714, would have surpassed by 221 years the maximum antediluvian age, that of Methusalah, 969 years, while, if Stephen would continue to live until he would attain that age in the year 3072 A.D., Bloom would have been obliged to have been alive 83,300 years, having been obliged to have been born in the year 81,396 B.C.

What events might nullify these calculations?

The cessation of existence of both or either, the inauguration of a new era or calendar, the annihilation of the world and consequent extermination of the human species, inevitable but impredictable.

How many previous encounters proved their preexisting acquaintance?

Two. The first in the lilacgarden of Matthew Dillon's house, Medina Villa, Kimmage road, Roundtown, in 1887, in the company of Stephen's mother, Stephen being then of the age of 5 and reluctant to give his hand in salutation. The second in the coffeeroom of Breslin's hotel on a rainy Sunday in the January of 1892, in the company of Stephen's father and Stephen's granduncle, Stephen being then 5 years older.

Did Bloom accept the invitation to dinner given then by the son and afterwards seconded by the father?

Very gratefully, with grateful appreciation, with sincere appreciative gratitude, in appreciatively grateful sincerity of regret, he declined.

Did their conversation on the subject of these reminiscences reveal a third connecting link between them?

Mrs Riordan (Dante), a widow of independent means, had resided in the house of Stephen's parents from 1 September 1888 to 29 December 1891 and had also resided during the years 1892, 1893 and 1894 in the City Arms Hotel owned by Elizabeth O'Dowd of 54 Prussia street where, during parts of the years 1893 and 1894, she had been a constant informant of Bloom who resided also in the same hotel, being at that time a clerk in the employment of Joseph Cuffe of 5 Smithfield for the superintendence of sales in the adjacent Dublin Cattle market on the North Circular road.

Had he performed any special corporal work of mercy for her?

He had sometimes propelled her on warm summer evenings, an infirm widow of independent, if limited means, in her convalescent bathchair with slow revolutions of its wheels as far as the corner of the North Circular road opposite Mr Gavin Low's place of business where she had remained for a certain time scanning through his onelensed binocular fieldglasses unrecognisable citizens on tramcars, roadster bicycles, equipped with inflated pneumatic tyres, hackney carriages, tandems, private and hired landaus, dogcarts, ponytraps and brakes passing from the city to the Phoenix Park and *vice versa*.

Why could he then support that his vigil with the greater equanimity?

Because in middle youth he had often sat observing through a rondel of bossed glass of a multicoloured pane the spectacle offered with continual changes of the thoroughfare without, pedestrians, quadrupeds, velocipedes, vehicles, passing slowly, quickly, evenly, round and round and round the rim of a round and round precipitous globe.

What distinct different memories had each of her now eight years deceased?

The older, her bezique cards and counters, her Skye terrier, her supposititious wealth, her lapses of responsiveness and incipient catarrhal deafness: the younger, her lamp of colza oil before the statue of the Immaculate Conception, her green and maroon brushes for Charles Stewart Parnell and for Michael Davitt, her tissue papers.

Were there no means still remaining to him to achieve the rejuvenation which these reminiscences divulged to a younger companion rendered the more desirable?

The indoor exercises, formerly intermittently practised, subsequently abandoned, prescribed in Eugen Sandow's *Physical Strength and How to Obtain It* which, designed particularly for commercial men engaged in sedentary occupations, were to be made with mental concentration in front of a mirror so as to bring into play the various families of muscles and produce successively a pleasant rigidity, a more pleasant relaxation and the most pleasant repristination of juvenile agility.

Had any special agility been his in earlier youth?

Though ringweight lifting had been beyond his strength and the full circle gyration beyond his courage yet as a High school scholar he had excelled in his stable and protracted execution of the half lever movement on the parallel bars in consequence of his abnormally developed abdominal muscles.

Did either openly allude to their racial difference?
Neither.

What, reduced to their simplest reciprocal form, were Bloom's thoughts about Stephen's thoughts about Bloom and Bloom's thoughts about Stephen's thoughts about Bloom's thoughts about Stephen?

He thought that he thought that he was a jew whereas he knew that he knew that he knew that he was not.

What, the enclosures of reticence removed, were their respective parentages?

Bloom, only born male transubstantial heir of Rudolf Virag (subsequently Rudolph Bloom) of Szombathely, Vienna, Budapest, Milan, London and Dublin and of Ellen Higgins, second daughter of Julius Higgins (born Karoly) and Fanny Higgins (born Hegarty); Stephen, eldest surviving male consubstantial heir of Simon Dedalus of Cork and Dublin and of Mary, daughter of Richard and Christina Goulding (born Grier).

Had Bloom and Stephen been baptised, and where and by whom, cleric or layman?

Bloom (three times) by the reverend Mr Gilmer Johnston M. A. alone, in the protestant church of Saint Nicolas Without, Coombe; by James O'Connor, Philip Gilligan and James Fitzpatrick, together, under a pump in the village of Swords; and by the reverend Charles Malone C. C., in the church of the Three Patrons, Rathgar. Stephen (once) by the reverend Charles Malone C. C., alone, in the church of the Three Patrons, Rathgar.

Did they find their educational careers similar?

Substituting Stephen for Bloom Stoom would have passed successively through a dame's school and the high school. Substituting Bloom for Stephen Blephen would have passed successively through the preparatory, junior, middle and senior grades of the intermediate and through the matriculation, first arts, second arts and arts degree courses of the royal university.

Why did Bloom refrain from stating that he had frequented the university of life?

Because of his fluctuating incertitude as to whether this observation had or had not been already made by him to Stephen or by Stephen to him.

What two temperaments did they individually represent?
The scientific. The artistic.

What proofs did Bloom adduce to prove that his tendency
was towards applied, rather than towards pure, science?

Certain possible inventions of which he had cogitated when
reclining in a state of supine repletion to aid digestion, stimulated by his appreciation of the importance of inventions now
common but once revolutionary for example, the aeronautic
parachute, the reflecting telescope, the spiral corkscrew, the
safety pin, the mineral water siphon, the canal lock with winch
and sluice, the suction pump.

Were these inventions principally intended for an improved
scheme of kindergarten?

Yes, rendering obsolete popguns, elastic airbladders,
games of hazard, catapults. They comprised astronomical
kaleidoscopes exhibiting the twelve constellations of the
zodiac from Aries to Pisces, miniature mechanical orreries,
arithmetical gelatine lozenges, geometrical to correspond
with zoological biscuits, globemap playingballs, historically
costumed dolls.

What also stimulated him in his cogitations?

The financial success achieved by Ephraim Marks and
Charles A. James, the former by his 1d. bazaar at 42 George's
street, South, the latter at his 6 1/2d. shop and world's fancy
fair and waxwork exhibition at 30 Henry street, admission 2d.,
children 1d.; and the infinite possibilities hitherto unexploited
of the modern art of advertisement if condensed in triliteral
monoideal symbols, vertically of maximum visibility (divined),
horizontally of maximum legibility (deciphered) and of mag-
netising efficacy to arrest involuntary attention, to interest, to
convince, to decide.

Such as?

K. 11. Kino's 11/- Trousers.

House of Keys. Alexander J. Keyes.

Such as not?

Look at this long candle. Calculate when it burns out and you receive gratis 1 pair of our special non-compo boots, guaranteed 1 candle power. Address: Barclay and Cook, 18 Talbot street.

Bacilikil (Insect Powder).

Veribest (Boot Blacking).

Uwantit (Combined pocket twoblade penknife with corkscrew, nailfile and pipecleaner).

Such as never?

What is home without Plumtree's Potted Meat?

Incomplete.

With it an abode of bliss.

Manufactured by George Plumtree, 23 Merchants' quay, Dublin, put up in 4 oz. pots, and inserted by Councillor Joseph P. Nannetti, M. P., Rotunda Ward, 19 Hardwicke street, under the obituary notices and anniversaries of deceases. The name on the label is Plumtree. A plumtree in a meatpot, registered trade mark. Beware of imitations. Peatmot. Trumplee. Montpat. Plamtroo.

Which example did he adduce to induce Stephen to deduce that originality, though producing its own reward, does not invariably conduce to success?

His own ideated and rejected project of an illuminated showcart, drawn by a beast of burden, in which two smartly dressed girls were to be seated engaged in writing.

What suggested scene was then constructed by Stephen?

Solitary hotel in mountain pass. Autumn. Twilight. Fire lit. In dark corner young man seated. Young woman enters. Restless. Solitary. She sits. She goes to window. She stands. She sits. Twilight. She thinks. On solitary hotel paper she writes. She thinks. She writes. She sighs. Wheels and hoofs. She hurries out. He comes from his dark corner. He seizes solitary paper. He holds it towards fire. Twilight. He reads. Solitary.

What?
In sloping, upright and backhands: Queen's Hotel, Queen's Hotel, Queen's Ho . . .

What suggested scene was then reconstructed by Bloom?
The Queen's Hotel, Ennis, County Clare, where Rudolph Bloom (Rudolf Virag) died on the evening of the 27 June 1886, at some hour unstated, in consequence of an overdose of monkshood (aconite) selfadministered in the form of a neuralgic liniment, composed of 2 parts of aconite liniment to 1 of chloroform liniment (purchased by him at 10.20 a.m. on the morning of 27 June 1886 at the medical hall of Francis Dennehy, 17 Church street, Ennis) after having, though not in consequence of having, purchased at 3.15 p.m. on the afternoon of 27 June 1886 a new boater straw hat, extra smart (after having, though not in consequence of having, purchased at the hour and in the place aforesaid, the toxin aforesaid), at the general drapery store of James Cullen, 4 Main street, Ennis.

Did he attribute this homonymity to information or coincidence or intuition?
Coincidence.

Did he depict the scene verbally for his guest to see?
He preferred himself to see another's face and listen to another's words by which potential narration was realised and kinetic temperament relieved.

Did he see only a second coincidence in the second scene narrated to him, described by the narrator as *A Pisgah Sight of Palestine* or *The Parable of the Plums*?

It, with the preceding scene and with others unnarrated but existent by implication, to which add essays on various subjects or moral apothegms (e.g. *My Favourite Hero* or *Procrastination is the Thief of Time*) composed during schoolyears, seemed to him to contain in itself and in conjunction with the personal equation certain possibilities of financial, social, personal and sexual success, whether specially collected and selected as model pedagogic themes (of cent per cent merit) for the use of preparatory and junior grade students or contributed in printed form, following the precedent of Philip Beaufoy or Doctor Dick or Heblon's *Studies in Blue*, to a publication of certified circulation and solvency or employed verbally as intellectual stimulation for sympathetic auditors, tacitly appreciative of successful narrative and confidently augurative of successful achievement, during the increasingly longer nights gradually following the summer solstice on the day but three following, videlicet, Tuesday, 21 June (S. Aloysius Gonzaga), sunrise 3.33 a.m., sunset 8.29 p.m.

Which domestic problem as much as, if not more than, any other frequently engaged his mind?

What to do with our wives.

What had been his hypothetical singular solutions?

Parlour games (dominos, halma, tiddledywinks, spillikins, cup and ball, nap, spoil five, bezique, twentyfive, beggar my neighbour, draughts, chess or backgammon): embroidery, darning or knitting for the policeaided clothing society: musical duets, mandoline and guitar, piano and flute, guitar and piano: legal scrivenery or envelope addressing: biweekly visits to variety entertainments: commercial activity as pleasantly commanding and pleasingly obeyed mistress proprietress in a cool dairy shop or warm cigar divan: the clandestine satisfaction of

erotic irritation in masculine brothels, state inspected and med-
ically controlled: social visits, at regular infrequent prevented
intervals and with regular frequent preventive superintendence,
to and from female acquaintances of recognised respectability
in the vicinity: courses of evening instruction specially designed
to render liberal instruction agreeable.

What instances of deficient mental development in his wife
inclined him in favour of the lastmentioned (ninth) solution?

In disoccupied moments she had more than once covered
a sheet of paper with signs and hieroglyphics which she stated
were Greek and Irish and Hebrew characters. She had interro-
gated constantly at varying intervals as to the correct method
of writing the capital initial of the name of a city in Canada,
Quebec. She understood little of political complications, internal, or balance of power, external. In calculating the addenda of
bills she frequently had recourse to digital aid. After completion
of laconic epistolary compositions she abandoned the imple-
ment of calligraphy in the encaustic pigment exposed to the
corrosive action of copperas, green vitriol and nutgall. Unusual
polysyllables of foreign origin she interpreted phonetically or by
false analogy or by both: metempsychosis (met him pike hoses),
alias (a mendacious person mentioned in sacred scripture).

What compensated in the false balance of her intelligence
for these and such deficiencies of judgment regarding persons,
places and things?

The false apparent parallelism of all perpendicular arms of
all balances, proved true by construction. The counterbalance
of her proficiency of judgment regarding one person, proved
true by experiment.

How had he attempted to remedy this state of comparative
ignorance?

Variously. By leaving in a conspicuous place a certain book

open at a certain page: by assuming in her, when alluding explanatorily, latent knowledge: by open ridicule in her presence of some absent other's ignorant lapse.

With what success had he attempted direct instruction?
She followed not all, a part of the whole, gave attention with interest comprehended with surprise, with care repeated, with greater difficulty remembered, forgot with ease, with misgiving reremembered, rerepeated with error.

What system had proved more effective?
Indirect suggestion implicating self-interest.

Example?
She disliked umbrella with rain, he liked woman with umbrella, she disliked new hat with rain, he liked woman with new hat, he bought new hat with rain, she carried umbrella with new hat.

Accepting the analogy implied in his guest's parable which examples of postexilic eminence did he adduce?
Three seekers of the pure truth, Moses of Egypt, Moses Maimonides, author of *More Nebukim* (Guide of the Perplexed) and Moses Mendelssohn of such eminence that from Moses (of Egypt) to Moses (Mendelssohn) there arose none like Moses (Maimonides).

What statement was made, under correction, by Bloom concerning a fourth seeker of pure truth, by name Aristotle, mentioned, with permission, by Stephen?
That the seeker mentioned had been a pupil of a rabbinical philosopher, name uncertain.

Were other anapocryphal illustrious sons of the law and children of a selected or rejected race mentioned?

Felix Bartholdy Mendelssohn (composer), Baruch Spinoza (philosopher), Mendoza (pugilist), Ferdinand Lassalle (reformer, duellist).

What fragments of verse from the ancient Hebrew and ancient Irish languages were cited with modulations of voice and translation of texts by guest to host and by host to guest?

By Stephen: *suil, suil, suil arun, suil go siocair agus suil go cuin* (walk, walk, walk your way, walk in safety, walk with care).

By Bloom: *Kifeloch, harimon rakatejch m'baad l'zamatejch* (thy temple amid thy hair is as a slice of pomegranate).

How was a glyphic comparison of the phonic symbols of both languages made in substantiation of the oral comparison?

By juxtaposition. On the penultimate blank page of a book of inferior literary style, entitled *Sweets of Sin* (produced by Bloom and so manipulated that its front cover came in contact with the surface of the table) with a pencil (supplied by Stephen) Stephen wrote the Irish characters for gee, eh, dee, em, simple and modified, and Bloom in turn wrote the Hebrew characters ghimel, aleph, daleth and (in the absence of mem) a substituted qoph, explaining their arithmetical values as ordinal and cardinal numbers, videlicet 3, 1, 4, and 100.

Was the knowledge possessed by both of each of these languages, the extinct and the revived, theoretical or practical?

Theoretical, being confined to certain grammatical rules of accidence and syntax and practically excluding vocabulary.

What points of contact existed between these languages and between the peoples who spoke them?

The presence of guttural sounds, diacritic aspirations, epenthetic and servile letters in both languages: their antiquity, both having been taught on the plain of Shinar 242 years after the deluge in the seminary instituted by Fenius Farsaigh, descendant of Noah, progenitor of Israel, and ascendant of Heber and Heremon, progenitors of Ireland: their archaeological, genealogical, hagiographical, exegetical, homiletic, toponomastic, historical and religious literatures comprising the works of rabbis and culdees, Torah, Talmud (Mischna and Ghemara), Massor, Pentateuch, Book of the Dun Cow, Book of Ballymote, Garland of Howth, Book of Kells: their dispersal, persecution, survival and revival: the isolation of their synagogical and ecclesiastical rites in ghetto (S. Mary's Abbey) and masshouse (Adam and Eve's tavern): the proscription of their national costumes in penal laws and jewish dress acts: the restoration in Chanah David of Zion and the possibility of Irish political autonomy or devolution.

What anthem did Bloom chant partially in anticipation of that multiple, ethnically irreducible consummation?

Kolod balejwaw pnimah
Nefesch, jehudi, homijah.

Why was the chant arrested at the conclusion of this first distich?
In consequence of defective mnemotechnic.

How did the chanter compensate for this deficiency?
By a periphrastic version of the general text.

In what common study did their mutual reflections merge?
The increasing simplification traceable from the Egyptian epigraphic hieroglyphs to the Greek and Roman alphabets and the anticipation of modern stenography and telegraphic code in the cuneiform inscriptions (Semitic) and the virgular quinquecostate ogham writing (Celtic).

Did the guest comply with his host's request?

Doubly, by appending his signature in Irish and Roman characters.

What was Stephen's auditive sensation?

He heard in a profound ancient male unfamiliar melody the accumulation of the past.

What was Bloom's visual sensation?

He saw in a quick young male familiar form the predestination of a future.

What were Stephen's and Bloom's quasisimultaneous volitional quasisensations of concealed identities?

Visually, Stephen's: The traditional figure of hypostasis, depicted by Johannes Damascenus, Lentulus Romanus and Epiphanius Monachus as leucodermic, sesquipedalian with winedark hair.

Auditively, Bloom's: The traditional accent of the ecstasy of catastrophe.

What future careers had been possible for Bloom in the past and with what exemplars?

In the church, Roman, Anglican or Nonconformist: exemplars, the very reverend John Conmee S. J., the reverend T. Salmon, D. D., provost of Trinity college, Dr Alexander J. Dowie. At the bar, English or Irish: exemplars, Seymour Bushe, K. C., Rufus Isaacs, K. C. On the stage, modern or Shakespearean: exemplars, Charles Wyndham, high comedian, Osmond Tearle († 1901), exponent of Shakespeare.

Did the host encourage his guest to chant in a modulated voice a strange legend on an allied theme?

Reassuringly, their place, where none could hear them talk, being secluded, reassured, the decocted beverages, allowing for subsolid residual sediment of a mechanical mixture, water plus sugar plus cream plus cocoa, having been consumed.

Recite the first (major) part of this chanted legend.

Little Harry Hughes and his schoolfellows all
Went out for to play ball.

And the very first ball little Harry Hughes played
He drove it o'er the jew's garden wall.
And the very second ball little Harry Hughes played
He broke the jew's windows all.

How did the son of Rudolph receive this first part?

With unmixed feeling. Smiling, a jew, he heard with pleasure and saw the unbroken kitchen window.

Recite the second part (minor) of the legend.

Then out there came the jew's daughter
And she all dressed in green.
"Come back, come back, you pretty little boy,
And play your ball again."

"I can't come back and I won't come back
Without my schoolfellows all.
For if my master he did hear
He'd make it a sorry ball."

She took him by the lilywhite hand
And led him along the hall
Until she led him to a room
Where none could hear him call.

She took a penknife out of her pocket
And cut off his little head.
And now he'll play his ball no more
For he lies among the dead.

How did the father of Millicent receive this second part?

With mixed feelings. Unsmiling, he heard and saw with wonder a jew's daughter, all dressed in green.

Condense Stephen's commentary.

One of all, the least of all, is the victim predestined. Once by inadvertence, twice by design he challenges his destiny. It comes when he is abandoned and challenges him reluctant and, as an apparition of hope and youth, holds him unresisting. It leads him to a strange habitation, to a secret infidel apartment, and there, implacable, immolates him, consenting.

Why was the host (victim predestined) sad?

He wished that a tale of a deed should be told of a deed not by him should by him not be told.

Why was the host (reluctant, unresisting) still?

In accordance with the law of the conservation of energy.

Why was the host (secret infidel) silent?

He weighed the possible evidences for and against ritual murder: the incitation of the hierarchy, the superstition of the populace, the propagation of rumour in continued fraction of veridicity, the envy of opulence, the influence of retaliation, the sporadic reappearance of atavistic delinquency, the mitigating circumstances of fanaticism, hypnotic suggestion and somnambulism.

From which (if any) of these mental or physical disorders was he not totally immune?

From hypnotic suggestion: once, waking, he had not recognised his sleeping apartment: more than once, waking, he had been for an indefinite time incapable of moving or uttering sounds. From somnambulism: once, sleeping, his body had risen, crouched and crawled in the direction of a heatless fire and, having attained its destination, there, curled, unheated, in night attire had lain, sleeping.

Had this latter or any cognate phenomenon declared itself in any member of his family?

Twice, in Holles street and in Ontario terrace, his daughter Millicent (Milly) at the ages of 6 and 8 years had uttered in sleep an exclamation of terror and had replied to the interrogations of two figures in night attire with a vacant mute expression.

What other infantile memories had he of her?

15 June 1889. A querulous newborn female infant crying to cause and lessen congestion. A child renamed Padney Socks she shook with shocks her moneybox: counted his three free moneypenny buttons, one, tloo, tlee: a doll, a boy, a sailor she cast away: blond, born of two dark, she had blond ancestry, remote, a violation, Herr Hauptmann Hainau, Austrian army, proximate, a hallucination, lieutenant Mulvey, British navy.

What endemic characteristics were present?

Conversely the nasal and frontal formation was derived in a direct line of lineage which, though interrupted, would continue at distant intervals to more distant intervals to its most distant intervals.

What memories had he of her adolescence?

She relegated her hoop and skippingrope to a recess. On the duke's lawn entreated by an English visitor, she declined to permit him to make and take away her photographic image (objection not stated). On the South Circular road in the company of Elsa Potter, followed by an individual of sinister aspect, she went half way down Stamer street and turned abruptly back (reason of change not stated). On the vigil of the 15th anniversary of her birth she wrote a letter from Mullingar, county

Westmeath, making a brief allusion to a local student (faculty and year not stated).

Did that first division, portending a second division, afflict him?

Less than he had imagined, more than he had hoped.

What second departure was contemporaneously perceived by him similarly, if differently?

A temporary departure of his cat.

Why similarly, why differently?

Similarly, because actuated by a secret purpose the quest of a new male (Mullingar student) or of a healing herb (valerian). Differently, because of different possible returns to the inhabitants or to the habitation.

In other respects were their differences similar?

In passivity, in economy, in the instinct of tradition, in unexpectedness.

As?

Inasmuch as leaning she sustained her blond hair for him to ribbon it for her (cf. neckarching cat). Moreover, on the free surface of the lake in Stephen's green amid inverted reflections of trees her uncommented spit, describing concentric circles of waterrings, indicated by the constancy of its permanence the locus of a somnolent prostrate fish (cf. mousewatching cat). Again, in order to remember the date, combatants, issue and consequences of a famous military engagement she pulled a plait of her hair (cf. earwashing cat). Furthermore, silly Milly, she dreamed of having had an unspoken unremembered conversation with a horse whose name had been Joseph to whom (which) she had offered a tumblerful of lemonade which it (he) had appeared to have accepted (cf. hearthdreaming cat). Hence, in passivity, in economy, in the instinct of tradition, in unexpectedness, their differences were similar.

In what way had he utilised gifts 1) an owl, 2) a clock, given as matrimonial auguries, to interest and to instruct her?

As object lessons to explain: 1) the nature and habits of oviparous animals, the possibility of aerial flight, certain abnormalities of vision, the secular process of imbalsamation: 2) the principle of the pendulum, exemplified in bob, wheelgear and regulator, the translation in terms of human or social regulation of the various positions of clockwise moveable indicators on an unmoving dial, the exactitude of the recurrence per hour of an instant in each hour when the longer and the shorter indicator were at the same angle of inclination, *videlicet*, 5 5/11 minutes past each hour per hour in arithmetical progression.

In what manners did she reciprocate?

She remembered: on the 27th anniversary of his birth she presented to him a breakfast moustachecup of imitation Crown Derby porcelain ware. She provided: at quarter day or thereabouts if or when purchases had been made by him not for her she showed herself attentive to his necessities, anticipating his desires. She admired: a natural phenomenon having been explained by him not for her she expressed the immediate desire to possess without gradual acquisition a fraction of his science, the moiety, the quarter, a thousandth part.

What proposal did Bloom, diambulist, father of Milly, somnambulist, make to Stephen, noctambulist?

To pass in repose the hours intervening between Thursday (proper) and Friday (normal) on an extemporised cubicle in the apartment immediately above the kitchen and immediately adjacent to the sleeping apartment of his host and hostess.

What various advantages would or might have resulted from a prolongation of such an extemporisation?

For the guest: security of domicile and seclusion of study. For the host: rejuvenation of intelligence, vicarious satisfaction. For the hostess: disintegration of obsession, acquisition of correct Italian pronunciation.

Why might these several provisional contingencies between a guest and a hostess not necessarily preclude or be precluded by a permanent eventuality of reconciliatory union between a schoolfellow and a jew's daughter?

Because the way to daughter led through mother, the way to mother through daughter.

To what inconsequent polysyllabic question of his host did the guest return a monosyllabic negative answer?

If he had known the late Mrs Emily Sinico, accidentally killed at Sydney Parade railway station, 14 October 1903.

What inchoate corollary statement was consequently suppressed by the host?

A statement explanatory of his absence on the occasion of the interment of Mrs Mary Dedalus (born Goulding), 26 June 1903, vigil of the anniversary of the decease of Rudolph Bloom (born Virag).

Was the proposal of asylum accepted?

Promptly, inexplicably, with amicability, gratefully it was declined.

What exchange of money took place between host and guest?

The former returned to the latter, without interest, a sum of money (£ 1. 7s. 0.), one pound seven shillings sterling, advanced by the latter to the former.

What counterproposals were alternately advanced, accepted, modified, declined, restated in other terms, reaccepted, ratified, reconfirmed?

To inaugurate a prearranged course of Italian instruction, place the residence of the instructed. To inaugurate a course of vocal instruction, place the residence of the instructress. To inaugurate a series of static, semistatic and peripatetic intellectual dialogues, places the residence of both speakers (if both speakers were resident in the same place), the Ship hotel and tavern, 6 Lower Abbey street (W. and E. Connery, proprietors), the National Library of Ireland, 10 Kildare street, the National Maternity Hospital, 29, 30 and 31 Holles street, a public garden, the vicinity of a place of worship, a conjunction of two or more public thoroughfares, the point of bisection of a right line drawn between their residences (if both speakers were resident in different places).

What rendered problematic for Bloom the realisation of these mutually selfexcluding propositions?

The irreparability of the past: once at a performance of Albert Hengler's circus in the Rotunda, Rutland square, Dublin, an intuitive particoloured clown in quest of paternity had penetrated from the ring to a place in the auditorium where Bloom, solitary, was seated and had publicly declared to an exhilarated audience that he (Bloom) was his (the clown's) papa. The imprevidibility of the future: once in the summer of 1898 he (Bloom) had marked a florin (2s.) with three notches on the milled edge and tendered it in payment of an account due to and received by J. and T. Davy, family grocers, 1 Charlemont Mall, Grand Canal, for circulation on the waters of civic finance, for possible, circuitous or direct, return.

Was the clown Bloom's son?
No.

Had Bloom's coin returned?
Never.

Why would a recurrent frustration the more depress him?
Because at the critical turningpoint of human existence
he desired to amend many social conditions, the product of
inequality and avarice and international animosity.

He believed then that human life was infinitely perfectible,
eliminating these conditions?
There remained the generic conditions imposed by natural,
as distinct from human law, as integral parts of the human
whole: the necessity of destruction to procure alimentary
sustenance: the painful character of the ultimate functions of
separate existence, the agonies of birth and death: the monot-
onous menstruation of simian and (particularly) human
females extending from the age of puberty to the menopause:
inevitable accidents at sea, in mines and factories: certain very
painful maladies and their resultant surgical operations, innate
lunacy and congenital criminality, decimating epidemics: cat-
astrophic cataclysms which make terror the basis of human
mentality: seismic upheavals the epicentres of which are
located in densely populated regions: the fact of vital growth,
through convulsions of metamorphosis, from infancy through
maturity to decay.

Why did he desist from speculation?
Because it was a task for a superior intelligence to substi-
tute other more acceptable phenomena in the place of the less
acceptable phenomena to be removed.

Did Stephen participate in his dejection?
He affirmed his significance as a conscious rational animal
proceeding syllogistically from the known to the unknown and

a conscious rational reagent between a micro- and a macrocosm ineluctably constructed upon the incertitude of the void.

Was this affirmation apprehended by Bloom?
Not verbally. Substantially.

What comforted his misapprehension?
That as a competent keyless citizen he had proceeded energetically from the unknown to the known through the incertitude of the void.

In what order of precedence, with what attendant ceremony was the exodus from the house of bondage to the wilderness of inhabitation effected?

Lighted Candle in Stick borne by
BLOOM
Diaconal Hat on Ashplant borne by
STEPHEN

With what intonation secreto of what commemorative psalm?
The 113th, *modus peregrinus: In exitu Israël de Egypto: domus Jacob de populo barbaro.*

What did each do at the door of egress?
Bloom set the candlestick on the floor. Stephen put the hat on his head.

For what creature was the door of egress a door of ingress?
For a cat.

What spectacle confronted them when they, first the host, then the guest, emerged silently, doubly dark, from obscurity by a

passage from the rere of the house into the penumbra of the garden?
The heaventree of stars hung with humid nightblue fruit.

With what meditations did Bloom accompany his demonstration to his companion of various constellations?

Meditations of evolution increasingly vaster: of the moon invisible in incipient lunation, approaching perigee: of the infinite lattiginous scintillating uncondensed milky way, discernible by daylight by an observer placed at the lower end of a cylindrical vertical shaft 5000 ft deep sunk from the surface towards the centre of the earth: of Sirius (alpha in Canis Maior) 10 lightyears (57,000,000,000,000 miles) distant and in volume 900 times the dimension of our planet: of Arcturus: of the precession of equinoxes: of Orion with belt and sextuple sun theta and nebula in which 100 of our solar systems could be contained: of moribund and of nascent new stars such as Nova in 1901: of our system plunging towards the constellation of Hercules: of the parallax or parallactic drift of socalled fixed stars, in reality evermoving wanderers from immeasurably remote eons to infinitely remote futures in comparison with which the years, threescore and ten, of allotted human life formed a parenthesis of infinitesimal brevity.

Were there obverse meditations of involution increasingly less vast?

Of the eons of geological periods recorded in the stratifications of the earth: of the myriad minute entomological organic existences concealed in cavities of the earth, beneath removable stones, in hives and mounds, of microbes, germs, bacteria, bacilli, spermatozoa: of the incalculable trillions of billions of millions of imperceptible molecules contained by cohesion of molecular affinity in a single pinhead: of the universe of human serum constellated with red and white bodies, themselves universes of void space constellated with other bodies, each, in continuity, its universe of divisible component bodies of which each was again divisible in divisions of redivisible component bodies, dividends and divisors ever diminishing without actual division till, if the progress were carried far enough, nought nowhere was never reached.

Why did he not elaborate these calculations to a more precise result?

Because some years previously in 1886 when occupied with the problem of the quadrature of the circle he had learned of the existence of a number computed to a relative degree of accuracy to be of such magnitude and of so many places, e.g., the 9th power of the 9th power of 9, that, the result having been obtained, 33 closely printed volumes of 1000 pages each of innumerable quires and reams of India paper would have to be requisitioned in order to contain the complete tale of its printed integers of units, tens, hundreds, thousands, tens of thousands, hundreds of thousands, millions, tens of millions, hundreds of millions, billions, the nucleus of the nebula of every digit of every series containing succinctly the potentiality of being raised to the utmost kinetic elaboration of any power of any of its powers.

Did he find the problems of the inhabitability of the planets and their satellites by a race, given in species, and of the possible social and moral redemption of said race by a redeemer, easier of solution?

Of a different order of difficulty. Conscious that the human organism, normally capable of sustaining an atmospheric pressure of 19 tons, when elevated to a considerable altitude in the terrestrial atmosphere suffered with arithmetical progression of intensity, according as the line of demarcation between troposphere and stratosphere was approximated, from nasal hemorrhage, impeded respiration and vertigo, when proposing this problem for solution he had conjectured as a working hypothesis which could not be proved impossible that a more adaptable and differently anatomically constructed race of beings might subsist otherwise under Martian, Mercurial, Veneral, Jovian, Saturnian, Neptunian or Uranian sufficient and equivalent conditions, though an apogean humanity of beings created in varying forms with finite differences resulting similar to the whole and to one another would probably there as here remain inalterably and inalienably attached to vanities, to vanities of vanities and to all that is vanity.

And the problem of possible redemption?
The minor was proved by the major.

Which various features of the constellations were in turn considered?
The various colours significant of various degrees of vitality (white, yellow, crimson, vermilion, cinnabar): their degrees of brilliancy: their magnitudes revealed up to and including the 7th: their positions: the waggoner's star: Walsingham way: the chariot of David: the annular cinctures of Saturn: the condensation of spiral nebulae into suns: the interdependent gyrations of double suns: the independent synchronous discoveries of Galileo, Simon Marius, Piazzi, Le Verrier, Herschel, Galle: the systematisations attempted by Bode and Kepler of cubes of distances and squares of times of revolution: the almost infinite compressibility of hirsute comets and their vast elliptical egressive and reentrant orbits from perihelion to aphelion: the sidereal origin of meteoric stones: the Libyan floods on Mars about the period of the birth of the younger astroscopist: the annual recurrence of meteoric showers about the period of the feast of S. Lawrence (martyr, 10 August): the monthly recurrence known as the new moon with the old moon in her arms: the posited influence of celestial on human bodies: the appearance of a star

(1st magnitude) of exceeding brilliancy dominating by night and day (a new luminous sun generated by the collision and amalgamation in incandescence of two nonluminous exsuns) about the period of the birth of William Shakespeare over delta in the recumbent neversetting constellation of Cassiopeia and of a star (2nd magnitude) of similar origin but of lesser brilliancy which had appeared in and disappeared from the constellation of the Corona Septentrionalis about the period of the birth of Leopold Bloom and of other stars of (presumably) similar origin which had (effectively or presumably) appeared in and disappeared from the constellation of Andromeda about the period of the birth of Stephen Dedalus, and in and from the constellation of Auriga some years after the birth and death of Rudolph Bloom, junior, and in and from other constellations some years before or after the birth or death of other persons: the attendant phenomena of eclipses, solar and lunar, from immersion to emersion, abatement of wind, transit of shadow, taciturnity of winged creatures, emergence of nocturnal or crepuscular animals, persistence of infernal light, obscurity of terrestrial waters, pallor of human beings.

His (Bloom's) logical conclusion, having weighed the matter and allowing for possible error?

That it was not a heaventree, not a heavengrot, not a heavenbeast, not a heavenman. That it was a Utopia, there being no known method from the known to the unknown: an infinity renderable equally finite by the suppositious apposition of one or more bodies equally of the same and of different magnitudes: a mobility of illusory forms immobilised in space, remobilised in air: a past which possibly had ceased to exist as a present before its probable spectators had entered actual present existence.

Was he more convinced of the esthetic value of the spectacle? Indubitably in consequence of the reiterated examples of poets in the delirium of the frenzy of attachment or in the abasement of rejection invoking ardent sympathetic constellations or the frigidity of the satellite of their planet.

Did he then accept as an article of belief the theory of astrological influences upon sublunary disasters?

It seemed to him as possible of proof as of confutation and the nomenclature employed in its selenographical charts as attributable to verifiable intuition as to fallacious analogy: the lake of dreams, the sea of rains, the gulf of dews, the ocean of fecundity.

What special affinities appeared to him to exist between the moon and woman?

Her antiquity in preceding and surviving successive tellurian generations: her nocturnal predominance: her satellitic dependence: her luminary reflection: her constancy under all her phases, rising and setting by her appointed times, waxing and waning: the forced invariability of her aspect: her indeterminate response to inaffirmative interrogation: her potency over effluent and refluent waters: her power to enamour, to mortify, to invest with beauty, to render insane, to incite to and aid delinquency: the tranquil inscrutability of her visage: the terribility of her isolated dominant implacable resplendent propinquity: her omens of tempest and of calm: the stimulation of her light, her motion and her presence: the admonition of her craters, her arid seas, her silence: her splendour, when visible: her attraction, when invisible.

What visible luminous sign attracted Bloom's, who attracted Stephen's, gaze?

In the second storey (rere) of his (Bloom's) house the light of a paraffin oil lamp with oblique shade projected on a screen of roller blind supplied by Frank O'Hara, window blind, curtain pole and revolving shutter manufacturer, 16 Aungier street.

How did he elucidate the mystery of an invisible attractive person, his wife Marion (Molly) Bloom, denoted by a visible splendid sign, a lamp?

With indirect and direct verbal allusions or affirmations: with subdued affection and admiration: with description: with impediment: with suggestion.

Both then were silent?

Silent, each contemplating the other in both mirrors of the reciprocal flesh of theirhisnothis fellowfaces.

Were they indefinitely inactive?

At Stephen's suggestion, at Bloom's instigation both, first Stephen, then Bloom, in penumbra urinated, their sides contiguous, their organs of micturition reciprocally rendered invisible by manual circumposition, their gazes, first Bloom's, then Stephen's, elevated to the projected luminous and semiluminous shadow.

Similarly?

The trajectories of their, first sequent, then simultaneous, urinations were dissimilar: Bloom's longer, less irruent, in the incomplete form of the bifurcated penultimate alphabetical letter, who in his ultimate year at High School (1880) had been capable of attaining the point of greatest altitude against the whole concurrent strength of the institution, 210 scholars: Stephen's higher, more sibilant, who in the ultimate hours of the previous day had augmented by diuretic consumption an insistent vesical pressure.

What different problems presented themselves to each concerning the invisible audible collateral organ of the other?

To Bloom: the problems of irritability, tumescence, rigidity, reactivity, dimension, sanitariness, pilosity. To Stephen: the problem of the sacerdotal integrity of Jesus circumcised (1st January, holiday of obligation to hear mass and abstain from unnecessary servile work) and the problem as to whether the divine prepuce, the carnal bridal ring of the holy Roman catholic apostolic church, conserved in Calcata, were deserving of simple hyperduly or of the fourth degree of latria accorded to the abscission of such divine excrescences as hair and toenails.

What celestial sign was by both simultaneously observed?

A star precipitated with great apparent velocity across the firmament from Vega in the Lyre above the zenith beyond the stargroup of the Tress of Berenice towards the zodiacal sign of Leo.

How did the centripetal remainer afford egress to the centrifugal departer?

By inserting the barrel of an arruginated male key in the hole of an unstable female lock, obtaining a purchase on the bow of the key and turning its wards from right to left, withdrawing a bolt from its staple, pulling inward spasmodically an obsolescent unhinged door and revealing an aperture for free egress and free ingress.

How did they take leave, one of the other, in separation?

Standing perpendicular at the same door and on different sides of its base, the lines of their valedictory arms, meeting at any point and forming any angle less than the sum of two right angles.

What sound accompanied the union of their tangent, the disunion of their (respectively) centrifugal and centripetal hands?

The sound of the peal of the hour of the night by the chime of the bells in the church of Saint George.

What echoes of that sound were by both and each heard?
By Stephen:

> *Liliata rutilantium. Turma circumdet.*
> *Iubilantium te virginum. Chorus excipiat.*

By Bloom:

> *Heigho, heigho,*
> *Heigho, heigho.*

Where were the several members of the company which with Bloom that day at the bidding of that peal had travelled from Sandymount in the south to Glasnevin in the north?

Martin Cunningham (in bed), Jack Power (in bed), Simon Dedalus (in bed), Tom Kernan (in bed), Ned Lambert (in bed), Joe Hynes (in bed), John Henry Menton (in bed), Bernard Corrigan (in bed), Patsy Dignam (in bed), Paddy Dignam (in the grave).

Alone, what did Bloom hear?

The double reverberation of retreating feet on the heavenborn earth, the double vibration of a jew's harp in the resonant lane.

Alone, what did Bloom feel?

The cold of interstellar space, thousands of degrees below freezing point or the absolute zero of Fahrenheit, Centigrade or Réaumur: the incipient intimations of proximate dawn.

Of what did bellchime and handtouch and footstep and lonechill remind him?

Of companions now in various manners in different places defunct: Percy Apjohn (killed in action, Modder River), Philip

Gilligan (phthisis, Jervis Street hospital), Matthew F. Kane (accidental drowning, Dublin Bay), Philip Moisel (pyemia, Heytesbury street), Michael Hart (phthisis, Mater Misericordiæ hospital), Patrick Dignam (apoplexy, Sandymount).

What prospect of what phenomena inclined him to remain?
The disparition of three final stars, the diffusion of daybreak, the apparition of a new solar disk.

Had he ever been a spectator of those phenomena?
Once, in 1887, after a protracted performance of charades in the house of Luke Doyle, Kimmage, he had awaited with patience the apparition of the diurnal phenomenon, seated on a wall, his gaze turned in the direction of Mizrach, the east.

He remembered the initial paraphenomena?
More active air, a matutinal distant cock, ecclesiastical clocks at various points, avine music, the isolated tread of an early wayfarer, the visible diffusion of the light of an invisible luminous body, the first golden limb of the resurgent sun perceptible low on the horizon.

Did he remain?
With deep inspiration he returned, retraversing the garden, reentering the passage, reclosing the door. With brief suspiration he reassumed the candle, reascended the stairs, reapproached the door of the front room, hallfloor, and reentered.

What suddenly arrested his ingress?
The right temporal lobe of the hollow sphere of his cranium came into contact with a solid timber angle where, an infinitesimal but sensible fraction of a second later, a painful sensation was located in consequence of antecedent sensations transmitted and registered.

Describe the alterations effected in the disposition of the articles of furniture.

A sofa upholstered in prune plush had been translocated from opposite the door to the ingleside near the compactly furled Union Jack (an alteration which he had frequently intended to execute): the blue and white checker inlaid majolicatopped table had been placed opposite the door in the place vacated by the prune plush sofa: the walnut sideboard (a projecting angle of which had momentarily arrested his ingress) had been moved from its position beside the door to a more advantageous but more perilous position in front of the door: two chairs had been moved from right and left of the ingleside to the position originally occupied by the blue and white checker inlaid majolica-topped table.

Describe them.

One: a squat stuffed easychair, with stout arms extended and back slanted to the rere, which, repelled in recoil, had then upturned an irregular fringe of a rectangular rug and now displayed on its amply upholstered seat a centralised diffusing and diminishing discolouration. The other: a slender splayfoot chair of glossy cane curves, placed directly opposite the former, its frame from top to seat and from seat to base being varnished dark brown, its seat being a bright circle of white plaited rush.

What significances attached to these two chairs?

Significances of similitude, of posture, of symbolism, of circumstantial evidence, of testimonial supermanence.

What occupied the position originally occupied by the sideboard?

A vertical piano (Cadby) with exposed keyboard, its closed coffin supporting a pair of long yellow ladies' gloves and an emerald ashtray containing four consumed matches, a partly consumed cigarette and two discoloured ends of cigarettes, its musicrest supporting the music in the key of G natural for voice and piano of *Love's Old Sweet Song* (words by G. Clifton Bingham, composed by J. L. Molloy, sung by Madam Antoinette Sterling) open at the last page with the final indications *ad libitum*, *forte*, pedal, *animato*, sustained pedal, *ritirando*, close.

With what sensations did Bloom contemplate in rotation these objects?

With strain, elevating a candlestick: with pain, feeling on his right temple a contused tumescence: with attention, focussing his gaze on a large dull passive and a slender bright active: with solicitation, bending and downturning the upturned rugfringe: with amusement, remembering Dr Malachi Mulligan's scheme of colour containing the gradation of green: with pleasure, repeating the words and antecedent act and perceiving through various channels of internal sensibility the consequent and concomitant tepid pleasant diffusion of gradual discolouration.

His next proceeding?

From an open box on the majolicatopped table he extracted a black diminutive cone, one inch in height, placed it on its circular base on a small tin plate, placed his candlestick on the right corner of the mantelpiece, produced from his waistcoat a folded page of prospectus (illustrated) entitled Agendath Netaim, unfolded the same, examined it superficially, rolled it into a thin cylinder, ignited it in the candleflame, applied it when ignited to the apex of the cone till the latter reached the stage of rutilance, placed the cylinder in the basin of the candlestick disposing its unconsumed part in such a manner as to facilitate total combustion.

What followed this operation?

The truncated conical crater summit of the diminutive

volcano emitted a vertical and serpentine fume redolent of aromatic oriental incense.

What homothetic objects, other than the candlestick, stood on the mantelpiece?

A timepiece of striated Connemara marble, stopped at the hour of 4.46 a.m. on the 21 March 1896, matrimonial gift of Matthew Dillon: a dwarf tree of glacial arborescence under a transparent bellshade, matrimonial gift of Luke and Caroline Doyle: an embalmed owl, matrimonial gift of Alderman John Hooper.

What interchanges of looks took place between these three objects and Bloom?

In the mirror of the giltbordered pierglass the undecorated back of the dwarf tree regarded the upright back of the embalmed owl. Before the mirror the matrimonial gift of Alderman John Hooper with a clear melancholy wise bright motionless compassionate gaze regarded Bloom while Bloom with obscure tranquil profound motionless compassionated gaze regarded the matrimonial gift of Luke and Caroline Doyle.

What composite asymmetrical image in the mirror then attracted his attention?

The image of a solitary (ipsorelative) mutable (aliorelative) man.

Why solitary (ipsorelative)?

Brothers and sisters had he none.
Yet that man's father was his grandfather's son.

Why mutable (aliorelative)?

From infancy to maturity he had resembled his maternal

procreatrix. From maturity to senility he would increasingly resemble his paternal procreator.

What final visual impression was communicated to him by the mirror?

The optical reflection of several inverted volumes improperly arranged and not in the order of their common letters with scintillating titles on the two bookshelves opposite.

Catalogue these books.

Thom's Dublin Post Office Directory, 1886.

Denis Florence M'Carthy's *Poetical Works* (copper beechleaf bookmark at p. 5).

Shakespeare's *Works* (dark crimson morocco, goldtooled).

The Useful Ready Reckoner (brown cloth).

The Secret History of the Court of Charles II (red cloth, tooled binding).

The Child's Guide (blue cloth).

The Beauties of Killarney (wrappers).

When We Were Boys by William O'Brien M. P. (green cloth, slightly faded, envelope bookmark at p. 217).

Thoughts from Spinoza (maroon leather).

The Story of the Heavens by Sir Robert Ball (blue cloth).

Ellis's *Three Trips to Madagascar* (brown cloth, title obliterated).

The Stark-Munro Letters by A. Conan Doyle, property of the City of Dublin Public Library, 106 Capel street, lent 21 May (Whitsun Eve) 1904, due 4 June 1904, 13 days overdue (black cloth binding, bearing white letternumber ticket).

Voyages in China by "Viator" (recovered with brown paper, red ink title).

Philosophy of the Talmud (sewn pamphlet).

Lockhart's *Life of Napoleon* (cover wanting, marginal

annotations, minimising victories, aggrandising defeats
of the protagonist).

Soll und Haben by Gustav Freytag (black boards, Gothic
characters, cigarette coupon bookmark at p. 24).

Hozier's *History of the Russo-Turkish War* (brown cloth,
2 volumes, with gummed label, Garrison Library,
Governor's Parade, Gibraltar, on verso of cover).

Laurence Bloomfield in Ireland by William Allingham
(second edition, green cloth, gilt trefoil design, previous
owner's name on recto of flyleaf erased).

A Handbook of Astronomy (cover, brown leather, detached,
5 plates, antique letterpress long primer, author's footnotes nonpareil, marginal clues brevier, captions small
pica).

The Hidden Life of Christ (black boards).

In the Track of the Sun (yellow cloth, titlepage missing,
recurrent title intestation).

Physical Strength and How to Obtain It by Eugen Sandow
(red cloth).

Short but yet Plain Elements of Geometry written in French by
F. Ignat. Pardies and rendered into Englifh by John Harris
D. D. London, printed for R. Knaplock at the Bishop's
Head, MDCCXI, with dedicatory epiftle to his worthy
friend Charles Cox, efquire, Member of Parliament for
the burgh of Southwark and having ink calligraphed
statement on the flyleaf certifying that the book was the
property of Michael Gallagher, dated this 10th day of
May 1822 and requefting the perfon who should find
it, if the book should be loft or go aftray, to reftore it to
Michael Gallagher, carpenter, Dufery Gate, Ennifcorthy,
county Wicklow, the fineft place in the world.

What reflections occupied his mind during the process of
reversion of the inverted volumes?

The necessity of order, a place for everything and everything in its place: the deficient appreciation of literature possessed by females: the incongruity of an apple incuneated in a tumbler and of an umbrella inclined in a closestool: the insecurity of hiding any secret document behind, beneath or between the pages of a book.

Which volume was the largest in bulk?
Hozier's *History of the Russo-Turkish War.*

What among other data did the second volume of the work in question contain?
The name of a decisive battle (forgotten), frequently remembered by a decisive officer, major Brian Cooper Tweedy (remembered).

Why, firstly and secondly, did he not consult the work in question?
Firstly, in order to exercise mnemotechnic: secondly, because after an interval of amnesia, when seated at the central table, about to consult the work in question, he remembered by mnemotechnic the name of the military engagement, Plevna.

What caused him consolation in his sitting posture?
The candour, nudity, pose, tranquility, youth, grace, sex, counsel of a statue erect in the centre of the table, an image of Narcissus purchased by auction from P. A. Wren, 9 Bachelor's Walk.

What caused him irritation in his sitting posture?
Inhibitory pressure of collar (size 17) and waistcoat (5 buttons), two articles of clothing superfluous in the costume of mature males and inelastic to alterations of mass by expansion.

How was the irritation allayed?
He removed his collar, with contained black necktie and

collapsible stud, from his neck to a position on the left of the table. He unbuttoned successively in reversed direction waist-coat, trousers, shirt and vest along the medial line of irregular incrispated black hairs extending in triangular convergence from the pelvic basin over the circumference of the abdomen and umbilicular fossicle along the medial line of nodes to the intersection of the sixth pectoral vertebræ, thence produced both ways at right angles and terminating in circles described about two equidistant points, right and left, on the summits of the mammary prominences. He unbraced successively each of six minus one braced trouser buttons, arranged in pairs, of which one incomplete.

What involuntary actions followed?

He compressed between 2 fingers the flesh circumjacent to a cicatrice in the left infracostal region below the diaphragm resulting from a sting inflicted 2 weeks and 3 days previously (23 May 1904) by a bee. He scratched imprecisely with his right hand, though insensible of prurition, various points and surfaces of his partly exposed, wholly abluted skin. He inserted his left hand into the left lower pocket of his waistcoat and extracted and replaced a silver coin (1 shilling), placed there (presumably) on the occasion (17 October 1903) of the inter-ment of Mrs Emily Sinico, Sydney Parade.

Compile the budget for 16 June 1904.

Debit

	£.	s.	d.
1 Pork kidney	0	0	3
1 Copy *Freeman's Journal*	0	0	1
1 Bath and Gratification	0	1	6
Tramfare	0	0	1
1 In Memoriam Patrick Dignam	0	5	0

2 Banbury cakes	0—0—1
1 Lunch	0—0—7
1 Renewal fee for book	0—1—0
1 Packet Notepaper and Envelopes	0—0—2
1 Dinner and Gratification	0—2—0
1 Postal Order and Stamp	0—2—8
Tramfare	0—0—1
1 Pig's Foot	0—0—4
1 Sheep's Trotter	0—0—3
1 Cake Fry's Plain Chocolate	0—0—1
1 Square Soda Bread	0—0—4
1 Coffee and Bun	0—0—4
Loan (Stephen Dedalus) refunded	1—7—0
BALANCE	0—17—5
	2—19—3

Credit

	£. s. d.
Cash in hand	0—4—9
Commission recd. *Freeman's Journal*	1—7—6
Loan (Stephen Dedalus)	1—7—0
	2—19—3

Did the process of divestiture continue?

Sensible of a benignant persistent ache in his footsoles he extended his foot to one side and observed the creases, protuberances and salient points caused by foot pressure in the course of walking repeatedly in several different directions, then, inclined, he disnoded the laceknots, unhooked and loosened the laces, took off each of his two boots for the second time, detached the partially moistened right sock through the fore part of which the nail of his great toe had again effracted, raised his right foot and, having unhooked a purple elastic sock suspender, took off his right sock, placed his unclothed right foot on the margin of the seat of his chair, picked at and gently lacerated the protruding part of the great toenail, raised the part lacerated to his nostrils and inhaled the odour of the quick, then, with satisfaction, threw away the lacerated unguical fragment.

Why with satisfaction?

Because the odour inhaled corresponded to other odours inhaled of other unguical fragments, picked and lacerated by Master Bloom, pupil of Mrs Ellis's juvenile school, patiently each night in the act of brief genuflection and nocturnal prayer and ambitious meditation.

In what ultimate ambition had all concurrent and consecutive ambitions now coalesced?

Not to inherit by right of primogeniture, gavelkind or borough English, or possess in perpetuity an extensive demesne of a sufficient number of acres, roods and perches, statute land measure (valuation £ 42), of grazing turbary surrounding a baronial hall with gatelodge and carriage drive nor, on the other hand, a terracehouse or semidetached villa, described as *Rus in Urbe* or *Qui si sana*, but to purchase by private treaty in fee simple a thatched bungalowshaped 2 storey dwellinghouse of southerly aspect, surmounted by vane and lightning conductor, connected with the earth, with porch covered by parasitic plants (ivy or Virginia creeper), halldoor, olive green, with smart carriage finish and neat doorbrasses, stucco front with gilt tracery at eaves and gable, rising, if possible, upon a gentle eminence with agreeable prospect from balcony with stone pillar parapet over unoccupied and unoccupyable interjacent pastures and standing in 5 or 6 acres of its own ground, at such a distance from the nearest public thoroughfare as to render its houselights visible at night above and through a quickset hornbeam hedge of topiary cutting, situate at a given point not less than 1 statute mile from the periphery of the metropolis, within a time limit of not more than 15 minutes from tram or train line (e.g., Dundrum, south, or Sutton, north, both localities equally reported by trial to resemble the terrestrial poles in being favourable climates for phthisical subjects), the premises to be held under feefarm grant, lease 999 years, the messuage to consist of 1 drawingroom with baywindow (2 lancets), thermometer affixed, 1 sittingroom, 4 bedrooms, 2 servants' rooms, tiled kitchen with close range and scullery, lounge hall fitted with linen wallpresses, fumed oak sectional bookcase containing the Encyclopaedia Britannica and New Century Dictionary, transverse obsolete medieval and oriental weapons, dinner gong, alabaster lamp, bowl pendant, vulcanite automatic telephone receiver with adjacent directory, handtufted Axminster carpet with cream ground and trellis border, loo table with pillar and claw legs, hearth with massive firebrasses and ormolu mantel chronometer clock, guaranteed timekeeper with cathedral chime, barometer with hygrographic chart, comfortable lounge settees and corner fitments, upholstered in ruby plush with good springing and sunk centre, three banner Japanese screen and cuspidors (club style, rich winecoloured leather, gloss renewable with a minimum of labour by use of linseed oil and vinegar) and pyramidically prismatic central chandelier lustre, bentwood perch with fingertame parrot (expurgated language), embossed mural paper at 10/- per dozen with transverse swags of carmine floral design and top crown frieze, staircase, three continuous flights at successive right angles, of varnished cleargrained oak, treads and risers, newel, balusters and handrail, with steppedup panel dado, dressed with camphorated wax: bathroom, hot and cold supply, reclining and shower: water closet on mezzanine provided with opaque singlepane oblong window, tipup seat, bracket lamp, brass tierod and brace, armrests, footstool and artistic oleograph on inner face of door: ditto, plain: servants' apartments with separate sanitary and hygienic necessaries for cook, general and betweenmaid (salary, rising by biennial unearned increments of

£ 2, with comprehensive fidelity insurance, annual bonus (£ 1) and retiring allowance (based on the 65 system) after 30 years' service), pantry, buttery, larder, refrigerator, outoffices, coal and wood cellarage with winebin (still and sparkling vintages) for distinguished guests, if entertained to dinner (evening dress), carbon monoxide gas supply throughout.

What additional attractions might the grounds contain?

As addenda, a tennis and fives court, a shrubbery, a glass summerhouse with tropical palms, equipped in the best botanical manner, a rockery with waterspray, a beehive arranged on humane principles, oval flowerbeds in rectangular grassplots set with eccentric ellipses of scarlet and chrome tulips, blue scillas, crocuses, polyanthus, sweet William, sweet pea, lily of the valley (bulbs obtainable from sir James W. Mackey (Limited) wholesale and retail seed and bulb merchants and nurserymen, agents for chemical manures, 23 Sackville street, upper), an orchard, kitchen garden and vinery, protected against illegal trespassers by glasstopped mural enclosures, a lumbershed with padlock for various inventoried implements.

As?

Eeltraps, lobsterpots, fishingrods, hatchet, steelyard, grindstone, clodcrusher, swatheturner, carriagesack, telescope ladder, 10 tooth rake, washing clogs, haytedder, tumbling rake, billhook, paintpot, brush, hoe and so on.

What improvements might be subsequently introduced?

A rabbitry and fowlrun, a dovecote, a botanical conservatory, 2 hammocks (lady's and gentleman's), a sundial shaded and sheltered by laburnum or lilac trees, an exotically harmonically accorded Japanese tinkle gatebell affixed to left lateral gatepost, a capacious waterbutt, a lawnmower with side delivery and grassbox, a lawnsprinkler with hydraulic hose.

What facilities of transit were desirable?

When citybound frequent connection by train or tram from their respective intermediate station or terminal. When countrybound velocipedes, a chainless freewheel roadster cycle with side basketcar attached, or draught conveyance, a donkey with wicker trap or smart phaeton with good working solidungular cob (roan gelding, 14 h).

What might be the name of this erigible or erected residence? Bloom Cottage. Saint Leopold's. Flowerville.

Could Bloom of 7 Eccles street foresee Bloom of Flowerville? In loose allwool garments with Harris tweed cap, price 8/6, and useful garden boots with elastic gussets and wateringcan, planting aligned young firtrees, syringing, pruning, staking, sowing hayseed, trundling a weedladen wheelbarrow without excessive fatigue at sunset amid the scent of newmown hay, ameliorating the soil, multiplying wisdom, achieving longevity.

What syllabus of intellectual pursuits was simultaneously possible?

Snapshot photography, comparative study of religions, folklore relative to various amatory and superstitious practices, contemplation of the celestial constellations.

What lighter recreations?

Outdoor: garden and fieldwork, cycling on level macadamised causeways, ascents of moderately high hills, natation in secluded fresh water and unmolested river boating in secure wherry or light curricle with kedge anchor on reaches free from weirs and rapids (period of estivation), vespertinal perambulation or equestrian circumprocession with inspection of sterile landscape and contrastingly agreeable cottagers' fires of smoking peat turves (period of hibernation). Indoor: discussion in tepid security of unsolved historical and criminal problems: lecture of unexpurgated exotic erotic masterpieces: house carpentry with toolbox containing hammer, awl, nails, screws, tintacks, gimlet, tweezers, bullnose plane and turnscrew.

Might he become a gentleman farmer of field produce and live stock?

Not impossibly, with 1 or 2 stripper cows, 1 pike of upland hay and requisite farming implements, e.g., an end-to-end churn, a turnip pulper etc.

What would be his civic functions and social status among the county families and landed gentry?

Arranged successively in ascending powers of hierarchical order, that of gardener, groundsman, cultivator, breeder, and at the zenith of his career, resident magistrate or justice of the peace with a family crest and coat of arms and appropriate classical motto (*Semper paratus*), duly recorded in the court directory (Bloom, Leopold P., M. P., P. C., K. P., L. L. D. (*honoris causa*), Bloomville, Dundrum) and mentioned in court and fashionable intelligence (Mr and Mrs Leopold Bloom have left Kingstown for England).

What course of action did he outline for himself in such capacity?

A course that lay between undue clemency and excessive rigour: the dispensation in a heterogeneous society of arbitrary classes, incessantly rearranged in terms of greater and lesser social inequality, of unbiassed homogeneous indisputable justice, tempered with mitigants of the widest possible latitude but exactable to the uttermost farthing with confiscation of estate, real and personal, to the crown. Loyal to the highest constituted power in the land, actuated by an innate love of rectitude his aims would be the strict maintenance of public order, the repression of many abuses though not of all simultaneously (every measure of reform or retrenchment being a preliminary solution to be contained by fluxion in the final solution), the upholding of the letter of the law (common, statute and law merchant) against all traversers in covin and trespassers acting in contravention of bylaws and regulations, all resuscitators (by trespass and petty larceny of kindlings) of venville rights, obsolete by desuetude, all orotund instigators of international persecution, all perpetuators of international animosities, all menial molestors of domestic conviviality, all recalcitrant violators of domestic connubiality.

Prove that he had loved rectitude from his earliest youth.

To Master Percy Apjohn at High School in 1880 he had divulged his disbelief in the tenets of the Irish (protestant) church (to which his father Rudolf Virag (later Rudolph Bloom) had been converted from the Israelitic faith and communion in 1865 by the Society for promoting Christianity among the jews) subsequently abjured by him in favour of Roman catholicism at the epoch of and with a view to his matrimony in 1888. To Daniel Magrane and Francis Wade in 1882 during a juvenile friendship (terminated by the premature emigration of the former) he had advocated during nocturnal perambulations the political theory of colonial (e.g. Canadian) expansion and the evolutionary theories of Charles Darwin, expounded in *The Descent of Man* and *The Origin of Species*. In 1885 he had publicly expressed his adherence to the collective and national economic programme advocated by James Fintan Lalor, John Fisher Murray, John Mitchel, J. F. X. O'Brien and others, the agrarian policy of Michael Davitt, the constitutional agitation of Charles Stewart Parnell (M. P. for Cork City), the programme of peace, retrenchment and reform of William Ewart Gladstone (M. P. for Midlothian, N. B.) and, in support of his political convictions, had climbed up into a secure position amid the ramifications of a tree on Northumberland road to see the entrance (2 February 1888) into the capital of a demonstrative torchlight procession of 20,000 torchbearers, divided into 120 trade corporations, bearing 2000 torches in escort of the marquess of Ripon and (honest) John Morley.

How much and how did he propose to pay for this country residence?

As per prospectus of the Industrious Foreign Acclimatised Nationalised Friendly Stateaided Building Society (incorporated 1874), a maximum of £ 60 per annum, being 1/6 of an assured income, derived from giltedged securities, representing at 5 % simple interest on capital of £ 1200 (estimate of price at 20 years' purchase), of which 1/3 to be paid on acquisition and the balance in the form of annual rent, viz. £ 800 plus 2 1/2 % interest on the same, repayable quarterly in equal annual instalments until extinction by amortisation of loan advanced for purchase within a period of 20 years, amounting to an annual rental of £ 64, headrent included, the titledeeds to remain in possession of the lender or lenders with a saving clause envisaging forced sale, foreclosure and mutual compensation in the event of protracted failure to pay the terms assigned, otherwise the messuage to become the absolute property of the tenant occupier upon expiry of the period of years stipulated.

What rapid but insecure means to opulence might facilitate immediate purchase?

A private wireless telegraph which would transmit by dot and dash system the result of a national equine handicap (flat or steeplechase) of 1 or more miles and furlongs won by an outsider at odds of 50 to 1 at 3 hr 8 m. p.m. at Ascot (Greenwich time), the message being received and available for betting purposes in Dublin at 2.59 p.m. (Dunsink time). The unexpected discovery of an object of great monetary value (precious stone, valuable adhesive or impressed postage stamps (7 schilling, mauve, imperforate, Hamburg, 1866: 4 pence, rose, blue paper, perforate, Great Britain, 1855: 1 franc, stone, official, rouletted, diagonal surcharge, Luxemburg, 1878), antique dynastical ring, unique relic) in unusual repositories or by unusual means: from the air (dropped by an eagle in flight), by fire (amid the carbonised remains of an incendiated edifice), in the sea (amid flotsam, jetsam, lagan and derelict), on earth (in the gizzard of a comestible fowl). A Spanish prisoner's donation of a distant treasure of valuables or specie or bullion lodged with a solvent banking corporation 100 years previously at 5% compound interest of the collective worth of £ 5,000,000 stg (five million pounds sterling). A contract with an inconsiderate contractee for the delivery of 32 consignments of some given commodity in consideration of cash payment on delivery per delivery at the initial rate of 1/4d to be increased constantly in the geometrical progression of 2 (1/4d, 1/2d, 1d, 2d, 4d, 8d, 1s 4d, 2s 8d to 32 terms). A prepared scheme based on a study of the laws of probability to break the bank at Monte Carlo. A solution of the secular problem of the quadrature of the circle, government premium £ 1,000,000 sterling.

Was vast wealth acquirable through industrial channels?

The reclamation of dunams of waste arenary soil, proposed in the prospectus of Agendath Netaim, Bleibtreustrasse, Berlin, W. 15, by the cultivation of orange plantations and melonfields and reafforestation. The utilisation of waste paper, fells of sewer rodents, human excrement possessing chemical properties, in view of the vast production of the first, vast number of the second and immense quantity of the third, every normal human being of average vitality and appetite producing annually, cancelling byproducts of water, a sum total of 80 lbs. (mixed animal and vegetable diet), to be multiplied by 4,386,035, the total population of Ireland according to census returns of 1901.

Were there schemes of wider scope?

A scheme to be formulated and submitted for approval to the harbour commissioners for the exploitation of white coal (hydraulic power), obtained by hydroelectric plant at peak of tide at Dublin bar or at head of water at Poulaphouca or Powerscourt or catchment basins of main streams for the economic production of 500,000 W. H. P. of electricity. A scheme to enclose the peninsular delta of the North Bull at Dollymount and erect on the space of the foreland, used for golf links and rifle ranges, an asphalted esplanade with casinos, booths, shooting galleries, hotels, boardinghouses, readingrooms, establishments for mixed bathing. A scheme for the use of dogvans and goatvans for the delivery of early morning milk. A scheme for the development of Irish tourist traffic in and around Dublin by means of petrolpropelled riverboats, plying in the fluvial fairway between Island bridge and Ringsend, charabancs, narrow gauge local railways, and pleasure steamers for coastwise navigation (10/- per person per day, guide (trilingual) included). A scheme for the repristination of passenger and goods traffics over Irish waterways, when freed from weedbeds. A scheme to connect by tramline the Cattle Market (North Circular road and Prussia street) with the quays (Sheriff street, lower, and East Wall), parallel with the Link line railway laid (in conjunction with the Great Southern and Western railway line) between the cattle park, Liffey junction, and terminus of Midland Great Western Railway 43 to 45 North Wall, in proximity to the terminal stations or Dublin branches of Great Central Railway, Midland Railway of England, City of Dublin Steam Packet Company, Lancashire and Yorkshire Railway Company, Dublin and Glasgow Steam Packet Company, Glasgow, Dublin and Londonderry Steam Packet Company (Laird line), British and Irish Steam Packet Company, Dublin and Morecambe Steamers, London and North Western Railway Company, Dublin Port and Docks Board Landing Sheds and transit sheds of Palgrave,

Murphy and Company, steamship owners, agents for steamers from Mediterranean, Spain, Portugal, France, Belgium and Holland and for Liverpool Underwriters' Association, the cost of acquired rolling stock for animal transport and of additional mileage operated by the Dublin United Tramways Company, limited, to be covered by graziers' fees.

Positing what protasis would the contraction for such several schemes become a natural and necessary apodosis?

Given a guarantee equal to the sum sought, the support, by deed of gift and transfer vouchers during donor's lifetime or by bequest after donor's painless extinction, of eminent financiers (Blum Pasha, Rothschild, Guggenheim, Hirsch, Montefiore, Morgan, Rockefeller) possessing fortunes in 6 figures, amassed during a successful life, and joining capital with opportunity the thing required was done.

What eventuality would render him independent of such wealth?

The independent discovery of a goldseam of inexhaustible ore.

For what reason did he meditate on schemes so difficult of realisation?

It was one of his axioms that similar meditations or the automatic relation to himself of a narrative concerning himself or tranquil recollection of the past when practised habitually before retiring for the night alleviated fatigue and produced as a result sound repose and renovated vitality.

His justifications?

As a physicist he had learned that of the 70 years of complete human life at least 2/7ths, viz., 20 years are passed in sleep. As a philosopher he knew that at the termination of any allotted life only an infinitesimal part of any person's desires has been realised. As a physiologist he believed in the artificial placation of malignant agencies chiefly operative during somnolence.

What did he fear?

The committal of homicide or suicide during sleep by an aberration of the light of reason, the incommensurable categorical intelligence situated in the cerebral convolutions.

What were habitually his final meditations?

Of some one sole unique advertisement to cause passers to stop in wonder, a poster novelty, with all extraneous accretions excluded, reduced to its simplest and most efficient terms not exceeding the span of casual vision and congruous with the velocity of modern life.

What did the first drawer unlocked contain?

A Vere Foster's handwriting copybook, property of Milly (Millicent) Bloom, certain pages of which bore diagram drawings, marked Papli, which showed a large globular head with 5 hairs erect, 2 eyes in profile, the trunk full front with 3 large buttons, 1 triangular foot: 2 fading photographs of queen Alexandra of England and of Maud Branscombe, actress and professional beauty: a Yuletide card, bearing on it a pictorial representation of a parasitic plant, the legend *Mizpah*, the date Xmas 1892, the name of the senders: from Mr + Mrs M. Comerford, the versicle: *May this Yuletide bring to thee, Joy and peace and welcome glee*: a butt of red partly liquefied sealing wax, obtained from the stores department of Messrs Hely's, Ltd., 89, 90, and 91 Dame street: a box containing the remainder of a gross of gilt "J" pennibs, obtained from same department of same firm: an old sandglass which rolled containing sand which rolled: a sealed prophecy (never unsealed) written by Leopold Bloom in 1886 concerning the consequences of the passing into law of William Ewart Gladstone's Home Rule

bill of 1886 (never passed into law): a bazaar ticket, N° 2004, of
S. Kevin's Charity Fair, price 6d, 100 prizes: an infantile epis-
tle, dated, small em monday, reading: capital pee Papli comma
capital aitch How are you note of interrogation capital eye I am
very well full stop new paragraph signature with flourishes capital em Milly no stop: a cameo brooch, property of Ellen Bloom
(born Higgins), deceased: a cameo scarfpin, property of Rudolph
Bloom (born Virag), deceased: 3 typewritten letters, addressee,
Henry Flower, c/o. P. O. Westland Row, addresser, Martha
Clifford, c/o. P. O. Dolphin's Barn: the transliterated name and
address of the addresser of the 3 letters in reversed alphabetic
boustrophedonic punctated quadrilinear cryptogram (vowels
suppressed) N. IGS./WI.UU. OX/W. OKS. MH/Y. IM: a press
cutting from an English weekly periodical *Modern Society*, subject
corporal chastisement in girls' schools: a pink ribbon which had
festooned an Easter egg in the year 1899: two partly uncoiled
rubber preservatives with reserve pockets, purchased by post from
Box 32, P. O., Charing Cross, London, W. C.: 1 pack of 1 dozen
creamlaid envelopes and feintruled notepaper, watermarked, now
reduced by 3: some assorted Austrian-Hungarian coins: 2 cou-
pons of the Royal and Privileged Hungarian Lottery: a lowpower
magnifying glass: 2 erotic photocards showing a) buccal coition
between nude senorita (rere presentation, superior position) and
nude torero (fore presentation, inferior position) b) anal violation
by male religious (fully clothed, eyes abject) of female religious
(partly clothed, eyes direct), purchased by post from Box 32, P.
O., Charing Cross, London, W. C.: a press cutting of recipe for
renovation of old tan boots: a 1d adhesive stamp, lavender, of the
reign of Queen Victoria: a chart of the measurements of Leopold
Bloom compiled before, during and after 2 months' consecutive
use of Sandow-Whiteley's pulley exerciser (men's 15/-, athlete's
20/-) viz. chest 28 in and 29 1/2 in, biceps 9 in and 10 in, forearm 8 1/2 in and 9 in, thigh 10 in and 12 in, calf 11 in and 12 in:
1 prospectus of The Wonderworker, the world's greatest remedy

for rectal complaints, direct from Wonderworker, Coventry
House, South Place, London E C, addressed (erroneously) to
Mrs L. Bloom with brief accompanying note commencing (erro-
neously): Dear Madam.

Quote the textual terms in which the prospectus claimed
advantages for this thaumaturgic remedy.

It heals and soothes while you sleep, in case of trouble in
breaking wind, assists nature in the most formidable way, insur-
ing instant relief in discharge of gases, keeping parts clean and
free natural action, an initial outlay of 7/6 making a new man
of you and life worth living. Ladies find Wonderworker especially useful, a pleasant surprise when they note delightful result
like a cool drink of fresh spring water on a sultry summer's day.
Recommend it to your lady and gentlemen friends, lasts a lifetime. Insert long round end. Wonderworker.

Were there testimonials?

Numerous. From clergyman, British naval officer, well-
known author, city man, hospital nurse, lady, mother of five,
absentminded beggar.

How did absentminded beggar's concluding testimonial
conclude?

What a pity the government did not supply our men with
wonderworkers during the South African campaign! What a
relief it would have been!

What object did Bloom add to this collection of objects?

A 4th typewritten letter received by Henry Flower (let H. F.
be L. B.) from Martha Clifford (find M. C.).

What pleasant reflection accompanied this action?

The reflection that, apart from the letter in question, his

magnetic face, form and address had been favourably received during the course of the preceding day by a wife (Mrs Josephine Breen, born Josie Powell), a nurse, Miss Callan (Christian name unknown), a maid, Gertrude (Gerty, family name unknown).

What possibility suggested itself?

The possibility of exercising virile power of fascination in the not immediate future after an expensive repast in a private apartment in the company of an elegant courtesan, of corporal beauty, moderately mercenary, variously instructed, a lady by origin.

What did the 2nd drawer contain?

Documents: the birth certificate of Leopold Paula Bloom: an endowment assurance policy of £ 500 in the Scottish Widows' Assurance Society, intestated Millicent (Milly) Bloom, coming into force at 25 years as with profit policy of £ 430, £ 462-10-0 and £ 500 at 60 years or death, 65 years or death and death, respectively, or with profit policy (paidup) of £ 299-10-0 together with cash payment of £ 133-10-0, at option: a bank passbook issued by the Ulster Bank, College Green branch showing statement of a/c for halfyear ending 31 December 1903, balance in depositor's favour: £ 18-14-6 (eighteen pounds, fourteen shillings and sixpence, sterling), net personalty: certificate of possession of £ 900, Canadian 4% (inscribed) government stock (free of stamp duty): dockets of the Catholic Cemeteries' (Glasnevin) Committee, relative to a graveplot purchased: a local press cutting concerning change of name by deedpoll.

Quote the textual terms of this notice.

I, Rudolf Virag, now resident at no 52 Clanbrassil street, Dublin, formerly of Szombathely in the kingdom of Hungary, hereby give notice that I have assumed and intend henceforth

upon all occasions and at all times to be known by the name of
Rudolph Bloom.

What other objects relative to Rudolph Bloom (born Virag)
were in the 2nd drawer?

An indistinct daguerreotype of Rudolf Virag and his father
Leopold Virag executed in the year 1852 in the portrait ate-
lier of their (respectively) 1st and 2nd cousin, Stefan Virag of
Szesfehervar, Hungary. An ancient haggadah book in which a
pair of hornrimmed convex spectacles inserted marked the passage of thanksgiving in the ritual prayers for Pessach (Passover):
a photocard of the Queen's Hotel, Ennis, proprietor, Rudolph
Bloom: an envelope addressed: *To My Dear Son Leopold*.

What fractions of phrases did the lecture of those five whole
words evoke?

Tomorrow will be a week that I received . . . it is no use Leopold
to be . . . with your dear mother . . . that is not more to stand . . .
to her . . . all for me is out . . . be kind to Athos, Leopold . . . my
dear son . . . always . . . of me . . . *das Herz . . . Gott . . . dein . . .*

What reminiscences of a human subject suffering from progressive melancholia did these objects evoke in Bloom?

An old man, widower, unkempt of hair, in bed, with head
covered, sighing: an infirm dog, Athos: aconite, resorted to by
increasing doses of grains and scruples as a palliative of recru-
descent neuralgia: the face in death of a septuagenarian, suicide
by poison.

Why did Bloom experience a sentiment of remorse?

Because in immature impatience he had treated with disre-
spect certain beliefs and practices.

As?

The prohibition of the use of fleshmeat and milk at one meal: the hebdomadary symposium of incoordinately abstract, perfervidly concrete mercantile coexreligionist excompatriots: the circumcision of male infants: the supernatural character of Judaic scripture: the ineffability of the tetragrammaton: the sanctity of the sabbath.

How did these beliefs and practices now appear to him?

Not more rational than they had then appeared, not less rational than other beliefs and practices now appeared.

What first reminiscence had he of Rudolph Bloom (deceased)?

Rudolph Bloom (deceased) narrated to his son Leopold Bloom (aged 6) a retrospective arrangement of migrations and settlements in and between Dublin, London, Florence, Milan, Vienna, Budapest, Szombathely with statements of satisfaction (his grandfather having seen Maria Theresia, empress of Austria, queen of Hungary), with commercial advice (having taken care of pence, the pounds having taken care of themselves). Leopold Bloom (aged 6) had accompanied these narrations by constant consultation of a geographical map of Europe (political) and by suggestions for the establishment of affiliated business premises in the various centres mentioned.

Had time equally but differently obliterated the memory of these migrations in narrator and listener?

In narrator by the access of years and in consequence of the use of narcotic toxin: in listener by the access of years and in consequence of the action of distraction upon vicarious experiences.

What idiosyncracies of the narrator were concomitant products of amnesia?

Occasionally he ate without having previously removed his hat. Occasionally he drank voraciously the juice of gooseberry fool from an inclined plate. Occasionally he removed from his lips the traces of food by means of a lacerated envelope or other accessible fragment of paper.

What two phenomena of senescence were more frequent?

The myopic digital calculation of coins, eructation consequent upon repletion.

What object offered partial consolation for these reminiscences?

The endowment policy, the bank passbook, the certificate of the possession of scrip.

Reduce Bloom by cross multiplication of reverses of fortune, from which these supports protected him, and by elimination of all positive values to a negligible negative irrational unreal quantity.

Successively, in descending helotic order: Poverty: that of the outdoor hawker of imitation jewellery, the dun for the recovery of bad and doubtful debts, the poor rate and deputy cess collector. Mendicancy: that of the fraudulent bankrupt with negligible assets paying 1/4d in the £, sandwichman, distributor of throwaways, nocturnal vagrant, insinuating sycophant, maimed sailor, blind stripling, superannuated bailiff's man, marfeast, lickplate, spoilsport, pickthank, eccentric public laughingstock seated on bench of public park under discarded perforated umbrella. Destitution: the inmate of Old Man's House (Royal Hospital), Kilmainham, the inmate of Simpson's Hospital for reduced but respectable men permanently disabled by gout or want of sight. Nadir of misery: the aged impotent disfranchised ratesupported moribund lunatic pauper.

With which attendant indignities?

The unsympathetic indifference of previously amiable females, the contempt of muscular males, the acceptance of fragments of bread, the simulated ignorance of casual acquaintances, the latration of illegitimate unlicensed vagabond dogs, the infantile discharge of decomposed vegetable missiles, worth little or nothing or less than nothing.

By what could such a situation be precluded?
By decease (change of state): by departure (change of place).

Which preferably?
The latter, by the line of least resistance.

What considerations rendered departure not entirely undesirable?

Constant cohabitation impeding mutual toleration of personal defects. The habit of independent purchase increasingly cultivated. The necessity to counteract by impermanent sojourn the permanence of arrest.

What considerations rendered departure not irrational?

The parties concerned, uniting, had increased and multiplied, which being done, offspring produced and educed to maturity, the parties, if not disunited were obliged to reunite for increase and multiplication, which was absurd, to form by reunion the original couple of uniting parties, which was impossible.

What considerations rendered departure desirable?

The attractive character of certain localities in Ireland and abroad, as represented in general geographical maps of polychrome design or in special ordnance survey charts by employment of scale numerals and hachures.

In Ireland?

The cliffs of Moher, the windy wilds of Connemara, lough Neagh with submerged petrified city, the Giant's Causeway, Fort Camden and Fort Carlisle, the Golden Vale of Tipperary, the islands of Aran, the pastures of royal Meath, Brigid's elm in Kildare, the Queen's Island shipyard in Belfast, the Salmon Leap, the lakes of Killarney.

Abroad?

Ceylon (with spicegardens supplying tea to Thomas Kernan, agent for Pulbrook, Robertson and Co, 2 Mincing Lane, London, E. C., 5 Dame street, Dublin), Jerusalem, the holy city (with mosque of Omar and gate of Damascus, goal of aspiration), the straits of Gibraltar (the unique birthplace of Marion Tweedy), the Parthenon (containing statues of nude Grecian divinities), the Wall street money market (which controlled international finance), the Plaza de Toros at La Linea, Spain (where O'Hara of the Camerons had slain the bull), Niagara (over which no human being had passed with impunity), the land of the Eskimos (eaters of soap), the forbidden country of Thibet (from which no traveller returns), the bay of Naples (to see which was to die), the Dead Sea.

Under what guidance, following what signs?

At sea, septentrional, by night the polestar, located at the point of intersection of the right line from beta to alpha in Ursa Maior produced and divided externally at omega and the hypotenuse of the rightangled triangle formed by the line alpha omega so produced and the line alpha delta of Ursa Maior. On land, meridional, a bispherical moon, revealed in imperfect varying phases of lunation through the posterior interstice of the imperfectly occluded skirt of a carnose negligent perambulating female, a pillar of the cloud by day.

What public advertisement would divulge the occultation of the departed?

£ 5 reward, lost, stolen or strayed from his residence 7 Eccles street, missing gent about 40, answering to the name of Bloom, Leopold (Poldy), height 5 ft 9 1/2 inches, full build, olive complexion, may have since grown a beard, when last seen was wearing a black suit. Above sum will be paid for information leading to his discovery.

What universal binomial denominations would be his as entity and nonentity?

Assumed by any or known to none. Everyman or Noman.

What tributes his?

Honour and gifts of strangers, the friends of Everyman. A nymph immortal, beauty, the bride of Noman.

Would the departed never nowhere nohow reappear?

Ever he would wander, selfcompelled, to the extreme limit of his cometary orbit, beyond the fixed stars and variable suns and telescopic planets, astronomical waifs and strays, to the extreme boundary of space, passing from land to land, among peoples, amid events. Somewhere imperceptibly he would hear and somehow reluctantly, suncompelled, obey the summons of recall. Whence, disappearing from the constellation of the Northern Crown he would somehow reappear reborn above delta in the constellation of Cassiopeia and after incalculable eons of peregrination return an estranged avenger, a wreaker of justice on malefactors, a dark crusader, a sleeper awakened, with financial resources (by supposition) surpassing those of Rothschild or the silver king.

What would render such return irrational?

An unsatisfactory equation between an exodus and return in

time through reversible space and an exodus and return in space through irreversible time.

What play of forces, inducing inertia, rendered departure undesirable?

The lateness of the hour, rendering procrastinatory: the obscurity of the night, rendering invisible: the uncertainty of thoroughfares, rendering perilous: the necessity for repose, obviating movement: the proximity of an occupied bed, obviating research: the anticipation of warmth (human) tempered with coolness (linen), obviating desire and rendering desirable: the statue of Narcissus, sound without echo, desired desire.

What advantages were possessed by an occupied, as distinct from an unoccupied bed?

The removal of nocturnal solitude, the superior quality of human (mature female) to inhuman (hotwaterjar) calefaction, the stimulation of matutinal contact, the economy of mangling done on the premises in the case of trousers accurately folded and placed lengthwise between the spring mattress (striped) and the woollen mattress (biscuit section).

What past consecutive causes, before rising preapprehended, of accumulated fatigue did Bloom, before rising, silently recapitulate?

The preparation of breakfast (burnt offering): intestinal congestion and premeditative defecation (holy of holies): the bath (rite of John): the funeral (rite of Samuel): the advertisement of Alexander Keyes (Urim and Thummim): the unsubstantial lunch (rite of Melchisedek): the visit to museum and national library (holy place): the bookhunt along Bedford row, Merchants' Arch, Wellington Quay (Simchath Torah): the music in the Ormond Hotel (Shira Shirim): the altercation with a truculent troglodyte in Bernard Kiernan's premises (holocaust): a blank period of time including a cardrive, a visit to a house of mourning, a leavetaking (wilderness): the eroticism produced by feminine exhibitionism (rite of Onan): the prolonged delivery of Mrs Mina Purefoy (heave offering): the visit to the disorderly house of Mrs Bella Cohen, 82 Tyrone street, lower, and subsequent brawl and chance medley in Beaver street (Armageddon): nocturnal perambulation to and from the cabman's shelter, Butt Bridge (atonement).

What selfimposed enigma did Bloom about to rise in order to go so as to conclude lest he should not conclude involuntarily apprehend?

The cause of a brief sharp unforeseen heard loud lone crack emitted by the insentient material of a strainveined timber table.

What selfinvolved enigma did Bloom risen, going, gathering multicoloured multiform multitudinous garments, voluntarily apprehending, not comprehend?

Who was M'Intosh?

What selfevident enigma pondered with desultory constancy during 30 years did Bloom now, having effected natural obscurity by the extinction of artificial light, silently suddenly comprehend?

Where was Moses when the candle went out?

What imperfections in a perfect day did Bloom, walking, charged with collected articles of recently divested male wearing apparel, silently, successively, enumerate?

A provisional failure to obtain renewal of an advertisement: to obtain a certain quantity of tea from Thomas Kernan (agent for Pulbrook, Robertson and C°, 5 Dame Street, Dublin, and 2 Mincing Lane, London E. C.): to certify the presence or absence of posterior rectal orifice in the case of Hellenic female divinities: to obtain admission (gratuitous or paid) to the performance of *Leah* by Mrs Bandmann Palmer at the Gaiety Theatre, 46, 47, 48, 49 South King street.

What impression of an absent face did Bloom, arrested, silently recall?

The face of her father, the late Major Brian Cooper Tweedy, Royal Dublin Fusiliers, of Gibraltar and Rehoboth, Dolphin's Barn.

What recurrent impressions of the same were possible by hypothesis?

Retreating, at the terminus of the Great Northern Railway, Amiens street, with constant uniform acceleration, along parallel lines meeting at infinity, if produced: along parallel lines, reproduced from infinity, with constant uniform retardation, at the terminus of the Great Northern Railway, Amiens street, returning.

What miscellaneous effects of female personal wearing apparel were perceived by him?

A pair of new inodorous halfsilk black ladies' hose, a pair of new violet garters, a pair of outsize ladies' drawers of India mull, cut on generous lines, redolent of opoponax, jessamine and Muratti's Turkish cigarettes and containing a long bright steel safety pin, folded curvilinear, a camisole of batiste with thin lace border, an accordion underskirt of blue silk moirette, all these objects being disposed irregularly on the top of a rectangular trunk, quadruple battened, having capped corners, with multi-coloured labels, initialled on its fore side in white lettering B. C. T. (Brian Cooper Tweedy).

What impersonal objects were perceived?

A commode, one leg fractured, totally covered by square

cretonne cutting, apple design, on which rested a lady's black straw hat. Orangekeyed ware, bought of Henry Price, basket, fancy goods, chinaware and ironmongery manufacturer, 21, 22, 23 Moore street, disposed irregularly on the washstand and floor and consisting of basin, soapdish and brushtray (on the washstand, together), pitcher and night article (on the floor, separate).

Bloom's acts?
He deposited the articles of clothing on a chair, removed his remaining articles of clothing, took from beneath the bolster at the head of the bed a folded long white nightshirt, inserted his head and arms into the proper apertures of the nightshirt, removed a pillow from the head to the foot of the bed, prepared the bedlinen accordingly and entered the bed.

How?
With circumspection, as invariably when entering an abode (his own or not his own): with solicitude, the snakespiral springs of the mattress being old, the brass quoits and pendent viper radii loose and tremulous under stress and strain: prudently, as entering a lair or ambush of lust or adders: lightly, the less to disturb: reverently, the bed of conception and of birth, of consummation of marriage and of breach of marriage, of sleep and of death.

What did his limbs, when gradually extended, encounter?
New clean bedlinen, additional odours, the presence of a human form, female, hers, the imprint of a human form, male, not his, some crumbs, some flakes of potted meat, recooked, which he removed.

If he had smiled why would he have smiled?
To reflect that each one who enters imagines himself to be

the first to enter whereas he is always the last term of a preceding series even if the first term of a succeeding one, each imagining himself to be first, last, only and alone whereas he is neither first nor last nor only nor alone in a series originating in and repeated to infinity.

What preceding series?

Assuming Mulvey to be the first term of his series, Penrose, Bartell d'Arcy, professor Goodwin, Julius Mastiansky, John Henry Menton, Father Bernard Corrigan, a farmer at the Royal Dublin Society's Horse Show, Maggot O'Reilly, Matthew Dillon, Valentine Blake Dillon (Lord Mayor of Dublin), Christopher Callinan, Lenehan, an Italian organ-grinder, an unknown gentleman in the Gaiety Theatre, Benjamin Dollard, Simon Dedalus, Andrew (Pisser) Burke, Joseph Cuffe, Wisdom Hely, Alderman John Hooper, Dr Francis Brady, Father Sebastian of Mount Argus, a bootblack at the General Post Office, Hugh E. (Blazes) Boylan and so each and so on to no last term.

What were his reflections concerning the last member of this series and late occupant of the bed?

Reflections on his vigour (a bounder), corporal proportion (a billsticker), commercial ability (a bester), impressionability (a boaster).

Why for the observer impressionability in addition to vigour, corporal proportion and commercial ability?

Because he had observed with augmenting frequency in the preceding members of the same series the same concupiscence, inflammably transmitted, first with alarm, then with understanding, then with desire, finally with fatigue, with alternating symptoms of epicene comprehension and apprehension.

With what antagonistic sentiments were his subsequent reflections affected?

Envy, jealousy, abnegation, equanimity.

Envy?

Of a bodily and mental male organism specially adapted for the superincumbent posture of energetic human copulation and energetic piston and cylinder movement necessary for the complete satisfaction of a constant but not acute concupiscence resident in a bodily and mental female organism, passive but not obtuse.

Jealousy?

Because a nature full and volatile in its free state, was alternately the agent and reagent of attraction. Because attraction between agent(s) and reagent(s) at all instants varied, with inverse proportion of increase and decrease, with incessant circular extension and radial reentrance. Because the controlled contemplation of the fluctuation of attraction produced, if desired, a fluctuation of pleasure.

Abnegation?

In virtue of a) acquaintance initiated in September 1903 in the establishment of George Mesias, merchant tailor and outfitter, 5 Eden Quay, b) hospitality extended and received in kind, reciprocated and reappropriated in person, c) comparative youth subject to impulses of ambition and magnanimity, colleagual altruism and amorous egoism, d) extraracial attraction, intraracial inhibition, supraracial prerogative, e) an imminent provincial musical tour, common current expenses, net proceeds divided.

Equanimity?

As as natural as any and every natural act of a nature

expressed or understood executed in natured nature by natural
creatures in accordance with his, her and their natured natures,
of dissimilar similarity. As not so calamitous as a cataclysmic
annihilation of the planet in consequence of a collision with
a dark sun. As less reprehensible than theft, highway robbery,
cruelty to children and animals, obtaining money under false
pretences, forgery, embezzlement, misappropriation of public
money, betrayal of public trust, malingering, mayhem, corrup-
tion of minors, criminal libel, blackmail, contempt of court,
arson, treason, felony, mutiny on the high seas, trespass, bur-
glary, jailbreaking, practice of unnatural vice, desertion from
armed forces in the field, perjury, poaching, usury, intelligence
with the king's enemies, impersonation, criminal assault, man-
slaughter, wilful and premeditated murder. As not more abnor-
mal than all other parallel processes of adaptation to altered
conditions of existence, resulting in a reciprocal equilibrium
between the bodily organism and its attendant circumstances,
foods, beverages, acquired habits, indulged inclinations, significant disease. As more than inevitable, irreparable.

Why more abnegation than jealousy, less envy than
equanimity?

From outrage (matrimony) to outrage (adultery) there arose
nought but outrage (copulation) yet the matrimonial violator
of the matrimonially violated had not been outraged by the
adulterous violator of the adulterously violated.

What retribution, if any?

Assassination, never, as two wrongs did not make one right.
Duel by combat, no. Divorce, not now. Exposure by mechanical artifice (automatic bed) or individual testimony (concealed
ocular witnesses), not yet. Suit for damages by legal influence
or simulation of assault with evidence of injuries sustained
(selfinflicted), not impossibly. Hushmoney by moral influence,

possibly. If any, positively, connivance, introduction of emulation (material, a prosperous rival agency of publicity: moral,
a successful rival agent of intimacy), depreciation, alienation,
humiliation, separation protecting the one separated from the
other, protecting the separator from both.

By what reflections did he, a conscious reactor against the
void of incertitude, justify to himself his sentiments?

The preordained frangibility of the hymen: the presup-
posed intangibility of the thing in itself: the incongruity and
disproportion between the selfprolonging tension of the thing
proposed to be done and the selfabbreviating relaxation of the
thing done: the fallaciously inferred debility of the female: the
muscularity of the male: the variations of ethical codes: the natural grammatical transition by inversion involving no alteration
of sense of an aorist preterite proposition (parsed as masculine
subject, monosyllabic onomatopoeic transitive verb with direct
feminine object) from the active voice into its correlative aorist
preterite proposition (parsed as feminine subject, auxiliary verb
and quasimonosyllabic onomatopoeic past participle with com-
plementary masculine agent) in the passive voice: the continued
product of seminators by generation: the continual production
of semen by distillation: the futility of triumph or protest
or vindication: the inanity of extolled virtue: the lethargy of
nescient matter: the apathy of the stars.

In what final satisfaction did these antagonistic sentiments
and reflections, reduced to their simplest forms, converge?

Satisfaction at the ubiquity in eastern and western terrestrial
hemispheres, in all habitable lands and islands explored or unex-
plored (the land of the midnight sun, the islands of the blessed,
the isles of Greece, the land of promise), of adipose anterior
and posterior female hemispheres, redolent of milk and honey
and of excretory sanguine and seminal warmth, reminiscent of

secular families of curves of amplitude, insusceptible of moods of impression or of contrarieties of expression, expressive of mute immutable mature animality.

The visible signs of antesatisfaction?
An approximate erection: a solicitous adversion: a gradual elevation: a tentative revelation: a silent contemplation.

Then?
He kissed the plump mellow yellow smellow melons of her rump, on each plump melonous hemisphere, in their mellow yellow furrow, with obscure prolonged provocative melons-mellonous osculation.

The visible signs of postsatisfaction?
A silent contemplation: a tentative velation: a gradual abasement: a solicitous aversion: a proximate erection.

What followed this silent action?
Somnolent invocation, less somnolent recognition, incipient excitation, catechetical interrogation.

With what modifications did the narrator reply to this interrogation?
Negative: he omitted to mention the clandestine correspondence between Martha Clifford and Henry Flower, the public altercation at, in and in the vicinity of the licensed premises of Bernard Kiernan and Co, Limited, 8, 9 and 10 Little Britain street, the erotic provocation and response thereto caused by the exhibitionism of Gertrude (Gerty), surname unknown. Positive: he included mention of a performance by Mrs Bandmann Palmer of *Leah* at the Gaiety Theatre, 46, 47, 48, 49 South King street, an invitation to supper at Wynn's (Murphy's) Hotel, 35, 36 and 37 Lower Abbey street, a volume of peccaminous

pornographical tendency entituled *Sweets of Sin*, anonymous author a gentleman of fashion, a temporary concussion caused by a falsely calculated movement in the course of a postcenal gymnastic display, the victim (since completely recovered) being Stephen Dedalus, professor and author, eldest surviving son of Simon Dedalus, of no fixed occupation, an aeronautical feat executed by him (narrator) in the presence of a witness, the professor and author aforesaid, with promptitude of decision and gymnastic flexibility.

Was the narration otherwise unaltered by modifications?
Absolutely.

Which event or person emerged as the salient point of his narration?
Stephen Dedalus, professor and author.

What limitations of activity and inhibitions of conjugal rights were perceived by listener and narrator concerning themselves during the course of this intermittent and increasingly more laconic narration?
By the listener a limitation of fertility inasmuch as marriage had been celebrated 1 calendar month after the 18th anniversary of her birth (8 September 1870), viz. 8 October, and consummated on the same date with female issue born 15 June 1889, having been anticipatorily consummated on the 10 September of the same year and complete carnal intercourse, with ejaculation of semen within the natural female organ, having last taken place 5 weeks previous, viz. 27 November 1893, to the birth on 29 December 1893 of second (and only male) issue, deceased 9 January 1894, aged 11 days, there remained a period of 10 years, 5 months and 18 days during which carnal intercourse had been incomplete, without ejaculation of semen within the natural female organ. By the narrator a limitation of activity,

mental and corporal, inasmuch as complete mental intercourse between himself and the listener had not taken place since the consummation of puberty, indicated by catamenic hemorrhage, of the female issue of narrator and listener, 15 September 1903, there remained a period of 9 months and 1 day during which, in consequence of a preestablished natural comprehension in incomprehension between the consummated females (listener and issue), complete corporal liberty of action had been circumscribed.

How?

By various reiterated feminine interrogation concerning the masculine destination whither, the place where, the time at which, the duration for which, the object with which in the case of temporary absences, projected or effected.

What moved visibly above the listener's and the narrator's invisible thoughts?

The upcast reflection of a lamp and shade, an inconstant series of concentric circles of varying gradations of light and shadow.

In what directions did listener and narrator lie?

Listener, S. E. by E.; Narrator, N. W. by W.: on the 53rd parallel of latitude, N., and 6th meridian of longitude, W.: at an angle of 45° to the terrestrial equator.

In what state of rest or motion?

At rest relatively to themselves and to each other. In motion being each and both carried westward, forward and rereward respectively, by the proper perpetual motion of the earth through everchanging tracks of neverchanging space.

In what posture?

Listener: reclined semilaterally, left, left hand under head, right leg extended in a straight line and resting on left leg, flexed, in the attitude of Gea-Tellus, fulfilled, recumbent, big with seed. Narrator: reclined laterally, left, with right and left legs flexed, the index finger and thumb of the right hand resting on the bridge of the nose, in the attitude depicted in a snapshot photograph made by Percy Apjohn, the childman weary, the manchild in the womb.

Womb? Weary?
He rests. He has travelled.

With?
Sinbad the Sailor and Tinbad the Tailor and Jinbad the Jailer and Whinbad the Whaler and Ninbad the Nailer and Finbad the Failer and Binbad the Bailer and Pinbad the Pailer and Minbad the Mailer and Hinbad the Hailer and Rinbad the Railer and Dinbad the Kailer and Vinbad the Quailer and Linbad the Yailer and Xinbad the Phthailer.

When?
Going to dark bed there was a square round Sinbad the Sailor roc's auk's egg in the night of the bed of all the auks of the rocs of Darkinbad the Brightdayler.

Where?

●

Samuel Beckett

The End

'Nothing is funnier than unhappiness', declares Nell in Samuel Beckett's play *Endgame*. The coupling of comedy and misery informs much of Beckett's work, which included novels, short stories, plays, radio and televisual plays, and poems. Awarded the Nobel Prize in Literature in 1969, Beckett produced works that increasingly pared away the external trappings to penetrate the essence of human existence. Alongside Franz Kafka, Beckett's work offers perhaps the most sustained and pure expression of mankind's condition in the twentieth century: bewildered, adrift, and despairing on a planet scorched by war and holocaust. Living much of his life in France and writing his most famous works in French, Beckett took as his subjects human failure, helplessness, distress, and disintegration. The literary critic Hugh Kenner says of Beckett: 'He is the non-maestro, the anti-virtuoso, a habitué of non-form and anti-matter, Euclid of the dark zone where all signs are negative, the comedian of utter disaster.'

Samuel Beckett was born in Foxrock, an affluent Dublin suburb, in 1906, to Anglo-Irish Protestant parents. Suffering from depression as a teenager, he excelled in his studies of Romance languages at Trinity College, and in 1928 moved for the first time to Paris, where he met his artistic hero James Joyce. Joyce's work was to have a powerful, at times oppressive influence on the young Beckett. In the 1930s he wrote his first story collection, *More Pricks than Kicks*, and the novel *Murphy*. It was not until after the Second World War, during which Beckett served in the French resistance, that he began writing in French.

Finally transcending the influence of Joyce, he enjoyed the great five-year surge of work on which his global reputation rests. Beckett's funny, often scatological, enigmatic, and playfully self-deconstructing trilogy of novels, *Molloy*, *Malone Dies*, and *The Unnameable*, were written during this period.

In his magisterial survey of Irish literature, *Inventing Ireland*, the critic Declan Kiberd insists that it is for his prose work that Beckett will be celebrated centuries hence, and indeed Beckett himself considered prose his primary art form. Be that as it may, it is his plays that are currently more widely known, especially *Waiting for Godot*, whose enormously successful run in the Théâtre de Babylone in 1953 marked the beginning of Beckett's international fame. After the earlier stories written in the shadow of Joyce, Beckett's short fiction became increasingly spare and forbidding, reaching an extreme with his 'closed space' fictions of the 1960s.

Beckett shunned publicity, declining even to attend his Nobel award ceremony in Stockholm. In his final decades he wrote mostly in a secluded house in the Marne Valley, near Paris. He continued to live in Paris, with his wife Suzanne Dechevaux-Dumesnil, enjoying friendships with numerous artists, writers, and others. He died in 1989, months after the death of his wife, and is buried in Montparnasse Cemetery.

The story anthologised here, 'The End', is one of four short stories Beckett wrote during the same period as the novel trilogy and *Waiting for Godot*. It has been described by the critic Christopher Ricks as 'the best possible introduction to Beckett's fiction'.

The End

THEY CLOTHED ME and gave me money. I knew what the money was for, it was to get me started. When it was gone I would have to get more, if I wanted to go on. The same for the shoes, when they were worn out I would have to get them mended, or get myself another pair, or go on barefoot, if I wanted to go on. The same for the coat and trousers, needless to say, with this difference, that I could go on in my shirtsleeves, if I wanted. The clothes—shoes, socks, trousers, shirt, coat, hat—were not new, but the deceased must have been about my size. That is to say, he must have been a little shorter, a little thinner, for the clothes did not fit me so well in the beginning as they did at the end, the shirt especially, and it was many a long day before I could button it at the neck, or profit by the collar that went with it, or pin the tails together between my legs in the way my mother had taught me. He must have put on his Sunday best to go to the consultation, perhaps for the first time, unable to bear it any longer. Be that as it may the hat was a bowler, in good shape. I said, Keep your hat and give me back mine. I added, Give me back my greatcoat. They replied that they had burnt them, together with my other clothes. I understood then that the end was near, at least fairly near. Later on I tried to exchange this hat for a cap, or a slouch which could be pulled down over my face, but without much success. And yet I could not go about bare-headed, with my skull in the state it was. At first this hat was too small, then it got used to me. They gave me a tie, after long discussion. It seemed a pretty tie to me, but I didn't like it. When it came at last I was too tired to send it back. But in the end it came in useful. It was blue, with kinds of little stars. I didn't feel well, but they told me I was well enough. They didn't say in so many words that I was as well as I would ever be, but that was the implication. I lay inert on the bed and it took three women to put on my trousers. They didn't seem to take much interest in my private parts which to tell the truth were nothing to write home about, I didn't take much interest in them myself. But they might have passed some remark. When they had finished I got up and finished dressing unaided. They told me to sit on the bed and wait. All the bedding had disappeared. It made me angry that they had not let me wait in the familiar bed, instead of leaving me standing in the cold, in these clothes that smelt of sulphur. I said, You might have left me in the bed till the last moment. Men all in white came in with mallets in their hands. They dismantled the bed and took away the pieces. One of the women followed them out and came back with a chair which she set before me. I had done well to pretend I was angry. But to make it quite clear to them how angry I was that they had not left me in my bed, I gave the chair a kick that sent it flying. A man came in and made a sign to me to follow him. In the hall he gave me a paper to sign. What's this, I said, a safe-conduct? It's a receipt, he said, for the clothes and money you have received. What money? I said. It was then I received the money. To think I had almost departed without a penny in my pocket. The sum was not large, compared to other sums, but to me it seemed large. I saw the familiar objects, companions of so many bearable hours. The stool, for example, dearest of all. The long afternoons together, waiting for it to be time for bed. At times I felt its wooden life invade me, till I myself became a piece of old wood. There was even a hole for my cyst. Then the window pane with the patch of frosting gone, where I used to press my eye in the hour of need, and rarely in vain. I am greatly obliged to you, I said, is there a law which prevents you from throwing me out naked and penniless? That would damage our reputation in the long run, he replied. Could they not possibly keep me a little longer, I said, I could make myself useful. Useful, he said, joking apart you would be willing to make yourself useful? A moment later he went on, If they believed you were really willing to make yourself useful they would keep you, I am sure. The number of times I had said I was going to make myself useful, I wasn't going to start that again. How weak I felt! Perhaps, I said, they would consent to take back the money and keep me a little longer. This is a charitable institution, he said, and the money is a gift you receive when you leave. When it is gone you will have to get more, if you want to go on. Never come back here whatever you do, you would not be let in. Don't go to any of our branches either, they would turn you away. Exelmans! I cried. Come come, he said, and anyway no one understands a tenth of what you say. I'm so old, I said. You are not so old as all that, he said. May I stay here just a little longer, I said, till the rain is over? You may wait in the cloister, he said, the rain will go on all day. You may wait in the cloister till six o'clock, you will hear the bell. If anyone challenges you, you need only say you have permission to shelter in the cloister. Whose name will I give? I said. Weir, he said.

I had not been long in the cloister when the rain stopped and the sun came out. It was low and I reckoned it must be getting on for six, considering the season. I stayed there looking through the archway at the sun as it went down behind the cloister. A man appeared and asked me what I was doing. What do you want? were the words he used. Very friendly. I replied that I had Mr. Weir's permission to stay in the cloister till six o'clock. He went away, but came back immediately. He must have spoken to Mr. Weir in the interim, for he said, You must not loiter in the cloister now the rain is over.

Now I was making my way through the garden. There was that strange light which follows a day of persistent rain, when the sun comes out and the sky clears too late to be of any use. The earth makes a sound as of sighs and the last drops fall from the emptied cloudless sky. A small boy, stretching out his hands and looking up at the blue sky, asked his mother how such a thing was possible. Fuck off, she said. I suddenly remembered I had not thought of asking Mr. Weir for a piece of bread. He would surely have given it to me. I had as a matter of fact thought of it during our conversation in the hall, I had said to myself, Let us first finish our conversation, then I'll ask. I knew well they would not keep me. I would gladly have turned back, but I was afraid one of the guards would stop me and tell me I would never see Mr. Weir again. That might have added to my sorrow. And anyway I never turned back on such occasions.

In the street I was lost. I had not set foot in this part of the city for a long time and it seemed greatly changed. Whole buildings had disappeared, the palings had changed position, and on all sides I saw, in great letters, the names of tradesmen I had never seen before and would have been at a loss to pronounce. There were streets where I remembered none, some I did remember had vanished and others had completely changed their names. The general impression was the same as before. It is true I did not know the city very well. Perhaps it was quite a different one. I did not know where I was supposed to be going. I had the great good fortune, more than once, not to be run over. My appearance still made people laugh, with that hearty jovial laugh so good for the health. By keeping the red part of the sky as much as possible on my right hand I came at last to the river. Here all seemed at first sight more or less as I had left it. But if I had looked more closely I would doubtless have discovered many changes. And indeed I subsequently did so. But the general appearance of the river, flowing between its quays and under its bridges, had not changed. Yes, the river still gave the impression it was flowing in the wrong direction. That's all a pack of lies I feel. My bench was still there. It was shaped to fit the curves of the seated body. It stood beside a watering trough, gift of a Mrs. Maxwell to the city horses, according to the inscription. During the short time I rested there several horses took advantage of this monument. The iron shoes approached and the jingle of the harness. Then silence. That was the horse looking at me. Then the noise of pebbles and mud that horses make when drinking. Then the silence again. That was the horse looking at me again. Then the pebbles again. Then the silence again. Till the horse had finished drinking or the driver deemed it had drunk its fill. The horses were uneasy. Once, when the noise stopped, I turned and saw the horse looking at me. The driver too was looking at me. Mrs. Maxwell would have been pleased if she could have seen her trough rendering such services to the city horses. When it was night, after a tedious twilight, I took off my hat which was paining me. I longed to be under cover again, in an empty place close and warm, with artificial light, an oil lamp for choice, with a pink shade for preference. From time to time someone would come to make sure I was all right and needed nothing. It was long since I had longed for anything and the effect on me was horrible.

In the days that followed I visited several lodgings, without much success. They usually slammed the door in my face, even when I showed my money and offered to pay a week in advance, or even two. It was in vain I put on my best manners, smiled and spoke distinctly, they slammed the door in my face before I could even finish my little speech. It was at this time I perfected a method of doffing my hat at once courteous and discreet, neither servile nor insolent. I slipped it smartly forward, held it a second poised in such a way that the person addressed could not see my skull, then slipped it back. To do that naturally, without creating an unfavorable impression, is no easy matter. When I deemed that to tip my hat would suffice, I naturally did no more than tip it. But to tip one's hat is no easy matter either. I subsequently solved this problem, always fundamental in time of adversity, by wearing a kepi and saluting in military fashion, no, that must be wrong, I don't know, I had my hat at the end. I never made the mistake of wearing medals. Some landladies

were in such need of money that they let me in immediately
and showed me the room. But I couldn't come to an agreement with any of them. Finally I found a basement. With this
woman I came to an agreement at once. My oddities, that's the
expression she used, did not alarm her. She nevertheless insisted
on making the bed and cleaning the room once a week, instead
of once a month as I requested. She told me that while she was
cleaning, which would not take long, I could wait in the area.
She added, with a great deal of feeling, that she would never
put me out in bad weather. This woman was Greek, I think, or
Turkish. She never spoke about herself. I somehow got the idea
she was a widow or at least that her husband had left her. She
had a strange accent. But so had I with my way of assimilating
the vowels and omitting the consonants.

Now I didn't know where I was. I had a vague vision, not
a real vision, I didn't see anything, of a big house five or six
stories high, one of a block perhaps. It was dusk when I got
there and I did not pay the same heed to my surroundings as
I might have done if I had suspected they were to close about
me. And by then I must have lost all hope. It is true that when I
left this house it was a glorious day, but I never look back when
leaving. I must have read somewhere, when I was small and still
read, that it is better not to look back when leaving. And yet I
sometimes did. But even without looking back it seems to me
I should have seen something when leaving. But there it is. All
I remember is my feet emerging from my shadow, one after
the other. My shoes had stiffened and the sun brought out the
cracks in the leather.

I was comfortable enough in this house, I must say. Apart
from a few rats I was alone in the basement. The woman did
her best to respect our agreement. About noon she brought me
a big tray of food and took away the tray of the previous day.
At the same time she brought me a clean chamber-pot. The
chamber-pot had a large handle which she slipped over her arm,

so that both her hands were free to carry the tray. The rest of the day I saw no more of her except sometimes when she peeped in to make sure nothing had happened to me. Fortunately I did not need affection. From my bed I saw the feet coming and going on the sidewalk. Certain evenings, when the weather was fine and I felt equal to it, I fetched my chair into the area and sat looking up into the skirts of the women passing by. Once I sent for a crocus bulb and planted it in the dark area, in an old pot. It must have been coming up to spring, it was probably not the right time for it. I left the pot outside, attached to a string I passed through the window. In the evening, when the weather was fine, a little light crept up the wall. Then I sat down beside the window and pulled on the string to keep the pot in the light and warmth. That can't have been easy, I don't see how I managed it. It was probably not the right thing for it. I manured it as best I could and pissed on it when the weather was dry. It may not have been the right thing for it. It sprouted, but never any flowers, just a wilting stem and a few chlorotic leaves. I would have liked to have a yellow crocus, or a hyacinth, but there, it was not to be. She wanted to take it away, but I told her to leave it. She wanted to buy me another, but I told her I didn't want another. What lacerated me most was the din of the newspaper boys. They went pounding by every day at the same hours, their heels thudding on the sidewalk, crying the names of their papers and even the headlines. The house noises disturbed me less. A little girl, unless it was a little boy, sang every evening at the same hour, somewhere above me. For a long time I could not catch the words. But hearing them day after day I finally managed to catch a few. Strange words for a little girl, or a little boy. Was it a song in my head or did it merely come from without? It was a sort of lullaby, I believe. It often sent me to sleep, even me. Sometimes it was a little girl who came. She had long red hair hanging down in two braids. I didn't know who she was. She lingered awhile in the room, then went away without

a word. One day I had a visit from a policeman. He said I had
to be watched, without explaining why. Suspicious, that was it,
he told me I was suspicious. I let him talk. He didn't dare arrest
me. Or perhaps he had a kind heart. A priest too, one day I had
a visit from a priest. I informed him I belonged to a branch of
the reformed church. He asked me what kind of clergyman I
would like to see. Yes, there's that about the reformed church,
you're lost, it's unavoidable. Perhaps he had a kind heart. He
told me to let him know if I needed a helping hand. A helping
hand! He gave me his name and explained where I could reach
him. I should have made a note of it.

One day the woman made me an offer. She said she was in
urgent need of cash and that if I could pay her six months in
advance she would reduce my rent by one fourth during that
period, something of that kind. This had the advantage of saving six weeks'(?) rent and the disadvantage of almost exhaust-
ing my small capital. But could you call that a disadvantage?
Wouldn't I stay on in any case till my last penny was gone, and
even longer, till she put me out? I gave her the money and she
gave me a receipt.

One morning, not long after this transaction, I was awakened by a man shaking my shoulder. It could not have been
much past eleven. He requested me to get up and leave his
house immediately. He was most correct, I must say. His surprise, he said, was no less than mine. It was his house. His
property. The Turkish woman had left the day before. But I
saw her last night, I said. You must be mistaken, he said, for she
brought the keys to my office no later than yesterday afternoon.
But I just paid her six months' rent in advance, I said. Get a
refund, he said. But I don't even know her name, I said, let
alone her address. You don't know her name? he said. He must
have thought I was lying. I'm sick, I said, I can't leave like this,
without any notice. You're not so sick as all that, he said. He
offered to send for a taxi, even an ambulance if I preferred. He

said he needed the room immediately for his pig which even
as he spoke was catching cold in a cart before the door and no
one to look after him but a stray urchin whom he had never set
eyes on before and who was probably busy tormenting him. I
asked if he couldn't let me have another place, any old corner
where I could lie down long enough to recover from the shock
and decide what to do. He said he could not. Don't think I'm
being unkind, he added. I could live here with the pig, I said,
I'd look after him. The long months of peace, wiped out in an
instant! Come now, come now, he said, get a grip on yourself,
be a man, get up, that's enough. After all it was no concern of
his. He had really been most patient. He must have visited the
basement while I was sleeping.

I felt weak. Perhaps I was. I stumbled in the blinding light.
A bus took me into the country. I sat down in a field in the sun.
But it seems to me that was much later. I stuck leaves under my
hat, all the way round, to make a shade. The night was cold. I
wandered for hours in the fields. At last I found a heap of dung.
The next day I started back to the city. They made me get off
three buses. I sat down by the roadside and dried my clothes
in the sun. I enjoyed doing that. I said to myself, There's nothing more to be done now, not a thing, till they are dry. When
they were dry I brushed them with a brush, I think a kind of
currycomb, that I found in a stable. Stables have always been
my salvation. Then I went to the house and begged a glass of
milk and a slice of bread and butter. They gave me everything
except the butter. May I rest in the stable? I said. No, they said.
I still stank, but with a stink that pleased me. I much preferred
it to my own which moreover it prevented me from smelling,
except a waft now and then. In the days that followed I took
the necessary steps to recover my money. I don't know exactly
what happened, whether I couldn't find the address, or whether
there was no such address, or whether the Greek woman was
unknown there. I ransacked my pockets for the receipt, to try

and decipher the name. It wasn't there. Perhaps she had taken it back while I was sleeping. I don't know how long I wandered thus, resting now in one place, now in another, in the city and in the country. The city had suffered many changes. Nor was the country as I remembered it. The general effect was the same. One day I caught sight of my son. He was striding along with a briefcase under his arm. He took off his hat and bowed and I saw he was as bald as a coot. I was almost certain it was he. I turned round to gaze after him. He went bustling along on his duck feet, bowing and scraping and flourishing his hat left and right. The insufferable son of a bitch.

One day I met a man I had known in former times. He lived in a cave by the sea. He had an ass that grazed winter and summer, over the cliffs, or along the little tracks leading down to the sea. When the weather was very bad this ass came down to the cave of his own accord and sheltered there till the storm was past. So they had spent many a night huddled together, while the wind howled and the sea pounded on the shore. With the help of this ass he could deliver sand, sea-wrack, and shells to the townsfolk, for their gardens. He couldn't carry much at a time for the ass was old and small and the town was far. But in this way he earned a little money, enough to keep him in tobacco and matches and to buy a piece of bread from time to time. It was during one of these excursions that he met me, in the suburbs. He was delighted to see me, poor man. He begged me to go home with him and spend the night. Stay as long as you like, he said. What's wrong with your ass? I said. Don't mind him, he said, he doesn't know you. I reminded him that I wasn't in the habit of staying more than two or three minutes with anyone and that the sea did not agree with me. He seemed deeply grieved to hear it. So you won't come, he said. But to my amazement I got up on the ass and off we went, in the shade of the red chestnuts springing from the sidewalk. I held the ass by the mane, one hand in front of the other. The little boys jeered and threw stones, but their aim was poor, for they only hit me once, on the hat. A policeman stopped us and accused us of disturbing the peace. My friend replied that we were as nature had made us, the boys too were as nature had made them. It was inevitable, under these conditions, that the peace should be disturbed from time to time. Let us continue on our way, he said, and order will soon be restored throughout your beat. We followed the quiet, dustwhite inland roads with their hedges of hawthorn and fuchsia and their footpaths fringed with wild grass and daisies. Night fell. The ass carried me right to the mouth of the cave, for in the dark I could not have found my way down the path winding steeply to the sea. Then he climbed back to his pasture.

I don't know how long I stayed there. The cave was nicely arranged, I must say. I treated my crablice with salt water and seaweed, but a lot of nits must have survived. I put compresses of seaweed on my skull, which gave me great relief, but not for long. I lay in the cave and sometimes looked out at the horizon. I saw above me a vast trembling expanse without islands or promontories. At night a light shone into the cave at regular intervals. It was here I found the phial in my pocket. It was not broken, for the glass was not real glass. I thought Mr. Weir had confiscated all my belongings. My host was out most of the time. He fed me on fish. It is easy for a man, a proper man to live in a cave, far from everybody. He invited me to stay as long as I liked. If I preferred to be alone he would gladly prepare another cave for me further on. He would bring me food every day and drop in from time to time to make sure I was all right and needed nothing. He was kind. Unfortunately I did not need kindness. You wouldn't know of a lake dwelling? I said. I couldn't bear the sea, its splashing and heaving, its tides and general convulsiveness. The wind at least sometimes stops. My hands and feet felt as though they were full of ants. This kept me awake for hours on end. If I stayed here something awful would happen to me, I said, and a lot of good that would do me. You'd get drowned, he said. Yes, I said, or jump off the cliff. And to think I couldn't live anywhere else, he said, in my cabin in the mountains I was wretched. Your cabin in the mountains? I said. He repeated the story of his cabin in the mountains, I had forgotten it, it was as though I were hearing it for the first time. I asked him if he still had it. He replied he had not seen it since the day he fled from it, but that he believed it was still there, a little decayed no doubt. But when he urged me to take the key I refused, saying I had other plans. You will always find me here, he said, if you ever need me. Ah people. He gave me his knife.

What he called his cabin in the mountains was a sort of wooden shed. The door had been removed, for firewood, or for some other purpose. The glass had disappeared from the window. The roof had fallen in at several places. The interior was divided, by the remains of a partition, into two unequal parts. If there had been any furniture it was gone. The vilest acts had been committed on the ground and against the walls. The floor was strewn with excrements, both human and animal, with condoms and vomit. In a cowpad a heart had been traced, pierced by an arrow. And yet there was nothing to attract tourists. I noticed the remains of abandoned nosegays. They had been greedily gathered, carried for miles, then thrown away, because they were cumbersome or already withered. This was the dwelling to which I had been offered the key.

The scene was the familiar one of grandeur and desolation.

Nevertheless it was a roof over my head. I rested on a bed of ferns, gathered at great labour with my own hands. One day I couldn't get up. The cow saved me. Goaded by the icy mist she came in search of shelter. It was probably not the first time. She can't have seen me. I tried to suck her, without much success. Her udder was covered with dung. I took off my hat and, summoning all my energy, began to milk her into it. The milk fell to the ground and was lost, but I said to myself, No matter, it's free. She dragged me across the floor, stopping from time to time only to kick me. I didn't know our cows too could be so inhuman. She must have recently been milked. Clutching the dug with one hand I kept my hat under it with the other. But in the end she prevailed. For she dragged me across the threshold and out into the giant streaming ferns, where I was forced to let go.

As I drank the milk I reproached myself with what I had done. I could no longer count on this cow and she would warn the others. More master of myself I might have made a friend of her. She would have come every day, perhaps accompanied by other cows. I might have learnt to make butter, even cheese. But I said to myself, No, all is for the best.

Once on the road it was all downhill. Soon there were carts, but they all refused to take me up. In other clothes, with another face, they might have taken me up. I must have changed since my expulsion from the basement. The face notably seemed to have attained its climacteric. The humble, ingenuous smile would no longer come, nor the expression of candid misery, showing the stars and the distaff. I summoned them, but they would not come. A mask of dirty old hairy leather, with two holes and a slit, it was too far gone for the old trick of please your honour and God reward you and pity upon me. It was disastrous. What would I crawl with in future? I lay down on the side of the road and began to writhe each time I heard a cart approaching. That was so they would not think I was sleeping or resting. I tried to groan, Help! Help! But the tone that came out was that of polite conversation. My hour was not yet come and I could no longer groan. The last time I had cause to groan I had groaned as well as ever, and no heart within miles of me to melt. What was to become of me? I said to myself, I'll learn again. I lay down across the road at a narrow place, so that the carts could not pass without passing over my body, with one wheel at least, or two if there were four. But the day came when, looking round me, I was in the suburbs, and from there to the old haunts it was not far, beyond the stupid hope of rest or less pain.

So I covered the lower part of my face with a black rag and went and begged at a sunny corner. For it seemed to me my eyes were not completely spent, thanks perhaps to the dark glasses my tutor had given me. He had given me the *Ethics* of Geulincx. They were a man's glasses, I was a child. They found him dead, crumpled up in the water closet, his clothes in awful disorder, struck down by an infarctus. Ah what peace. The *Ethics* had his name (Ward) on the fly-leaf, the glasses had belonged to him. The bridge, at the time I am speaking of, was of brass wire, of the kind used to hang pictures and big mirrors, and two long black ribbons served as wings. I wound them round my ears and then down under my chin where I tied them together. The lenses had suffered, from rubbing in my pocket against each other and against the other objects there. I thought Mr. Weir had confiscated all my belongings. But I had no further need of these glasses and used them merely to soften the glare of the sun. I should never have mentioned them. The rag gave me a lot of trouble. I got it in the end from the lining of my greatcoat, no, I had no greatcoat now, of my coat then. The result was a grey rag rather than a black, perhaps even chequered, but I had to make do with it. Till afternoon I held my face raised towards the southern sky, then towards the western till night. The bowl gave me a lot of trouble. I couldn't use my hat because of my skull. As for holding out my hand, that was quite out of the question. So I got a tin and hung it from a button of my greatcoat, what's the matter with me, of my coat, at pubis level. It did not hang plumb, it leaned respectfully towards the passer-by, he had only to drop his mite. But that obliged him to come up close to me, he was in danger of touching me. In the end I got a bigger tin, a kind of big tin box, and I placed it on the sidewalk at my feet. But people who give alms don't much care to toss them, there's something contemptuous about this gesture which is repugnant to sensitive natures. To say nothing of their having to aim. They are prepared to give, but not for their gift to go rolling under the passing feet or under the passing wheels, to be picked up perhaps by some undeserving person. So they don't give. There are those, to be sure, who stoop, but generally speaking people who give alms don't much care to stoop. What they like above all is to sight the wretch from afar, get ready their penny, drop it in stride and hear the God bless you dying away in the distance. Personally I never said that, nor anything like it, I wasn't much of a believer, but I did make a noise with my mouth. In the end I got a kind of board or tray and tied it to my neck and waist. It jutted out just at the right height, pocket height, and its edge was far enough from my person for the coin to be bestowed without danger. Some days I strewed it with flowers, petals, buds and that herb which men call fleabane, I believe, in a word whatever I could find. I didn't go out of my way to look for them, but all the pretty things of this description that came my way were for the board. They must have thought I loved nature. Most of the time I looked up at the sky, but without focussing it, for why focus it? Most of the time it was a mixture of white, blue and grey, and then at evening all the evening colours. I felt it weighing softly on my face, I rubbed my face against it, one cheek after the other, turning my head from side to side. Now and then to rest my neck I dropped my head on my chest. Then I could see the board in the distance, a haze of many colours. I leaned against the wall, but without nonchalance, I shifted my weight from one foot to the other and my hands clutched the lapels of my coat. To beg with your hands in your pockets makes a bad impression, it irritates the workers, especially in winter. You should never wear gloves either. There were guttersnipes who swept away all I had earned, under cover of giving me a coin. It was to buy sweets. I unbuttoned my trousers discreetly to scratch myself. I scratched myself in an upward direction, with four nails. I pulled on the hairs, to get relief. It passed the time, time flew when I scratched myself. Real scratching is superior to masturbation, in my opinion. One can masturbate up to the age of seventy, and even beyond, but in the end it becomes a mere habit. Whereas to scratch myself properly I would have needed a dozen hands. I itched all over, on the privates, in the bush up to the navel, under the arms, in the arse, and then patches of eczema and psoriasis that I could set raging merely by thinking of them. It was in the arse I had the most pleasure. I stuck my forefinger up to the knuckle. Later, if I had to shit, the pain was atrocious. But I hardly shat any more. Now and then a flying machine flew by, sluggishly it seemed to me. Often at the end of the day I discovered the legs of my trousers all wet. That must have been the dogs. I personally pissed very little. If by chance the need came on me a little squirt in my fly was enough to relieve it. Once at my post I did not leave it till nightfall. I had no appetite, God tempered the wind to me. After work I bought a bottle of milk and drank it in the evening in the shed. Better still, I got a little boy to buy it for me, always the same, they wouldn't serve me, I don't know why. I gave him a penny for his pains. One day I witnessed a strange scene. Normally I didn't see a great deal. I didn't hear a great deal either. I didn't pay attention. Strictly speaking I wasn't there. Strictly speaking I believe I've never been anywhere. But that day I must have come back. For some time past a sound had been scarifying me. I did not investigate the cause, for I said to myself, It's going to stop. But as it did not stop I had no choice but to find out the cause. It was a man perched on the roof of a car and haranguing the passers-by. That at least was my interpretation. He was bellowing so loud that snatches of his discourse reached my ears. Union . . . brothers . . . Marx . . . capital . . . bread and butter . . . love. It was all Greek to me. The car was drawn up against the kerb, just in front of me, I saw the orator from behind. All of a

sudden he turned and pointed at me, as at an exhibit. Look at
this down and out, he vociferated, this leftover. If he doesn't go
down on all fours, it's for fear of being impounded. Old, lousy,
rotten, ripe for the muckheap. And there are a thousand like
him, worse than him, ten thousand, twenty thousand———. A
voice, Thirty thousand. Every day you pass them by, resumed
the orator, and when you have backed a winner you fling them
a farthing. Do you ever think? The voice, God forbid. A penny,
resumed the orator, tuppence———. The voice, Thruppence. It
never enters your head, resumed the orator, that your charity
is a crime, an incentive to slavery, stultification and organized
murder. Take a good look at this living corpse. You may say
it's his own fault. Ask him if it's his own fault. The voice, Ask
him yourself. Then he bent forward and took me to task. I had
perfected my board. It now consisted of two boards hinged together, which enabled me, when my work was done, to fold it
and carry it under my arm. I liked doing little odd jobs. So I
took off the rag, pocketed the few coins I had earned, untied the
board, folded it and put it under my arm. Do you hear me, you
crucified bastard! cried the orator. Then I went away, although
it was still light. But generally speaking it was a quiet corner,
busy but not overcrowded, thriving and well-frequented. He
must have been a religious fanatic, I could find no other explanation. Perhaps he was an escaped lunatic. He had a nice face,
a little on the red side.
    I did not work every day. I had practically no expenses. I
even managed to put a little aside, for my very last days. The
days I did not work I spent lying in the shed. The shed was on
a private estate, or what had once been a private estate, on the
riverside. This estate, the main entrance to which opened on a
narrow, dark and silent street, was enclosed with a wall, except
of course on the river front, which marked its northern boundary for a distance of about thirty yards. From the last quays beyond the water the eyes rose to a confusion of low houses,

wasteland, hoardings, chimneys, steeples and towers. A kind of
parade ground was also to be seen, where soldiers played football all the year round. Only the ground-floor windows—no, I
can't. The estate seemed abandoned. The gates were locked and
the paths were overgrown with grass. Only the ground-floor
windows had shutters. The others were sometimes lit at night,
faintly, now one, now another. At least that was my impression.
Perhaps it was reflected light. In this shed, the day I adopted it,
I found a boat, upside down. I righted it, chocked it up with
stones and pieces of wood, took out the thwarts and made my
bed inside. The rats had difficulty in getting at me, because of
the bulge of the hull. And yet they longed to. Just think of it,
living flesh, for in spite of everything I was still living flesh. I
had lived too long among rats, in my chance dwellings, to share
the dread they inspire in the vulgar. I even had a soft spot in my
heart for them. They came with such confidence towards me, it
seemed without the least repugnance. They made their toilet
with catlike gestures. Toads at evening, motionless for hours,
lap flies from the air. They like to squat where cover ends and
open air begins, they favour thresholds. But I had to contend
now with water rats, exceptionally lean and ferocious. So I made
a kind of lid with stray boards. It's incredible the number of
boards I've come across in my lifetime, I never needed a board
but there it was, I had only to stoop and pick it up. I liked doing
little odd jobs, no, not particularly, I didn't mind. It completely
covered the boat, I'm referring again to the lid. I pushed it a
little towards the stern, climbed into the boat by the bow,
crawled to the stern, raised my feet and pushed the lid back
towards the bow till it covered me completely. But what did my
feet push against? They pushed against a cross bar I nailed to the
lid for that purpose, I liked these little odd jobs. But it was
better to climb into the boat by the stern and pull back the lid
with my hands till it completely covered me, then push it forward in the same way when I wanted to get out. As holds for my

hands I planted two spikes just where I needed them. These little odds and ends of carpentry, if I may so describe it, carried out with whatever tools and material I chanced to find, gave me a certain pleasure. I knew it would soon be the end, so I played the part, you know, the part of—how shall I say, I don't know. I was comfortable enough in this boat, I must say. The lid fitted so well I had to pierce a hole. It's no good closing your eyes, you must leave them open in the dark, that is my opinion. I am not speaking of sleep, I am speaking of what I believe is called waking. In any case, I slept very little at this period, I wasn't sleepy, or I was too sleepy, I don't know, or I was afraid, I don't know. Flat then on my back I saw nothing except, dimly, just above my head, through the tiny chinks, the grey light of the shed. To see nothing at all, no that's too much. I heard faintly the cries of the gulls ravening about the mouth of the sewer nearby. In a spew of yellow foam, if my memory serves me right, the filth gushed into the river and the slush of birds above screaming with hunger and fury. I heard the lapping of water against the slip and against the bank and the other sound, so different, of open wave, I heard it too. I too, when I moved, felt less boat than wave, or so it seemed to me, and my stillness was the stillness of eddies. That may seem impossible. The rain too, I often heard it, for it often rained. Sometimes a drop, falling through the roof of the shed, exploded on me. All that composed a rather liquid world. And then of course there was the voice of the wind or rather those, so various, of its playthings. But what does it amount to? Howling, soughing, moaning, sighing. What I would have liked was hammer strokes, bang bang bang, clanging in the desert. I let farts to be sure, but hardly ever a real crack, they oozed out with a sucking noise, melted in the mighty never. I don't know how long I stayed there. I was very snug in my box, I must say. It seemed to me I had grown more independent of recent years. That no one came any more, that no one could come any more to ask me if I was all right and needed

nothing, distressed me then but little. I was all right, yes, quite
so, and the fear of getting worse was less with me. As for my
needs, they had dwindled as it were to my dimensions and become, if I may say so, of so exquisite a quality as to exclude all
thought of succour. To know I had a being, however faint and
false, outside of me, had once had the power to stir my heart.
You become unsociable, it's inevitable. It's enough to make you
wonder sometimes if you are on the right planet. Even the
words desert you, it's as bad as that. Perhaps it's the moment
when the vessels stop communicating, you know, the vessels.
There you are still between the two murmurs, it must be the
same old song as ever, but Christ you wouldn't think so. There
were times when I wanted to push away the lid and get out of
the boat and couldn't, I was so indolent and weak, so content
deep down where I was. I felt them hard upon me, the icy, tu-
multuous streets, the terrifying faces, the noises that slash,
pierce, claw, bruise. So I waited till the desire to shit, or even to
piss, lent me wings. I did not want to dirty my nest! And yet it
sometimes happened, and even more and more often. Arched
and rigid I edged down my trousers and turned a little on my
side, just enough to free the hole. To contrive a little kingdom,
in the midst of the universal muck, then shit on it, ah that was
me all over. The excrements were me too, I know, I know, but
all the same. Enough, enough, the next thing I was having visions, I who never did, except sometimes in my sleep, who
never had, real visions, I'd remember, except perhaps as a child,
my myth will have it so. I knew they were visions because it was
night and I was alone in my boat. What else could they have
been? So I was in my boat and gliding on the waters. I didn't
have to row, the ebb was carrying me out. Anyway I saw no
oars, they must have taken them away. I had a board, the remains of a thwart perhaps, which I used when I came too close
to the bank, or when a pier came bearing down on me or a
barge at its moorings. There were stars in the sky, quite a few. I

didn't know what the weather was doing, I was neither cold nor warm and all seemed calm. The banks receded more and more, it was inevitable, soon I saw them no more. The lights grew fainter and fewer as the river widened. There on the land men were sleeping, bodies were gathering strength for the toil and joys of the morrow. The boat was not gliding now, it was tossing, buffeted by the choppy waters of the bay. All seemed calm and yet foam was washing aboard. Now the sea air was all about me, I had no other shelter than the land, and what does it amount to, the shelter of the land, at such a time. I saw the beacons, four in all, including a lightship. I knew them well, even as a child I had known them well. It was evening, I was with my father on a height, he held my hand. I would have liked him to draw me close with a gesture of protective love, but his mind was on other things. He also taught me the names of the mountains. But to have done with these visions I also saw the lights of the buoys, the sea seemed full of them, red and green, and to my surprise even yellow. And on the slopes of the mountain, now rearing its unbroken bulk behind the town, the fires turned from gold to red, from red to gold. I knew what it was, it was the gorse burning. How often I had set a match to it myself, as a child. And hours later, back in my home, before I climbed into bed, I watched from my high window the fires I had lit. That night then, all aglow with distant fires, on sea, on land and in the sky, I drifted with the currents and the tides. I noticed that my hat was tied, with a string I suppose, to my buttonhole. I got up from my seat in the stern and a great clanking was heard. That was the chain. One end was fastened to the bow and the other round my waist. I must have pierced a hole beforehand in the floor-boards, for there I was down on my knees prying out the plug with my knife. The hole was small and the water rose slowly. It would take a good half hour, everything included, barring accidents. Back now in the stern-sheets, my legs stretched out, my back well propped against the sack stuffed with grass I used as a cushion, I swallowed my calmative. The sea, the sky, the mountains and the islands closed in and crushed me in a mighty systole, then scattered to the uttermost confines of space. The memory came faint and cold of the story I might have told, a story in the likeness of my life, I mean without the courage to end or the strength to go on.

Eimar O'Duffy

From *King Goshawk and the Birds*

NOW LARGELY FORGOTTEN, THE satirist, socialist, republican, and economic theorist Eimar O'Duffy can be seen as the missing link between Jonathan Swift and Flann O'Brien, Ireland's two greatest satirists. Among O'Duffy's key works are *The Wasted Island*—an autobiographical novel describing the coming to nationalist consciousness of a young republican, and his subsequent disillusionment with the 1916 Rising—and the 'Cuanduine' trilogy of satirical novels published between 1926 and 1933: *King Goshawk and the Birds, The Spacious Adventures of the Man in the Street*, and *Asses in Clover.*

Eimar O'Duffy was born in 1893 to a father of Anglo-Irish stock who, when the Great War commenced, demanded that his son enlist in the British Army. O'Duffy's refusal, and the sense of deracination that drove him to study at University College Dublin rather than the Protestant Trinity College, provoked his family into ostracising him. He studied dental surgery, though he never became a dentist, and spent much of his time in college reading Irish history, nurturing his budding nationalism. He joined the Irish Republican Brotherhood and was a captain in the Irish Volunteers but, like a number of republicans of the era, was opposed to the planned Rising of 1916, fearing it would be a disaster. A week before the Rising, O'Duffy informed the Volunteers' Chief-of-Staff Eoin MacNeill, who had had no part in its planning, of what was to come. This prompted MacNeill to place advertisements in the newspapers advising Volunteers not to take part.

After the War of Independence, disillusioned with life in the

Free State, O'Duffy moved with his family to England in 1925. There he began writing his Cuanduine trilogy, and fed a growing interest in economic theory which led to his 1932 treatise, *Life and Money*. In an effort to make ends meet, O'Duffy wrote numerous detective thrillers, potboilers, and light novels, none of which found much success. He died in 1935 of the stomach ulceration that had long caused him severe pain.

The satirical newspaper stories included here from *King Goshawk and the Birds*—the fantastical, near-future novel that opens his trilogy—demonstrate the satiric bite and playfulness that place O'Duffy in a lineage with Swift and Flann O'Brien. The novel includes astral travel, a Dublin philosopher who encounters both Socrates and the mythological figure of Cuchulainn, and a future world degraded by 'king capitalists'. The interplanetary and futuristic elements of the trilogy merited O'Duffy an inclusion in the *Encyclopaedia of Science Fiction*. The historian Diarmaid Ferriter has noted that O'Duffy's economic ideas and critique of capitalism and the banking system resonate in today's economically troubled climate. According to the writer and comedian Kevin Gildea, 'The economic and social concerns of Eimar O'Duffy are as relevant today as they were when they were written in the 1920s and '30s.'

From *King Goshawk and the Birds*

CHAPTER IV

Cuanduine reads a Newspaper

THE PHILOSOPHER'S ATTIC HAD not changed much in the years that had passed, save that it was grown older and the rent higher. The old man had a new suit of clothes waiting for Cuanduine, of a nice pattern of tweed, and fashionably cut, with snow-white shirt and tie of poplin. When he was dressed in these the Philosopher served them a breakfast of milk and bread and cheese, as he had done before when Cuchulain came to Earth; after which he offered the young man a newspaper, and himself opened another.

"What is this?" asked Cuanduine.

"That," said the Philosopher, "is one of the marvels of human civilisation." Cuanduine turned the newspaper over in his hands; looked at it right way up, wrong way up, and sideways; opened it and counted the pages; and finally looked at the Philosopher with an expression of bewilderment on his godlike countenance. "It is called a newspaper" the Philosopher explained. "In it is written down the news of all the things that happened yesterday in the world: and to-morrow I shall get another which will relate all that happened to-day."

"But how," asked Cuanduine, "can the truth be ascertained in so short a time?"

"I did not say that it told the truth," replied the Philosopher. "I only said it told the news."

Then Cuanduine began to read aloud from the newspaper: "Social and Personal. King Goshawk gave a garden party at

211

Tuscaloosa yesterday . . . The Duke of Dudborough is fifty-one to-day.' Who is the Duke of Dudborough?"

"I don't know," said the Philosopher.

Cuanduine held his peace after that. These are some of the things he read:

Mr. Cyrus Q. Moneybags has had to cancel his European trip owing to an attack of leprosy.

———

Miss Dinkie Filmy has recovered from her fit of the blues, and has consented to resume her part in the great film "Kisses of Fire," the production of which will now proceed.

———

If your breath is bad in the morning, try Punk's Pills. (Advt.)

———

LIMELIGHT CINEMA
All This Week
RODERICK REDLIP and BETTY BRIGHTEYE
in
TAVY'S BROKEN HEART
Adapted from Shaw's touching romance *Man and Superman.*

———

Dashblank & Co.'s New List of Masterpieces
Henry Heavynib's Great Novel, *Daisy* . . . . . . .10s.
Amy Slosh's Great Novel, *Girlish Hearts* . . . . 10s.
Lady Dishwater's Great Novel, *Riviera Romps* . . . 10s.

Daisy Deepend's Great Novel, *Fiametta's Frillies* . . . 10s.
Millions of other Great Novels. See our Catalogue.

"All Dashblank's novels are Masterpieces" *(vidt* Press).

DASHBLANK & Co. "Masterpieces Only."

———

A STRAIGHT ISSUE

Once again it becomes our duty to tell the Government in
plain and unmistakable language what the best elements in
the country—and we speak in no undemocratic sense—think
of the way it is handling the present situation. This is a time
for plain speaking; a time to search men's souls, and to apply
to every word and action the acid test of Truth and Justice.
We do not count ourselves among those—if there are any
such—who would deny that there is never an occasion when
the cause of true Justice might not be less disadvantageously
served by a not overinflexible adhesion to the strict *litera vere-
cundiae* than by a too inopportune application of those solemn
precepts which are the concrete foundation on which morality
and true civilisation subsist. But nevertheless there are occasions such as the present, when the whole fabric of Society . . .

———

THE WOLFO-LAMBIAN CRISIS

It is a matter of exceeding difficulty to estimate, at the present
stage of the proceedings, the true light in which to regard the
unfortunate misunderstanding that now threatens to involve
the Not-Very-Far-East in chaos and possibly bloodshed. To
hold the balance evenly between causes in which so many questions, not only of national principle and international morality,

but of widespread interests and deep aspects of policy and diplomacy, are inextricably intertwined, might possibly at this moment, when even the parties primarily concerned have not yet put their case fully before the public, militate unfavourably against those very principles of reconciling the effectuating of rightful action with the non-impairment of national privileges and financial interests, which it is the first duty of the organs of public opinion to safeguard, secure, and protect.

———

UP AND DOWN
Royal Resource.

When King Henry was driving down the Strand yesterday, a sudden breeze almost blew the royal hat from the royal head. Nothing daunted, his Majesty caught the royal brim with the royal fingers, and by this display of royal resourcefulness saved an awkward situation.

A Prince's Joke.

Prince Reggie, son and heir of the Jute King, is renowned for his sense of humour. The other day his Highness paid a surprise visit to one of his father's slums in Liverpool. As soon as his presence was known, dense crowds came swarming round to feast their eyes on his princely countenance. "They look like sardines in a box," remarked the Prince to an aide-de-camp. Screams of laughter greeted this ready sally.

———

A GREAT SPORTSMAN

Lord Puddlehead, who died last Monday, was almost as distinguished in the field of sport as in that of politics. His greatest kill was on his own estate at Puddlington about five years ago, when he shot 850 brace of pheasants in a day. But his performance in Scotland last year runs it close. On that occasion he shot 3600 head of grouse in five days, an average of 690 per day. Altogether over one million birds and beasts have fallen to his gun during his amazingly active life.

———

ATROCIOUS MURDER
AIRMAN DONE TO DEATH IN JUNGULAY

A murder of a peculiarly dastardly character was perpetrated to-day by tribesmen in the neighbourhood of Jhamjhar, Jungulay. The victim was Lieut. Derek Blacktan, an officer in King Goshawk's Air Force stationed at Brahmbuhl Jhelli. Entirely unarmed save for a loaded revolver, he happened to be strolling in the vicinity of Jhamjhar, when he was set upon by three natives and beaten to death. The village had been bombed from the air a few days before, and it is believed that the assassination was an act of vengeance. Reprisals are already in preparation.

———

THE FAIRLY-NEAR-EASTERN CRISIS
LAMBIAN REPLY TO THE WOLFIAN NOTE
WOLFOPOLIS, *Thursday.*

The reply of the Lambian Government to the Wolfian Note demanding reparation for the alleged negligence of a Lambian lighterman in damaging the paint of a Wolfian steamer in Micropolis harbour last week, was delivered here this morning. The Wolfian Note, it will be remembered, embodied the following demands:

1. The Lambian Government to send a grovelling apology to the Wolfian Government.

2. The guilty lighterman, or, if he cannot be discovered, any

other Lambian lighterman, to be executed at once without trial, and the trade of lightermanship to be suppressed in Lambia.

3. The Lambian flag to be lowered seven times on all public buildings in Micropolis whenever a Wolfian citizen passes by.

4. All citizens of Lambia to prostrate themselves for five minutes at sight of a Wolfian citizen.

5. Lambia to pay an indemnity of £900,000,000,000 in three yearly instalments.

6. The members of the Lambian Cabinet, and the Committee of the Lambian Lightermen's Union, to proceed at once to Wolfopolis and publicly prostrate themselves before Nervolini, the Wolfian Dictator, afterwards accepting his boot in the part prescribed in the Annex.

The Lambian reply is understood to accede to all these demands, with the exception of No. 6. It also asks that the period for the payment of the indemnity be extended to five years.

The Wolfian Fleet has already put to sea in readiness for any eventuality.

LAMBOPOLIS, *Thursday*.
It is reported that the Wolfian Fleet has been sighted off Micronetta.

———

HOW I DID IT

ACQUITTED MURDERER TELLS HOW HE KILLED HIS WIFE, DAUGHTER, AND SOLICITOR

THE BLANKSTOWN MYSTERY SOLVED AT LAST

WILLIAM BADSTUFF'S OWN STORY

EXCLUSIVE TO THE "ILLUSTRATED SUNDAY SURVEY"

GORY DETAILS   *SENSATIONAL REVELATIONS*

GENUINE NARRATIVE AS ISSUED
FROM THE MURDERER'S REFUGE
IN THE WILDS OF CENTRAL ASIA,
SECURED BY "SUNDAY SURVEY"
AT A COST OF
TWO MILLION POUNDS

MR. BADSTUFF.

First Instalment Next Sunday Tells
HOW BADSTUFF WON THE AFFECTIONS
OF HIS SOLICITOR'S CHIROPODIST

ORDER YOUR COPY AT ONCE

OTHER CONTENTS OF THIS ISSUE

RURITANIA *MUST* PAY – – – – – By Frantic Blair
IS THERE A HELL? – – – – By Rev. Simon Broadhead
DARNING THE PRINCE'S SOCKS – – By Sylvia Slop

ALL THE LATEST PHOTOS OF SPORT AND SOCIETY
CONCLUSION OF SPLENDID SERIAL, "LAWLESS
LOVE" LONG OR SHORT KNICKERS? MORE VIEWS

FROM OUR READERS ON THIS ABSORBING TOPIC

READ THE
"ILLUSTRATED SUNDAY SURVEY"

SPORTING NEWS

It is understood that the soccer match between Wondrous Wanderers and Sturdy Stickers has been cancelled owing to the refusal of the latter team to play for less than £5000 per man. The Wanderers had contracted for £3500.

———

A record entry is expected for the Amateur Golf Championship, £1000 having been guaranteed to each competitor. There is a rumour, however, that Mr. Niblick, the present holder, will refuse to play unless guaranteed £20,000, win, lose, or draw.

———

Yesterday's great fight between Bruiser Burke and Slogger Samson for the Middleweight Championship of the World was a magnificent display of fistic talent. Every precaution had been taken to ensure a genuine contest. A sum of one million pounds was to be divided equally between the combatants on condition that the fight should last at least ten rounds, that a full pint of blood should be spilt, and that not less than two eyes should be completely bunged. In addition, the winner was to receive a further quarter of a million, and the loser a further four hundred thousand. The result was highly satisfactory. After six rounds each man had a darkened peeper, and in the eighth the referee announced that the blood measure was full. The next two rounds were uneventful, but as the gong sounded for the eleventh, every nerve in the vast audience was tense with excitement. The two bruisers faced each other for a moment. Then simultaneously each tipped the chin of the other with his left, and, quick as lightning, flung himself backwards on the floor. Burke, being the heavier man, reached it first, and was accordingly declared the loser. Frantic cheering greeted the result. The blood was subsequently auctioned, and was knocked down at £120, which will be divided equally between the pugilists.

————

Bashing Burton has declared himself ready to accept £2,000,000 as a preliminary fee for discussing the conditions under which he might be prepared to fight Kid Coffey for the Heavyweight Championship, without prejudice to his right to refuse to fight him on any conditions.

————

BRITISH LABOUR TROUBLE
A general strike is threatened in British coal mines as a result of the proposed cut of two shillings per week in wages. The Coal Trust have issued a statement that it will be impossible to work the mines at a profit unless the cut is accepted.

————

CENSORS' GOOD WORK
IMMODEST WOMEN PENALISED
In Wolfe Tone Street yesterday two young women wearing immodest dresses, which revealed their throats and ankles, were arrested by Censors, stripped, and taken before the District Court. They were sentenced to a year's hard labour. We hope this will be a lesson to those young persons that the world-wide

reputation of Irish womanhood for modesty and chastity is not a thing to be lightly imperilled.

——

BUY THE

"SUNDAY MUCKHEAP"

THE BEST TUPPENCEWORTH
ON THE MARKET

LARGER IRISH CIRCULATION
THAN ANY NATIVE PAPER

SUPPORT HOME TALENT

DUBLIN SPICE
IS JUST AS GOOD AS ANY IMPORTED FILTH

——

OUR LITERARY CORNER
A Novel with a Purpose.
"Blood and Fire," by B. S. T. Sellar. Charlatan & Co. 10s.

This gifted and popular author breaks new ground in his latest and greatest book. Is war right? Is there not something inequitable in the present unequal distribution of wealth? Is marriage what it might be? These are the startling questions which the trials and sufferings of the last few years have moved Mr. Sellar to ask. The author faces them courageously and without flinching. There is a new note of thought in this remarkable book, and if Mr. Sellar does not answer any of the great questions he raises, his message is perhaps all the more effective in consequence.

———

DUBLIN DISTRICT COURT

Percy MacGoldbags, 22, was summoned before Mr. Donkey yesterday on the charge of killing three children when motoring through Cuffe Street on the 15th inst. Constable Ryan testified that accused went down the street at a speed of one hundred miles an hour—twenty beyond the limit. Accused pleaded contributory negligence, and said that he had never driven a car before. Mr. Donkey, fining the young man five pounds, advised him to take lessons before again driving through crowded thoroughfares.

———

CENTRAL CRIMINAL COURT

The concluding stage of the trial of Bill Bungle, 40, bricklayer, for the murder of his wife, was heard yesterday. Prisoner read a statement in which he declared that his wife drank, and neglected the home and children. He had tried to get a divorce by setting up a sham domicile in England, but the subterfuge had been discovered. After five minutes' consideration the jury returned a verdict of guilty, and prisoner was sentenced to be hanged.

———

PROVINCIAL NEWS

The Ballycatandog Urban District Council met yesterday to discuss the resolution forwarded by the Ballymess Council, condemning the proposal of the Government to establish the metric system in Ireland.

Mr. Brady, proposing the motion, said that it was the duty of every Irishman worthy of the name to denounce the most tyrannous piece of legislation ever introduced into a democratic country. The action of the Government made the deeds of Nero, Queen Elizabeth, and Oliver Cromwell look mild and benignant in comparison.

MR. GRADY: Where was your grandfather in 1916?

MR. THADY: Under the bed.

MR. BRADY: I defy any man here to say my grandfather was a funk.

MR. GRADY: The Bradys were always great heroes.

MR. BRADY: They're every bit as good as the Gradys anyhow.

MR. GRADY: You old fool.

THE CHAIRMAN: Order! Order!

Mr. Grady: Don't you start putting in your oar.

THE CHAIRMAN: I will if I like. And who has a better right? My grandfather was out in 1916.

MR. GRADY: Yes. Right out of it.

THE CHAIRMAN: No. That's where yours was.

MR. GRADY: Do you call my grandfather a funk?

The meeting broke up in disorder.

———

HOUSES TO LET

A five-roomed house to let. South suburbs. Moderate rent. No children.

Cosy house. Two bedrooms, sitting-room, kitchen, bath. £150 and taxes. No dogs. No children.

Delightful house. Five miles from city. Six bed., four reception rooms. Billiard room, conservatory, stables, garage, kennels, garden and kitchen garden. No children.

Fine house, beautifully situated in own ground ten miles from city. Children objected.

Gate lodge to let. Five rooms. No dogs, no poultry, no children. Suit married couple.

Perfect house. Situated in own grounds. Beautiful scenery. Healthy climate. Five bedrooms, four reception. Day and night nursery. School-room. Large flower garden. Playing field, with goal-posts., etc. Tennis-court. Suit married couple. No children.

Pigstye to let. 10s. weekly. Suit large family.

Victorian mansion. Beyond repair. Situated in formerly fashionable quarter in heart of city. Reasonable rent. No objection to dogs, cats, poultry, canaries, tortoises, goldfish, axolotls, or even children.

––––

LATEST NEWS
Micronetta shelled
Strong action of Nervolini.

Micronetta has been shelled by the Wolfian Fleet. The first shell struck an infant school in the centre of the town, killing the teacher and eleven children. The white Flag was at once hoisted. The Wolfian admiral, landing soon afterwards, fainted with relief on learning that no British or American citizens were among the casualties. All lightermen in the town have been Bogged and boiled in oil.

Máirtín Ó Cadhain

From *The Dirty Dust*

'Cunty gash', 'piss-flaps', 'fuck me pink'—like works by
Beckett and Joyce, Máirtín Ó Cadhain's 1949 novel *The Dirty
Dust* has managed to garner acclaim as a modernist masterpiece
while boasting a lexicon of eyebrow-raising fruitiness; at least, it
does in Alan Titley's raucous 2015 translation. The novel, originally titled *Cré na Cille*, was written in Irish, and more than
six decades passed before it was translated into English, despite
it having been translated into Norwegian and Danish. In the
same year as it published *The Dirty Dust*, Yale University Press
published a second, more scholarly translation of *Cré na Cille*,
Graveyard Clay, a collaboration between Liam Mac Con Iomaire
and Tim Robinson. In his introduction to his translation, Alan
Titley calls *The Dirty Dust* 'the greatest Irish novel, just as *Ulysses*
is recognised as the greatest Anglo-Irish novel', and says of Ó
Cadhain that, 'He was both traditional and experimental as he
willed'. Writing in *The Irish Times*, Colm Tóibín suggested that
the novel, 'in all its aleatory music, is closer to John Cage than
to sean-nós'.

Set six feet under the soil of a Connemara graveyard, *The
Dirty Dust* is comprised almost entirely of dialogue—the incessant, caustic, petty chatter of a host of corpses. Unflaggingly the
dead gossip, rant, and banter about the same quotidian concerns that exercised them above ground. The dominant voice
is that of Caitriona Paudeen, an acid-tongued woman rife with
loathing for her sister Nell, who she reckons stole the man she
desired. Amid the cacophony is a voice that repeatedly declares
its allegiance to Hitler, a pompous literary man, and a guy who

repeatedly brags of the night he drank forty-two pints. There is little plot to speak of, and many pages are torrents of bilious imprecations—according to a writer in *The New Yorker*, the Titley translation is 'a minefield strewn with the words "cunt" and "fuck"'. Kevin Barry, an author whose fiction shares a certain amount of pungent, rural-grotesque DNA with *The Dirty Dust*, has described it as a 'splendidly batty' novel.

Cré na Cille is regularly cited as the greatest Irish-language novel of the twentieth century, but Máirtín Ó Cadhain produced plenty more well-regarded work besides, including six short-story collections, further novels, essays, polemics, and satires. He was born in Spiddal, County Galway, in 1906. Growing up amid speakers of the Irish language, he became a lifelong activist for its preservation and revitalisation. He worked as a schoolteacher and was imprisoned between 1939 and 1944 in an internment camp by the Irish Free State. The intensive reading of European, Irish, and Russian literature that he undertook during his years of captivity laid the foundations for his key works. *Cré na Cille* was first serialised in *The Irish Press* in 1949 to huge popularity, and published in a single volume the following year by an Irish-language press. Ó Cadhain wrote a regular column in *The Irish Times* between 1953 and 1956, and began lecturing in Irish at Trinity College Dublin in 1956. He was elected to the chair of Irish, and a lecture hall at the college now bears his name.

Included here is the opening section of Alan Titley's translation of Máirtín Ó Cadhain's relentlessly gabbling, shit-tongued novel in voices.

From *The Dirty Dust*
Interlude 1
The Black Earth

1.

DON'T KNOW IF I am in the Pound grave, or the Fifteen Shilling grave? Fuck them anyway if they plonked me in the Ten Shilling plot after all the warnings I gave them. The morning I died I calls Patrick in from the kitchen. "I'm begging you Patrick, I'm begging you, put me in the Pound grave, the Pound grave! I know some of us are buried in the Ten Shilling grave, but all the same . . ."

I tell them to get me the best coffin down in Tim's shop. It's a good oak coffin anyway. I am wearing the scapulars. And the winding sheet . . . I had them ready myself. There's a spot on this sheet! Like a smudge of soot. No, not that. A daub of finger. Who else but my daughter-in-law! 'Tis like her dribble. Oh, my God, did Nell see it? I suppose she was there. Not if I had anything to do with it . . .

Look at the mess Kitty made of my covering clothes. I always said that that one and the other one, Biddy Sarah, should never be given a drop to drink until the corpse was gone from the road outside the house. I warned Patrick not to let them near my winding sheet if they had a drop taken. All they ever wanted was a corpse here, there, or around the place. The fields could be bursting with crops, and they'd stay there, if she could cadge a few pence at a funeral . . .

I have the crucifix on my breast anyway, the one I bought myself at the mission . . . But where's the black one that Tom's wife, Tom the crawthumper, brought me from Knock, that last time they had to lock him up? I told them to put that one on me too. It's far nicer than this one. Since Patrick's kids dropped it the Saviour looks a bit crooked. He's beautiful on this one, though. What's this? My head must be like a sieve. Here it is, just under my neck. 'Tis a pity they didn't put it on my breast.

They could have wrapped the rosary beads better on my fingers. Nell, obviously, did that. She'd love it if it fell to the ground just as they were putting me in the coffin. O Lord God, she better stay miles away from me . . .

I hope to God they lit the eight candles on my coffin in the church. I left them in the corner of the press under the rent book. You know, that's something that was never ever on any coffin in the church, eight candles! Curran had only four. Tommy the Tailor's lad, Billy, had only six, and he has a daughter a nun in America.

I tells them to get three half-barrels of porter, and Ned the Nobber said if there was drink to be got anywhere at all, he'd get it, no bother. It had to be that way, given the price of the altar. Fourteen or fifteen pounds at least. I spent a shilling or two, I'm telling you, or sent somebody to all kinds of places where there was going to be a funeral, especially for the last five or six years when I felt myself failing. I suppose the Hillbillies came. A pity they wouldn't. We went to theirs. That's how a pound works in the first place. And the shower from Derry Lough, they'd follow their in-laws. Another pound well spent. And Glen Booley owed me a funeral too . . . I'd be surprised if Chalky Steven didn't come. We were at every single one of his funerals. But he'd say he never heard about it, 'til I was buried.

And then the bullshit: "I'm telling you Patrick Lydon, if I could help it at all, I would have been at her funeral. It wouldn't have been right if I wasn't at Caitriona Paudeen's funeral, even if I had to crawl on my naked knees. But I heard nothing, not a

bit, until the night she was buried. Some young scut . . ." Steven
is full of crap! . . .

I don't even know if they keened me properly. Yes, I know
Biddy Sarah has a nice strong voice she can go at it with if she
is not too pissed drunk. I'm sure Nell was sipping and supping
away there also. Nell whining and keening and not a tear to be
seen, the bitch! They wouldn't have dared come near the house
when I was alive . . .

Oh, she's happy out now. I thought I'd live for another couple of years, and I'd bury her before me, the cunt. She's gone
down a bit since her son got injured. She was going to the doctor for a good bit before that, of course. But there's nothing
wrong with her. Rheumatism. Sure, that wouldn't kill her for
years yet. She's very precious about herself. I was never that way.
And it's now I know it. I killed myself working and slaving away
. . . I should have watched that pain before it got stuck in me.
But when it hits you in the kidneys, actually, you're fucked . . .

I was two years older than Nell anyway . . . Baba. Then me,
and Nell. Last year's St. Michael's Day, I got the pension. But I
got it before I should have. Baba's nearly ninety-three, for God's
sake. She'll soon die, despite her best efforts. None of us live
that long. When she hears that I'm dead, she'll know she's done
for too, and then maybe she'll make her will . . . She'll leave
every bit to Nell. The bitch will have one up on me after all.
She has Baba primed. But if I had lived another bit until Baba
had made her will, she'd have given me half the money despite
Nell. Baba is quick enough. She wrote to me mostly for the last
three years since she abandoned Blotchy Brian's place and took
off to Boston. It's a great start that she has shagged off from that
poisonous rats' nest anyway.

But she never forgave Patrick that he married that cow from
Gort Ribbuck, and that he left Blotchy Brian's Maggie in the
lurch. She would never have gone next or near Nell's house that
time she was home from America if it wasn't for the fact that

her daughter married Blotchy Brian. And why would she? . . .
A real kip of a house. A real crap kip of a house it was too.
Certainly not a house for a Yank. I haven't a clue how she put
up with it having been in our house and in fancy homes all over
America. She didn't stay there long though, she soon shagged
off home . . .

She'll never come back to Ireland again. She's finished with
us. But you'd never know what kind of a fit would hit her when
this war is over, if it suited her. She'd steal the honey from a
bee's hive, she is so smarmy and sweet. She's gutsy and spirited
enough to do it. Fuck her anyway, the old hag! After she buggered off from Blotchy Brian's place in Norwood, well she still
had a lot of time for Maggie. Patrick was the real eejit that he
didn't listen to her, and didn't marry the ugly bitch's daughter. "I
wouldn't marry Meg if she had all of Ireland . . ." Baba hurried
off up to Nell's place as if you had clocked her on the ear. She
never came near our place again, but just about stood on the
floor the day she was returning to the States.

—. . . Hitler's my darling. He's the boy for them . . .

—If England is beaten, the country will be in a bad way. The
economy has already gone to the dogs . . .

—. . . You left me here fifty years before my time, you One
Eared Tailor git! You lot were always twisted. Couldn't trust
you. Knives, stones, bottles, it didn't matter. You wouldn't fight
like a man, but just stab me . . .

—. . . Let me talk, let me talk.

—Christ's cross protect me!—Am I alive or dead? Are the
people here alive or dead? They are all rabbiting on exactly the
same way as they were above the ground! I thought that when I
died that I could rest in peace, that I wouldn't have to work, or
worry about the house, or the weather, that I would be able to
relax . . . But why all this racket in the dirty dust?

2.

—. . . Who are you? How long are you here? Do you hear me? Don't be afraid. Say the same things here as you said at home. I'm Maggie Frances.

—O may God bless you. Maggie Frances from next door. This is Caitriona. Caitriona Paudeen. Do you remember me, or do you forget everything down here? I haven't forgotten anything yet, anyway.

—And you won't. This is much the same as the "ould country" except that we only see the grave we are in, and we can't leave our coffin. Or you won't hear any live person either, and you won't have a clue what they're up to, except when the newly buried crowd tell you. But, hey, look Caitriona, we are neighbours again. How long are you here? I never noticed you coming.

—I don't know, Maggie, if it was St. Patrick's Day, or the day after that I died. I was too weak. I don't know how long I'm here either. Not that long, anyway . . . You've been buried a long time now, Maggie . . . Too true. Four years this Easter. I was spreading a bit of manure for Patrick down in Garry Dyne when one of Tommy's young ones came up to me. "Maggie Frances is dying," she said. And what do you know, Kitty, the young one, was just going in the door when I reached the end of the haggard. You were gone. I closed your eyes. Myself and Kitty laid you out. And thanks to us, well, everyone said that you looked gorgeous on the bed. Nobody had any need to complain. Everyone who saw you, Maggie, everyone said you were a lovely corpse. Not a bit of you, not a hair out of place. You were as clean and smooth as if they had ironed you out on the bed . . .

. . . No, I didn't hang on that long, Maggie. The kidneys had packed up a long time ago. Constipation. I got a sharp pain five or six weeks ago. And then, on top of that I got a cold. The pain went into my stomach and then on my chest. I only lasted about a week . . . I wasn't that old either, Maggie, just seventy-one. But I had a hard life. I really had a hard life, and I looked every bit of it. When it hit me, it really hit me, left its mark on me. I had no fight left . . .

You might say that Maggie, alright. That hag from Gort Ribbuck didn't help me a bit. Whatever possessed my Patrick to marry the likes of her in the first place? . . . God bless you, Maggie, you have a heart of gold, but you don't know the half of it, and a word about it never passed my lips. A full three months now and she hasn't done a stroke . . . The young one. She just about made it this time. The next one will really put her to the pin of her collar, though . . . Her brood of kids out of their minds except for Maureen, the eldest one, and she was in school every day. There I was slaving away washing them and keeping them from falling into the fire, and throwing them a bit of grub whenever I could . . . Too true, too true. Patrick's house will be a mess now that I am gone. Of course that hag couldn't keep a decent house any way, any woman who spends every second day in bed . . . O, now you're talking, tell me more . . . Patrick and the kids, that's the real tragedy . . .

It was so. I had everything ready, Maggie, the clothes, the scapulars, the lot . . . 'Tis true, they lit eight candles for me in the church, not a word of a lie. I had the best coffin from Tim's place. It cost at least fifteen pounds . . . and, wait for it, not two plates on it, but three, believe me . . . And every one of them the spitting image of the fancy mirror in the priest's house . . .

Patrick promised he'd put a cross of Connemara marble on my grave: just like the one on Peter the Publican, and written in Irish: "Caitriona, wife of John Lydon . . ." He said it himself, not a word of a lie. You don't think I'd ask him do you, I wouldn't dream of it . . . And he said he'd put a rail around it just like the one on Huckster Joan's, and that he'd decorate it with flowers—I can't remember what he called them, now—the kind that the School Mistress wore on her black dress after the

School Master died . . . "That's the least we could do for your," Patrick said, "after all you did for us throughout your life." . . .

But listen to me, what kind of place is this at all, at all? . . . Too true, too true, the Fifteen Shilling plot . . . Now, come on Maggie, you know in your heart of hearts that I wouldn't want to be stuck up in the Pound plot. Of course, if they had put me in there, I could have done nothing about it, but to think that I might want that . . .

Nell, was it . . . I nearly buried her. If I had lived just a tiny little bit more . . . That accident to her boy, that really shook her . . . A lorry hit him over near the Strand about a year or a year and a half ago, and it made bits of his hip. The hospital didn't know whether he would live or die for about a week . . .

O, you heard about it already, did you? . . . He spent another six months on the flat of his back . . . He hasn't done a thing since he got home, just hobbling around on two crutches. Everyone thought he was a goner . . .

He can't do anything for the kids, Maggie, except for the eldest fucker and he's a bollocks . . . that might be the case alright . . . Like his grandfather, same name Big Blotchy Brian, a total asshole. Who cares, but then, his grandma, Nell . . . Nell and her crowd never harvested anything for the last two years . . . That injury has really shagged the two of them, Nell and that Brian Maggie one. I got great satisfaction from that bitch. We had three times as many spuds as her this year. Ah, for God's sake, Maggie Frances, wasn't the road wide enough for him just as it was for everybody else to avoid the lorry? . . . Nell's boy was thrown, Maggie. "I wouldn't give you the steam of my piss," the judge said . . . He let the lorry driver come to court in the meantime, but he didn't allow Nell's youngfella to open his mouth. He's bringing it to the High Court in Dublin soon, but that won't do him any good either . . . Mannix the lawyer told me that Nell's crowd wouldn't get a brass farthing. "And why would he," he said, "wrong side of the road." . . . No truer word, Maggie. Nell won't get a hairy cent from the law. It's what she deserves. I'm telling you, she won't be going past our house so easily from now on singing "Ellenmore Morune" . . .

Ara, poor Jack isn't that well either, Maggie. Sure, Nell never minded him one bit, nor did Blotchy Brian's daughter since she went into their house . . . Isn't Nell my own sister, Maggie, and why on earth would I not know? She never paid a blind bit of attention to Jack, and not a bit of it. She was wrapped up in herself. She didn't give a flying fuck about anyone, apart from herself . . . I'm telling you, that's the God's honest truth, Jack suffered endlessly because of her, the slut . . . Fireside Tom, Maggie. Just as he always was . . . In his hole of a hovel all the time. But it will fall down on him someday soon . . . Ah, for God's sake didn't my Patrick go and offer to put some thatch on it . . . "Look, Pat," I said to him, "you have absolutely no business sticking thatch on Tom's wreck of a house. Nell can do it if she wants. And if she does so, then so will we" . . .

"But Nell has nobody at all now since Peter's leg was smashed," said Pat.

"Everybody has enough to do for himself," I said, "everyone has to thatch their own place, even a kip like that prick Fireside Tom."

"But the house will collapse on him," he says.

"It can if it wants to," I says, "Nell has enough on her plate without filling up Tom's mouth with shite. That's it, Pat, my boy, keep at it. Fireside Tom is like rats being drowned in a bath. He comes crawling to us to keep out of the rain" . . .

Nora Johnny, is it? . . . It's a queer thing to find out more about her here . . . I know far too much about her, and every single one of her breed and seed, Maggie . . . Listening to the Master every single day, is that it . . . The Old Master himself, the wretch . . . the Old Master reading to Nora Johnny! . . . Nora Johnny! . . . ah, for Christ's sake . . . he doesn't think much of himself, does he, the master . . . Reading stuff to Nora

Johnny . . . Of course, that one has nothing between her ears. Where would she get it from? A woman that never darkened the door a school, unless it was to vote . . . I'm telling you it's a queer world if a schoolmaster spends his time talking to the likes of her . . . What's that, Maggie? . . . that he fancies her . . . I don't know who she is . . . If her daughter lived in the same house as him for the last sixteen years, as she has here, he sure as hell would know who she was then. But I'll tell him yet . . . I'll tell him about the sailor, and the rest of it . . .

—"Johnny Martin had a daughter
    As big as any other man . . ."

—Five-eight's forty; five-nine's forty-five, five ten's . . . sorry sir, I don't remember . . .

—"As I roved out to the market, seeking for a woman to find"

—I had twenty, and I played the ace of hearts. I took the king from your partner. Mrukeen topped me with the jack. But I had a nine, and my partner out of luck . . .

—But I had the queen, and was defending . . .

—Mrukeen was going to play the five of trumps, and he'd beat your nine. Wasn't that what you were going to do, Mrukeen?

—But then the mine blew our house up into the air . . .

—But we'd have won the game anyway . . .

—No way. If it wasn't for the mine . . .

—. . . A lovely white-headed mare. She was gorgeous . . .

—I can't hear a thing, Maggie. O my God almighty and His precious mother . . . a white-headed mare . . . The five of trumps . . . I can't listen to this . . .

—I was fighting for the Republic . . .

—Who asked you anyway . . .

—He stabbed me . . .

—Then he didn't stab you in the tongue anyway. Bugger the lot of you. My head is totally screwed up since I came here. Oh, Maggie, if you could just slink away. In the other world, if you didn't like someone's company you could just leave them there, and shag off somewhere else. But unfortunately, the dead can't budge an inch in the dirty dust . . .

3.

. . . And after all that they shagged me into the Fifteen Shilling Place. After all my warnings . . . Nell had a grin on her as wide as a barn door! She'll surely get buried in the Pound Place now. I wouldn't be a bit surprised if it was she put Patrick up to sticking me in the Fifteen Shilling Place instead of the Pound. She wouldn't have the neck to darken the door of my house, only that I was dead. She didn't put a foot on my floor since the day I married . . . that is, if she didn't sneak in unknown to me while I was dying.

But, Patrick is a bit of a simpleton. He'd give in to her crap. And his wife would agree: "To tell God's truth, but you're right Nell. The Fifteen Shilling Place is good enough for anybody. We're not millionaires . . ."

The Fifteen Shilling Place is good enough for anyone. She would say that. She would say that, wouldn't she? Nora Johnny's One. I'll get her yet! She'll be here for sure at her next delivery. I'll get her yet, I'm telling you. But I'll get her mother first— Nora Johnny herself—in the meantime.

Nora Johnny. Over from Gort Ribbuck. Gort Ribbuck of the Puddles. It was always said they milk the ducks there. Doesn't she just fancy herself. Now she's learning from the Master. It was about time for her to start anyway. No schoolmaster in the world would speak to her, except in the graveyard, and even then he wouldn't if he knew who she was . . .

It is her daughter's fault that I'm here twenty years too soon. I was washed out for the last six months looking after her mangy children. She's sick when she's expecting a child, and sick when she's not. The next one will take her away. Take here away, no doubt about it . . . She was no good for my Patrick anyway, however he would get on without her . . . You couldn't talk to him. "It's the only one thing I'm going to do," he said, "I'll feck off to America and I'll leave the place go to hell, seeing as you don't give a toss about it . . ."

That was when Baba was home from America. She did everything she could to get him to marry Blotchy Brian's Maggie. She really took a fancy to that little ugly hussy of Blotchy Brian's for some reason. "She looked after me well when I was in the States," she said, "especially when I was very sick, and all my own people miles away. Blotchy Brian's Maggie is an able little smarty, and she has a bit put aside herself, as well as what I could give her. I had more time for you, Caitriona," she says, "than for any other of my sisters. I'd prefer to leave my money in your house than to anyone else belonging to me. I'd love to see your own Paddy get on in the world. You have two choices now," she said to him, "I'm in a hurry back to America, but I won't go until I see Blotchy Brian's young girl fixed up here, as she is having no luck at all over there. Marry her, Paddy. Marry Brian's Maggie and I won't see you stuck. I have more than enough to see me out. Nell's son has asked her already. Nell herself was talking to me about her only the other day. She'll marry him, Nell's son, I'm telling you, if she doesn't marry you. Marry her, or marry who you like, but if you marry who you like yourself . . ."

"I'd sooner take to the roads," said Patrick. "I won't marry any other woman who ever sniffed the air other than Johnny Nora's daughter from Gort Ribbuck."

He did.

I had to put the clothes on her back myself. She didn't have as much as a penny towards the wedding, not to mention a dowry. A dowry from the crowd of the Toejam trotters? A dowry in Gort Ribbuck of the puddles where they milk the

ducks? . . . He married her, and she is like death warmed up
ever since. She couldn't raise a pig or a calf, or a hen or a
goose, or even a duck, and she knew all about them from Gort
Ribbuck. Her house is filth. Her kids are filthy. She's totally
clueless whether she's working the land or scavenging stuff on
the shore . . .

There was some decent stuff in that house until she came
along. I kept it as clean as a whistle. Every single Saturday night
without fail I washed the stools and the chairs and the tables out
in the stream. I spun and I carded. I had bags of everything. I
raised pigs and calves and fowl . . . as long as I had the go in me
to do it. And when I hadn't I shamed Johnny Nora's one enough
that she didn't sit on her arse completely . . .

But what will happen to the house now without me? . . .
Nell will get great satisfaction anyway . . . She can afford to.
She has a fine woman to make bread and spin yarn on the
floor of her house now: Blotchy Brian's Maggie. She can easily
be jeering about my own son who only was a bit of a waster,
a messer. She'll be going up past our house every second day
now saying: "Bejaysus, we got thirty pounds for the pigs . . . It
was a great fair if you had some cattle. We got sixteen pounds
for the two calves" . . . Even though the hens aren't laying right
now, our Maggie has always a few tricks up her sleeve. She
brought eighty eggs to the Fancy City on Saturday. We had
four clutches of chicks this year. The hens are laying twice as
many eggs. I had another clutch yesterday. "The little speckled
oat coloured clutch," Jack called them, when he saw me handling them . . . She'll have ants in her pants when she's going
past our house. She'll know I'm not there. Nell! The Bitch! She
might be my sister, alright, but I hope and pray that not one
other corpse will come to the graveyard before her . . . !

4.

—. . . I was fighting for the Irish Republic, and you had me executed, you traitor. You fought for the English, just the same as fighting for the Free State . . . You had an English gun in your hand, English money in your pocket, and love of England in your heart. You sold your soul and your ancient heritage for a mess of porridge, for a "soft bargain," for a job . . .

—That's a lie! You were a criminal, fighting against the legitimate Government . . .

—. . . I swear by the oak of this coffin, Margaret, I swear I gave her, I gave Caitriona the pound . . .

—. . . I drank forty-two pints . . .

—I remember it well, you scumbag. I bollixed my ankle that day . . .

—. . . You stuck the knife in me, straight between my gut and the top of my ribs. Through the skin of my kidneys. Then you twisted it. The foul stroke always by the Dog Eared crowd.

—. . . Let me speak. Free speech . . .

—Are you ready now for an hour's reading, Nora Johnny? We'll start a new novelette today. We finished "Two Men and the Powder Puff" the other day, don't you remember? This one is called "The Berry Kiss." Listen carefully now:

"Nuala was an innocent young girl until she met Charles ap Rice in the nightclub . . ." Yes, I know. There isn't any chance to get away here, or to talk about culture . . . and just as you say, Nora, they are always talking about small stupid insignificant stuff here . . . cards, horses, booze, violence . . . we are totally pissed off about his racing mare every bloody day . . . that's the whole truth, undoubtedly, Nora . . . Nobody has a snowball's chance in hell of developing their intellect here . . . Right on, that's the complete truth . . . this place is as bad-mannered, as thicko, as barbaric as whatever happens over in the dregs of the Half Guinea place . . . we are really back in the dark ages since the *sansculottes* started scrimping money together from the dole to be put in the Fifteen Shilling Place . . . I'll tell you how I would divide this place up, if I had my way: those who went to university in the Pound Place, those who . . . No, no, that's not it Nora! Yes, it's a crying shame that some of my own past pupils are lying next to me here . . . It really depresses me to learn how ignorant they still are, after all I burst my guts for them . . . and sometimes they are pig ignorant rude with me . . . I just don't know what's happening to the young crowd . . . that's it, Nora . . . no chance whatsoever of culture . . .

"Nuala was an innocent young girl until she met Charles ap Rice in the nightclub . . ." A nightclub, Nora? . . . You were never in a nightclub? . . . Well, a nightclub isn't that different from this place . . . Ah, no, Nora, ah no. Nightclubs aren't the same places as sailors hang out. They are "dives" really, but cultured people go to the nightclubs . . . You'd like to go to one of them . . . Not a bad idea really to put the finishing touch, the last notch, to bring a proper *cachet* to your education . . . I was in a nightclub once, just that time when they had raised teachers' salaries, just before they reduced them again, twice. I saw an African prince there . . . He was as black as the sloe and was drinking champagne . . . You'd love to go to a nightclub, Nora! Aren't you the brazen hussy . . . oh, the "naughty girl" . . . Oh Nora, so "naughty . . ."

—You thieving bollocks! Johnny the Robin's daughter out from Gort Ribbuck! Where did she say she wanted to go, Master . . . ? Her tricks will get her yet! Don't take a gnat fart's notice of her, I'm telling you. If you knew her like I do you'd keep your trap firmly shut. I've been dealing with herself and her daughter for the last sixteen years. You shouldn't bother your arse wasting your time with Toejam Nora. She was hardly a day at school, and she wouldn't know the difference between the ABC and a plague of fleas in her armpit . . .

—Who's this? Who are you . . . ? Caitriona Paudeen. I don't believe you're here at last . . . Well, however long it takes, this is where you end up . . . Welcome anyway, Caitriona, you're welcome . . . I'm afraid, Caitriona, that you are . . . How will I put it . . . You are a bit hard on Toejam No—. . . Nora Johnny . . . She has come on a bomb since you used to be . . . What's the way you put it . . . That's it . . . dealing with her . . . We find it hard to measure time, but if I get you correctly, she's three years here already under the positive influence of culture . . . But listen here, Caitriona . . . Do you remember the letter I wrote for you to your sister Baba in America . . . 'Twas the last one I wrote . . . The day after that, my last sickness hit me . . . Is that will still in dispute . . . ?

—I got many letters from Baba since you were writing them for me, Master. But she never said "yea" or "nay" about the money. Yes we got an answer from her about that letter, alright. That was the last time she mentioned the will: "I haven't completed my will yet," she said. "I hope I do not pass away suddenly or by happenstance, as you have suggested in your letter. Do not be concerned in this matter. I'll execute my will in due course, when I know what is required of me." I know what I told her when I caught up with her. "I'm sure the schoolmaster wrote that for you. No one of us ever spoke like that."

The Young Master—he succeeded you—he writes the letters for us now. But I'm afraid that the priest writes for Nell. That hag can pull the wool over his eyes with her chickens and knitted socks and her twisted tricks. She is a dab hand it, Master. I thought I'd live another few years yet and see her buried, the maggot . . . !

You did your best for me anyway, Master, about the will. You could handle the pen. I often saw you writing a letter, and do you know what I thought? I thought that you could knit words together just as well as I could put a stitch in a stocking . . . "May God have mercy on the Old Master," I'd say to myself. "He would always do you a good turn. If God allowed him to live, he'd have got the money for me . . ."

I'd say it won't be long now until the Mistress—that is to say, your good wife, Master—it won't be long until she gets her act together. No doubt about it. She's a fine good-looking young thing yet . . . Oh, I'm very sorry Master! Don't take a bit of notice of anything I say. I'm often romancing like that to myself, but sure, no one can help who they are themselves . . . I know, Master, I shouldn't have told you at all. You'll be worried about it. And I thought you'd be absolutely thrilled to hear that the Mistress was getting her act together . . .

Ah, come on, don't blame me, Master . . . I'm not a gossip . . . I can't tell you who the man is . . . Ah, please, Master, don't push me . . . If I thought it would really make you so cranky I wouldn't have said as much as a word . . .

She swore blind that she wouldn't marry another man, did she, Master? Oh, come on! . . . Did you never hear it said that married women are the best . . . You were hardly cold in your grave when she had cocked her eye at another guy. I think, honestly, that she was always a bit flighty . . .

Ah, no, certainly not the Foxy Policeman either. He has a lump of a nurse hanging out of him in the Fancy City, or so they say . . . nor the spuds guy . . . Go on, have another guess, Master. I'll give you as many as you want . . . Paddy is gone to England. They took the lorry from him, and sold it. He never went up a road for turn without letting a string of debts behind him. Guess again, Master . . . That's him, dead on, exactly, Billy the Postman. Well done getting it like that, just as a pure guess. Never mind what anyone else says, Master, I think you have a great head on your shoulders . . .

Careful now with Nora Johnny. I could tell you things, Master . . .

Ah, forget about that now, get over it Master, and don't let it bother you . . . Maybe you are dead right . . . It wasn't just letters that had him coming to the house . . . Ah, come off it, Master . . . She was always a bit flighty, your wife . . .

5.

—. . . They were sent as plenipotentiaries to make a peace treaty between Ireland and England . . .

—I'm telling you you're a filthy liar. They were only sent over as messenger boys, they exceeded their authority, and betrayed us, and the country is buggered up ever since . . .

—A white mare. She was a beauty. No bother for her to carry a ton and a half . . .

—. . . By the oak of this coffin, I swear Nora Johnny, I swear I gave Caitriona the pound . . .

—. . . "That daughter of Big Martin John
        Was just as tall as any man
        When she stood up on the hill . . ."

—. . . Why don't you go stuff your England and its markets. You're just scared shitless of the few pence you have in the bank. Hitler's the boy! . . .

—. . . Now, Coley, I'm a writer. I read fifty books for every one that you read. I'll see you if you think I am not a writer. Did you read my last book, "The Dream of the Jelly Fish?" . . . You didn't Coley . . . My apologies Coley. I'm very sorry. I forgot that you couldn't read . . . It's a great story though . . . And I had three and a half novels, two and a half plays, and nine and a half translations with the publishers, The Goom,* and another short story and a half "The Setting Sun." I never got over the fact that "The Setting Sun" wasn't published before I died . . .

—If you're going to be a writer, Coley, remember that it's taboo for The Goom* to publish anything that a girl would hide from her father . . . Apologies, Coley. I'm sorry. I thought

---

* The Goom (An Gúm) was a state publishing house established in 1927 to publish books in Irish for the general public and for schools. Máirtín Ó Cadhain's early stories were published by An Gúm, but he always had a fractious relationship with them. This is one of the asides in the novel where he is poking fun at his literary adversaries.

you intended becoming a writer. But just in case you get that blessed itch . . . There isn't an Irish speaker who doesn't get that itch sometime in his life . . . they say it's the stuff on the coast around here that causes it . . . Now, Coley, don't be rude . . . It's the duty of every Irish speaker to find out if he has the gift of writing, especially the gift of the short story, plays, poetry . . . These last two are far commoner than the gift of the short story, even. Take poetry, for example. All you have to do is start at the bottom of the page and to work your way up to the top . . . either that, or scribble from right to left, leave a huge margin, but that isn't half as poetic as the other way . . .

Apologies again, Coley. I'm really sorry. I didn't remember that you can't read or write . . . But the short story, Coley . . . I'll put it like this . . . You've drunk a pint, haven't you? . . . Yes, I understand . . . You drank lots of pints of stout, and often . . . Don't mind how much you drank, Coley . . .

—I drank forty-four pints one after the other . . .

—I know that . . . Just hang on a minute . . . Good man. Let me speak . . . Get an ounce of sense, Coley, and let me speak . . . You've seen what's on the top of a pint of stout. The head, isn't it? A head of useless dirty froth. And yet, the more of it that's there on the pint, the more your tongue is hanging out for the pint itself. And if your tongue is hanging out for it you'll drink it all the way down to the dregs, even though it tastes flat. Do you see now, Coley, the beginning, the middle and the end of the short story . . . Be careful now that you don't forget that the end has to leave a sour taste in your mouth, the taste of the holy drink, the wish to steal the fire from the gods, to take another bite of the apple of knowledge . . . Look at the way I'd have finished that other short story—"Another Setting Sun," the one I was working on if I hadn't died suddenly from an attack of writer's cramp:

"Just after the girl had uttered that fateful word, he turned on his heels, departed the claustrophobic atmosphere of the room, and went out into the fresh air. The sky was dark with threatening clouds that were coming in from the sea. A weak faceless sun was entering the earth behind the mountains of the Old Town . . ." That's the *tour de force* Coley: "a weak faceless sun entering the earth"; and there should be no need for me to remind you that the last line after the last word has to be richly splattered with dots, writer's dots as I call them . . . But maybe you'll have the patience to listen to me reading it all to you from start to finish . . .

—Wait now, my good man. I'll tell you a story:

"Once upon a time there were three men . . ."

—Coley! Coley! There's no art in that story: "Once upon a time there were three men . . ." That's a hackneyed start . . . Wait now a minute, Coley, patience one minute. Let me speak. I think that I'm a writer . . .

—Shut your mouth you old windbag. Keep going, Coley . . .

—Once upon a time there were three men, and it was a long time ago. Once upon a time there were three men . . .

—Yes, go on, Coley, go on . . .

—Once upon a time there were three men . . . ah yes, there were three men a long time ago. I don't know what happened to them after that . . .

—". . . I swear by the book, Jack the Lad . . ."

—. . . Five elevens fifty-five; five thirteens . . . five thirteens . . . nobody learns that . . . Now, Master, don't I know them! Five sevens . . . was that what you asked me, Master? Five sevens, was it? . . . five sevens . . . five by seven . . . wait now a second . . . five ones is one . . .

Translated from the Irish by Alan Titley

Flann O'Brien

Scenes in a Novel

THWARTED, ALCOHOLIC, SELF-DEFEATING, AND brilliant, Flann O'Brien—one of the numerous pseudonyms of Brian O'Nolan—lived a life emblematic of the stifled, post-idealist Ireland that emerged from the smoke and rubble of our liberation from British rule. Part of a generation of Irish writers that included James Joyce, Samuel Beckett, Frank O'Connor, and Maeve Brennan, Flann O'Brien differed from his celebrated contemporaries in that he chose not to exile himself from Ireland, a country he found drab and repressive.

Published when he was twenty-eight, O'Brien's first novel, *At Swim-Two-Birds*, is astonishingly original: both a key modernist novel and, with its manifold metafictional layerings and intertextuality, presaging postmodernism. Jorge Luis Borges, one of the novel's first international readers, wrote in a review, 'I have enumerated many verbal labyrinths, but none so complex as the recent book by Flann O'Brien, *At Swim-Two-Birds*'. O'Brien's other major novel, *The Third Policeman*, is likewise uncommon: a disturbing rural-ontological comedy, walking a blade's edge between dread and hilarity.

O'Brien's first language was Irish, and his official career was in the civil service. He was born in Tyrone in 1911, and raised in Dublin, where he learned English at Blackrock College. He studied German, Irish, and English at University College Dublin, where he briefly co-edited the student journal *Blather*. O'Brien's debut novel was published following the emphatic endorsement of Graham Greene, who was then reading manuscripts at the publishing house Longman. Although it found further admirers in Samuel Beckett and James Joyce, both then living in Paris, the outbreak of war retarded sales of the novel. In 1940, O'Brien's next novel, *The Third Policeman*, was rejected by its publishers for being too fantastical, though it is now considered a classic. Humiliated by the rejection, O'Brien put out the story that the novel's only manuscript had been lost. It was finally published in 1967, winning O'Brien, recently deceased, yet more illustrious fans, including Anthony Burgess, who belligerently declared that, 'If we don't cherish the work of Flann O'Brien we are stupid fools who don't deserve to have great men'.

Flann O'Brien considered himself a failure. From 1940 he wrote a near-daily column for *The Irish Times* under the *nom de plume* Myles na gCopaleen. Satirical, absurdist, and imaginative, the column was beloved by many readers until its termination in 1966, the year when its author died of a heart attack following years of health problems relating to his chronic alcoholism. (The newspaper columns have been collected as *The Best of Myles*, and in numerous other volumes.)

Notable among Flann O'Brien's other works—which include plays and short stories—are the novels *The Poor Mouth* (published in Irish as *An Béal Bocht*), *The Dalkey Archive*, and *The Hard Life*. Acknowledged as an inspiration by many later Irish writers, including John Banville, Joseph O'Neill, and Kevin Barry (for whom he was 'Ireland's late-modernist godhead and the arch upsetter of our sacred literature'), Flann O'Brien is possibly the only Irish writer to have been honoured with a 'Google Doodle'.

'Scenes in a Novel', the short story included here, features some of the key effects that O'Brien would later employ in his great novels: self-reflexive framing, errant footnotes, and the uprising of his characters against a despotic author.

Scenes in a Novel

by Brother Barnabas
(Probably Posthumous)

I AM PENNING THESE lines, dear reader, under conditions of great emotional stress, being engaged, as I am, in the composition of a posthumous article. The great blots of sweat which gather on my brow are instantly decanted into a big red handkerchief, though I know the practice is ruinous to the complexion, having regard to the open pores and the poisonous vegetable dyes that are used nowadays in the Japanese sweat-shops. By the time these lines are in neat rows of print, with no damn over-lapping at the edges, the writer will be in Kingdom Come.[1] (See Gaelic quotation in 8-point footnote.) I have rented Trotsky's villa in Paris, though there are four defects in the lease (three reckoning by British law) and the drains are—what shall I say?—just a *leetle* bit Gallic. Last week, I set about the melancholy task of selling up my little home. Auction followed auction. Priceless books went for a mere song, and invaluable songs, many of them of my own composition, were ruthlessly exchanged for loads of books. Stomach-pumps and stallions went for next to nothing, whilst my ingenious home-made typewriter, in perfect order except for two faulty characters,

---

1. "Traugh sin, a leabhair bhig bháin
   Tiocfaidh lá, is ba fíor,
   Déarfaidh neach os cionn do chláir
   Ní mhaireann an lámh do scríobh."

   ["It is a pity, beloved little book
   A day will come, to be sure,
   Someone will inscribe over your contents
   'The hand that wrote this lives not'" (Trans. Jack Fennell)]

249

was knocked down for four and tuppence. I was finally stripped of all my possessions, except for a few old articles of clothing upon which I had waggishly placed an enormous reserve price. I was in some doubt about a dappled dressing-gown of red fustian, bordered with a pleasing grey piping. I finally decided to present it to the Nation. The Nation, however, acting through one of its accredited Sanitary Inspectors, declined the gift—rather churlishly I thought—and pleading certain statutory prerogatives, caused the thing to be burnt in a yard off Chatham Street within a stone's throw of the house where the Brothers Sheares played their last game of *taiplis* [draughts]. Think of that! When such things come to pass, as Walt Whitman says, you re-examine philosophies and religions. Suggestions as to compensation were pooh-poohed and sallies were made touching on the compulsory acquisition of slum property. You see? If a great mind is to be rotted and deranged, no meanness or no outrage is too despicable, no maggot of officialdom is too contemptible to perpetrate it . . . the ash of my dressing-gown, a sickly wheaten colour, and indeed, the whole incident reminded me forcibly of Carruthers McDaid.[2] Carruthers McDaid is a man I created one night when I had swallowed nine stouts and felt vaguely blasphemous. I gave him a good but worn-out mother and an industrious father, and coolly negativing fifty years of eugenics, made him a worthless scoundrel, a betrayer of women and a secret drinker. He had a sickly wheaten head, the watery blue eyes of the weakling. For if the truth must be told I had started to compose a novel and McDaid was the kernel or the fulcrum of it. Some writers have started with a good and noble hero and traced his weakening, his degradation and his eventual downfall; others have introduced a degenerate villain to be ennobled and uplifted to the tune of twenty-two chapters, usually at the hands of a woman—"She was not beautiful, but a shortened nose, a slightly crooked mouth and eyes that seemed brimful of a

---

2. Who is Carruthers McDaid, you ask?

simple complexity seemed to spell a curious attraction, an inexplicable charm." In my own case, McDaid, starting off as a rank waster and a rotter, was meant to sink slowly to absolutely the last extremities of human degradation. Nothing, absolutely nothing, was to be too low for him, the wheaten-headed hound . . .

I shall never forget the Thursday when the thing happened. I retired to my room at about six o'clock, fortified with a pony of porter and two threepenny cigars, and manfully addressed myself to the achievement of Chapter Five. McDaid, who for a whole week had been living precariously by selling kittens to foolish old ladies and who could be said to be existing on the immoral earnings of his cat, was required to rob a poor-box in a church. But no! Plot or no plot, it was not to be.

"Sorry, old chap," he said, "but I absolutely can't do it."

"What's this, Mac," said I, "getting squeamish in your old age?"

"Not squeamish exactly," he replied, "but I bar poor-boxes. Dammit, you can't call me squeamish. Think of that bedroom business in Chapter Two, you old dog."

"Not another word," said I sternly, "you remember that new shaving brush you bought?"

"Yes."

"Very well, you burst the poor-box or it's anthrax in two days."

"But, I say, old chap, that's a bit thick."

"You think so? Well, I'm old-fashioned enough to believe that your opinions don't matter."

We left it at that. Each of us firm, outwardly polite, perhaps, but determined to yield not one tittle of our inalienable rights. It was only afterwards that the whole thing came out. Knowing that he was a dyed-in-the-wool atheist, I had sent him to a revivalist prayer-meeting, purely for the purpose of scoffing and showing the reader the blackness of his soul. It appears that he remained to pray. Two days afterwards I caught him sneaking out to Gardiner Street at seven in the morning. Furthermore, a contribution to the funds of a well-known charity, a matter of four-and-sixpence in the name of Miles Caritatis was not, I understand, unconnected with our proselyte. A character ratting on his creator and exchanging the pre-destined hangman's rope for a halo is something new. It is, however, only one factor in my impending dissolution. Shaun Svoolish, my hero, the composition of whose heroics have cost me many a sleepless day, has formed an alliance with a slavey in Griffith Avenue; and Shiela, his "steady," an exquisite creature I produced for the sole purpose of loving him and becoming his wife, is apparently to be given the air. You see? My carefully thought-out plot is turned inside out and goodness knows where this individualist flummery is going to end. Imagine sitting down to finish a chapter and running bang into an unexplained slavey at the turn of a page! I reproached Shaun, of course.

"Frankly, Shaun," I said, "I don't like it."

"I'm sorry," he said. "My brains, my brawn, my hands, my body are willing to work for you, but the heart! Who shall say yea or nay to the timeless passions of a man's heart? Have you ever been in love? Have you ever—?"

"What about Shiela, you shameless rotter? I gave her dimples, blue eyes, blonde hair and a beautiful soul. The last time she met you, I rigged her out in a blue swagger outfit, brand new. You now throw the whole lot back in my face . . . Call it cricket if you like, Shaun, but don't expect me to agree."

"I may be a prig," he replied, "but I know what I like. Why can't I marry Bridie and have a shot at the Civil Service?"

"Railway accidents are fortunately rare," I said finally, "but when they happen they are horrible. Think it over."

"You wouldn't dare!"

"O, wouldn't I? Maybe you'd like a new shaving brush as well."

And that was that.

Treason is equally widespread among the minor characters. I have been confronted with a Burmese shanachy, two corner-boys, a barmaid, and five bus-drivers, none of whom could give a satisfactory explanation of their existence or a plausible account of their movements. They are evidently "friends" of my characters. The only character to yield me undivided and steadfast allegiance is a drunken hedonist who is destined to be killed with kindness in Chapter Twelve. *And he knows it!* Not that he is any way lacking in cheek, of course. He started nagging me one evening.

"I say, about the dust-jacket—"

"Yes?"

"No damn vulgarity, mind. Something subtle, refined. If the thing was garish or cheap, I'd die of shame."

"Felix," I snapped, "mind your own business."

Just one long round of annoyance and petty persecution. What is troubling me just at the moment, however, is a paper-knife. I introduced it in an early scene to give Father Hennessy something to fiddle with on a parochial call. It is now in the hands of McDaid. It has a dull steel blade, and there is evidently something going on. The book is seething with conspiracy and there have been at least two whispered consultations between all the characters, including two who have not yet been officially created. Posterity taking a hand in the destiny of its ancestors, if you know what I mean. It is too bad. The only objector, I understand, has been Captain Fowler, the drunken hedonist, who insists that there shall be no foul play until Chapter Twelve has been completed; and he has been over-ruled.

Candidly, reader, I fear my number's up.

* * * * * * *

I sit at my window thinking, remembering, dreaming. Soon I go to my room to write. A cool breeze has sprung up from the west, a clean wind that plays on men at work, on boys at play and on women who seek to police the corridors, live in Stephen's Green and feel the heat of buckshee turf . . .

It is a strange world, but beautiful. How hard it is, the hour of parting. I cannot call in the Guards, for we authors have our foolish pride. The destiny of Brother Barnabas is sealed, sealed for aye.

I must write!

These, dear reader, are my last words. Keep them and cherish them. Never again can you read my deathless prose, for my day that has been a good day is past.

Remember me and pray for me.

Adieu!

Alf MacLochlainn

From *Out of Focus*

Born in Dublin in 1926, Alf MacLochlainn studied at University College Dublin and trained as a librarian, with internships at the Library of Congress in Washington DC and Simmons College in Boston. In 1949 he began working at the National Library of Ireland, and eventually became its director in 1962. He also held the post of Librarian at University College, Galway, and was the chairman of the James Joyce Institute of Ireland, and a trustee of Dublin's Chester Beatty Library. MacLochlainn's first book, the surrealist novella *Out of Focus*, was published in 1978. It was followed in 1996 by a collection titled *The Corpus in the Library: Stories and Novellas*, and another collection in 2015, *Past Habitual: Stories*. Highly literary and formally ambitious, his work bears the influence of Samuel Beckett, and particularly of Flann O'Brien.

In addition to his books of fiction, MacLochlainn has also produced scripts for radio and television, short films, criticism, and essays on a variety of subjects. Included here is the second of the four sections that make up *Out of Focus*, the novella which was republished by Dalkey Archive in 1985.

From *Out of Focus*

On a Strangely Synchronous Afternoon

As I NOW RECALL, I should have realised early that it was a strangely synchronous day. Walking down the street that morning I strode quickly along close to the wall, my usual practice, and on turning a corner came face to face with another man of the same espalier habit. I slackened speed and shuffled slightly sideways, beginning a half-smile of self-deprecation, embarrassment and apology. My protagonist followed like a mirror image my every shuffle and grin, slipping to his right as I slipped to the left, to his left as I altered course to starboard, and we finished eyeball to eyeball, rotating slowly as we moved through matched arcs of one hundred and eighty degrees, figures in an antique dance.

A few minutes later I undertook the crossing of a one-way street. Before stepping off the pavement I glanced both right and left, trusting no-one, and descried a single motor-car approaching at moderate speed in the permitted direction. The street was otherwise free of traffic and I stepped forward onto the roadway, moving slowly to allow the motorist time to drive past before I should reach any point on his planned path. The motorist, however, perhaps attributing my slowness to infirmity and anxious to extend courtesy to the disabled, reduced speed and wagged his head in token that I should have precedence in use of the road. Noting his reduced speed but having no knowledge of the reasons for it—perhaps mechanical failure, perhaps excess of caution, perhaps the charitable motive suggested above—I decided to adopt a pace more normal for my years and strength and marched boldly forward. The motorist now, seeing perhaps that a gesture of courtesy had been misplaced and imagining in his turn that the few feet of roadway I had traversed left him still generous room for passing without danger to either of us, accelerated. Rapid consideration left me convinced that his previous retardation and my having pushed forward into the traffic-way together left me in a position to complete the traverse before he could reach me, and I accordingly speeded up my walk still further to make sure of safety; but his continuing acceleration rendered collision a distinct possibility so I again slackened speed only to note that he, placing the same interpretation on the data available to us mutually, had also slowed down. It was now a matter of unwilling bluff and double-bluff, two movable objects in the grip of a ridiculous but irresistible force and we proceeded by a series of stop-go accelerations, slowings-down and head-waggings until the front wing of his car, almost at a stand-still, struck me on the thigh. I had barely steerage way but unfortunately tripped and fell, striking my back heavily on the ground.

The motorist was solicitous in the extreme and insisted on taking me to hospital for a full assessment of my condition and on informing my next of kin.

Normally, to peer at your feet you peer downwards, but one lying flat on his back and peering at his feet can only be described as peering along or across at them. This I did, with some difficulty, as the bruises on my back made even the slight head-movement required fairly strenuous. There the feet were, evidenced by two ridged prominences in the snowy wastes of the bed-spread. Couloirs, cwms and crevasses shuddered and changed shape as I waggled my toes. Next, I carefully flexed one knee, thus bringing its foot, one would have presumed, nearer to my head than the other foot. The presumption was borne out by optical evidence collated in the course of the elaborate ensuing experiment. Continuing to peer in the general direction of the feet, I closed an eye briefly and as it reopened closed the other, equally briefly, repeating the procedure a number of times, left, right, left, right. The left- and right-eyed view-points presented quite different bed-scapes. Left eye surveyed (reading from left to right) left foot, right foot and right knee. Right eye saw only left foot and raised knee, the knee occluding or eclipsing the right foot. So far so good. I straightened the knee again, reproducing the earlier configuration. I was then disturbed to find that further closings and openings of the eyes failed to produce any significant alteration in the occlusions of the remoter landscapes behind (hardly below) the feet. As the opposite wall of the ward was, like the bedspread, of a neutral tinge, it was not possible to establish coordinates which would be of any use to me in determining the length of my legs, or even, indeed, if they were of the same length. A smart lateral striking together of the balls of the great toes, while both knees were straight, disposed of the amendment to the motion, but even if the legs were of the same length, was that length twelve inches or twelve feet or even perhaps as many miles?

My planning of further experiments in optical orientation and leg-measurement was interrupted by the arrival of a nurse, who told me a young lady had rung up to say she would try to get in on the afternoon train to see me.

I resented the suggestion that a few bruises on the back called for such elaborate arrangements 'to see me'.

'Would you like a bath?' the nurse asked.

Indeed I would and a few minutes later I was standing alone in my pelt in a narrow bathroom. The nurse with some misgiving had finally accepted my assurance that I could look after myself.

I leant with both hands for security on the side of the bath, the conventional enamelled type, about five feet long and two feet wide. I was standing beside one of its longer sides, a short side equipped with twin taps to my right, the sloping and curved short side, fitted for accommodating human backs, to my left.

Considerable planning would be necessary, I realised. My real, if slight and temporary, disablement required the avoidance of the necessity for sudden and violent movement. Hence I must not attempt to enter a bath already full of water which might prove too hot for comfort. It seemed logical to me therefore that I should enter the bath at my leisure while it was still empty and control the inflow of hot and cold supply in such fashion that comfort was assured. A rapid glance around confirmed access to soap, sponge and towel and ignoring the steps which hospitals thoughtfully supply I stepped easily over the side, turned on the hot tap, and sat down.

Initial hot inflow is subject to perceptible heatloss through the warming of the metal of the bath (specific heat 1.03 recurring). A nice adjustment is necessary of this first inrush, the gradual lowering of the thighs against the bottom of the bath proving an excellent test for the even heating of the highly conductive steel sheeting.

At the critical moment, my hands reached out to grasp hot and cold taps, ready to reduce hot delivery and allow cold. Again, so far so good. An even and comfortable temperature was being maintained, depth was increasing at a satisfactory rate, I could sit back, straighten my legs (memo: measure bath to establish length of legs), lay my spine, still a little sensitive, to the sloped area at the back and survey the gradual rise of the water-surface. As the water crept up the side of the bath I noted the delicate meniscus of the interface. Ankle-knobs disappeared, water lapped about the knee-caps.

Suddenly a distant clashing was heard, followed by the mingled hiss, gurgle and rattle of water being drawn from some remote central cistern. The cold tap faltered, gargled, spat and revived, but its delivery-rate had slackened noticeably. Unless corrective measures were undertaken as a matter of urgency, temperature would alter perceptibly upwards. I reached forward again towards the taps, but too quickly and the muscles of my back convulsed. Unnerved, I had to hang for a moment on the two taps. I twisted the hot one slightly, reducing its flow successfully and quickly let go as it was too hot for comfortable touching. I rested then with both hands on the cold tap and found my face close to an interesting orifice placed in the wall of the bath between the taps. It was in the shape of a miniature rose window and from its centre a light chrome chain connected with the rubber stopper sealing the vent-hole in the floor of the bath.

I recognised the orifice as an overflow, though any somnolent or otherwise inactive reclining bather would be well drowned before the engulfing water would reach its threshold. Consideration for damaged floors, ceilings, plaster and wall-paper, if not for a few drowned patients, should have made the designers place this orifice at least a foot lower. My ear was near it and I could hear, super-imposed on the gurgling of my two taps, a distant quiet sizzling. I turned my head to bring eye rather than ear to bear on the rose window and was surprised to notice a distinct if tiny glow emanating from its interior. My back was by now accommodated to its position and I could move fairly freely. I brought my eye close to the hole and peered in.

The view was in part obscured by the metal rays or spokes of the rose-window pattern but the details of the high-angle distant prospect were unmistakable: she was getting off a train. Good heavens, I thought, can it be so late already?

She stood on the platform, glancing up and down in indecision. She was carrying in her right hand a medium-sized travelling-case. Its medium size was plainly the cause of her indecision. A large bag would have required the assistance of a porter or of one of the silently-running articulated luggage-trolleys supplied by Messrs. Northern Engineering, Gateshead, of which several were to be seen whirring up and down the station. A small bag she would unhesitatingly have taken with her at a brisk walk. As it was, most of the passengers had preceded her to the exit when at last she emerged and approached the one remaining taxi. The driver, sitting at the wheel, was hunched over a newspaper. She spoke to him.

'Can you take me to the City Hospital, please?'

She elicited no response. She spoke again and he looked up with an annoyed frown, then with a twist of the lips and a wave of his hand dismissed her. The newspaper before him was folded neatly to expose a diagram presenting a two-move chess problem hinging on a promotion risking stale-mate.

Water was rising to operational levels so I withdrew my head from the vicinity of the rose window and in gingerly consideration for my back retreated along the bath, checking, before leaving, that the cold tap had returned to normal delivery. The water I found on reaching the full-back position and stretching out was now comfortably deep and hot and with two swift leftward swipes of the right toes I closed off both hot and cold taps (memo: further evidence of leg-length) but not so firmly that toes would be unable to reopen them.

Cogitate as I might I could find no explanation for the light emanating from the overflow nor for the strange view it afforded of relatively distant places. So far there was no evidence that distant times too were being brought under my gaze for it was perfectly in order that she should at that particular moment be dismounting from a train at a city terminal.

The unnecessary height of the overflow above the bath floor I had already noticed. Several other practical aspects of the matter required review. What of those baths, admittedly not nowadays so frequently met with, which combine overflow and vent-hole-stopper in a single metal tube, which fits into the vent-hole and effectively prevents escape of water until drawn up by means of a neat piston-like handle marked 'pull' set mid-way between the two taps? Such tubes function as overflows by having their upper ends open, the 'pull' handle being attached to a diametrical bar across the upper end. Taps and 'pull' handle on a bath so fitted must be set in a wide lip overhanging the interior of the bath. It would be quite impossible for the bather to insert his head beneath this lip and above the sealing-tube. *A fortiori* it would be quite impossible for him or her to determine whether or not such an overflow was acting as light-trap, periscope and telescope, and indeed the tubular structure of such overflows might lead to appreciably improved performance as all three.

Ratiocination on these and associated lines of enquiry occupied my mind for a considerable time and a minor water-reheating operation had to be undertaken. I reached my left foot out and up and grasped the lugs of the hot tap carefully (memo: note leg-length), engaging the knuckle of the great toe about a lug pointing so to speak towards four o'clock, that is considering the inscribed 'H' on a red ground on top of the tap as clock-centre. My no. 2 toe was inserted behind a lug pointing to eight o'clock and made to exert a supporting pressure. The tap obediently delivered water, cool at first but almost immediately hot enough to rewarm my bath. Enquiringly I attempted at the same time to engage the cold tap with my right foot but found to my surprise that it was extremely difficult to turn the two taps in the same direction at the same time. The attempt to do so involved a multiplying torque reaching, by the linkage of my legs, the sensitive areas of my spine. To turn hot on and cold off at the same moment was perfectly simple. The pressures required were in fact equal and opposite, half-torque was balanced by counter-vailing half-torque and spine was left unmolested; but only hot water was delivered. I had perforce to turn off the hot tap but already my right toes, still hooked on the cold tap, had acquired a reflex and carried out an involuntary movement in the opposite direction. Filing away the perplexing results of this experiment I decided that manual overdrive was called for in the interests of my spine, recalled my legs and reached forward with my two hands to the taps. This concatenation of movements again brought my head into the vicinity of the tiny rose window.

'Hanging about' is the only word to describe her behaviour. She wandered a few steps forward and back, near the rear of the single taxi with its immobile chess-playing driver. She put down her bag, picked it up again, looked back towards the railway-platform, over towards the exit leading to the city, put down her bag, bit her nail meditatively, made small erratic gestures with her shoulders and head. Two boys were sitting on the sun-baked pavement by the taxi-rank. She glanced at them, peered farther afield, then returned her gaze to them. They were playing jack-stones*; and one of them was approaching the climax.

---

* This game can be either an exercise of skill and patience for an individual or a contest between two. The skill and patience are exploited in prescribed manipulations of five small stones or pebbles, each about the size of the top joint of a little finger. Participants sit or squat upon the ground, a level area of a few feet square being required, free from extraneous pebbles or vegetation. A city pavement is an admirable location.

The stones are dropped from the hand onto the ground so that they lie within a compass of a few inches. Competitor A (let us say) commences. He takes one of the pebbles, tosses it in the air and allows it to land on the back of his hand. If he is successful he tosses it from the back of his hand and catches it in his palm. If he fails to catch at any point his right to continue play lapses and his rival begins. If A has been successful in the two stages of his work with the single stone, he proceeds, tossing it again in the air and *while it is aloft grabbing a second stone from those lying on the ground* and then catching the first as it descends. He now tosses the two stones which are in his palm and tries to catch them on the back of his hand; if he succeeds he tosses them from the back of the hand and catches them on the palm; and further proceeding tosses the two, grabs a third and so on.

When he has successfully tossed and grabbed all up to and including the fifth he progresses to grabbing two at a time, then two and three, then four

He examined the five pebbles lying on the ground, carefully appraising their dispersal, their several rotundities and angularities, and his mind made up, quickly picked one up, tossed it in the air and as it sailed up shot his hand with lightning speed across the group of four left on the ground, sweeping them into his clutching palm in time to switch his hand back, turn and open it just as the first tossed stone arrived to join its fellows safely on the palm. He sighed briefly with relief, allowing the five stones to cradle themselves comfortably in his curved fingers. He had now to launch these upwards in as tight a formation as possible and allow them to land on the back of his hand. A smooth rising glide of the hand, with his fingers forming an upward-pointing funnel, shot them gently in the air; his hand flicked over following them, descended below them just as they began to fall, wavering with spread knuckles as they spread slightly in their fall until one, two, three, four, five had clicked safely home as his hand came to rest without a tremor not an inch from the ground. The game was almost over. It only remained for him to toss the five now safely ensconced on the back of his palm. He tossed and grabbed and a vicious click told that one of the stones had knocked another. It knocked it three or four feet away and he was left with the useless four in his

---

and then five. Competitors of international class have further requirements added; the falling stone must not be allowed to make a click against those already in the palm, for example. Initial choice of pebbles is clearly a matter of grave import. Pebbles which are too rounded will roll too easily from the back of the hand, those which are too flat are difficult to grab quickly from the ground. Mathematicians might tentatively express the game in some such form as $T(1\rightarrow5)G[(1\rightarrow(1+4)]$ where 'T' means 'toss' and 'G' means 'grab'.

The foregoing summary gives little idea of the skill and competitive spirit which may be engaged in so seemingly simple a game. One of the two boys mentioned above had reached the penultimate and critical point at which he was faced with the problem of grabbing four stones from the ground and thereafter tossing five from the back of the hand (T5G4 in the notation suggested).

hand which put him back to the very beginning again. At this point the girl asked him would he carry her bag for her.

I began to fear that the nurse might return soon and expect to find me with my ablutions completed. Crouched as I was at the tap end of the bath I had several options open to me. I could stay where I was, convenient to my peephole, and by a slight adjustment of knees, etc., assume the normal posture of sitting on the ground, with my legs flat on the floor of the bath, my feet pointed towards the sloped end. There would be an undoubted if slight advantage in depth of water about the buttocks but the position was definitely at variance with the method of using the bath intended by the designers. As, however, I had already noted several design-faults in this bath, and indeed in baths in general, perhaps this was not even persuasive. I decided finally that sitting with my right and left shoulders in imminent danger of sharp contact with hot and cold taps respectively would be a gross perversion and eased myself into the designed position with my back to the slope. Now another design fault became apparent.

The soap was sitting in a small depression beside the hot tap and I could not reach it with my outstretched hand. It would be necessary to flex my knees, bringing my whole body forward, to leave the soap within range. A number of possible design improvements immediately occurred to me, some I knew already available through commercial outlets. First, the Bailey bridge type of soap-tray. This is a plastic or metal tray equal in length to the width of the bath. It is furnished with projecting moulded handles at both ends which sit firmly on the bath-rims. The tray provides adequate accommodation for face-cloths, sponges, if desired, soaps, light plastic containers for proprietary brands of shampoo, cubes of so-called bath salts of a mildly detergent character which impart a faint sliminess to the water, appreciated by some bathers. On the whole, one might think, a useful device; but profoundly inhibiting to pedal operation of taps as outlined above.

Floating soap might seem a solution to the accessibility problem and could be readily manufactured by the incorporation in each tablet of a vacant air-bubble. Decomposition of such tablets, permanently in contact with warm water, would inevitably be rapid and a point would soon be reached when the soap-skin would become perilously thin and finally pierced at one or more points. At that stage the soap would inevitably fill with water and sink. A floating and sealed soap-container then occurred to me and I rapidly sketched out in my mind a suitable design, lined with sponge or aerated plastic foam, consisting of two halves hinged together and held closed or open by, springs easily tripped by pressure on external nodules.

Worthwhile exploitation of this device would require fitting it with some motive power and directional navigation remotely controlled to ensure its recovery from the farther (normally the tap) end of the bath, whither it might so easily drift under the impulsion of convection currents as the bath water changed temperature. Sophisticated miniaturised hardware, perhaps strapped to the head of the bather, seemed called for. The container could of course be fitted with a magnet and the bather equipped with a belt and anklets magnetised to appropriate polarities. Successive attractions and repulsions would drive the container in any required direction. Again, directional jets loaded with liquid soap could be placed at strategic points around the bath-rim.

Unfortunately time and material resources did not permit the execution of any or all of these projects and against the possible arrival of the nurse I felt the agonising need to act. I reached forward, flexing the knees to grasp the soap. To my dismay it refused to lift with my fingers. I tugged harder and was horrified when it finally gave, to hear a squelching, popping noise and to see attached to the bath a soap-retainer of yet another kind. It was a thin piece of rubber, flat, oval; three or four inches in its longer axis, two or three in its shorter, fitted on both surfaces with a large number of tiny suction-cups. When the device was pressed on a bath surface, even a vertical one, these cups adhered aggressively. A soap-tablet pressed upon the upper surface would now adhere equally closely and could be removed only by such tugging as would cause a large number of lacerated wounds on the soap surface.

It was soap so scarred that I held in my hand with some revulsion and I paused still crouched near the tap end. I noticed again the faint gleam in the over-flow hole.

The boy was hefting her case in his hand. It was certainly not too heavy for a man to carry, perhaps slightly uncomfortable for a girl, difficult for a twelve-year-old boy. His difficulty was compounded by the necessity to transport as well his bicycle, which was lying near where he had been playing with his friend. With the case in his right hand, he grasped the head of the bicycle with his left midway between the handlebars. He attempted to lift the machine but its centre of gravity was far from his point of contact and the head twisted in his hand, the front wheel swivelling upwards, and the frame and rear wheel fell heavily to the ground. He relinquished his hold on the case, stood the bicycle up correctly and grasped the case again. As it left the ground and became part of his gravitational system his centre of gravity changed and he leant over in compensation. The bicycle slid downwards, its front wheel again twisting, rolling away from him, and the cross-bar slipping down along his thigh.

He released both bicycle and case, took the bicycle firmly, walked to a nearby wall and planted the bicycle firmly against it. Returning he took the case in his hands and brought it to the bicycle, then set about placing it carefully at a slant in the notional triangle formed by the front of the saddle, the cross-bar and the head. The case measured 15" x 24" x 4", was notably

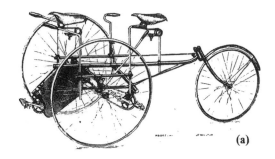

(a)

*Alternative means (a) and (b) of cycle transport
for carrying small travelling cases from main
station to city hospital.*

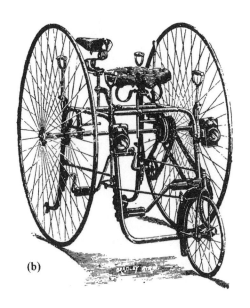

(b)

shallow that is to say for its height and length, and fitted but
ill into the allotted place. Further, the eight points at which its
six sides converged in corners were reinforced with metal shoes
which gave to the whole a readiness to slide when these shoes
came in contact with other metal surfaces.

Slowly and carefully, with his right hand on the right-hand
handle-bar and his left steadyingly on the case, he piloted the
bicycle away from the wall, propelling it by pressure on the rear
portions of the saddle from the front of his left hip. He began to
follow the girl. As they came to the exit proper from the station
premises she stopped abruptly to check on approaching traffic
before crossing the street. The boy stopped equally abruptly and
the resultant jerk dislodged the case from its precarious em-
placement. It slipped heavily sideways, coming to rest askew
in the angle formed by the turning of the head-bar into the
left handle-bar. The centre of gravity had again changed and
the late attempt to establish equilibrium caused the case to slip
formlessly to the ground on the farther side of the machine
from the perplexed boy. Resourcefully he wheeled the bike in a
long circle, so approaching the case as he came around that it
was again convenient to his right hand. This time, he poised the
case transversely on a small carrier behind the saddle, its lower 4" x 24" side (that is the narrow side opposite the handle),
resting on the carrier, a light spring hinged at the back of the
carrier exerting some pressure on the whole. In stable conditions the arrangement was ideal, but the centre of gravity was
dangerously high and the transverse arrangement of the longer
axis of the case gave little prospect of trouble-free locomotion.
The potential danger became cruelly actual when the journey
was recommenced. Bumping his bicycle off the pavement to
follow the girl across the street, the boy again lost control of the
machine, the case slipping sideways. He grabbed frantically at
it, yet again altering the centre of gravity of the whole boy-bike-
case system. The bike slid away from him landing flat on its side

and in the final inches of its fall dealing him a smart blow on the left ankle with its saddle. The involuntary spasm in his ankle plunged him into still further disequilibrium, and case, bike and boy finished in a sprawled heap on the roadway.

With the soap in my hand I had to decide which particular phase of the ablutions to undertake first. There would seem to be some linear logic in starting at either head or feet, but considerations other than mere linearity had to be borne in mind. There was bound to be substantial difference between the dirt-deliveries of head and feet. Justifiable objection might be made to rinsing the head in water already fouled by the off-scouring of perspiratory feet. On the other hand, the hair is a notable dust trap and washing it first would transfer a perceptible quantity of mechanical dirt and other atmospheric pollutants to the water. Again, the hands are notoriously the most efficient dirt-collectors of all the human members and many bathers would not be prepared to use them for working the other members until they themselves had been thoroughly washed and rinsed, even though such washing and rinsing would transfer to the water a quantity of dirt unreasonably out of proportion with the superficial area cleansed.

'Tisk, tisk,' said the nurse, sticking her head round the door, 'aren't you ready yet? I'll come back in a minute.'

Haste was necessary and as I had the soap in my hand I began there, lathering furiously. Feet, legs, buttocks, torso followed quickly and heedless of foot-sweat I plunged my head into the now-tepid water. As my ears breached the surface on the way down I was suddenly conscious of a distant altercation dimly heard. Undoubtedly sound travels more easily through water than through air but what frog-men in distant reservoir could be arguing so loudly that their querulous tones could reach me here? I was now leaning forward in the posture of one making a profound obeisance and when my hair had been sufficiently rinsed I raised my head slowly, allowing adequate time for run-off drainage. Paused thus with my head forward I again noticed the gleam in the rose window. The argument was clearly coming from that source. I peered in.

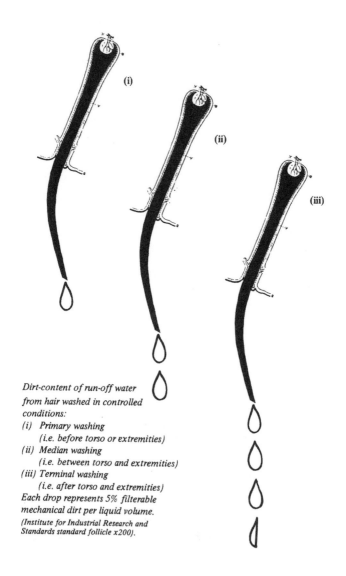

Dirt-content of run-off water from hair washed in controlled conditions:

(i) Primary washing
    (i.e. before torso or extremities)
(ii) Median washing
    (i.e. between torso and extremities)
(iii) Terminal washing
    (i.e. after torso and extremities)
Each drop represents 5% filterable mechanical dirt per liquid volume.
(Institute for Industrial Research and Standards standard follicle x200).

The girl was now frighteningly near. I was looking down at the spacious front hall of the hospital. She was standing at the doorway of the porter's glass-walled enquiry kiosk. The porter was gesticulating urgently towards a notice which announced visiting-hours. Her voice was shrouded in a cavernous gurgling and I could not discern the words spoken. The porter lifted a telephone hand-set and spoke briefly. Almost immediately a large nun arrived and further disputation with the girl ensued. She, however, was clearly one not easily rebuffed.

I heard the nurse at the door again, tapping loudly.

'Come now,' she said, 'If you can't manage better than that we'll have to give you a blanket bath in future.'

I knew the end was approaching and my hand dangled the fine chain connecting the centre of the overflow with the rubber plug in the vent-hole. There remained an opportunity to undertake one further experiment. Science had failed to establish the causes for the rotation of the whirlpool frequently noted around bath-vents. Many scholars held that the water should be expected to fall evenly over all points on the circular edge of the vent-hole, setting up a volume of immobile water exactly over the centre of the hole. Such immobile volume would presumably be in the form of an inverted cone and no-one had yet explained why this cone should prove so inherently unstable, falling constantly to one side or the other and setting up the whirlpool effect. And why should the whirlpool spin clockwise (if clockwise) or anti-clockwise (if anti-clockwise)? Was it, as some held, an effect of terrestrial axial rotation, differing with latitude, clockwise in one hemisphere, anti-clockwise in the other? Could human intervention alter whatever mysterious factors effect these tremendous cosmic movements?

I chucked on the chain and the plug came up. A gathering rattle sounded in the drain-pipe as the water plunged down, but it was still too deep for any sign of a whirlpool. Clearly over the deepening rumble I could hear the squeaking of the girl and the nun below, now raised to still greater volume and shrillness. I moved my head again towards the overflow and stared through it in amazement.

Great vertical rivers of water were plunging down on the hallway. Nun, girl and porter were buffeted and swirled about by the cascading torrents. Streaming freshets of sudsy grey effluent slopped about them, engulfing their feeble gestures of resistance in deluvian power. Surges of foam lapped about their feet, their

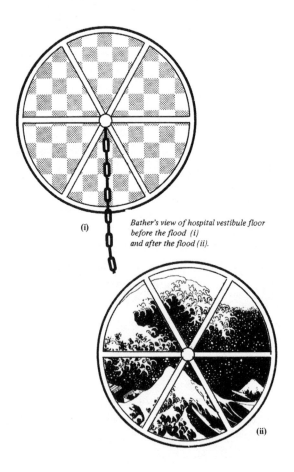

Bather's view of hospital vestibule floor before the flood (i) and after the flood (ii).

knees, their waists. The black and white tiled floor disappeared in the grey depths. A watery vapour swayed over the flood and obscured the tearing vortex in which the three frail humans struggled ineffectually.

The nurse came in and clucked imperiously. 'Finished at last?' she said. 'I hope we did behind our ears.'

The whirlpool was clockwise.

Lip-top and end-wall overflow bathoscope
by Wright, Sutcliffe and Son,
Halifax, 1900.
(Note dead-end overflow 0
and open-end vent-hole V).

Aidan Higgins

Helsingør Station

AMONG THE MOST AMBITIOUS and inventive Irish writers of the twentieth century, Aidan Higgins never achieved the renown of James Joyce or Samuel Beckett, although in recent years there has been an upsurge of interest in his work, thanks to reissues published by Dalkey Archive and other presses. Born in Celbridge, County Kildare in 1927, Higgins died in 2015 in Kinsale, County Cork, where he had been living with his wife, the writer Alannah Hopkin. Over the course of his life, Higgins travelled extensively, and his oeuvre is permeated with a cosmopolitanism that set him apart from his contemporaries. Higgins's widely acclaimed first novel, *Langrishe, Go Down* (1966), was adapted as a screenplay for the BBC by Harold Pinter. Elegiacally tracing the decline of a once-wealthy family through the lives of four daughters, the novel has been described by John Banville and others as Higgins's masterpiece. Later works, such as the sun-drenched *Balcony of Europe* and the epistolary novel *Bornholm Night-Ferry*, eschew the conventions of plot and fabulation in favour of an autobiographical, allusive, discursive style. 'No one else has blurred the gap between fact and fiction quite like Ireland's unconventional octogenarian', wrote a reviewer in *The Guardian* in 2008.

In a late-career creative surge, Higgins wrote his 'Bestiary' autobiographical trilogy, *Donkey's Years*, *Dog Days*, and *The Whole Hog*. As with his novels, these books playfully roam the liminal territory between fiction and memoir. Aidan Higgins is a precursor to the recent international writers who have re-energised prose by similarly splicing non-fiction and fiction, such as Karl Ove Knausgaard, Geoff Dyer, and W. G. Sebald. A rich example of Higgins's hard-to-categorise, romantic, sensuous work, 'Helsingør Station' can be found in *Flotsam & Jetsam*, a collection of Higgins's writings published by Dalkey Archive.

Helsingør Station

Matterly Light

IN DENMARK EVERY DAY is different; so say the old books. It's made up of islands, every island different, and a witch on each. There are over 300 of them. I knew one of them once. She lived in Copenhagen, that port up there on Kattegat. We were fire and water, like Kafka and Milena, a daring combination only for people who believe in transformations, or like boiling water. You were Mathilda de la Mole.

No, you were you to the end of your days. Why should I complain? The other day I was thinking of you.

The pale Swedish dramatist who lives over on Sortedam Dossering with a distinguished Danish theatrical lady claims that he has learnt Danish in bed. Across the long wall of the Kommune Hospital a solicitous female hand had inscribed a proclamation to the effect that many of the nurses there are lesbians, too. Ten years ago the nurses of this city were regarded as being no better than common whores.

Down there in a basement you had lived like a rat with good old Psycho, in a lice-ridden hole below street level in a kind of cellar, the walls green with mould. Water dripped from above, you suffered, Petrusjka was but a babe. The place was full of furnace fumes by day, rats ran about at night, chewed up your stockings. Drunks fell down into the area. You lived there then. I didn't know you. Where was I?

This Danish capital is a tidy well-run place. The little grey city is relatively free of the subversive aerosol squirt and graffiti-smeared walls of West Berlin; though the pedestrian underpass near Bar Lustig is marked with a daring axiom to the effect that *Kusse er godt for hodet* or cunt is good for the head, with a crude heart pierced by an arrow.

You wrapped newspapers inside your clothes, crouched behind Psycho Kaare, your arms about him, bound for Sweden. That was your life then. All the associations with your lovers seem to have been pre-ordained, moving rapidly towards consummation. He was the third man in your life. Blind in one eye, 192 centimetres tall, a failed dramatist turned carpenter, transvestite, father-to-be of little Petrusjka Kaare.

You lied to the shop-girls. The outsize dresses were not for 'a big mum', but for Psycho, wanting the impossible, garbed in female attire, ill, unshaven, chain-smoking, drinking Luksus beer, looking out the window into the street of whores. There was a strange smell off his breath. Both of you were under-nourished, half starving. You left him, lived with an alcoholic pianist for three weeks. Then you couldn't stand it any more— there was an even worse smell off *him*. Empty turps bottles crowded the WC. You swallowed your pride and approached your mother for a loan. Mrs Edith Olsen gave it grudgingly. You returned to Psycho, the tall unshaven figure in the chair, dressed as a woman, looking out the window.

Then you were standing for an endless time with your hand on the red Polish kettle that was getting warmer and warmer; knowing that an important moment had arrived for you. You would go to bed with him. He would be the father of your only child. So nothing is ever entirely wasted, nothing ever entirely spent. Something always remains. What? Shall I tell you?

Oh he was a young man once, and very thin. He knew Sweden, had been there before. He arranged the papers for rent-ing a house. It was cheap there then. He was writing one-act plays, a mixture of Dada and Monty Python. They were funny. He sat cross-legged on a chair, typing away, laughing. As a child he had done homework with frozen feet stuck to the cold floor.

The Royal Theatre rejected the plays. You loved him. Light came from his face. He was young once; not any more. In his early forties he had begun to grow old. Now he is a dead man.

The motorbike, covered in sacks, hid under snow. All the boards in the hut creaked. Winter pressed down on the roof. In the *dacha*, you and Psycho began starving again. A plump partridge strutted up and down in the garden every evening. Each evening it returned. Armed with a stick Psycho waited behind a tree. You watched from the window. The bird was too clever, Psycho too weak with hunger, the cooking pot stayed empty. You wept.

Then Psycho couldn't stand it any longer and left for Copenhagen, the cellar and the rats. He couldn't take it any longer. You couldn't bear to return and stayed on. You were alone for weeks, made a fire at night, to keep off the living men, and the dead men too. The dead were full of guile and slippery as eels.

Going into Sweden on the back of Psycho's motorbike you had almost died of cold. Motorcyclists are known to experience a sense of detachment, and *may not even recall arriving at their destination*. St Brendan the Navigator saw Judas chained to an iceberg in the middle of the Atlantic. It happened once a year, by God's mercy, a day's relief for the betrayer from his prison in the everlasting fires of Hell.

But you accepted all the buffetings of fate. You walked into the forest. You said: 'It's difficult to think in a forest. I am thinking *av karse*, but the thought never finds its end, as near the mountains or by the sea. It's heavy in there, the wall of trees keeps out the sun. There is absolute silence in the Swedish forest, no singing birds there. Even the *uuuls* are silent. Oh that was a miss for me.'

In the forest you came face to face with an elk. The great prehistoric head was suddenly there, the mighty span of horns, the mossy tines, set like an ancient plough into the weighty head.

You glared, separated by only the breadth of a bedroom. The great beast was grey all over, like a certain type of small Spanish wild flower found in the hills. The dead flower in the jar of the Cómpeta bedroom.

Then, without a sound, without breaking a twig, the elk faded away into the forest. It was very quiet there. Heavy too, like the Swedes themselves. They worked all day, raced home in identical Volvos in the evening, closed their doors. It was a *Shakespearean* forest, you thought, with no dead leaves, no undergrowth, but mossy underfoot. The light there was very dim, angled in, then draining away. *Matterly light*, you thought. Elks moved always in 'matterly light', fading back into the silence out of which they had come. The Swedish-Shakespearean wilderness.

Perhaps the best idea is to imagine a country, never going there. Otherwise you end up writing impressionistic letters from abroad, while feeling superior to those who stayed home.

We were in Spain, in a *pueblo* in the sierras. It was raining. Outside, a narrow wet street of glistening umbrellas. We sat in a window annexe, waited an hour for a poor meal. You didn't mind, drinking *vino*, telling me about your flat, where I had never been. You described it. The Russian icon with the bullet-hole. It had been torn from a Moscow wall during the Revolution. You described the delicate colours of a Chinese scroll. The pewter candlesticks of 1840 with a lump of lead soldered into it, making it less valuable. Your apartment overlooked the lake. Your landlady was unhinged. From a ground-floor window she watched you come and go, wanted to get you out. You rode a tall old bike. Psycho worked as a self-employed carpenter above the brothel quarter.

'I always talk in showers,' you said, 'and then I am sad.' Your green eyes, as if never seeing clearly what they looked at, looked at me, took me in. Who was this? You seemed to be chewing on memories of other times, places, situations, other loves.

You travelled about, to Venice, the Scilly Isles, Greece, finally Spain, where I was to meet you. At Naxos you saw the seabed of the most delicate, and 'there was the finest sands I have ever seen'. In Tripoli, of all places, you found timelessness. You felt at home there in its endless evenings, far from the Western mess.

Pastel was your favourite shade. The long evenings on Naxos, where you had mourned a lost love, were pastel coloured. Not mauve, not lilac, nor scarlet as on the Algarve. You, Misery's Mistress, grown beautiful, in sunglasses, walked through the pastel shades. The 'Greekish' men chased scantily clad foreign women into the sea or through the pine woods. Hippies copulated in the most public places. On the beach, in the backs of crowded buses.

You told me of your first love. It wasn't really love. His name had been Olsen too, a married man. You went to bed with him in Olsen's Hotel because he had spoken lovingly to you of his wife, then in childbed. You were on a cycling trip with your plain friend Alice. You were sixteen, become attractive after endless puberty. It was Easter 1958 at Holbaek, sixty kilometres from Copenhagen. Hymns were relayed from a loudspeaker into the square. You ordered Tuborg, an orange juice for Alice. You wore jeans and an anorak, a late developer, flat-chested. You entered the men's toilet by mistake after the Tuborg and came out whistling to hide your embarrassment. 'I thought it were a boy,' remarked a rustic.

Bjørn Olsen was a commercial traveller in perfumes. He was kind. At first you said no and then yes. You were shocked by the size of his prick. This was serious stuff. But it wasn't love.

You were nineteen in the country, with the plainness of puberty gone. You spent a weekend with a couple of friends and ended up in bed with them. Andersen the painter was 'insatiable and fucked all the good-looking girls'. He wanted you in bed with his beautiful redheaded wife. First her and then you. Andersen would not take no. The whole house creaked.

You tried to take your life by opening a vein in your wrist with the point of a pencil. It had nothing to do with Andersen, you didn't want to live, had nothing to live for, you opened the vein, closed your eyes, covering yourself with your overcoat.

'But, as you see, I recovered. Afterwards you feel worse than before. I felt so ashamed. You are still alive and the bed soaked with blood.'

Things will never be the same again. No, things are the same as they always were, only you're the same too, so things will never be the same again. I say things but I may mean times and places. Times with you. Is the memory of things better than the things themselves? We will never know. But no matter what happens I still love you very much, though obviously in my life 'love' has to be betrayed, and many times. I do not know why this is so. I only know I am relieved to have finished, yet in a perverse way I'm still the same, and nothing has changed.

In a stand of oak a leaf falls. Queen Caroline Mathilde, dressed as a man, goes out riding. She is on the lookout for the son of the German cobbler Struensee with whom she is besotted. He enjoys her favours, in between advising the king—and who is himself insane and knows full well that the queen's condition is incurable.

We stayed in a hotel in Málaga, coming and going like marine creatures in a grotto of transparent water, in the depths of the fine old mirrors set into the doors of two hanging cupboards in room *número* 37 on the fourth floor of Hotel Residencia Cataluña on Plaza del Obispo facing the cathedral. The gonging bell galvanized us at every stroke. At the corner some stonemasons were chipping away tirelessly at tombstones, covered in fine white dust.

You told me of Diana's mirrors, Nero's sunken brothelship. We went out. You found it was cold and returned for your poncho. The lift attendant asked were you married. I bought a small hand mirror for Petrusjka, whom I had never seen. I told you

about the red spot on Jupiter. When daylight struck the bev-
elled edges, the mirrors threw out rainbow hues. We came and
went in them, nude as newts, as in a deep-focus medium shot
thrown on the black-and-white screen by Toland. They were
fine old-fashioned mirrors such as you do not come across today.
Whatever has happened to those far-off happy days? Were they
happy days? Was being with you happiness for me? And with
me for you? Were we happy then?

One morning you said it was beginning to end, you could
feel it. You had to go away again. The return flight was booked.
The stonemasons continued chipping away, covered in fine
dust, as we went past for the last time. Málaga was Yo-Yo-mad.
It was the day of the *Subnormales*. A child dressed up as a bride
was being photographed in the Alameda Gardens as we passed
through, climbing up through the levels of the Alcazaba, past
the cruising gays anxious as whippets. Below appeared the bull-
ring, the sanded oval, tiers of empty seats; beyond it the port. A
long rusty Soviet oil tanker lay to in the dazzling bay. Covered
in sweat we climbed to the Hotel Gibralfaro, which belongs
to another European time. Maids in black taffeta were waiting
at table. I was charged 400 pesetas for a half-bottle of chilled
Valdapenas. Over by the bar stood von Strohein, the great director of *Greed*, with his back to us, in riding-breeches, whip under
one arm, a monocle screwed into one eye-socket, throwing back
double Scotch. We returned to our room late.

A seal-like hooded statue of Rasmussen in stone stands on the
Strandjev promenade, a memorial to the hero of Thule. We
walked hand in hand down the promenade, which was the
length of your own childhood. To our left the seal-like hooded
figure stared out towards Kattegat. An ever-alert eye peered out
under bushy eyebrows stick with hoar-frost. We took a number
1 bus to Central Station, and walked out from there. You said
you wanted to show me places from your past. We presently

found one and went in. It was full of Danes. A pianist crouched over the keyboard and sang like a woman, high and mocking. Then a burly friend from the past came in, embraced you. He sat at the piano, began to play. It was part of the past when you had lived like a rat with good old Psycho. Someone had tried to cook their semen in a frying-pan. Perhaps the pianist?

Danish was very much a language of the stomach, you told me. *Mave* had a 'stomach-sound', as Mogens Glistrup was a most Danish name, Danish as Trudholm. 'Everything is dangerous to a Dane.' By Thulevej, a signpost above a small cliff, more chine than cliff, warns wanderers of *livsfare jordeskred*, unsteady earth.

Your apartment did not disappoint. It was the sort of nest you would find to live in, irregular in shape, with windows overlooking the lake. Your abode. I was there with you. The last swallows flew over the yacht basin and a skiff with two active oarsmen went skimming by. It was a bright September Sunday. Light scudded off the water, the clouds drifted up high.

You had read Walter Schubart's *Religion og Erotik* in translation and were full of it, spoke slightingly of St Paul, convert and martyr. He whom you called Paulus of Tarsus had 'fucked up' the teachings of Christ and changed Christendom.

And then? The wind threshing the hedges at Melby. A blue crossing over Kattegat (for we were *en route* for Rørvig). Six passengers sat silently in the narrow cabin as we crossed a thoroughly Danish sea to Skanse Hage. In the *fiskhus* the flounders caught that morning at Isefjord were breathing their last.

In the *bodega* at Hundested, that Place of Dogs, the recorded voice of Kathleen Ferrier sang 'Jesu, Joy of Man's Desiring' on the muted transistor. You had sung this at the top of your voice as a child, standing on a chair, to the astonishment of Papa Olsen, who played a cornet from the back of a truck with his group on Labour Day. In the yard an outsize dog frisked about our table. From another table an unsober Dane asked you:

'Why don't you come over and sit with us, and tell that fellow to go back to wherever he came from?'

And now we are approaching the Rasmussenhus. The signs have become vague and weathered; we are nearing the homestead of the hero of Thule. The dormer windows overlook Kattegat. He had built the house with his own hands. Before entering these hallowed precincts I enter you near the cliff face in the long grass, removing the minimum of clothes. We hear Danish voices passing amicably through the hidden paths.

He died in hospital outside Copenhagen in 1934, when I was seven years old and you not yet born. He died of flu and eating rotten seal-meat. He was fifty-four. His rare windswept spirit abides at Thulevej, in the Rasmussenhus set back among fir trees, protected from the elements. It looks out always at Kattegat's tides, sails, gulls, swans, the air and peace. A great pot-bellied stove occupies the study where he wrote up his diary, where a large white cat followed us silently from room to room.

Lev Lesbisk is painted prominently athwart the bridge approaches at Peblingessen. For fine young women live husbandless today in Denmark, with single children secure in carriers, cycling home from Klampenborg. The young mothers are turned their backs on menfolk. Or marriage. Venus (Lesbia) rules hereabouts.

In the little red train that takes us to Hundested from Hillerod, a woman no longer young is immersed in her book. The deliberating eyes are fixed steadfastly on the text, her slow right hand turns another page, as we move through this ordered countryside. A lynx-faced cat mews miserably in a basket. A drunk raises a Hof beer on a passing platform. The head of the cat is pushed out of sight by an abstracted female hand. Single dogs go prowling in the fields so bare of livestock or any living thing. Even bird life is missing. The wheat stubble is burning, scarring the fields with long black lines. The windbreaks are odd-looking things, if they are windbreaks. What else could they be?

Last spring we passed Kokkedal's cut hayfields. The dry hay was lying in neat swaths. Mown wheat. Cyclists drifted alongside the train, waving, thoroughly Danish, as the train traversed a region of lilac woods.

Now Vedbaek Rungstedlund where Baroness Blixen lies buried under her favourite tree; the Danish poets give Sunday readings there. We sat at a table under a tree at Humlebaek, coffee and Cognac before us, looked across at the white Swedish shore: a nuclear plant.

Thobin Thimm

It is an early September day in Copenhagen, sunny after yesterday's rain. Over Øster Søgade the mews make their cries of secateurs cutting. It's seventeen feet deep in the middle, and thus cannot be man-made, says the Swedish dramatist. Trust a Swede to notice that.

Handsome jogging couples pass in jogging outfits. Drained with fever I sleep. You nurse me. Plain yoghurt, purple grapes, chilled Rioja. For review comes *Wise Blood*. Sandra Holm arrives late and covers the bed in flowers. She is a little bull. I have some kind of virus. My temperature is 'midway between normal and where you die', the nurse tells me, studying the thermometer. I spend three days in bed.

Then, after washing off the death-sweat, I sally forth, feeling frail, unshaven. Into the thin sunlight, the *Kondilovers* go by, one attached to a dog on a lead. Muddy carp-like fish hang comatose in the shallow brown waters by the footpaths. The bomb shelters are overgrown. In the middle of the lake a small islet is covered in vegetation. In the garden of Bar Lustig a boy sells us grapes. It is autumn now in Denmark, the air cold and bracing. The foliage hangs stiffly. I feel unwell. Cyclists drift by. A crab-red sun sinks over the pseudo-bridge, a causeway for ingoing and outgoing traffic. The sky is clear as yesterday. Music drifts over the water. Though unwell, I feel irrationally happy, *feverishly* so. Green neon from the Finanbanken spills into Øster Søgade lake. Ambulance sirens sound off incessantly between the two hospitals. Danish dead are being hustled in and out.

Four white dray horses pull a Carlsberg wagon over the 'bridge', out of the past. A municipal cleaner in orange Day-Glo sweeps the path. The rush of air from fast cars—angelic wings. I start into the second American title: *Everything That Rises Must Converge*. Feeble things. My fever returns.

It has all come back: coughing, lemon drinks, bed-sweats, dry throat. The nude nurse is in bed with the feverish patient clasped in her arms. An enlarged harvest moon sinks over the pseudo-bridge. Traffic lights wink and blink like mooring lights lost in the trees. Tiny Brodini has no peace because of the magnitude of his task. You told me that your grandmother's name had been Lemm, which signifies Prick. She was Pomeranian, made good soups. So you had Hungarian-Pomeranian blood coursing in your veins.

You sat on the sofa, crossed your long stylish legs, stared at me. No one could have guessed what was in that grey-green look, even I did not know. You dialed a number, listened, replaced the receiver. Your transistor played low. Now you are stalking about before the long mirror, dressed only in Italian shoes with five-inch stiletto heels. You are 'paying the world a gleaming lie'.

Italians applaud at the end of every movement, I tell you. Danes slow-clap to show their appreciation. If the English do it it means the opposite, censure. The Chinese are fond of noise, and find silence oppressive. Similarly Greeks and Spaniards. Not so the Danes, you say, rolling your hips at me.

Then, lo and behold, I am well again. An old flame arrives from Jutland. Thobin Thimm is a painter, he and his sister run a rose farm in Jutland. He invites us to dine with him at a new

Italian place. Shape of the frog in the sauce. Grapy flavor of Italian wine, tang of the cheese. Petrusjka sits with us, a lady.

I stood you a haircut at Frisor Kirsten's near the Gyldne And or Golden Duck. Kirsten herself cut our hair; she dressed in black leather trousers, her hips bulged seductively as she snipped away with small scissors, and your slanted eyes watched me in the mirror. Thimm had gone to bed with Kirsten Arboll. She had lived in Johannesburg, thought that the blacks had not much to complain about. The sun shone through the glass annexe of the Gyldne. And where we drank gin. A numbing wind from Østersoen was sweeping the streets clean. Lutheran bells rang grudgingly in their belfries.

Dyrehaven was a woody place where few people went, with mole-casts between the trees and in the open, where there were low mounds. Baroness Blixen used to walk there. 'A life of sniffing and sleeping and fear,' you said, of the moles. 'What sort of existence was that?' Thobin had departed to Jutland.

Killian Turner

An Investigation into My Own Disappearance

THE DISTURBED AND DISTURBING writings and cross-disciplinary work of Killian Turner have exerted a covert influence on the arts in Ireland. Although his work remains largely out of print, the myth that has grown around Turner's strange life has led to a growing interest in his relatively short career. With a creative output curtailed by his mysterious disappearance (and probable suicide) in 1985, Turner is a somewhat uncanny figure who devoted himself to a strange, solitary artistic project in an era smothered by oppressive religious and moral structures. Like many of Ireland's writers, Turner achieved much of his work abroad.

Killian Turner was born in Dublin in 1948, and raised in the coastal suburb of Dalkey. From the outset his life was marked by unhappy circumstances. Turner was an only child whose mother died in childbirth. His father, a history teacher, succumbed to a long struggle with depression when Turner was eighteen, taking his own life. Turner lived on his inheritance for a number of years, moving between a series of addresses around Dublin and Wicklow. Although he did not pursue third-level studies, he was a prodigious reader and autodidact, conversant with the currents of contemporary continental philosophy and critical theory, as well as mythology and the mystical traditions. He was fascinated by the literature of drugs, psychedelic exploration, and extreme experience. The cosmic horror of H. P. Lovecraft was an early and abiding influence. Turner's first novel, *Edge of Voices*, was published in 1979. A bizarre, at times funny hybrid work, containing elements of sci-fi, scantly veiled memoir, and

metaphysical speculation, it has drawn comparisons to Philip
K. Dick's *VALIS*, which was published two years later.

Aged thirty-three, Turner spent a period travelling around
Europe before settling in West Berlin, where he would remain
until his disappearance in 1985. His provocative second novel,
The Garden, imagined an alternative present in which National
Socialism has triumphed across Europe, and a Nazified Ireland
has been converted into the 'granary' of the continent. One reviewer described the deadpan, plotless book as 'either a joke in
questionable taste, or the nostalgic, vindictive fantasy of a confused and lonely man, whose bitterness has bred a disingenuous
sympathy for the Nazis and for Hitler'. *The Garden* was to be
Turner's final novel; his writings thereafter became more fragmentary, obscure, and disturbing, dealing with extremes of sexuality and psychology. Published in numerous zines, journals,
and periodicals, Turner's shorter writings were published post-
humously as the collections *Erased Horizons, Forgotten Shores:
Essays 1975–1982*, and *Visions of Cosmic Squalor/The Upheaval*.

Turner is part of a European anti-canon of troubled, visionary authors that includes Antonin Artaud, Georges Bataille
(of whom Turner once speculated that he himself was the re-
incarnation), Friedrich Nietzsche, and the Marquis de Sade.
Conceived during the same period as his notorious late prose
work, the so-called 'House Sequence', the piece included here,
'Investigation Into My Own Disappearance', can be found in
Visions of Cosmic Squalor/The Upheaval.

Following a period of severe delusions, Killian Turner vanished in West Berlin in October of 1985. Officially declared a
missing person by the West German authorities some months
later, various conspiracy theories have emerged in the intervening years, but as has been documented elsewhere, it is likely that
Turner took his own life.

An Investigation Into My Own Disappearance

Editor's Note

IN WHAT HAS been called his 'suicide note' Killian Turner left detailed instructions, in the form of an annotated map of Berlin, detailing where and how to gather the materials that would make up his 'final literary work'. These materials included handwritten notes left in the apartments of four different friends and/or lovers (none of whom were acquainted with one another), several distinct lines of graffiti scrawled on the wall of holding cell no. 3 in Polizeiabschnitt 22 in Charlottenburg, and sheaves of paper secreted inside various items that Turner had left on long-term deposit in an array of pawnshops all over West Berlin. Turner did not leave any indication as to how the pieces should be arranged, only that the work as a whole—however arranged—should be called An Investigation Into My Own Disappearance. *In the instructions, Turner made it clear that the work comprised not only the texts found at the locations across Berlin, but the locations themselves, the efforts made to gather them, and any incidents, encounters, or conversations that took place during this process. In January 1986, Turner's friend and former collaborator, the experimental poet Evelyn Miles, gained possession of the map and proceeded to gather the scraps and fragments it led to, eventually releasing the material to the Turner Archive in 2014. The arrangement below is the current editor's. It is not intended to be final or definitive.* An Investigation Into My Own Disappearance *appears to have been composed in the months leading up to Turner's disappearance in October 1985 (therefore at approximately the same time as or slightly before the composition of the 'House Sequence'). Turner's mental state at the time of composition was thus one of extreme deterioration; there is evidence that Turner was convinced that the figments of his literary imagination were becoming real. As Thomas Duddy wrote in an essay on the convergences between the work of Turner and Georges Bataille published in* Radical Philosophy *in 1999: 'Given the troubling nature of Turner's visions, we might provisionally conclude that he killed himself out of moral duty, in order to prevent the terrible things he was writing about erupting into true existence.'*

An Investigation into my own disappearance.

Q: WHAT IS THE impossible task?
A: To be alive & dead. To be & not-be.

My First-Born Bastard

Romy's one of those people who spends all week enthusiastically raping the planet, because that's her job, & discovers her feeling for the oppressed when she's pissed at the weekend. *But hell, we all have to earn a buck.* Bobby Sands. A hero & a poet. Which is meant to impress me because i am Irish, although i have gone off the IRA & don't believe in such a thing, in real life, as heroes. Or poets, or the Irish. Romy had, earlier on in the evening, when she was still struggling to repress her wish to be fucked, & in reference to a passing remark i had made about a recently deceased celebrity junkie, accused (accused?) me of 'casual cruelty'. Where did this casual cruelty stand in the hierarchy of cruelty as opposed to planting no-warning bombs in public houses, i inquired? She didn't or pretended she didn't hear or understand in the din of the mangled throng. On the floor, her skirt lifted, my pants around my ankles. & afterwards, for days, i felt that minor guilt, persistent under everything i did, which i think i have picked-up like a mental disease from too many visits to cathedrals & libraries. Why did i fuck someone i do not love? That i hate, mildly - although this does not make her special . The ridiculous idea that i should marry her. A fully formed, glowing, perfectly happy child romping through summer meadows in my imagination whenever i let my guard down. A child whom i know or at least wish for its own sake cannot be born.

The shit-eater Jingle

let's call it a dream, & not something i sing to myself about every morning in the shower, if there is a shower. A toilet which flushes down into a dark cage. In the cage are two naked men. Specially selected from a whole army of captives, kept in a very large cage somewhere off-track on a vast estate in Bavaria. Two different naked men to shit on from a height every couple of days. Until they drown in it or die of disgust or the plague or whatever you die from eventually in such situations. The shower-song, which does not exist, & in any case is hardly a song, the little jingle say, the little jingle goes like this (*allegro andante*) 'oh who's a shit-eater, who's a shit-eater, who's a shit-eater today . . .' which is repeated until the end of the shower.

Phenakistoscope

the sense from the polizei the other night that they had captured an exotic non-native specimen. A specimen that had stepped through the TV screen out of a foreign, dubbed, made-for-TV movie, talking German in a voice not quite its own, lips not quite syncing. The one thing about being terribly intoxicated while under arrest is it doesn't hurt as much, although yes you wake up with bruises not knowing wherefore, like excellent sex. i have been arrested in daylight hours stone cold sober & i tell you it is no advantage to know you are being helplessly battered. The two uprights strained their gaze at me through a phenakistoscope in a 19th Century traveling fair. Two leery pigs out of a 1950's drive-in audience in the land of the hicks & the thicks - the appropriately credulous audience for such creations of the reactionary image-machine as *reefer madness* & *she shoulda said no* & *live fast die young.* I think they believed they had captured James Dean or Jim Morrison. As soon as they slammed & ratcheted the cell door I lay on the floor & masturbated thinking of James Dean as two cops either end of me & then fell asleep.

From Holding Cell 3

chronic envy syndrome. A rhapsody.

the bell we couldn't lay hands on.

We seek to dream. We dream to seek.

The search for God is the production of God.

Perhaps a writer is one who can mirror the whole world, and not commit suicide. Yet.

On the bridge

the real event will always disappoint because it has lost the sacred gleam of the imagined & foretold. Yet there are moments in many existences when the real gleams briefly ever so briefly with the rare & precious substance of the actualised foretold. It is for presence at one of these exceptional, ephemeral moments of transfiguration that the human being is seeking.

how he will get there

through the flashing, throbbing, blaring dark dense street-draining mouth of a nightclub on Winterfeldtplatz . . .

or down a disused manhole, the third one after the Cafe Kranzler, two thirds covered with a century of hardened, mineralising crowshit . . .

or some circular submarine access secreted in the labyrinth of pipes at the waterworks at Beelitzhof . . .

or in the underground car park of the Universität der Künste, behind the student union noticeboard . . .

or it will be a golden knob you turn half way up the cone of the radio tower . . .

or it will be a screen made of water inside the penthouse of the CEO, where there will be many people in silken bathrobes, smoking . . .

What it is

Some will say warehouse. Stock control centre. Zoo of the damned, the circumstantially abandoned, the utterly owned, sold-before-birth. Those whom destiny, dark legate of time, hates most. Karma sink. Holocaust Continuation Project. Apocalypse Threshold. Rendering Unit. Sade's show-house.

Santa-Never-Comes. Though deep underground, it is very bright. High roofed, as high as the Duomo of Florence, to accommodate the cages. Cages are piled upon cages to the height of the Duomo. Most stock can only be viewed by cranes. They are fed & hosed by crane also. They are not crowded, however. One per cage, 6 by 12. Cages all weaponised & electronically monitored. Communication between cages is punishable by summary execution by overwhelming electric shock.

Market Statistics

In this matter facts are difficult to accumulate. No specific accounting exists. A credible guess, after four years of study (those four years since *the suspicion* first gripped me), based on scattered police figures, articles in journals of radical sociology, UNESCO fact-files, sundry & often contradictory newspaper articles in various languages i can read or half-read, a good hundred ministerial dossiers . . . indicates that between the Urals & the Azores, between Lapland & Gavdos, annually, *circa* 25,000 children under 16 go missing & are not found. These are drawn from the most miserable layers, the bulk being escapees/runaways from orphanages, foster homes, half-way houses & or juvenile detention centres of various sorts. The rest come from other forlorn demographics & the most downtrodden immigrant communities. Curiously, these children are always described as *escaped* or *absconded* but never as *kidnapped*. Rich children do not go missing. In a ten year period we are talking about quarter of a million children of misery. Distraught, crazy Berga, who made it over the wall & whose entire family have subsequently been arrested, says that children are worth 6 figure dollar sums on the east-west interblocular black market & that before she got over the wall she had been working on a case where a claim had been made that two children from an orphanage in Leipzig had been exchanged for seven 4-axle truck-loads of Levi 501s. Do the maths—a business worth 25 million a year if it can be imagined that the children are rounded up by the same 'company' & brought to market in the same way. & it can be imagined. I have imagined it.

Lakshmi Logic

Saw Lakshmi speak last night at the Freie Universität. At the end of her presentation she cleared her throat & asked every-one to leave except black women. i obliged as did all other non-black women in the audience. Was i the only one put in mind of the last time in Germany groups of people were segre-gated according to gender, race . . . ? Horrid echoes. Lakshmi is not atypical of the international literati that are a kind of excrescence of the failure of '68 to make real change outside the university bubble. Her sentiments are noble, her poems atrocious. The Greeks had high sentiments, & great literature, & slaves who were not allowed to marry or to hold on to their children. It is not possible to make the recorded past nor the present cohere from a moral-aesthetic perspective. Only prehistory & the future, because they are entirely speculative realms, can be painted as morally just in the sense that the ones who produce the best art are the ones who deserve, by way of their exceptional suffering, to produce the best art. But let us imagine this to be the case in the present. Going by let's call it *Lakshmi Logic*, the million children kept in cages somewhere underneath Berlin would then be the greatest artists in exis-tence—& whoso believes in the transfiguring power of art, a power without the dream of which there can be no notion of art worth having, will be driven, at all costs, to witness this great work, even if it is only for a second or two before being shot or overwhelmingly electrocuted.

speaking out of the pain of having to live a difference that has no name says Lakshmi.

Why i must disappear

to render the impossible.

Gender & Race Neutral Story

Time vomited the market. The market attacked the boss. The boss disciplined the grown-up. The grown-up battered the child. The child bate the cat. The cat caught the rat. But the rat got away. Only the rat, only the rat, only the rat got away.

The other direction

Someone, apparently a man, was shot last night trying to get over the wall. First time in a couple of years. Radio now playing west-german border cop recording of the *grab vorfall.* Rifle Shots. Couple of cops or soldiers barking indecipherably as they approach. & then the guy, sounding cheerful believe it or not, *so you guys got me after all.* My thought: has anyone ever tried to get over the wall, which is also the wall between life & death for so many, in the other direction?

Hillary McTaggart

A Night on the Tiles

HILLARY MCTAGGART, A RELATIVE of the composer Ina Boyle, grew up in Enniskerry, County Wicklow. Born prematurely in 1949, she suffered throughout her short life from respiratory illness as well as nervous ailments. As a teenager she studied flute at the Royal Academy of Music, as well as drama, before reading French and English at Trinity College Dublin. Upon graduating McTaggart spent time in Paris and London. In Paris she became acquainted with feminist figures such as Luce Irigaray and Élisabeth Roudinesco. In London she made an unsuccessful attempt to enter stage acting. Upon returning to Ireland she lived for a few years at the family home in Enniskerry, where she committed herself to writing, before marrying an accountant and moving to Luxembourg, at which point she gave up her literary focus. After a year in Luxembourg she fell ill and died of tuberculosis, three days before her thirtieth birthday.

Little of McTaggart's writing was published during her lifetime, and the recent revival of interest in her work is due to research by Gerry Dukes of manuscripts held by David McTaggart, the writer's brother. Hillary McTaggart's only book, still unpublished, is *Address Book*, a remarkable series of prose pieces of varying lengths mostly written in the second person. Though the style is difficult to categorise, its basis in 'addresses' bears the influence of the stylised declamatory register of French prosody, as well as that of Beckett. The short prose piece 'A Night on the Tiles' was McTaggart's first published work, appearing in *The Honest Ulsterman* in 1973. An article on Edna

O'Brien's *Country Girls Trilogy* published in *The Irish Press* in 1974 effectively put paid to McTaggart's literary ambitions: scathing and mean-spirited, the article (according to Dukes) led to McTaggart being blackballed by UK and Irish publishers.

A Night on the Tiles

YOU TAKE IT EVERY night before dawn. Sometimes just one dose, sometimes two. The yellow pill on your plastic tongue—the living room carpet, the dull lamplight. But regardless of the dosage, and regardless of the particular crepuscular shade outside—rosy fingered or wintery white—that drug you take, Dottie, always has the same effect.

First one of your hands, whichever hand you've been eating with, starts to swell. Within a second that pink plastic hand has swollen so gigantically that, not only do your fingers now fill the living room—knuckles in the cornices and thumb squished under the windowsill and the grandfather clock and rocking chair akimbo—but that one-second measure in which your outlandish growth spurt happens dilates so much and subdivides into so many distinct durational segments that, really Dottie, it literally feels like an hour has passed, that singular second subdividing into so many distinct phases that, to be honest, I could probably count ninety distinct stages within your plastic hand's enormous drug-induced swelling.

Backstepping into the kitchen doorway, in the shadow of your now colossal plastic hand, I ponder what to do. Due to the abrupt change of scale, it's even tricky to tell whether your pink hand has grown to room-size or whether the wallpapered walls and everything within them, myself included, have shrunken to hand-size—no inertial frame of reference, you see. Like *Alice in Wonderland* in a house in Enniskerry. 'Queer' doesn't begin to cover it.

Guided by instinct I take a big empty shoebox and pass through the kitchen out to the garage. Without really thinking I place in the shoebox two kitchen tiles, several rashers of bacon and some red and yellow billiard balls, along with two green slugs from the ground. Back in the kitchen I lay this concatenation out on the table. My thinking is that in order to comprehend this unfortunate loss of domestic standards— in order to counteract the spiriting away of those day-to-day Cartesian coordinates by which we measure and balance and make sense of things—one must create a miniature model of the whole ghastly size-distorting process using this shoebox full of mundane bric-a-brac. For what better way of restoring domestic decorum than by finding the optimal geometrical relationship that obtains between some billiard balls and some strips of bacon?

As I lay out the bacon slice by slice on top of the dusty tiles you needn't tell me how ridiculous I look. All the other girls from Alexandra are safely tucked up in bed beside their husbands while here I am, unkempt, unslept, and greasy-haired, shunting around slugs and billiard balls at dawn for my beloved doll. In contrast to virtually everyone else, though, I never let some misplaced sense of modesty get in the way of really *living*; in all my years I've never let that voice that says *One must not do that!* obscure my discovery, in my native habitual solitude, of the unadulterated brilliance of objects and things. You and I are not like the others, Dottie, so let our walls veritably blossom with bacon if needs be; for despite what they say it is obvious to me, at least, that we have not tasted or tested nearly *half* enough. For all we know life's perennially sought-after alchemical elixir may well turn out to be not some cordial potion in a gilded goblet but the dank moisture in a stranger's armpit. Let us forgo mores and lick life's armpit, I say.

Where was I? O yes—the dawn, your gigantism, my shoebox.

Now, as I've said, the collection of objects in the shoebox comprises a small-scale model of what has happened to you. There are various ways to conceive how this works. One could say, for example, that my careful distribution around the house of this collection of objects—walking over and putting a slice of bacon behind the curtains, for example, and then grabbing a yellow billiard ball and placing it in the vase of red roses on the kitchen window—is much like the composition of a code that unlocks a safe. Or one could consider it like an interactive scale-model doll's house of the house we are now in. Each a valid analogy. For me, though, Dottie, the best way to think of the shoebox-issued configuration is as a *mathematical model* by which these lights and colours and messy real-world stuff are abstracted into a simpler, easier-to-grasp form—a symbolic arrangement of data one can shift and shimmy about in order to find the desired solution, as expressed in the form of an unknown quantity, a hidden yet very real function.

When I now put one of the slugs in my hair, for instance, then open the back door and cast a red billiard ball onto the gravel in the driveway with a scrunch, and then in the kitchen stuff five slices of bacon into one of the chipped china teacups from the larder—and carry out these three operations *in that exact order*—I know this will bring about a certain outcome; which in this case is to make your gigantic hand shrink somewhat, make the rest of your body correspondingly grow somewhat, and also make hair start sprouting from your oversized hand, making hand-hair sprout swiftly by a metre and then stop. If each operation is followed in a logical sequence by another such operation, and then another, and then another—well, Dottie, it's like standing at a blackboard with a piece of chalk and working through a complicated equation until, without having in the least been able to foresee it in advance, one suddenly lights upon an elegant solution—just like Euclid, I think to myself, as I place a yellow billiard ball in the fridge-freezer beside the peas.

What happens next is that, your hand-hair having sprouted, I'm obliged to go upstairs to my bedroom, take out my biggest comb from the dresser, come back down and comb your hair—*to spruce you up*. Standing there in the dim-lit threshold, listening to the birds now avidly chirping outside as I comb your swollen hand's dark locks, I muse that it's a bit like that scene in the movie *The Birds* where Tippi Hedren, in her green cocktail dress, slips upstairs in the house that's been subject to an avian siege and from the corridor glances into one of the bedrooms only to see slumped by the bed the corpse of a man with black holes where his eyes should be, his peepers horridly pecked hollow. Actually, no, it's not like that at all. I ruminate, combing your thick hand-hair. I suppose it *is* quite like that scene in *The Birds* in that, were I not writing all of this out, none of what I am describing—the big hand, the slug hair, the dawn rendering lamplight redundant—would really even be happening at all, while in *The Birds*, had Tippi Hedren not ascended the stairs in her olive-green dress, followed by the camera crew, and not glanced into the bedroom in a stylised way, in a sense the man's face in close-up with his eyes gouged out wouldn't have 'happened' either, for we wouldn't have seen him, would we?

A chime from the grandfather clock breaks me from this reverie.

Your straggly hair is now neater so I put away the comb now and take out the second of the slugs—the first slug still being in my hair—and place the slimy thing in the sink. Then I open the cupboard, take out the saltcellar and drench the slug in a bath of snow-white salt. O, no doubt about it, Dottie, it's thoroughly cruel. But really, in this case such cruelty is necessary. For, you see, as the slug, in intense, slow-sizzling disquiet, begins to dissolve into goo, the biological 'enormity' of that micro-event, in combination with your having had the pretence of normality restored through the 'normal everyday act' of combing your hair, serves to shift the locus of 'enormity' away from your hand and onto the disintegrating slug—out of the living room, into the sink, as one might say. In effect it effects a *transference of enormity.* And as a consequence, my dear doll, you now begin to shrink. What a relief! Behind your shrinking form the lucent living room curtains begin to reappear. Your shadow begins to shorten. Enormity has slinked off. My act of slug violence has restored order. Our interminable night is almost over.

All that remains, Dottie, as your plastic body shrinks, are the tiles, those two dusty green and purple tiles taken from the garage, now lying on the kitchen table. For without the correct placement of those two tiles, in concert with the already distributed items, unfortunately you will proceed in a quite heinous manner to shrink well past the human scale down into the miniscule, which needless to say would be inconvenient. Strange bedfellows, scale and tiles. Here we arrive at the *denouement* of the whole drama, where my immolation of the slug and your 'reverse growth' must be followed by an appropriate 'functionalisation' of the purple and green tiles. In my dressing gown in the brightening interior I dash about, from the sink to the front door, from the front door to the living room threshold, from the living room threshold back to the kitchen table—upon which I now notice a jar of nail polish. *Voilà!* I place the purple and green tiles on the threshold between the living room and kitchen. Making sure not only that you and I, Dottie, are in each other's line of vision, but furthermore that we form a straight line with the dissolving slug in the kitchen sink—I being the central vertex and each of you diameter points—I put my slippered feet now one by one on the tiles and, standing like this in the doorway, begin to paint my nails with the nail polish, applying the little brush, in careful dabs, to my enamel. This activates the functional destiny of those two tiles. As is obvious to anyone in the house with a pair of eyes, and even to those simply reading what I've written here, those two purple and green tiles salvaged from Daddy's shed are, within our lately coordinated system, the large scale counterparts of my small-scale fingernails. As my fingernails are to my hands—hard coloured ornaments—so those tiles are to the domestic interior. I dab and dab, fingers outstretched, and by affirming the blue nail varnish in this way I am affirming—in the most sartorially indubitable manner—the extension of the radius of social propriety all the way from Dublin's glimmering ballrooms to this homely living room in Enniskerry; I am affirming that, far from being absent, logic and decorum are absolutely with us here within these walls; I am affirming that, though at this hour our vision be grown bleary, nevertheless the unblinking eye of civic propriety sees us clearly, Dottie, and recognises us clearly; and, well, *why not let's all just settle down and exist together at the same scale once again!* In this way, heavy-limbed and tired but comfortably at the helm, I stand upright in the living room threshold, my feet on the two tiles, daubing my fingernails blue, blueing my pure nails and blueing them and blueing my nails some more. When the cap closes on the bottle of nail varnish, I look up and see you sat in the middle of the carpet at exactly the correct size once again. All's well that ends well.

Coda. Upon returning to your regular doll size and regular doll proportions, despite its having been inconvenient, nevertheless you still harbour a degree of regret for your lost monstrosity—since, admittedly, maladroitness notwithstanding, monstrosity does at least take one away from the horrible ubiquity of day-to-day *ennui*—the sun rising in the morning, the sun falling at night and everything tedious in between. Therefore, by way of compensation, through the radiant blue of my fingernails—which creates a basin of physical attraction— nature's genius deems that our living room and kitchen, in one last flourish, now be transformed into a vaulted dome of bluest wonder, I standing under the centre of this vast blue dome, you and the slug-puddle on the perimeters, a blue nocturnal eminence undulating from my nails, our domestic living space becoming a vaulted fake firmament full of twinkling stars, the night-sky of Mozart's *Zauberflöte*, and I the Queen of the Night in her extravagant gown, singing her acrobatic arias—I, on the tiles, in my dressing gown! Thus it concludes. Though your bodily explosion and your gigantic hand's girth has put our upright piano out of tune in the most ghastly way, nevertheless, in this enchanted moment under this vast blue dome in this vast blue dawn, let your fingers play on those ivory keys, Dottie—let the piano's little hammers valiantly strike the tautened strings in the sounding box—and—as outside the gravel scrunches under the postman's feet—let our whole blue house ring out now finally in a wonderfully hideous harmony! Let the house be drenched in beautifully harmonious discord at this, our scene's culmination, at this, our adventure's end, without which out-of-tune celebratory valedictory song, those slices of bacon in the chipped teacup would simply be so many slices of bacon in a chipped teacup, the slug in my hair would simply be a slug in my hair, and the billiard ball in the flowerpot would simply be a billiard ball in a flowerpot—so many loose tickets to a sideshow of madness—though you and I would know better!

Desmond Hogan

Kennedy

THROUGHOUT THE DECADE that followed the publication of Desmond Hogan's excellent debut novel, *The Ikon Maker*, in 1976, he looked poised to be a literary star. Living in London in the early eighties, Hogan shared an agent with Ian McEwan, Salman Rushdie, and Bruce Chatwin, and was a close friend of Kazuo Ishiguro. However, while these writers ascended to worldwide fame, Desmond Hogan's destiny was to be stranger and grimmer. Following a series of highly regarded short story collections and novels, he vanished from the literary world, trailing rumours of escalating paranoia and psychic disintegration while drifting around Europe. Only in recent years has he reemerged from obscurity, rekindling the prestige he enjoyed during his period of youthful promise.

Born in Ballinasloe, County Galway, in 1950, Desmond Hogan studied at University College Dublin, where he met the writer and filmmaker Neil Jordan. With the help of several other aspiring writers, Hogan and Jordan set up the Irish Writer's Co-operative, which published *The Ikon Maker*. The novel depicted the troubled, burgeoning homosexuality of an alienated young man, and his mother's anguish as he becomes increasingly alien to her. A reviewer in the *Cork Examiner* wrote, 'Like no other Irish writer just now, Hogan sets down what it's like to be a disturbed child of what seems a Godforsaken country in these troubled times'. Hogan was awarded the Rooney Prize for Irish Literature in 1977.

A restless traveller, Hogan left Ballinasloe young and drifted for years between rented rooms in London, and later, among various European and American cities. A book of his travel writings, *The Edge of the City*, was published by Faber & Faber in 1993. His fragmentary novel *A Farewell to Prague* further exploited Hogan's global wanderings to evocative effect, as do many of his short stories. Hogan's fascination with gypsy and traveller culture, with its ancient storytelling tradition, infuses his oeuvre.

In recent years there have been reissues of Hogan's books, translations (he is the first living Irish writer to have his entire oeuvre published in French), and plenty of new work. Robert McCrum, Hogan's former editor at Faber, stoked interest when he wrote a long *Observer* article titled 'The Vanishing Man', which portrayed Hogan as a solitary, troubled, gifted figure. Admired by such writers as Colm Tóibín, Desmond Hogan has lately influenced a younger generation of writers, including Dave Lordan and Kevin Barry.

Kennedy

A NINETEEN-YEAR-OLD youth is made to dig a shallow grave in waste ground beside railway tracks near Limerick bus station and then shot with an automatic pistol.

Eyes blue-green, brown-speckled, of blackbird's eggs.

He wears a hoodie jacket patterned with attack helicopters.

Murdered because he was going to snitch—go to the guards about a murder he'd witnessed—his friend Cuzzy had fired the shot. The victim had features like a Western stone wall. The murder vehicle—a stolen cobalt Ford Kuga—set on fire at Ballyneety near Lough Gur.

The hesitant moment by Lough Gur when blackthorn blossom and hawthorn blossom are unrecognizable from one another, the one expiring, the other coming into blossom.

Creeping willow grows in the waste ground near Limerick bus station—as it was April male catkins yellow, with pollen, on separate tree small greenish female stamens. In April also whitlow grass which Kennedy's grandmother Evie used to cure inflammation near fingernails and toenails.

In summer creeping cinquefoil grows in the waste ground.

He was called Kennedy by Michaela, his mother, after John F. Kennedy, and Edward Kennedy, both of whom visited this city, the latter with a silver dollar haircut and tie with small knot and square ends. He must have bought a large jar of Brylcreem with him, Kennedy's father, Bongo, remarked about him.

"When I was young and comely,
Sure, good fortune on me shone,
My parents loved me tenderly."

A pious woman found Saint Sebastian's body in a sewer and had a dream he told her to bury him in the catacombs.

Catacumbas. Late Latin word. Latin of Julian the Apostate who studied the Gospels and then returned to the Greek gods.

The Catacombs. A place to take refuge in. A place to scratch prayers on the wall in. A place to paint in.

Cut into porous tufa rock, they featured wall paintings such as one of the three officials whom Nebuchadnezzar flung in the furnace for not bowing before a golden image of him in the plain of Dura in Babylon but who were spared.

Three officials, arms outstretched, in pistachio-green jester's apparel amid flames of maple red.

The body of Sebastian the Archer refused death by arrows and he had to be beaten to death. Some have surmised the arrows were symbolic and he was raped.

As the crime boss brought Kennedy to be murdered he told a story:

"I shook hands with Bulldog who is as big as a Holstein Friesian and who has fat cheeks.

It was Christmas and we got a crate and had a joint.

He says, 'I have the stiffness.'

He slept in the same bed as me in the place I have in Ballysimon.

In the morning he says, 'Me chain is gone and it was a good chain. I got it in Port Mandel near Manchester.'

He pulled up all the bedclothes.

He says 'I'll come back later and if I don't get me chain, your Lexus with the wind-down roof will be gone.'

He came back later but he saw the squad car—'the scumbags,' he said—and he went away.

A week later I saw Cocka, a hardy young fellow, with Bulldog's chain, in Sullivan's Lane."

The crime boss, who is descended from the Black and Tans,

himself wears a white-gold chain from Crete, an American gold ring large as a Spanish grandee's ring, a silver bomber jacket, and pointy shoes of true white.

He has a stack of *Nude* magazines in his house in Ballysimon, offers you a custard and creams from a plate with John Paul II's—Karol Wojtyła's—head on it, plays Country and Western a lot:

Sean Wilson—"Blue Hills of Breffni," "Westmeath Bachelor."

Sean Moore—"Dun Laoghaire Can Be Such a Lonely Place."

Johnny Cash—"I Walk the Line."

Ballysimon is famed for a legitimate dumping site but some people are given money to dump rubbish in alternative ways.

"Millionaires from dumping rubbish," it is said of them.

By turning to violence, to murder, they create a history, they create a style for themselves. They become ikons as ancient as Calvary.

Matthew tells us his Roman soldier torturers put a scarlet robe on Christ, Mark and John a robe of purple.

Emerging from a garda car Kennedy's companion and accomplice Cuzzy, in a grey pinstripe jersey, is surprised into history.

Centurion's facial features. A flick of hair to the right above his turf cut makes him a little like a crested grebe.

South Hill boys like Cuzzy are like the man-eating mares of King Diomedes of the Bistones that Hercules was entrusted to capture—one of the twelve labours King Eurystheus imposed on him.

"If I had to choose between Auschwitz and here," he says of his cell, "I'd choose Auschwitz."

As Kennedy's body is brought to Janesboro Church some of his brothers clasp their hands in an attitude of prayer. Others simply drop their heads in grief.

Youths in suits with chest hammer pleats and cigarette-rolled shoulders. Mock-snake skin shoes. With revolver cufflinks.

One of the brothers has a prison tattoo—three Chinese letters in biro and ink—on the side of his right ear.

The youngest brother, who is the only one to demur jacket and tie, has his white shirt hanging over his trousers and wears a silver chain with boxing gloves.

Michaela's—Kennedy's mother—hair is pêle-mêle blanche-blonde, she wears horn-toed, fleur-de-lys patterned, lace-up black high heels, mandorla—oval—ring, ruby and gold diamante on fingernails against her black.

Her businessman boyfriend wears a Savile Row-style suit chosen from his wardrobe of dark lilac suits, grey and black lounge suits, suits with black collars, wine suits, plum jackets, claret red velvet one-button jackets.

Kennedy's father Bongo had been a man with kettle-black eyebrows, who was familiar with the juniper berries and the rowan berries and the scarlet berries of the bittersweet—the woody nightshade—sequestered his foal with magpie face and Talmud scholar's beard where these berries, some healing, some poisonous, were abundant. He knew how to challenge the witch's broom.

John Joe Criggs, the umbrella mender in Killeely, used to send boys who looked like potoroos—rat kangaroos with prehensile tails—to Weston where they lived, looking for spare copper.

"You're as well hung as a stallion like your father," Bongo would say to Kennedy. "Get a partner."

In Clare for the summer he once turned to Michaela in the night in Kilrush during a fight.

"Go into the Kincora Hotel and get a knife so I can kill this fellow."

He always took Kennedy to Ballyheigue at Marymass—September 8—where people in bare feet took water in bottles from the Holy Well, left scapulars, names, and photographs of people who were dead, children who'd been killed.

He fell in a pub fight. Never woke up.

His mother Evie had hung herself when they settled her.

Hair ivory grey at edges, then sienna, in a ponytail tied by a velvet ribbon, usually in tattersal coat, maxie skirt, heelless sandals.

On the road she'd loved to watch the mistle thrush who came to Ireland with the Act of Union of 1801, the Wee Willie Wagtail—blue tit—with black eyestripe and lemon breast, the chaffinch with pink lightings on its breast who would come up close to you, in winter in fraochán—ring ouzel, white crescent around its breast, bird of river, of crags.

On the footbridge at Doonass near Clondara she told Kennedy of the two Jehovah's Witnesses who were assaulted in Clondara, their bibles burned, the crowd cheered on by the Parish Priest, and then the Jehovah's Witnesses bound to the peace in court for blasphemy.

Michaela's father Billser had been in Glin Industrial School.

The Christian Brothers, with Abbey School of Acting voices, used to get them to strip naked and lash them with the cat of the nine tails. Boys with smidgen penises. A dust, a protest of pubic hair. Boys with pubes as red as the fox who came to steal the sickly chickens, orange as the beak of an Aylesbury duck, brown of the tawny owl.

Then bring them to the Shannon when the tide was in and force them to immerse in salt water.

The Shannon food—haws, dulse, barnacles—they ate them. They robbed mangels, turnips. They even robbed the pig's and bonham's—piglet's—food.

"You have eyes like the blackbird's eggs. You have eyes like the *céirseach's* eggs. You have eyes like the merie's eggs," a Brother, nicknamed the Seabhac—hawk—used to tell Billser.

Blue-green, brown speckled.

He was called Seabhac because he used to ravage boys the

way the hawk makes a sandwich of autumn brood pigeons or meadow pipits, leaving a flush of feathers.

He had ginger-beer hirsute like the rufous-barred sparrow-hawk that quickly gives up when it misses a target, lays eggs in abandoned crow's nests.

A second reason for his nickname was because he was an expert in Irish and the paper-covered Irish dictionary was penned by *an Seabhac*—the Hawk.

Father Edward J. Flanagan from Ballymoe, North Galway, who founded Boys Town in Omaha and was played by Spencer Tracy, came to Ireland in 1946 and visited Glin Industrial School.

The Seabhac gave him a patent hen's egg, tea in a cup with blackbirds on it, Dundee cake on a plate with the same pattern.

Billser used to cry salty tears when he remembered Glin.

Michaela's grandfather Torrie had been in the British Army and the old British names for places in Limerick City kept breaking into his conversation—Lax Weir, Patrick Punch Corner, Saint George's Street.

Cuzzy and Kennedy met at a Palaestra—boxing club.

Cuzzy was half-Brazilian.

"My father was Brazilian. He knocked my mother and went away."

"Are you riding any woman now?" he asked Kennedy, who had rabbit-coloured pubes, in the showers.

"You have nipples like monkey fingers," Kennedy said to Cuzzy, who had palomino-coloured pubes, in the showers.

The coach, who looked like a pickled onion with tattoos in the nude, was impugned for messing with the teenage boxers. HIV Lips was his nickname.

"Used to box for CIE Boxing Club," he said to himself, "would go around the country. They used to wear pink-lined vests, and I says no way am I going to wear that."

"He sniffed my jocks. And there were no stains on them," a

shaven headed boxer who looked like a defurred monkey or a peeled banana reported in denunciation of him.

A man who had a grudge against him used to scourge a statue of the Greek boxer Theagenes of Thasos until it fell on him, killing him.

The statue was thrown in the sea and fished up by fishermen.

Barrenness came on the country which the Delphic Oracle said wouldn't be removed until the statue was restored.

In the Palaestra was a poster of John Cena with leather wrappings on his forearm like the Terme Boxer—Pugile delle Terme—a first-century BC copy of a second-century BC statue which depicted Theagenes of Thasos.

John Cena in black baseball cap, briefs showing above trousers beside a lingering poster for Circus Vegas at Two Mile Inn—a kick-boxer in mini-bikini briefs and mock-crocodile boots.

Kennedy and Cuzzy were brought to the Garda Station one night when they were walking home from the Boxing Club.

"They'll take anyone in tracksuits."

Cuzzy, aged sixteen, was thrown in the girls' cell.

Kennedy was thumped with a mag lamp, a telephone book used to prevent his body from being bruised.

Cuzzy was thumped with a baton through a towel with soap in it.

A black guard put his tongue in Kennedy's ear. A Polish guard felt his genitals.

Kennedy punched the Polish guard and was jailed.

Solicitors bought parcels of heroin and cocaine into jail.

Youths on parole would swallow one eight heroin and €50 bags of heroin, thus sneak them in.

One youth put three hundred diazepam, three hundred steroids, three ounces of citric in a bottle, three needles up his anus.

Túr Cant for anus.

Ríspún Cant for jail.

Slop out in mornings.

Not even granule coffee for breakfast. Something worse.

Locked up most of the day.

One youth with a golf-ball face, skin-coloured lips of the young Dickie Rock, when his baseball cap was removed a pronounced bald patch on his blond head, had a parakeet in his cell.

Cuzzy would bring an adolescent Alsatian to the Unemployment Office.

Then he and Kennedy got a job laying slabs near the cement factory at Raheen.

Apart from work, Limerick routine.

Drugs in cling-foil or condoms put up their anuses, guards stopping them—fingers up their anuses.

Tired of the routine they both went to Donegal to train with AC Armalite rifles and machine guns in fields turned salmon-colour by ragged robin.

The instructor had a Vietnam veteran pepper-and-salt beard and wore Stars and Stripes plimsolls.

The farmer who used to own the house they stayed in would have a boy come for one month in the summer from an Industrial School, by arrangement with the Brothers.

The boy used to sleep in the same bed as him and the farmer made him wear girl's knickers.

In Kennedy's room was a Metallica poster—fuchsine bikini top, mini-bikini, skull locket on forehead, fuchsine mouth, belly button that looked like deep cleavage of buttocks, skeleton's arms about her.

"It was on Bermuda's island

That I met Captain Moore . . ."

"It's like the Albanians. They give you a bit of rope with a knot at the top.

Bessa they call it.

They will kill you or one of your family.

You know the Albanians by the ears. Their ears are taped back at birth.

And they have dark eyebrows.

I was raised on the island.

You could leave your doors open. They were the nicest people.

Drugs spoiled people."

Weston where Kennedy grew up was like Bedford-Stuyvesant or Brownsville, New York, where Mike Tyson grew up, his mother, who died when he was sixteen, regularly observing him with clothes he didn't pay for.

Kennedy once took a €150 tag off a golf club in a Limerick store, replaced it with a €20 tag, and paid for it.

As a small boy he had a Staffordshire terrier called Daisy.

Eyes a blue-coast watch, face a sea of freckles, he let the man from Janesboro who sucked little boys' knobs buy him 99s—ice cream cones with chocolate flakes stuck in them, syrup on top—or traffic-light cakes—cakes with scarlet and green jellies on the icing.

He'd play *knocker gawlai*—knock at doors in Weston and run away.

He'd throw eggs at taxis.

Once a taxi driver chased him with a baseball bat.

"I smoked twenty cigarettes a day since I was eleven.

Used to work as a mechanic part time then.

I cut it down to ten and then to five recently. My doctor told me my lungs were black and I'd be on an oxygen mask by the time I was twenty.

I'm nineteen."

The youth in the petrol-blue jacket spoke against the Island on which someone on a bicycle was driving horses.

A lighted motorbike was going up and down Island Field.

We were on the Metal Bridge side of the Shannon.

It was late afternoon, mid-December.

"They put barbed wire under the Metal Bridge to catch the bodies that float down. A boy jumped off the bridge, got caught in the barbed wire and was drowned.

They brought seventeen stolen cars here one day and burned all of them."

There were three cars in the water now, one upside down, with the wheels above the tide.

"When I was a child my mother used to always be saying, 'I promised Our Lady of Lourdes. I promised Our Lady of Lourdes.'

There's a pub in Heuwagen in Basel and I promised a friend I'd meet him there.

You can get accommodation in Paddington on the way for £20 a night. Share with someone else."

He turned to me. "Are you a Traveller? Do you light fires?"

He asked me where I was from and when I told him he said, "I stood there with seventeen Connemara ponies once and sold none of them."

On his fingers rings with horses' heads, saddles, hash plant.

His bumster trousers showed John Galliano briefs.

Two stygian hounds approached the tide followed by an owner with warfare orange hair, in a rainbow hoodie jacket, who called "Mack" after one of them.

He pulled up his jacket and underlying layers to show a tattoo MAKAVELI on his butter-mahogany abdomen.

"I got interested in Machiavelli because 2Pac was interested in him. Learnt all about him. An Italian philosopher. Nikolo is his first name. Put his tattoo all over my body. Spelt it Makaveli. Called my Rottweiler-Staffordshire terrier cross breed after him. Mack.

Modge is the long-haired black terrier.

Do you know that 2Pac was renamed Tupac Amaru Shakur by his mother after an Inca sentenced to death by the Spaniards?

In Inca language, Shining Serpent.

Do you know that when the Florentines were trying to recapture Pisa Machiavelli was begged because he was a philosopher to stay at headquarters but he answered," and the youth thrust out his chest like Arnold Schwarzenegger for this bit, "that he must be with his soldiers because he'd die of sadness behind the lines?

They say 2Pac was shot dead in Las Vegas. There was no funeral. He's as alive as you or me.

I'm reading a book about the Kray Twins now.

Beware of sneak attacks."

And then he went off with Mack and Modge singing the song 2Pac wrote about his mother, "Dear Mama."

"When I was a child my father used to take me to Ballyheigue every year.

There's a well there.

The priest was saying mass beside it during the Penal Days and the Red Coats turned up with hounds.

Three wethers jumped up from the well, ran towards the sea.

The hounds chased them, devoured them and were drowned.

The priest's life was spared."

They were of Thomond, neither of Munster nor Connaught, Thomond bodies, Thomond pectorals.

The other occasion I met Kennedy was on a warm February Saturday.

He was sitting in a Ford Focus on Hyde Road in red silky football shorts with youths in similar attire.

He introduced me to one of them, Razz, who had an arm tattoo of a centurion in a G-string.

"I was in Cloverhill. Remand prison near a courthouse in

Dublin. Then Mountjoy. You'd want to see the bleeding place. It was filthy. The warden stuck his head in the cell door one day and said, 'You're for Portlaoise.' They treat you well in Portlaoise."

"What were you in jail for?"

"A copper wouldn't ask me that."

A flank of girls in acid-pink and acid-green tops was hovering near this portmanteau of manhood like coprophagous— dung-eating—gulls near cows for the slugs in their dung.

A little girl in sunglasses with mint green frontal frames, flamingo wings, standing outside her house nearby, said to a little girl in a lemon and peach top who was passing:

"There are three birthday cards inside for you, Tiffany."

"It's not my birthday."

"It is your fucking birthday."

And then she began chasing the other girl like a skua down Hyde Road, in the direction of the bus station, screaming, "Happy Birthday to you. Happy Birthday to you."

Flowers of the magnolia come first in Pery Square Park near the Bus Station, tender yellow-green leaf later.

A Traveller boy cycled by the sweet chestnut blossoms of Pery Square Park the day they found Kennedy's body, firing heaped on his handlebars.

I am forced to live in a city of Russian tattooists, murderously shaven heads, Rumanian accordionists, the young in pallbearers' clothes—this is the hemlock they've given me to drink.

The Maigue in West Limerick, as I crossed it, was like the old kettles Kennedy's ancestors used to mend.

Travellers used to make rings from old teaspoons and sometimes I wondered if they could make rings from the discarded Hackenberg lager cans or Mr. Sheen All-Surface Polish cans beside the Metal Bridge.

I am living in the city for a year when a man who looks as if his face has been kicked in by a stallion approaches me on the street.

"I'm from Limerick city and you're from Limerick city. I know a Limerick city face. I haven't seen you there for a while. How many months did you get?"

Dorothy Nelson

From *In Night's City*

THE AUTHOR OF two short novels, *In Night's City* and *Tar and Feathers*, both published in the 1980s and now largely forgotten, Dorothy Nelson stood alone as an Irish female writer of her time in the intensity and darkness of her subject matter, and the severity with which she examined it. Nelson was awarded the Rooney Prize for Irish Literature for *In Night's City*. Though both of her books were well received, the time Nelson devoted to the guitar-making workshop she ran with her husband meant she never made the leap to become a full-time writer. In recent years, critics such as Eileen Battersby in *The Irish Times* have praised Nelson's work and called for her reinstatement among the luminaries of Irish literature. Eimear McBride discerned foreshadowings in Nelson of the linguistic inventiveness and troubling subject matter of her own debut novel, *A Girl Is a Half-Formed Thing*. Both of Nelson's novels have recently been republished in Dalkey Archive's Irish Literature Series.

Dorothy Nelson was born in Bray, County Wicklow, and now lives in Dun Laoghaire, a coastal suburb of South County Dublin. She has acknowledged Djuna Barnes, Carson McCullers, and Aidan Higgins as literary influences. Writing out of an oppressive, sexually tormented Catholic Ireland that was only then beginning to question itself and its institutions, Nelson's two novels are prescient in their painful interrogation of repression and internalised trauma. Paradoxically voicing the smothered communication and stifled emotion of Ireland's past and present, Sara, the young protagonist of *In Night's City*, implores, 'Can't you hear me, Ma? Can't you hear what I'm not saying, like I heard you?'

Included here is the opening section of that novel, which dwells on themes of emotional violence and familial anguish.

From *In Night's City*

Chapter 1
SARA—FEBRUARY 1970

"Tickle me the way you tickle my Mammy," I said. I climbed up on the bed and he smiled down. The colours were runnin' down his face like a river. Bright splashing colours. "Go on tickle me," I said. An' he tickled my belly with his colours. "I have a secret," I said. "Mammy says I've to tell no-one 'specially not you." "Are you goin' to tell me it?" he said. "Tickle me again an' I'll tell," I said. "It's a big secret." "I swear I won't tell anybody," he said laughin'. "Let me in beside you first," I said. I got in under the covers where it was soft. "Well then," he said. "What's the big secret?" "Me an' Mammy went down the town an' we turned a road an' then another road. We saw you sittin' in the car with a lady an' Mammy hurt my arm an' said I wasn't to tell no-one. 'Specially not you. I see your colours Daddy," I said. "I see them." He laughed down an' all the colours grew bright an' came runnin' down his face. "Say how old I am, say?" I said. "You're three!" he said, an' he tickled me. "No I'm not. Three is a baby. I'm four now. Say it Daddy. Say how old I am." "Three-and-a-half," he said. The laughin' came closer. "I'm not three-and-a-half. I just told you, I'm four now." He tickled me again an' I was laughin' into his colours. Then it was dark. I felt the Dark touchin' me funny an' I was cryin' so Maggie came an' he touched Maggie funny not me. Not me. Not me.

The Big Dark was grindin' the Little Dark's bones to smithereens. Then the bones were a white dust an' the dust began to whirl an' fall on my bed. It came higher an' higher until I was sucked down under it an' I couldn't breathe.

•

He was looking down on me and then he pulled the blankets off me an' touched me funny. Mammy came in an' I thought "It'll be all right now. It'll be all right." It was dark but she didn't turn the light on. She stood beside my pillow an' looked at him doin' the funny things. Her eyes were sort of glintin' and she looked real cold. I went to say "Mammy stop him hurtin' me" but she wasn't mindin' me. She was in the faraway place watchin' him doin' the funny things so I pretended I wasn't there. Then he went downstairs and she went into the toilet. When she came back she switched the light on an' I started to cry. "Look," I said. "Look is that red blood on the sheets? Is it Mammy?" She came over an' pulled the covers up and told me to lie down. "Go to sleep now," she said. "You had a bad dream." "It wasn't a dream, Mammy," I said. "It was real." She bent down over me. "It was a dream. Now go to sleep." "It wasn't Mammy," I cried. "Say it wasn't. Look." I pushed the covers down and showed her the red blood. "Look at that," I said. "It was a dream," she said. "Now lie down and go to sleep." "It wasn't, Mammy. Say it wasn't. Say it was real." When she was gone I switched the light on again to look at the blood. "Look at it, Maggie," I said. "She said it was a dream but it wasn't. It was real." Maggie came to have a look an' she started laughin' mad an' then I laughed too. I kept pointin' at the red blood and laughin' my head off.

Anne walked up the stairs ahead of me. I could see the sun streaming in through the window in the middle of the stairway. When she stepped into the stream of light it shone on her fuzzy hair an' I could see the nits climbin' in through the knots an' tangles.

"Anne!" I called up after her. She turned around in the sun. "Can they fly?" I asked.

"What did you say, Sara Kavanagh?"

"Them nits," I said, pointing with my finger. "Can they fly? You're not to sit beside me anymore if they can."

"There's no nits in my hair, you," she said. An' she ran on ahead of me up the stairs. The way she said that stopped me, as if she knew as well as I did but she was saying "No" 'cause if you say "No" it means they're not there.

She sat beside me as usual an' my eyes kept strayin' over to the tangles. When the sun wasn't shinin' you couldn't see but I kept scratchin' my head 'cause maybe they could an' she just wouldn't say. She bent over her copybook like she always did when she didn't know the answers. I couldn't stand to see the way she huddled over her book as if she was terrified, with her eyes dartin' around to see if everyone else was writing. So I wrote the answers down on a piece of paper as best I could and passed them over. She set the paper on her lap under the desk and wrote them into her book. It was a funny thing. She hardly ever spoke a word. She just came an' went like a piece of dust that didn't want to be seen. She was standin' by the window leanin' on the brush and lookin' out at the sky. The soft was there. I could see the blue an' pink soft like little lappin' waves an' then the grey came an' I shivered in the cold. The grey kept hopping in over the pink and blue washin' them away like the winter rain washin' the colours off the face of the world. "You all right, Mammy?" I asked. But she couldn't hear me so I tried to slide in to where the pink an' blue was but the grey kept gettin' in the way an' I couldn't find her.

I could see them again in the sun when she walked up the stairs. Millions crawlin' around in her hair like it was a playground.

"Hey you, Anne," I said. "Wait for me." She pressed in against the wall to let the other girls go by.

"Just tell me," I said. "Say, 'Yes' or 'No'. Can they fly?" Her face squeezed up real tight like a cryin' face.

"They're not there," she said. "Leave me alone you."

"Doesn't your mother wash your hair?"

"I haven't got a mother."

"'Course you have. Everyone has a mother."

"No I haven't. She's dead." She started to walk ahead of me but I ran to catch up.

"When'd she die then?"

"I don't know. A long time ago," she said.

"Mothers don't die. I never heard of anyone's mother dead before."

She sat me up on her lap an' held me against her cardigan. It smelled of her.

"I haven't got nits," she said. "I haven't." And she turned an' ran back down the stairs into the toilets.

She was a jewel. Anne was a jewel. I could see the sun shinin' on her hair an' the nits sparkled in the sun. "They can't fly because they are jewels," I said. Anne O'Sullivan has no mother, I wrote in my head, she has jewels but they can't fly.

When Ma told me he was dead I didn't think 'Father you are' but, 'Sweat and breath you are'. Not 'Father you are' but 'Sweat and breath mingling with my own you are'.

"Pull yourself together now," she said. When I looked around she was holding her hands to her head as if she was going to split down the middle at any second.

I went up to the toilet and sat on the edge of the bath. I had wanted him to die slow. He would be lying in bed under the white starched sheets. A face without a body. And the wheeze coming up his lungs filling that room and echoing from wall to wall. His large hands would reach out from under the bedclothes to touch mine. The tips of his fingers against the palms of my hands. The tears spurting out of his eyes and I saying, 'Too late. Too late. Let your tears turn to blood and drip down the walls and ceiling of this room. Bloody the four feet space between your bed and mine for the past twenty years.'

"Stop your dreaming," Maggie says chuckling.

"Go away, Maggie. You haven't stopped laughing since she told me. They'll hear you and think it's me."

"Whose mouth then?" she asks. "Whose mouth?" I stood up and looked in the mirror over the bath and saw the way my mouth was, curled up in a sneer and the chuckling coming from it. I clenched my lips real tight together so nothing could come out. She was quiet for a while and then she says, "Just you remember I'll be right here watching and waiting to see if you cry over that son-of-a-bitch."

But I couldn't cry because she was rising up so fast inside me and she wouldn't quieten down. I was afraid she might say something out of turn and I wouldn't be able to stop it coming. Maggie laughing because the man was dead. Man of the father. Not father you are but sweat and breath you are.

I washed my face with the end of the towel and then dried it. I looked in the mirror again and behind my eyes I could see her chuckling away to herself. I opened the door and went on down to the kitchen.

Willy leans back in his chair. The front legs rise up as he balances the weight of his body on the hind legs. The legs wobble from side to side as if they're about to give from under him but he manoeuvres them slowly back to the floor without letting them slip.

"I don't know what made me come on holidays this time of the year," he says. "I was plannin' on July. It was an impulse. Maybe I knew." His eyes move about the kitchen as he talks.

"You've changed the wallpaper then?"

"Yes," Ma says. "Last summer we got Pa Curran in to strip down the walls properly. Your Father wasn't able for it. It's the grease from the cooker makes it so dirty looking."

Ma has no taste. I remember when Pa Curran put the paper up I asked her why she didn't get a plain paper instead of gaudy flowers. "It'd make the room look bigger," I said.

"Are you complainin'?" she snapped. "Is this house not good enough for you now?"

"All I meant was . . ."

"I know what you meant," she said. "I happen to like gaudy wallpaper as you call it."

Did you ever laugh? Did you ever once crack your face laughin'?

"I'll make a pot of tea," she says. "It'll calm us down."

"I can't believe it," says Willy. "It's all happened so fast. He was stretched out on the floor stiff as ice. Must have been a good two hours before we came in."

"Stop thinkin' about it," Ma says. "It'll do no good. Get out the cups. Joseph, get another chair from the sitting room."

"Did you ever think about dyin'?" I asked him. He looked up over the rim of the paper. His eyes singing Sara, Sara.

"What makes you ask that? Do I look like I'm dying?" he said laughing over at me. "Can't wait to get rid of me, is that it then?"

"I was just wondering," I said. "Would you be afraid?" He looked up again. His eyes bright singing Sara, Sara.

"I suppose if I thought about it I would," he said, folding the paper and putting it on the back of the chair. "But I don't think about it. When you get to my age you won't either."

"I'll never be your age. You're an oul man now."

"Is that right," he said, leaning one arm on the table.

His eyes teasing me with the singing. The field was dizzy in my head. All the colours of the carnival wheeling down my mind where he was sitting. Waiting for me in the colours and I bursting with excitement.

"Anyway you must have thought about it," I said.

"What are you getting at?" His eyes narrowed.

"I'm just saying if you think you'd be afraid, you must have thought."

"Would you get outa that, you stupid lug. Are you reading them books again?"

"I'm reading them books because I'm not going to end up like you," I shouted at him. "I'm going to be somebody. I'm not going to end up in a council house."

His face got red and blotchy. He was going to lose his temper.

"I'm only tryin' to learn things," I said.

"Like what for instance?"

"I'm reading about this man dyin'. How afraid he is and then when he knows for sure he's not afraid anymore."

He leaned both arms on the table and spread his hands flat on the cloth. "When he knows?"

"Yes, you see according to this story it wasn't the dyin'. It was the fear of not knowing that terrified him."

"What do you mean you're not going to end up like me?"

"I'm going to do things. Like I might travel all over the world or become rich."

"Is that so now? And what if I say you're not going anywhere?"

I leaned over until my eyes were level with his. "In another five years I'll be twenty-one and there'll be nothing you can do about it."

"Show me that book," he said.

I went upstairs and brought the book down to him.

"This is what you read then?"

"No. Not all the time. I change around."

"You want to learn things, eh!" he jeered.

"Yes I want to be educated. I might start going to night school."

He flicked through the pages. Then he tore a fist of them out and threw them on the floor.

"What'd you do that for?" I shouted. "What's the harm in me readin'?"

"You're a gobshite, that's why. You'll never get anywhere. You haven't a brain in your head."

I picked up the book and he started laughing.

"You're not funny," I said. "You know that? You're not funny at all."

Willy stands up and goes over to the window to pull the curtains across.

"It's already dark out," he says. "What time is it?"

"It's five o'clock," Joseph says.

"Here sit down and drink your tea," Ma says, passing him the cup.

"God he was stiff as ice," says Willy.

Joseph goes over to the table and pours himself a cup.

"Did you make all the arrangements?" he asks, his voice crisp and harsh from trying to hold back the crying.

"I told you twice already, I've done everything." She shakes her head impatiently the way she does when she has to repeat herself.

"He's coming to get us Mammy," I said.

"Who, Sara, who?" she said, shaking me.

"Me and Maggie under the bed where you're a queen."

My Ma was under the bed where she was a queen and then she went off and left us. So the next time she called me I pretended not to hear.

"I hate everything," I said to Maggie. "I hate the whole world."

Willy gets up and walks around the kitchen.

"I thought if I shook him hard enough he'd come to," he says. "He looked so set on the floor like he'd decided he wasn't goin' to move off it. An' I kept shakin' an' shakin' him an' all the time I was shakin' a dead man."

"It was the way he fell," Ben says. "Must have gone flat down on his face. Over there," he says pointing to where Joseph is sitting.

Joseph gets up off the chair and sits down beside the fire.

"For Christ's sake would you two shut up," he says.

"It's a pure miracle I came home at all," Willy says.

"Ben, answer that knock, will ya?" Joseph says. Ben gets up and opens the back door. Two of the neighbours file past him with their heads bent low.

"Esther," Mrs. Turner says, pulling a chair up beside her. "I was on my way to the shops and Mary comes running down after me. 'Ma, Mr. Kavanagh dropped dead with a heart attack,' she says. And I come immediately." She clutches Ma's hand in her own like she was praying over her.

Ma looks up into her face and then looks away again as if there was something in that face she couldn't bear to see. Mrs. O'Brien nods her head in agreement with Mrs. Turner and sits down.

I make tea and listen to their goster.

Ben answers the second knock on the door and more neighbours file in. I make tea and listen to their goster. 'Oh humey fraw!'

Ma sits quiet like a thought in the back of your mind. She stares out through the window as if she is looking for something. Watching and waiting like she did all those years, as if now that it's happened it doesn't matter because she's still watching and waiting.

"What did you bring that priest into this house for?" she raged.

"I swear to God I never told him anything. I was depressed, that's all. He noticed it in class and said he'd call around to the house sometime."

"You little bitch." Her hand stung my face. "You were trying to make a show of me. God knows what lies you filled him up with."

I couldn't stop crying. She hit me again. And I thought, 'I could lift her quite easily. She's smaller than me. I could mash her into the ground.' But I couldn't because I smelled her. I smelled my mother where she couldn't cry.

And he lies in the hospital morgue on a trolley not giving a tinker's curse for the dark shadows under her eyes or the thin gaunt face staring into the blackness. And not a tinker's curse for me either, that bleeds inside listening to the hypocritical dumdums around me. To drive me insane is what they have come for. No more, no less than to see me ranting like a lunatic as well I may before this wake is over.

His skin was the colour of a pale translucent bulb and his eyes like two carefully drawn chalk lines. A faint tinge of purple showed through the skin on the flaccid mouth, lying flat like a dead fish on a sandy dune. And my eyes eating up every crease and line. Joseph bent over and kissed that mouth. He kissed that dead mouth! I thought my bones would fall out through my skin I shook so much. I thought, 'I'm goin' to drown now, right this minute.' It was the dead fish that did that to me. And Maggie was moaning. Oh! God, I could hear her getting louder and louder. And I turned and ran out into the corridor.

And now on this night. A carousel in a kitchen. Faces familiar. Tongues saying the right words. Bodies move listlessly side to side on the kitchen chairs. They leave one by one. Having said the correct soothing phrases. Relief in the flickering eyelids of my mother. Denies it with a smile. Her tongue says, "Thank you, thank you for coming." Relief, even the kitchen seems to breathe more easily. Always say the right things at the right time. Death is here now. In between the memories. Throbbing! Throbbing! For the only death that really matters, the one that sucks the blood—my own. All else a constant reminder of the ticking clock.

To sing a lullaby, hush now, hush now. It's not the words that flow from mouths. It's not the eyes that smile, or the hands that touch. Touch lightly now, touch lightly now. These people.

I have yet to hear one of them scream. Will someone please scrrrrrrrrrream?

Willy leans back on the chair. The front legs rise high. The hind legs swivel and turn, turn and swivel. They keel over like two drunken ballerinas and he sails over the chair and lands on his back. The hum of voices stops and everyone turns to look at Willy lying on the floor. Maggie starts to chuckle and I give a quick cough. He lies on his back looking up at the faces looking down at him. The tears storm down his cheeks. He starts gasping as if he's about to choke on his crying.

"He's dead. My Daddy's dead."

Joseph gives him a hand to get up but he shakes him off and struggles up himself, still crying. He runs through the hallway and up the stairs.

"Poor fella," Mrs. O'Brien says. "He must be terrible upset."

"Go after him an' see he's alright, Sara," Joseph says.

He lies on his old bed, his body stretched the full length, his feet dangling out over the edge. His eyes are all red and puffed.

"I kept thinkin'," he says. "The way he'd laugh when we'd queue up for pocket money on Sundays. And how sometimes he'd meet me after school and bring me for a drive."

When he went to England Ma said, "You drove him out of the house with your fists."

"He shouldn't have done it," Da said. "I won't put up with his carrying on like that."

"And the way we used to all sit around the wireless listenin' to the football results," Willy said.

"He thrashed us all the time when we were small," I say.

His hands thrashing me all over and I thinking this is better than being dead. Better. Better. Better.

"Only when we were bad," says Willy. A half-smile plays around his mouth as if he's gliding over the surface of memories, stopping and moving on over the polished surface, seeing and not feeling because he's moving so fast.

"Sara, do you remember the carnival?" he asks.

"Yes," I say. "I remember it." The carnival shone out through his skin, his dead eyes, his dead nose. And the music played on his purple tinged lips. The music flowing through the loud-speakers bobbing over people's heads like big coloured balls. And his colours spread like a rainbow across the field. Did you know? Did you know he was a man? Your father was a man. Did you know that?

Emer Martin

From *Breakfast in Babylon*

EMER MARTIN'S GLOBAL, anti-parochial novels reflect her wandering, transcontinental life. Born in Dublin, she published her first novel, *Breakfast in Babylon*, in 1995 at the age of twenty-six. The punkish, drug- and booze-soaked novel was selected as Book of the Year at the Listowel Writers' Week. Recalling Irvine Welsh's *Trainspotting* and writers such as Louis-Ferdinand Céline and Jean Genet, it delved into the aimless, embittered lives of international dropouts, junkies, beggars, and whores on the streets of Paris and other European cities. In 1999 Martin's second novel, *More Bread Or I'll Appear*, was published. That was followed in 2007 by *Baby Zero*, which explored the convergences and conflicts between Eastern and Western civilisations. For her raw and visceral subject matter, the writer and journalist Olaf Tyaransen claimed that Martin 'is to chick-lit what Shane MacGowan is to sobriety'.

Emer Martin has lived in London, Paris, the Middle East, and the United States. As well as writing fiction, she is a painter and filmmaker, with numerous exhibitions and short films to her name. In 2007 she produced Irvine Welsh's directorial debut, the short film *Nuts*. She was awarded a Guggenheim Fellowship in 2000, and is the founder of Rawmeash, a publishing collective based in California's Bay Area.

Martin began writing when she was nine, and has said of her education, 'The nuns in my convent school had spent so many years ranting about the dangers of drugs and sex that I couldn't wait to dive right in and try it for myself. I knew they

were obsessed for a reason.' Currently she lives in California,
and she is working on a novel spanning the prehistoric era to
the present day.

Included here is the opening section from *Breakfast in
Babylon*, the 1995 debut novel soon to be reissued by Rawmeash.

From *Breakfast in Babylon*

The Melon Murderer

"I AM NOT Jesus Christ. I left home younger than he, walked further and stayed out in the wilderness longer. I am a tinker. A tinker who could not stop tinking around this stretch of earth. The homecomings I have are the memories of certain events that penetrated my mind, that neither slowed nor startled me but that would not leave me. Think of the sound 'tink,' shallow and brief."

Isolt was talking to herself in the Garden of Gethsemane looking over Jerusalem. All her hard times in the city had almost turned her back into a Catholic. Standing here now she felt no Godly presence and was relieved to be spared the embarrassment of being born again. She took a last look at Jerusalem and left the garden to go home and pack.

The humidity had left the air, but she still hated Tel Aviv. She lay on the bed reading for three days. Intrusion from the outside world was neither volunteered nor sought for. The second morning she put her head in her hands and shuddered. Determined to shake her gloom, she made her way down the streets and walked along the beach feeling that something was ending in her. She bought a pack of cigarettes and sat on an iron chair on the promenade, reading and watching all the old Jewish ladies surrender their varicose veins to the evening sun.

That day she could not dissipate the thick layer of shadows that had stretched into her head, as if even her own ghosts were collapsing quietly in her soul. Stray dogs sniffed about the sand. She had a world where all the old ladies had bulging blue veins and all the dogs had cataract eyes. There were the usual conversations with the brigade of tanned, hairy perverts that maintain a diligent patrol of Tel Aviv's sea front.

"Where are you from?"

"Go away."

"English? American? Denmark?"

She settled her eyes on a battleship which was circling the horizon hypnotically. She wondered about the huge ship's motive for this rotating exercise.

"You have beautiful eyes."

"What book are you reading?"

It certainly seemed like a waste of petrol . . . Maybe the Syrians were invading.

"I think books open the mind, do you?"

"Go read one then."

"You want to come in my car for coffee in Jaffa?"

"Go away. I want to be alone."

"My friend has car, you come with us."

The ship was commencing yet another circle. She had made the mistake of acknowledging his presence.

"Please, I don't want to talk."

"You think I am a dog?"

"No, I like dogs."

"You want my friend give you books to read? My friend has books at the house."

"Fuck off!"

He jumped up in moral outrage. "You are not lady. You are stupid girl. There is not interesting talking to you and not special to look at you. You are fat and short."

She wondered if the captain of the ship had been looking overboard, dropped his contact lenses, and forced his whole crew to circle the spot in search of them. Small plastic floating through moving waves. The pervert was sulking in the distance, always alert for foreign girls who come to watch the sun go down. He was lighting a cigarette. She hoped he'd get cancer for calling her fat.

Two British lads who drank with her crowd came by. The smaller was covered in tattoos. Doomed stragglers who never got out when the summer had taken the Sunday boat from Haifa and the hostels closed and the jobs became scarce. They probably thought the same of her. She went for a beer with them but they seemed not to notice her presence so she relaxed and, savouring the one luxury of being invisible, she began to eavesdrop.

"Yeah, she's a mad cow. What age do you think she is?"

"Thirtyish, nice legs, she said she'd been to Egypt four months ago. She's been here ages."

"Probably drank the Nile dry."

"Got kids back in Leeds and everything, stupid cow. I met her on a moshav in the Golan Heights. She got fired. One morning she took the farmer's gun and went through the fields shooting all his bloody melons."

"Now the dumb bitch has invested in a metal detector and goes up and down the beach in the middle of the night looking for all the coins, watches and shit."

"Damn, if the police catch her at that . . ."

"I first met her in the Sinai. She goes to the desert a lot and smokes dope—bedouin dope—dirt cheap. Anyway I see her in the hostel and say, didn't I see you in the Sinai? She says, 'Probably, I'm always in the Sinai, I love it there, the Sinai's my garden.'"

The other shook his head, smiling. "Fucking metal detector."

"I'll drink to that," Isolt said, ordering three more beers. "But then I'll drink to anything."

At last she could leave Israel, forward into the soft rains of Europe, her body tired and her head shapeless, her thoughts less tense but without theme or direction. She spent two weeks on the Greek islands before she got to Athens. Two weeks in the company of the usual well-adjusted people one meets in budget travel. She would forget all their names soon. Their impressions would linger on, though, having found place to root throughout her brain, like unnoticed scrubweed.

In Athens she made inquiries about the infamous magic bus—a bus that for a meagre sum of gold would take her nonstop to cities in Northern Europe. Women had been known to give birth on this bus, Turkish immigrants had been stabbed and occasionally the company went bankrupt and the forever-drunken driver would bail out mid-way leaving everybody stranded on the wrong side of the Yugoslavian border. The man in the agency shook his head.

"They have gone bankrupt, there is a new bus under a different name."

"And what might that be?"

He shrugged glumly. "The not-so-magic bus?"

"Well, can I get it to Amsterdam?"

"Only Paris and Frankfurt."

Sitting down on the grotty travel agent's wooden bench she thought about it. She was sure some of her friends would be there hanging around. She knew the city well. She would take a train into Turkey while she was so close and afterwards go to Paris for a week, make some money begging, and head up to Holland for the winter.

She met a British guy who had Greek parents and spoke the language. They walked about the city together for a couple of days. It was in Athens when she first saw the rain and felt she was almost home. They got drunk in a fast food place. She ran back and forth to the toilet, each time looking at herself in the mirror. Each time a few minutes older. Which made her feel at least something was moving. If only the world.

The hotel room had plastic under the sheets and no locks on the door. An Irish couple cleaned the toilets in the morning.

There was a freezing lobby in which she sat all day, reading a book and waiting for her train. Grey Athens outside the window, clinging to her soul. At Istanbul she stopped because of the snows. She had a note in her pocket from the Irish cleaner to give to her sister in Paris. Isolt kept that note through all the years that followed.

Nobody got stabbed, born or abandoned on the not-so-magic bus. Isolt did get sick out of the window after a Tequila race with four German backpackers. While she was deep in a coma under the seat her money and passport were stolen. She suspected the Germans but they blamed the Turkish family in the back seat. She arrived slightly dismembered in Paris, that most forgiving of cities, with no money and no identification. Locking her battered rucksack in the train station lockers with the coins one of the Germans had given her she watched them all skip off to a café to get drunk on her money; she was momentarily overcome with a sense of *déjà vu*.

How to find a friend in Paris. Does your guide book tell you this? How to search every haunt, begging spot, and familiar park bench where people once congregated. How to take your jet-lagged eyes and roll them down each street, each gutter. How to grow your stiff legs long enough to see over every house and scan four roads at once.

On the brink of despair when night had turned her search to bewildered panic, she saw Jim at the Saint-Michel fountain through a circus of beggars and their half-wild dogs. He was leaning against a car drinking a beer. His eyes opened uncharacteristically wide as he saw her limp over.

"Well, well! The dead arose and appeared to many."

"Hallo, Jim. You look awful," she said. And he did.

"Looking pretty grubby yourself, you old tart. Where have you been? London?"

"No."

"Have you anywhere to stay tonight?"

"Emm . . . Not really. You see I'm just back from Israel. I've lost some shit, well I was robbed . . . anyway I don't feel very organised."

He laughed. Thank God for Jim, she thought.

"Welcome to the Twilight Zone. You can come back to the squat I suppose."

His friend, a small Englishman in his forties, groaned. "Jesus! You Irish multiply. Let one of you in and the next thing you've got all the clan, second cousins, blood brothers, half-sisters, crowding the place out and an end to the peace."

"Yep." Jim nodded happily and nudged Isolt. "Buy us both a beer and consider the rent paid."

"Shit . . . I'm broke . . . otherwise . . ."

The Englishman rolled his eyes and gave her a bottle of beer from the pocket of his dirty overcoat. Jim put his arm around her and looked into her tired not-so-magic face.

"From the first time I saw you . . ." he sighed in his drunken stupor.

A couple of hours later they climbed through the wire and took the chain off the squat door. Isolt turned to the English guy whose name was Larry. "I suppose I'm the only female as usual?"

Jim, lighting a match and making his way up the bare stairs laughed, "You're one of the lads at this stage. Christopher will probably have a fit. He kind of found this place and threw a tantrum when a girl moved in. He doesn't like girls, but he doesn't live here so we ignore him."

"Yeah, there's a bird from Leeds here. She's a wino but she's OK," Larry said.

Jim giggled, "Hey, dig this! The chick has a metal detector. She drags it around everywhere. It's no fucking use in Paris."

Larry and Jim glanced knowingly at each other. Larry opened a door. "She's been to Israel too."

"Good," Isolt said. "We can swap holiday snaps."

The place was candle-lit. The rooms were big but there was no water or electricity. Isolt saw her sitting there among the rubble drinking wine. The lads had described her as a wino. That was charitable of them. She was thin and long. Her nice legs were covered in sores and her slender hands had bitten nails. Her face was washed out and old-looking. All in all, in candlelight she struck Isolt as being chewed—her whole body, lovely needle-marked limbs, defeated face. Chewed. Something had swallowed her all right, devoured her, but now she had been spat out and was on the defensive for the last years of her life. Isolt knew who she was. She would have known her anywhere.

Isolt felt she was encountering a heroine in a story. A heroine on heroin—the melon murderer. And the Sinai desert was once her garden. They were introduced; her name was Becky, a Jewish English pauper from Leeds, and they would share a room. Isolt kicked about the rubbish on the floor: milk cartons, bottles of meths, discarded homemade pipes, soggy coffee filters, beer cans.

"Well, Jim. I see you brought your fungus collection with you, or do you just let the debris build up in each place of its own accord?" Her eye caught the plastic water carrier filled to the brim with cigarette butts. "Whoops! Ashtrays are full, time to move squats."

Becky looked at Isolt half-eyed. "Shit, Jim, who the hell is this? A miniature health inspector?"

Their room was the size of a grand piano. It was full of cigarette butts, wine bottles and syringes. Larry gave Isolt one of his blankets, a manky piece of cloth which smelt of hard times and no doubt previous encounters he had had under the offensive article. The nights were bitterly cold in this weary kingdom and she needed it. Two people living in the space of one piano was a bit like building a ship in a bottle. Becky's ship was sinking.

Isolt had only a raft, drifting. She hated Isolt's youth, though
Isolt insisted that she was on her side and growing old quickly.
She accused Isolt of being a Nazi, but Isolt assured her that
the room was too small to goosestep in, even for her stumpy,
Catholic legs. Becky hated Catholics.

They talked into the sorry nights while methylated fires
burned in the can for light and warmth. In a drunken stupor
Becky spilt the meths on her hand and set it alight. The
flames rolled off. She stared in surprise and tried it again,
like a child.

"You read a lot of books. Who said the Irish were stupid?"

"You did."

"I did?" She was puzzled.

"You, as in you the Brits."

"Christ, don't go on with this chip on your shoulder like the
bloody Scots."

"It is a well-deserved and ongoing chip on my shoulder."

"I'm not British, I'm Jewish, or at least that's what I thought
before going to Israel. They didn't want me there either. It's
good that you read all those books. I don't know much about
anything." She kicked over an empty milk carton. "Except
debris of course."

She drank some wine, sucking furiously at the mouth of the
bottle, again, like a child.

"I got pregnant at seventeen back in lovely Leeds. I got married and had four kids. I kept the kitchen kosher while my husband kept his distance. Ha! Ha! Ha!" Her face looked horrible
lit from beneath by the fire; she went on, "His name was Bertie,
not very Jewish eh? I'm no fanatic. Becky and Bertie, cute eh?"
She glared at Isolt.

Isolt nodded, waiting for more details.

"So there we were, he got drunk. I did not, then I started too.
Where was I? Oh yeah, so Becky keeps the kitchen kosher, kept
the kiddies and lost her looks. Man, I tell you I was beautiful

once. Nothing like you. Blond, tall, the lot. So I'm boozing all the time and one day I find out he's fucking some dozy little tart who actually was my hairdresser. I wouldn't have minded so much if he had gone groping after a forty-year-old of some substance called Maude or something. No, it was a curly-haired, sixteen-year-old, disco-fluff slut called, now listen to this . . ." She put her bony finger to her lips as if to quiet the already quiet Isolt. "She called herself Tricky."

They both tried to laugh.

"That bastard used to beat me too. He used to find that I drunk all his booze and slam me against the wall. He never gave me enough for the kids or nothing. Then he stuck his little dicky in Tricky. And Becky runs off and dies in Paris."

"Do you want to die in Paris?"

"It's not top on my list of priorities right now, no."

"Oscar Wilde died here."

"Yeah, he was a faggot though."

"So?"

"His wife ran off didn't she? With the kids? Changed their names. Don't talk to me about literary figures, I saw the mini-series. I wonder what they changed their names to? I hope it didn't end in 'y'."

"Not-so-wilde?" Isolt suggested. This appealed to Becky.

"Sure I can handle that, and they were probably drivers of your not-so-magic bus."

As they were settling to go to sleep Becky turned to Isolt. "It's Christmas Day tomorrow and you are not in Amsterdam as planned, my girl."

"You noticed?" Isolt cringed.

"Sure. You're not that fucking small."

"Well, I don't really mind. Amsterdam is just a faraway hill that's greener. Happy Christmas!" She tried to clink her bottle with Becky's, but Becky pulled hers away.

"Get lost." She looked at Isolt, the flames throwing shadows on the wall. The futility of the patterns they cast sucked at Isolt's head until she was about to scream. Becky's head drooped and she said, "Happy just another shitty day!"

"I'll drink to that." Isolt sat up and opened another bottle of wine. It was going to be a long night and they could sleep all day tomorrow.

When they were evicted the police came in with gas masks in the middle of the night and chased them all out as they slept. Jim had been cracked over the head with a baton and had to get stitches on his scalp. The doors and windows were bricked up. Anything they could not grab in the panic to get out was lost. They were all scattered on the streets for a couple of weeks hunting desperately for a new dwelling place. As they rolled their sleeping bags out under the bridge, Isolt was grateful for Larry and Jim and their constant banter.

"My friend Rory was a madman," said Jim. "He ran away from home when he was twenty-six . . ."

Larry grumbled, "Is this the guy that cooked that poor hedgehog?"

"I shared a place with him in London."

"What, with the hedgehog?"

"No, with Rory, he had a lot of stories attatched to him, a real ladies' man was Rory. We were all in London sharing a tiny room between six of us from Dublin and we all got scabies except Rory . . ."

"Oh I see," Larry said. "It was an English hedgehog and therefore an oppressor who deserved to get cooked by scabies-ridden Irishmen who came to fiddle the social security system."

Jim got serious. "No, you see Rory reckoned that eating the hedgehog stopped him getting scabies."

"Christ," said Larry. "A medical breakthrough by the Irish. That is a first. I thought you lot were still suffering from beri-beri and rickets."

An old Irishman called from the depths of the arches, "Don't you get cheeky about the Famine, young man, I was there."

Larry turned to him. "I'm not young, mate. I'm forty-five, and don't talk to me about the Irish potato famine, you may have lived through it but I read the book."

Jim peered at the old man through the darkness. "If you lived through it you must be at least one hundred and forty years old."

"I was one hundred and forty years old THEN," the old man snapped and promptly rolled over to sleep.

Nobody had seen Becky in two weeks. Somebody around the fountain said her liver had insisted on being taken to the hospital. It had occurred to Isolt last time she saw her that living did not come naturally to Becky. Her life seemed to make her awkward; she didn't know what to do with it. She was not sure if it was worth going on with all this breathing and consciousness. Then Becky never mentioned suicide, not for life's sake Isolt suspected, but perhaps because she felt that death offered nothing better. She was too tall and too blond and too worn to allow people to warm up to her. It was obvious that she had been a beauty and the way she never hid her needle-marked arms disturbed the lads. She was always bitching about men but seemed to prefer men's company to women's. She had slept with all the men in the squat at one time or another. They joked about this among themselves though they always were slightly ashamed of admitting it to each other. Everyone except Ali—no one slept with Ali—and Christopher because she hated him. Once when he was lying on the floor she took her precious metal detector and held it over his chest.

"If the bleeper goes off you have a heart."

It didn't.

"Yep. That figures," she said and strutted out of the room, Christopher staring after her slender shape with contemptuous, greedy eyes.

The only things she had taken with her from the now-demolished squat were her metal detector and her sleeping bag. She had stood on the side of the street that night when everyone was running from the police; she had not been part of the panic. Watching the action, leaning with one hand on her detector and one hand on her hip, the sleeping bag at her feet.

"The bare necessities," she told Isolt when Isolt came up to her out of the chaos. Isolt had raised her materialistic eyebrows at Becky's odd world.

Becky felt competitive with the younger girl because they were usually the only females around so many men. Isolt hated this. Becky was often rude to her, and then placated her by stealing books from Shakespeare and Co, the English book-shop. For a person who had never read a book in her life she had excellent taste.

"If the blurb on the back is depressing, complicated and obscure, I know you will read it."

Isolt inquired if Becky found her depressing, complicated and obscure.

"Oh baby! You are not complicated. I can read you like one of your damn books."

"I find the truth in the books I read, where do you find yours?"

"Listen, you are just a little kid now. I have been a woman for thirty-six years. We are the watchers and the waiters while men are busy being the doers and getters. If you get dumped on for all those years you begin to see through shit-coloured glasses, you see up the world's trouser leg, you see life as it is. Not like those damn books, what do those people know, they're all men. They're all educated people who have their acts together."

"Not all of them."

"They have their acts together enough to write and publish their shitty books."

"The watchers and the waiters, huh?"

"Yep, and the weight watchers. Ha! Ha!" She poked Isolt's beer belly.

Becky was now gone.

They found another squat just outside Paris and about twelve people moved in. This one had electricity but no water. Weeks later Becky arrived at the fountain. Isolt was at the cinema with Jim. Ali took her back and she moved straight into Isolt's room though there were plenty of others to spare. The first night she was shooting up and splattered blood on the wall. Isolt stood looking at it on her arrival.

"I took the liberty of doing some decorating while you were away, darling," she explained sluggishly.

Isolt shrugged. "Oh well, it's an improvement on the wallpaper I suppose."

"Oscar Wilde had a wallpaper problem in Paris too."

"How on earth did you know that—the mini-series?"

"You don't have a monopoly on dead faggots, you know."

Isolt did not embrace her though she was very glad to have her back and flattered that she chose her room. She sat down beside her and gave her a beer. Most of her blond hairs had turned grey in that short time. Isolt wanted to know where she had been all those weeks. She ventured to ask but Becky told her to mind her own business. Isolt wondered how she emerged from the down-hearted Parisian night with no sleeping bag, a different set of dirty clothes and the metal detector which had broken. Why carry a heavy, unfunctional machine with her when she disdained a change of clothes or a toothbrush?

"Just keeping the wolves from the door," Becky explained, though she didn't seem to have much chance, operating as she did in constant stupor.

When they were outside at the fountain the next evening she fell over. She stood up and fell over again. Jim picked her up and virtually cradled her.

"You've taken up break-dancing," he said.

"Break-dancing my arse," Larry frowned. "You've given yourself brain damage. That's epilepsy."

"Fuck you too, Larry," she said, all bravado. "It's this stupid country. The French refuse to obey the laws of gravity because an Englishman discovered it. They're fucking me up."

She remained at the fountain that night. Isolt ran back and forth getting bottles of wine at the Arab shop for her. She was terrified of standing up. In the end Larry and Jim carried her onto the last Metro. Isolt and Ali walked along beside them. Ali stood on the platform and shouted with his fist in the air to some curious onlookers.

"Kill the Arab."

"Shut up, Ali," Jim said. "You are an Arab."

Becky cried a little back at the squat. She snivelled and sucked on an empty wine bottle. Isolt sat on the floor and looked at her from across the room. Jim hugged her.

"It's cool to cry, Becky, we all cry sometimes."

"I don't," Larry said.

Every winter evening they would gather around Saint-Michel fountain, but in summer they would sit on the cobblestoned slope in front of the giant Pompidou Centre and watch the fire eaters, belly dancers and musicians. A huge man who was so fat his belly was rectangular would lounge about on a bed of nails, wearing a purple turban and taunting the passersby. The place was crawling with opportunistic Arabs, junkies, dealers, students, tourists and pickpockets. The Africans would congregate at the top of the slope making impassioned speeches and arguing back and forth. Usually the beggars Isolt knew would go to a self-service restaurant beside the square and have dinner. They sat at the back tables with all their bags, eating and drinking water after free water and discoursing loudly.

There were many beggars in the group. Some came and went

within a week, some stayed for years, most drifted back and forth between European countries, not always in the same life-style. On the streets people became friends quickly and adapted just as quickly to their absences. The Europeans and Ali pooled their money together while eating in the Melodine and one of the lads went off and bought hash or acid for the evening's entertainment. The left-overs were spent on beer. Everybody was invariably broke the next morning and would go out to beg and start again. There was a party every night.

The dealer was a tiny Puerto Rican American from Detroit. He was either on a bicycle or pulling a tartan shopping cart. He came to a bench beside the Pompidou fountain every evening at eight o'clock. If there was no one there at that time he would walk right by as briskly as the White Rabbit. He would mount the escalators of the Pompidou Centre and look through the tourist telescopes. If there were more clients at the bench than he could handle he would not come down till some left. Once when he was right on the top of the fifth floor looking down, Ali the Iranian looked up and caught the telescope dead in the eye. He started hopping up and down.

"Hey man! There's our man. There's the cat man."

Christopher saw the others strain to look up. He withdrew from the telescope abruptly and fled. When he arrived at the bench he denied he had been up there looking down at them.

"Ali's crazy, man. You know that."

It was usually better not to congregate at the bench so everybody preferred to wait in the Melodine or watch the action on the slope. Jim and Larry would go alone.

"Damn, he was paranoid today, we had to go off with him to where he stashed it in a phone box. There was some fucker in there making a call and Christopher is pacing around holding his bicycle over his head in complete panic. Then he just busts into the phone box and grabs the package. The poor bugger inside was scared stiff."

The first time Isolt had met Christopher was an autumn Sunday years ago when she was sixteen years old and had just left home. She was sitting on the bench in a dismal little park in Odon. He came dragging his tartan shopping cart and wearing an out-of-date long sheepskin coat. He had a mop of curly black hair and a drooping mustache. She had been with Jim, drinking a case of beer. He stopped beside them.

"Acid?" he hissed. "Scary clowns, the cleanest."

Jim bought two hits and gave one to Isolt. It was the first time she tripped and she did not know what to expect. Christopher exchanged a few words with Jim and went on his way.

"Do you know him?" Isolt had asked.

"No, not really. I've seen him around. He's a paranoid, acid head American who lives in Versailles."

Isolt looked at the acid; it was a tiny white square of paper with a clown's face on it.

"You can get all kind of designs. Put it on your tongue and let it dissolve."

She did as she was told. "What now?"

"Welcome home, baby!" he had said, handing her another beer.

Isolt had looked at him glumly as she sipped the beer. It sounded kind of sinister to her.

The lads told her that Christopher hated women. He had a French girlfriend, though he kept her off the circuit and in the background. She was meek and thin and worshipped him. They told Isolt if she came to score to keep her mouth shut. Isolt consequently avoided Christopher as she did not relish being silenced just because she was a girl. She and Becky would give their money and let the men do the strutting about and scoring. As long as they were high every night they didn't care.

Christopher lived in a big squat in Versailles which he shared with a bunch of beggars. He rented a room in Saint-Lazare where his girlfriend lived and he rented a *chambre de bonne* in the attic of a building in the sixteenth district. He had found the squat Isolt now lived in and he called around once in a blue moon. When he did Isolt felt the situation to be different and she did not feel too inhibited to join in the conversation. He never objected, though she confessed to Becky that she never felt at ease in his presence. Becky agreed.

"He gives me the creeps. I can never hear what he's saying, he talks so low and he's always so paranoid. One acid too many if you ask me. He hates me. I can't bear to be in the same room as him. He's always telling the lads to get rid of me behind my back. That I'm trouble and a junkie. As if they can throw me out of here. He has no rank over me, I don't fall for his bullshit. This is a squat. He hasn't the guts to say it to my face. He thinks he controls that place in Versailles, not letting any women through the door. He's just like the Arabs, he'd prefer women in veils. He's afraid of women if you ask me. Just look at that droopy little girl he's got. Fucking pathetic. Stuck up, pretty French cow. She's a poor little rich kid. Hanging on to him for something, probably to piss her parents off. I know that type a mile away. The cheek of him trying to oust me. I'd like to see him try it, the spic midget. I'd punch his fucking lights out if he ever tried anything. He says I'm a junkie and will bring the law in. He can talk. I see him score smack too—that Malaysian guy says he buys some every other day."

"Christopher is a junkie?" Isolt was shocked.

"Yeah. He's pretty controlled but you see him always slugging that codeine medicine. That's to relive his monkey. He's a junkie all right and I know one when I see one. I bet all that crowd out in Versailles are junkies. He should be more sympathetic to me, he knows what it's like, the little cunt. He never complains that you're here. Maybe he likes you. Maybe Christopher is in love. Ha! Ha!"

Isolt smiled. "That's a somewhat dubious privilege."

"Stay away, girl, that's all I can say."

Isolt was flattered all the same. It was always good to hear she had one less enemy than she had previously thought.

The days went on. The grey days. They dug deep. She fell asleep. It was too heavy. More like a small death. Dreamless and dark. A long howl, being wrenched away. When she awoke she did not feel right. It was as if she had awoken somewhere different from where she first lay. The weight in her head, her shaking hands. This was Isolt's afternoon nap.

It was summer in Paris. The tourists were swarming over the monuments. A French Arab had tried to commit suicide by throwing himself off Notre Dame cathedral and he survived by landing on a Canadian tourist. It was the tourist that died.

Two Afghan guys moved into the squat. Becky slept with one of them and then went into hermitage in her room, staring at the broken metal detector.

One night Christopher the dealer brought a Vietnamese man to the squat. He was small and gentle; he wore a top hat and walked barefoot on the dirty pavements. Christopher brought them all into the sitting room and told them that this smiling little man could levitate. They sat around while the man hummed with his thin eyelids shut over his watery brown eyes. Nothing happened. Larry shook his head.

"Christ, Christopher, it's a good job he doesn't do this for a living."

Nevertheless they were all amused. Ali had a pocket piano with a four-tune instruction manual and was playing "Joy to the World." It had a puny, empty, tin sound. They were all stoned and happy. Only Becky seemed detached and irritated. The Vietnamese man opened his eyes and turned his soft face to her as if sensing her lone disenchantment.

"You are an English flower," he whispered.

"And you are a Vietnamese weed," she snapped, going back to her room. Jim stopped her.

"Come on, Becky. Lighten up, it's only a bit of a laugh."

Becky winced. "I'm thirty years old."

"Thirty-six," Isolt corrected her.

"OK, thirty-six. I'm tired of all this shit. My liver is fucked, my brain is dead, my whole body is rotting. I've nothing to look forward to but death on the streets. My husband hates me and my kids have probably forgotten me and blame me for abandoning them and all my so-called friends are freaks and misfits . . ."

"Oh well," Jim said. "At least you have heroin to fall back on."

Christopher said something snide to the Afghans that nobody could hear and they said something in Farsi to Ali. They all laughed and looked at Becky. Becky caught it and glared at them. "I hate you and your primitive culture. You too, Christopher, especially you. You should know better. I hope you die poor and alone and I hope you die soon and I hope you die screaming."

She fled from the squat. Isolt followed her down onto the street.

"Leave me alone, Irish, sit this one out. I need to be alone."

Isolt walked with her in silence. Becky turned to her. "I hate men. I hate all their big, macho world. I hate their macho Gods. All the Bible and all the rest of the stuff they say is all just macho-shit-talk. This whole world . . . Oh no! . . . Oh God! . . ."

She closed her eyes and groaned. She dug her nails into Isolt's arms and said something else. Isolt didn't know what; still she acknowledged her wisdom and began to cry.

"Don't cry, Isolt. You will be OK. You never expect anything so how can you be disappointed?"

Isolt couldn't stop crying so Becky took her to a café and bought her a beer while she snivelled into a napkin. People were staring. The waiter took his time serving them. Isolt felt that he hated them. Everybody in the café hated them. The Parisians hated them. Their own countries hated them.

"Isolt?" Becky said.

"What?" Isolt sniffed.

"I'm glad you're not a man."

Isolt squeezed her hand but Becky withdrew it. "Because you would be a right fucker if you were."

The Vietnamese guy padded quietly in holding his top hat with his two tiny hands in front of him.

Becky smiled. "Christ, look who's here. The oriental acrobat. Jesus, they're going to love us three."

The waiter exchanged glances with the patron when the little man sat softly beside them.

"Do you speak English?" Becky asked.

The gentle man smiled but said nothing. Becky threw her eyes up to heaven.

"Oh God! His conversation is about as good as his levitation stunts."

The three of them sat. Isolt ordered three more beers. Eventually Jim and Larry came down and they had a good session of it. All of them promised never to speak to Christopher again. All of them broke the promise within the week; all except Larry who never spoke to him anyway. The Vietnamese moved in on Becky's insistence.

"We can put him on the mantelpiece," she explained.

They were thrown out of the café at three o'clock in the morning and told not to come back. Isolt realised that Becky had spent thirty-six years in a world that did not want her. The strain was beginning to show.

Isolt felt she was just an eternal witness. Brought up before the great court, she would stand in the box and tell the jury of a shabby world that was hard to live in, where all the old ladies had varicose veins and all the dogs had cataract eyes. That was not the way she always saw the world. Sometimes it was the only way she could see the world.

She said to herself, "I am not the son of God. Nor would I have had it that way. The daughter of something that was there once but no longer is. All I can say is, God love you, Jesus, if your father let them do that to you. I would not have let it happen to any friend of mine. If I had had any power I would have reached out and stopped them before they wove the very first thorns in that cruel crown. I would have broken their spines."

The lies. Those sacred lies. The dreary repetition in those dark high-ceiling classrooms. Prayers of all the wrong way of doing things. Still, for years she murmured them solemnly with all the rest of the daughters and sons, while they patiently waited for life to come trundling down the iron tracks like a noisy train. Nothing ever came.

About twenty of them were crouched in a circle on the grass around the Eiffel Tower. The drink had run out and having no miracle worker in their midst, Larry suggested that they go to an off-licence near Bastille and do a smash and grab. Jim, Becky and the infamous Rory went along—Rory who had arrived on the scene for the first time and who could not understand the undying interest Larry took in his eating habits and relationship with animals. They were back in the squat when the others came in. The smash and grab had been a success. Larry couldn't believe it.

"You really did it? I was only joking."

Everybody was laughing and slapping each other on the back. Jim and Rory were telling the story interrupting each other.

"I tell you the glass wouldn't break. Rory had to hit it about six times."

Rory shaking his head. "Ah no Jim, about ten bloody times I swear."

Isolt turned and saw Becky on the couch. She was very drunk and was sewing something with a needle and thread. Isolt looked closer over the candle-lit web of smokey air and

saw what it was that she was sewing so intently. It was her leg.
Jim saw Isolt's horror and hastened to explain.

"You see Rory did the smashing, Becky leapt into the window
to do the grabbing and her thigh got ripped on the glass . . ."

"What did you do, Jim?" Larry eyed him suspiciously.

"I did most of the running." Jim the ever-gallant hero.

They all did the drinking. Becky was so drunk that she confessed to not feeling a thing. She finished stitching the gash in
her thigh and poured some whiskey over the now-closed wound.

It was the next day that Isolt sat in the squat looking through
a crack in one of the shutters. She could see Becky limping up
the hill to the station with a bottle in her hand. Jim saw her
sitting there.

"You're not going out?" he said gently.

"No, I think I'll leave the economy alone today."

"Still looking for that bag of money to take you to
Amsterdam?"

"Still looking. This is the longest week in Paris I ever spent.
Eight bloody months now."

He was walking out: "Remember, if you leave, to put the
chain on the door."

Yes, she thought, the chain. The wolves are at each door. We
have to chain the door. Oh silent Christ, keep the wolves away
for a little while longer. I'll get to Amsterdam. Don't let the
wolves come in while I am here.

Becky woke her one night to tell her that the squat was on
fire. Isolt was reluctant to investigate but Becky was so insistent that she wearily got up and went to check all the rooms.
Only sleeping bodies, debris and the stale smell of smoke and
unwashed flesh. The Vietnamese was looking at Isolt from his
corner, his emaciated legs crossed. She shuddered. He never
seemed to sleep or eat. He gave her the creeps.

"Nothing, Becky, not even a lighted cigarette butt. Only an

anorexic, insomniac, shell-shocked Vietnamese trying to levitate. One of these days I'll come in and find him suspended in
mid-air. He's been at it long enough." Becky was not listening
to her but crouched up, hugging her thin legs and chanting,
"It's on fire, I swear and we don't want to see that happen . . .
I've seen a Greek whose face was melted from rotting fire. I
could get a bad smell from the room. Are you sick?, I asked
him, is it the sweet sickliness of cancer? Go away, he said, I clean
this house. I went, there is no ease to my flight. What good is
good? he said, when the cheating men take everything. So I
am here now but you know this is no long, yellow field, this is
the burnt street. This is no overgrown ditch, those are rows of
mean shops, overpriced . . . What's good is good. I remember
somebody told me to come back . . . Who was it?

"Look at me for there is another fire and I am already incin-
erated and the lipstick won't hide it. Will I carry these burnt
ashes home? Nobody believes it is human what I am. The Greek
told me, this town will eat you alive, but I said, you are too late,
rinse your mouth out and have them for dessert. Start again
after. It won't stop through me. There is a death beat running
through. Hide . . .

"My God we are all on fire . . . The hot winds prevent you
from walking, just as the cold stopped you from stepping outside . . . In Israel I wanted to get back where there is rain on the
windows . . . you were there too, did you? . . . Crushing insects
on your legs—did you notice how some won't die? . . . Please
bring me the silence, grant me some of that which you worked
for. Go now hurry! Put out the fire. Find me the God of which
you have spoken. He is gone from my room, leaving the smell
of disappointment behind . . . Hear the flames crackling? FIRE.
FIRE. FIRE. FIRE."

Isolt had not noticed that Becky's chanted whisper had
become a scream. The others were standing at the door.

"She thinks the place is on fire!" Isolt gasped. "That's what she's talking about. A fire."

Larry grabbed her. "Calm down, love. She's just got the DTs or something. Maybe she took some acid earlier. Sleep in my room. Jim will stay with her."

Isolt obeyed mutely. Larry gave her a cigarette but her hands were shaking too badly to light it.

"The wolves, Larry, the wolves are at the door."

"Don't you start," he said. "One mad bird is enough around here."

He put a blanket around her. The stench brought her to her senses. He seemed to have a collection of them.

Isolt did not sleep that night. What frightened her was beyond what was happening to Becky. What frightened her was the ranting speech. It was not in Becky's words. It was not Becky's language or imagery. These were Isolt's words, Isolt's recurring fearful imagery. It was Isolt's speech that Becky screamed at her.

Could her world have slipped away? Could it have gone without her noticing it? Just like that? So that her words could be screamed at her from another body? Is that madness? Had she gone mad and not noticed it? That was possible. Does the guide book tell you how to find a world that has slipped away? Does the guide book tell you how to know when to stop sightseeing and go home? Is there an index at the back listing cheap mental health clinics for when your mind finally goes and your subconscious slips into another head and shouts back at you?

Two months later, while Jim and Isolt were at the cinema, Rory was trying to fix the metal detector and left it in the hall. Becky walked from their room all strung out on heroin. While Isolt and Jim were at the cinema and Rory was at the shop and Larry was dozing in his room, their good friend Becky tripped over her beloved metal detector, fell down the stairs and broke her neck. She died instantly, without even knowing she was dying. Rory found the body on his return. Larry said he heard her fall but there was no scream and he assumed it was only the metal detector that fell.

They left the body in its exact position. Nobody touched her. They cleared their stuff out and went, leaving her passport on her chest for identification. They rang the police from a coin box.

The police would have found a corpse of a thirty-six-year-old female with needle-marked arms outstretched on the stairs and a semi-starved Vietnamese in the living room, emaciated legs crossed, no doubt a gentle smile on his face. They would have stepped over a metal detector at the head of the stairs.

The wolves had been fed.

Isolt went with Rory to Amsterdam the next week. Jim told them that he would join them in a couple of days. He never arrived. Larry remained in Paris. Rory and Isolt spent winter in Holland working in a hostel that was on a barge and in spring they bought tickets to London. It was only here in Amsterdam, among the cobblestones, the hurtling trams and the iced-over canals, that Isolt began to realize she had lost one of the main characters of her life. It was only here she knew that eight months sharing a room and exchanging thoughts was a long time. Becky's death was the first warning, a bleak premonition. She began to love her truly in the aftermath of her life for the lesson she had been taught. She often felt compelled in that time to write down Becky's story but after much deliberation she decided against it.

Better just never to forget. She would leave writing to the writers and rely on reading and waiting and watching and tinking.

Think of the sound "tink," shallow and brief.

Isolt stood ankle deep in the smooth waters of Paris, letting the idle waves lap about her feet. Outside, the vast oceans of loneliness were pointlessly singing.

She had watched Becky stumble out to work with a bottle in her hand under the doomed sky.

"God bless your eyesight—when you saw the flames from far away, you woke us all to warn us. Though we fled for shelter in the coming years, you stood as if caught in some childhood dream, unable to move."

Mike McCormack

The Occupation: A Guide for Tourists

Launching himself on the literary scene in 1996 with the short-story collection *Getting It in the Head*, Mike McCormack cut a lonely figure among Irish writers of his generation. His early work owed more to the experimentalism of J. G. Ballard, the gothic obsessions of Edgar Allan Poe, and the technomodernist theorising of Jean Baudrillard and Martin Heidegger, than to the domestic realists more commonly cited by his peers. McCormack was awarded the Rooney Prize for Literature for his debut, and since then has published a further story collection, *Forensic Songs*, and three novels, *Crowe's Requiem*, *Notes From a Coma*, and *Solar Bones*. Awarded the Goldsmiths Prize and the Bord Gaís Energy Irish Book of the Year in 2016, *Solar Bones* was described by Ian Samson in *The Guardian* as 'exceptional indeed; an extraordinary novel'. In 2010 John Waters in *The Irish Times* declared *Notes From a Coma* to be the greatest Irish novel of the preceding decade.

Mike McCormack was born in London in 1965, grew up in Louisburgh, County Mayo, and has lived for much of his adult life in Galway. He studied English and philosophy at University College, Galway, and after graduating spent much of his twenties immersed in the city's bohemian and visual-arts culture, eventually marrying the artist Maeve Curtis. McCormack has been a persistent advocate for a reanimation of the experimental ethos in Irish writing, arguing that without it the national literature will be rendered irrelevant in a globalised culture. In an interview with *Hot Press* magazine, he expressed pride in his commitment to an artistic vision that has not always translated into commercial success, saying, 'I've written the books I want to write, and nothing has really infringed upon them in any way'.

In an afterword he wrote for a reissue of *Getting It in the Head* years after it was first published, McCormack recalled making the resolution 'that there would be as little as possible of that pallid soul searching which slowed things up and too often tried to pass itself off as storytelling'. Eerily prescient of the geo-political snuff-movie horrors witnessed in the years subsequent to its publication, 'The Occupation: A Guide For Tourists' is from that collection.

The Occupation: A Guide for Tourists

My JEEP WAS one of a dozen vehicles tailed back from the checkpoint. It was the last vehicle in a convoy of three other jeeps, several marked container trucks carrying emergency medical aid and one transit van fitted with radio and signalling equipment. Up ahead, the border security were swarming over the first trucks, searching through the cabs and spilling the contents out onto the dusty road. One of the guards had disappeared into the security hut with a handful of our entry permits. An air of surly menace hung over the guards. They had the aspect of men completing a despicably menial task by way of punishment. Every one of them needed a shave and a new issue of fatigues. The thirty-year occupation showed in every filthy, frayed piece of webbing and in the corroded state of their antiquated weaponry; and this was the occupying army.

Ours were the first vehicles to gain entry to the occupation in fifteen years. We were a detail of Amnesty observers coming to verify rumours of horrific and systematic human rights abuses. During the last year details of work camps and smuggled photographic evidence of mass rape and torture had been finding its way into the western press. Eventually world conscience had been sufficiently moved to force a UN resolution which achieved a temporary opening of the border. We were the first entrants but, somewhere to our rear, a massive convoy of relief aid under UN guard was wending its way through the desert.

Evidently this border detail was taking the recent UN resolution as something of a personal insult. Only such lofty censure could account for the sheer sense of affront exuded by the soldier who was making his way towards me. He was a blunt hump of a man whose skin had been weathered to the texture of old leather. His corporal's stripes were barely visible beneath the mantle of dust that clung about him. He was handing back the visas to the other travellers without a word. When he stood before me I saw that he had also handed out a second document, a few xeroxed pages. I read it through and I quote it here in full. It was titled *The Occupation: A Guide for Tourists.* It went on:

I. While travelling in a foreign country you come upon a terrible scene. Atop a hill a young man is being put to death before a crowd of onlookers. He has recently been nailed to a cross. Blood streams from a wound in his side and his thin body is faced into the full glare of the sun. He does not have long to live. Do you:

A. Feel outrage and disgust and immediately cut the man down from the cross?

B. Pass quickly without saying a word? You will not presume to meddle in the judicial procedures of your host country. Besides, the man was obviously a notorious criminal who got what was coming to him.

C. Admire the skill with which the whole tableau has been staged and resolve to seek out the theatre company and make them a lavish contribution.

If your answer is **A**, then proceed to **2A**, if **B** to **2B**, if **C** to **2C** and so on.

2A. You take the man to a small hospital on the outskirts of the city and try to sign him in at casualty as your brother. While the man lies bleeding on a trolley you enter into a sordid dispute with the hospital bursar. You finally undertake to pay the medical fees in foreign currency, American dollars and Deutschmarks mainly. You also surrender your passport as security. The patient is wheeled away rapidly for emergency surgery and you spend the next few days in the city while the man is monitored in the intensive care unit.

2B. You have put the incident quickly out of your mind and spend a few days touring the outlying countryside and city. You discover terrible scenes of waste and devastation. The occupying armies have requisitioned crops and animals and the country's infrastructure is a shambles. Whole provinces have been isolated by cratered roads and demolished bridges; famine and disease are rife in the worst-hit areas. When you reach the city you find that it is crawling with paupers and wounded veterans, the thoroughfares of the commercial centre are a *chevaux-de-frise* of broken glass and strewn metal.

2C. You trace the theatre company to an abandoned warehouse by the railway station. They are a small company specialising in a particularly vivid brutalism. Productions of *Hamlet* and *Oedipus Rex* have taken a devastating toll on the players and their confidence is at a low ebb. They have recently had to pull out of an important production because of a shortage of funds. You make an offer to underwrite this new production and it is accepted with gratitude. You are treated as a messiah.

3A. After four days the young man regains consciousness. He is tended to by a retinue of a dozen men his own age. The surgeon introduces you as his saviour but he is singularly lacking in gratitude when told of your intervention. He accuses you of having thwarted his destiny and of arrogantly meddling in things of which you know nothing.

3B. An explosion in the commercial area of the city results in many casualties. A rebel attack on an army convoy has been completely mis-timed, the device goes off near a mobile soup kitchen killing mainly women and children, injuring hundreds. You sign up at a mobile blood transfusion unit and donate 500 mls of blood. Pandemonium reigns in the streets and you volunteer to do relief work in one of the field hospitals.

3C. As part of the underground art movement you learn that the company has a constant fear of infiltration by the authorities: it has been rightly identified as the source of resistance propaganda. Several productions in the past have been shut down by the security forces.

4A. After ten days your relationship with the patient has not improved. He is incommunicative and evasive. No one will reveal his identity and local police have no record of him having committed any crime. You decide to persevere with your efforts of friendship for a few more days.

4B. You are contacted at the hotel by the transfusion unit who inform you that you have a developed case of HIV. You spend the rest of the day drinking heavily at the hotel bar. Outside there is a heavy military presence. Patrols move continuously up and down the street, never resting except to disperse small gatherings and send people on their way with a cuff of their gun butts. Overhead, helicopters cross the sky and when night falls searchlights probe the streets. Everyone suspects that there are several more incendiary devices triggered to go off.

4C. The company has planned a final production of an ancient morality play. It will be a public performance with an overtly political theme; it is hoped that it will incite the city to all-out, unified resistance against the invaders. You are sworn to secrecy and at their request you take on a minor but significant role in the production.

5A. Psychological tests have shown that the patient suffers from a complex of neuroses ranging from severe paranoia to extreme credulity in occult and New Age religions, healing crystals and tarot cards. The psychologist remarks that this condition is not unusual, the character of the occupation has given rise to several such cases. He has treated several men, all with undocumented pasts, who claim to have healing and regenerative talents. He will not venture a prognosis.

5B. After four days wandering through the city in a drunken stupor you sober up near a brothel. It is the middle of the night, in heavy darkness, but your mind is now clear. You enter the brothel and promptly engage in several acts of anal intercourse with under-age boys. You then refuse to pay. There follows a tense moment when a search by bouncers reveals that you are carrying no currency whatsoever. You calmly await the arrival of the police.

5C. Rehearsals are continuing smoothly and you are now enjoying a privileged status within the company. You realise that there is an unspoken effort among the players to court your goodwill. They bring you small gifts of hard-to-get coffee and local craftware. Furthermore you have discovered a talent for acting and your performance has drawn genuine praise from the other players.

6A. The patient's attitude has now developed to outright hostility. You narrowly escape serious injury when he attacks you with scissors in the recreation room. You are rescued by four male nurses. The psychologist explains that you have now assumed demonic status in the patient's imagination. Not only are you responsible for a salvation he did not need but also for the political failure of his death. He suspects that you are an army spy.

6B. You co-operate fully with your interrogators and admit to having no funds whatsoever. You astonish them further by confessing to six attempted murders via the sexual act. Your captors are in a quandary; they need to prosecute but are unsure of the grounds on which to proceed: the emergency laws have no provisions for dealing with aliens. On a sheet of paper you outline the charges against yourself and draw up details of an emergency bill covering the crime of murder by sexually trans-mitted disease. You advise that the bill be made law as quickly as possible and waive the right to a preliminary hearing. You are scheduled to stand trial in three days.

6C. You have begun to covet the lead role in the play. The principal player is a buffoon whose every word and gesture grates on your soul. As a method actor he has immersed himself totally in the role. He has assumed a facile air of wisdom and his speech has become littered with anodyne, pastoral anecdotes. Several of the female players have begun to attest that he has a cure for menstrual cramp. You resolve to turn him over to the authorities. You begin to circulate information about him in various bars and cafeterias.

7A. You now have misgivings about the wisdom of your intervention. It is revealed to you that the patient is one of the leaders of the resistance and that you have interfered with a mythopoeic event essential to the salvation of the city. Your responsibility for the fate of the people weighs heavily on your conscience and after a night of soul searching you resolve to make amends.

7B. Your trial begins in the ruins of a religious museum. The witnesses testify from the pulpit and the judge is seated behind the altar. At his back, the door of the tabernacle has been recently shattered. The jury is made up of out-patients from a nearby infirmary. You conduct your own defence but limit your examination to apparently pointless questions on the history of the occupation. In your closing speech you plead guilty and urge that the maximum sentence be handed down. In his summative speech the judge congratulates you on the skill and clarity of your defence. He speaks at length on the ground-breaking nature of the trial and assures you that your name will merit a chapter to itself in the judicial history of his country.

7C. On his way home from rehearsals the principal actor is picked up by the security forces. After interrogations and beatings he signs a detailed confession outlining various subversive activities and connections. Morale in the company plummets when several more members are implicated. The company is now gutted of a large part of its artistic and administrative talent; its future is in real jeopardy. You move quickly to take charge of the production, promptly casting yourself in the principal role and allocating the lesser ones in such a way as to throw light on your performance. There is a feeling of renewed confidence.

8A. You outline your plan to the patient and after consultation with his cadre it is decided that it will go ahead. You are issued with a new identity which places you immediately in the pantheon of resistance heroes who have kept the flame of national salvation burning. Within days you are being greeted surreptitiously as the hidden king.

8B. After only two hours' deliberation the jury file back into the pews and the foreman returns a guilty verdict. You congratulate yourself on having conducted a successful defence. The judge commends the jury on their verdict and then draws a black cowl over his head before delivering the sentence. You hear that your execution will be expedited immediately and that there are no provisions for an appeal.

8C. The day of the production is drawing close. Flyers have been distributed and a large crowd is anticipated. The dressmaker works long into the night preparing your costume; there are numerous alterations to be made before it will fit. You spend the rest of the evening at a small restaurant with the rest of the cast.

9A. The patient briefs you on the details of your mission. Initially overcome by crippling fear, you surmount it with the knowledge that a whole nation is depending on you. Besides, events have now taken on a momentum of their own. You are robed in a regal gown and a makeshift crown is placed upon your head. You are paraded through the slums of the city to a summit on its outskirts, the site of your ascension. On your journey various thugs take the opportunity to indulge in indiscriminate violence, and there are several scuffles with your minders. By the time you reach the summit you have sustained injuries to your abdomen and your cloak has been ripped away.

9B. You are led from the museum into sunlight wearing a sign which details your crimes. When your eyes have adjusted to the sunshine you are taken through the streets where the crowds are gathering to view some sort of pageant. Upon reading your crimes they grow incensed and start to attack you. They seem to have a ready supply of whips and chains and start to rain blows down upon you. By the time you reach the execution summit your body is running with blood.

9C. The routes are lined by heavy crowds conspicuously armed with whips, chains and sticks. You move serenely at the head of your supporting cast and the production is going smoothly. Suddenly the onlookers play the part of persecutors. They work your body in passing and by the time you reach the summit your torso is a tracery of lacerations and you have begun to hallucinate. You try to hold your focus on the lines of your parting speech.

10. Beneath the cross you are given a final moment in which to address the crowd. The soldiers stand aside and an expectant hush descends upon the multitude. You have their full attention. You begin haltingly, it is your first public address and your voice lacks resonance. Gradually, however, you gain in confidence and your speech becomes a ringing affirmation of life, the sacredness of resistance through arms and art and the necessity of justice. The murmur of assent grows until a wave of applause breaks over you; it is sustained while the soldiers take you bodily and hoist you onto the cross. As the nails are driven in you feel no pain, your ecstasy has lifted you beyond sensation. From your perch you can see out over the crowd down onto the ruins of the city. Columns of smoke billow in several parts and food queues are visible in every quarter. This is your kingdom and auditorium, your panopticon, and it remains fixed in your imagination until consciousness, like the daylight, drains away to darkness.

I gazed past the checkpoint into the occupied country. The dirt road beyond the sentry post curved past an isolated grove of cedars, wending its way to the top of a low summit. Halfway up the slope a woman led a donkey carrying a huge bundle of kindling. Beyond the hill the city cast up a grey pall of smoke, shrouding the summit. Beneath the smoke vague shadows moved. I took my binoculars and gazed into the fug; I saw that the joiners were already working on the crosses.

Philip Ó Ceallaigh

The Song of Songs

PHILIP Ó CEALLAIGH is one in a long line of Irish writers who opted to get out and stay out. For years he has been living in Bucharest; the gritty post-Soviet cities of Eastern Europe dominate his two story collections to date, *Notes From a Turkish Whorehouse* and *The Pleasant Light of Day*. Born in rural Waterford in 1968, Ó Ceallaigh studied philosophy at University College Dublin, and after graduating began a roaming, factotum's life that would eventually see him settle in Romania in 2000. Previously he had lived in Russia, America, Kosovo, Spain, Georgia, and Egypt.

Ó Ceallaigh's debut collection, *Notes From a Turkish Whorehouse*, won the Rooney Prize for Literature in 2006, and his next book, *The Pleasant Light of Day*, was the first Irish collection to be shortlisted for the Frank O'Connor International Short Story Award. In a review of that book, Joseph O'Connor described Ó Ceallaigh as a writer 'already touched by greatness'.

Philip Ó Ceallaigh's fictions are almost exclusively set outside of Ireland—in locations as diverse as Romania, the United States, and indeed a Turkish whorehouse. On his decision to settle in Bucharest in his early thirties and devote himself to writing, Ó Ceallaigh has said, 'Writing seemed the only compensation for much of the shit that happened to me, and now I was committed to sitting in my little room and typing at the edge of a disintegrating and brutalised city.'

In 2010, Ó Ceallaigh edited *Sharp Sticks, Driven Nails*, an anthology of short stories published by Stinging Fly Press. His novel *And You Wake Up Laughing* was published in a Romanian translation in 2012. He wrote a screenplay adaptation of one of his stories, 'A Very Unsettled Summer', which was filmed in Romania in 2013. In 2015 Penguin Modern Classics published Ó Ceallaigh's translation of Mihail Sebastian's novel of the 1930s, *For Two Thousand Years*. He is currently working on a non-fiction book that examines the destruction of Eastern Europe's Jews through the lives and work of writers of the era. 'The Song of Songs' is from *The Pleasant Light of Day*.

The Song of Songs

SHE WAS GETTING OFF a bus with about twenty others when he saw her. If you don't fuck this one, thought Joey, you can toss yourself off the balcony. Though Joey did not like big asses specifically, there was something special in the vast twin rotundities atop short solid legs like triangles, down to the points of her heels tap-tapping the asphalt as she negotiated her way through the profane human mess. She wore loose semi-transparent cotton trousers—well, maybe cotton, he didn't really know—and her thong panties made a tiny triangle of fabric over her tailbone. He was looking at a big naked ass, basically.

Motion was the holy spirit that gave the language of the ass, the ass-song, its poetry, and hers was the soul of sex in motion, rolling and flowing to the mad music of the heavens. Joey mouthed the words:

> Love is as powerful as death;
> Passion is as strong as death itself.
> It bursts into flame
> And burns like a raging fire.
> Water cannot put it out;
> No flood can drown it.

It was a hot day. He felt that if he rose forward on his toes and held his breath, it would happen, that he would float above the people and the traffic.

Everybody was getting out of work, determined to get back to the buildings where they ate and slept. People struggled with each other to board buses and made it very hard for the people getting off. The people on the footpath hurried to connect with other buses, with trams, and walked into those going the opposite direction. Joey pushed his way through the human obstacles and followed her.

At the intersection she did not join the throng waiting to cross the road. She turned left. The people were fewer now and he followed at a discreet distance. Her generous haunches set off a slim waist, delicate back and narrow shoulders.

Some women had the shape but did not have the motion. This one, walking ahead of him, had that very pure lateral gyration, the sideways switch of the hips on the horizontal plane, inflected only slightly by the nodding vertical motion of each buttock. Women, Joey figured, didn't just bleed to the moon and wake to the sun: the movement of their backsides, like all heavenly bodies, could be described on a series of planes. The annual journey of the earth around the sun could be described on a horizontal plane, relative to which the daily rotation of the globe occurred on a vertical axis. These two axes intersected at the earth's centre. On the axis of the horizontal and lateral movements of the female backside, Joey also posited a central point. He did not know whether it was in her cunt or up her ass, but this was dead bones anyway, like mathematics, irrelevant to the fact that the world spun, women shook their buttocks, and it was all magical and sad.

About a hundred metres after a shack made of aluminium or some kind of metal, that sold booze, chocolate and cigarettes all night, she turned left towards the entrance of a block, rummaging in her handbag for keys.

Joey grunted and leapt the steps, caught the door with his fingertips just in time. As the ass disappeared round a corner, he slid into the cool shadows of the hallway and pressed his back against the cold wall. He heard her opening the lift door and entering and pulling the clunking door after her.

She ascended in the metal box, and Joey strode forward. He

watched the lighted display as she rode past the fourth, fifth, sixth floors. It stopped at the seventh.

He called the lift and rode to the seventh.

There were four apartments on the floor. He pressed his ears to the door closest to the lift. There was no sound. At the second door a man and a woman were talking. He reckoned a new gearbox. She thought the bathroom should be retiled. Joey moved on. At the third door the television was on. The newscaster said it would be a very hot week. Some people were going to the mountains, but most people were going to the coast. There would be a special report, random citizens giving their accounts of hot weather. Joey moved on to the last door. He heard a toilet flush. That was her. He knew it. He knocked.

—Whozat?

—Joey!

—Who?

—Joey! The windows man!

She opened the door. Her face was nothing special. Round and kind of stupid. No matter. Her hallway was still painted with the cheap greyish mud they sprayed on the walls when the block was first built, thirty-something years before. Linoleum on the floor. Probably she rented, and worked in a government office where there was not much to do.

—Special offer for PVC double-glazing, said Joey. Do it in the summer, you'll be glad in the winter.

—No, thank you.

—Colossal savings on utilities. Free estimates.

—Not interested.

—Here, let me give you my card, case you change your mind.

Joey went through his pockets but there was no card, because he never had any printed.

—I can come back.

She closed the door.

Joey took the stairs back down, two at a time.

That night he woke from the dream, the moon shining in his window.

> *I will stay on the hill of myrrh,*
> *The hill of incense*
> *Until the morning breezes blow*
> *And the darkness disappears.*

He stood up and knew it would happen even before it did. He rose up on his toes and just kept going, gently, like a balloon, and put a hand up and touched the ceiling. He pushed gently against the ceiling and came back to the floor. It was a simple matter of concentration. With practice he would learn to control it, surely, and fly as high as he liked. He could probably launch himself off the balcony and float down to the street, five floors down. But he did not think he should try that trick just yet.

He knocked on the door. He could hear the after-work of the television. He closed his eyes, ignoring the sound as best he could, and breathed, reciting:

> *I have come down among the almond trees*
> *To see the young plants in the valley,*
> *To see the new leaves on the vines*
> *And the blossoms on the pomegranate trees.*
> *I am trembling; you have made me as eager for love*
> *As a chariot driver is for battle.*

He felt the lightness and pushed off gently from the floor. The door opened.

—Holy fuck! said the woman.

He opened his eyes. He was levitating very slightly. He felt it wavering and brought himself back down.

She looked around the hallway.

—I come in peace, said Joey.

—Yeah right. How do you explain THAT?

Joey sighed.

—Do not be afraid. It's a gift. I don't understand it yet myself.

—Wait a minute, aren't you the windows man?

—It's true, I can do windows, but that's not why I'm here. Can I come in a minute?

She looked around, suspicious.

—Listen, said Joey, you're going to have to trust me. Do you believe in angels?

—Alright, then, you'd better come inside.

He entered the hall and she closed the door. He introduced himself. They shook hands. Her name was Maria.

—Pleased to meet you, Maria.

In the hallway the good smell of the meat and onions she had been frying in old grease. On the TV they were moving through the ads.

—So, get to the point, said Maria.

—I've chosen you, said Joey, from amongst all women.

She raised her eyebrows and opened her mouth.

—Is this some kinda—

—You saw me fly, didn't you? You think it's easy to do that?

—I saw some kinda trick, don't know what it was. Wasn't flying exactly. Floating a little bit maybe . . .

Hard to impress some of these ladies, thought Joey.

—Want me to do it again, huh?

—Wouldya?

—If I'm not interrupting your evening's viewing.

The television was on very loud, advertising instant soup. They went into the small room where she lived. There was a narrow mattress on the floor.

—Do it again, so, said Maria.

—Help me out a bit. Can you turn off that racket? Got anything to drink? Some nice music?

Maria switched off the set and indicated a small cassette player. She went to the kitchen and Joey looked through the cassettes. They all showed stocky men wearing tight tops, grinning horribly. Adrian the Wonder-Boy, one was called. Keyboard and drum-machine pop. He turned on the radio and tuned into a classical music programme and got lucky with a Chopin nocturne, in B-flat minor. The sun was going down and from the window it looked like half the city was on fire. Fine by him if it really was. The fire engines could howl down through the smoky twilight streets and they could all go to hell. Maria returned with a litre of red wine and two water glasses, and Joey felt it was going to all work out. He emptied a glass and poured another.

—Okay, then, you going to do it or what?

The piano notes surged upwards, sure of their direction.

—Yes, Maria, I certainly am. I'm going to fly specially for you, but you'll have to turn round for a moment.

—Hey! What's the big idea?

—Just for a moment, till I'm airborne, then you can look.

She turned to face the wall and Joey took another good swig. He stared at her miraculous ass. He felt it welling in him. He spoke softly:

> You, my love, excite men
> As a mare excites the stallions of pharaoh's chariots
> Your hair is beautiful upon your cheeks
> And falls along your neck like jewels.

He inhaled and pushed off and felt it, more surely this time, and was able to direct his body so that he tilted forwards a little as he gained height, floating in the middle of the room with his arms outspread.

Maria turned her head. Her eyes were popping.

—Jesus fucking Christ! Howja do that!

—Don't turn around!

Too late. Joey veered right, into the doorjamb, and crashed to the floor. Maria was beside him, her hands on his face.

—Sweetie! You OK?

—I'm still getting the hang of it.

He smiled wanly. Her hands caressed his sore head.

—Maybe you shouldn't drink when you fly, hon.

—Booze helps. Gimme some more.

He chugged another glass down, the two of them kneeling on the floor. Then he stuck his mouth on hers and reached around with his left hand and grabbed some haunch while working with his tongue. It was a good combination, with his eyes closed. When they took a break they were both breathing hard, and transfigured.

—Tell me how you do it, she murmured.

—Well, it's been a while coming, but I'm only learning how to harness my power. Actually it has something to do with you. With the essence of your womanliness.

—Hey, don't go poking fun.

—Really. When I saw you today in the street I knew you were special. But your face distracts me. Maybe I'm still a bit shy, but I need to see you from behind.

He got her onto the mattress and had his hand under the elastic of her trouser-things. He had almost worked a couple of digits into her snatch but she bucked him out of it.

—Hey, Joey, don't you think this is moving a bit fast? We haven't even talked about stuff.

—The speed feels about right. We've got something magic here, can't you feel it?

—Yeah, I can feel *something*. Joey, fly for me one more time, baby.

—Let's get it on, then I'll do loop-the-loops for you. I might leap from the balcony even.

—Listen, let me go freshen up. First you fly. Then we make love.

—Sounds good.

Maria went to the bathroom. Joey sat up on the mattress and drank some more red. He heard the water go on and thought about it flowing all over her.

When she came back she was wearing something see-through that came to just below her pussy, and fresh thong-panties.

She lowered herself onto the mattress and lay on her side. Her hips were a fine rounded mountain range with the bedside light making a Himalayan shadow onto the back wall. Her tits were nothing special.

—Listen, Joey. I want you to know this isn't something I usually do. I usually like to get to know a guy first. To go out to a restaurant and talk about things, like where we grew up and what we expect from life, and to find out if we're compatible. You know what I mean?

Yeah, I know exactly, thought Joey.

— Maria, you are the only woman I have ever flown for.

— Do it again, Joey. Do it for me.

— OK. Lie on your front. That's it. Take your panties off.

He could see it all anyway with the bit of material on but she obliged him. He took off his shoes and socks and trousers and shirt and stood there, lordly, in his shorts. Life would never be the same again for either of them, he was sure. Once he got this flying thing under control, there would be no looking back. Just ignore the face, he told himself. Concentrate on the centre of gravity. Luckily the station was doing a run of Chopin nocturnes and he had one in D-flat major that was just perfect.

The winter is over; the rains have stopped;
In the countryside the flowers are in bloom

This is the time for singing;
The song of doves is heard in the field.

He pushed off gently with his toes, giving a little more with the left for torque. He kept it going until he was right above her and felt his head graze the ceiling, then held it there above her. Gradually he came down until he was trembling above her, not touching, with his face before her ass. He rubbed his face against it and kissed it, reached down and caressed her hips, while his feet were hanging in the sky. This is it, thought Joey. This is how it is supposed to be. He felt her ass up for a good long time, not wanting it to end.

—It's OK, Joey, she said. I'm on the pill.

He murmured:

I have entered my garden,
My beloved, my bride.
I am gathering my spices and myrrh;
I am eating my honey and honeycomb;
I am drinking my wine and milk.

Flying was good, but when he was in her, giving it from behind and getting handfuls, feeling up the sun and the moon—all the stars in the sky sparking up his mind—that was the real thing too.

—OOH! UUH! Joey! Aaa!

—Huh! Huh! Huh!

—Right there!

—UH! Uh!

—Now, Joey! Now!

All the heavenly bodies rushed together and exploded briefly. There was complete darkness and one shooting star fell through the black sky like a drip from the ceiling. It went very quiet for a moment, then the radio said they would be back again at the same time next week. The ads came on. Does your deodorant ever let you down? Joey disengaged and fell off to the side, which was the floor, because the mattress was not big. The blood pounded in his head.

—You're a special guy, no doubt about it, said Maria, reaching for her smokes. She offered him one and they lit up.

He sat up properly on the linoleum and looked around. There was a row of paperbacks on a shelf of a unit. He couldn't read the titles properly but one was definitely by Paulo Coelho. On another shelf she had made up an arrangement of empty perfume bottles. It was some kind of shrine. He took a few drags of the cigarette. Maria was talking:

—Nobody ever flew for me before. I've met a lot of creepy guys. Most guys think they got a big dick or a car they're hot shit. Fuck them sons of bitches. You're the real thing, Joey. Flying, that's real magic. And you know poetry too. You don't look like much, but with this flying we've got it made. You just need a haircut and some decent clothes. Maybe if you got some exercise too, worked out or something.

Joey began to put on his clothes.

—Got to go, he said.

—Oh well. Here, gimme a big kiss.

He gave her a big kiss, just to be nice.

—Fly one more time for me, 'fore you go.

—I'd love to, Maria, but I'm pretty whacked.

—Just float a little. Nothing flashy. Here, I'll lie on my front the way you like.

She flopped onto her belly and stuck her ass in the air and wiggled it a little. He sighed.

—Why don't I leap off the balcony for you?

—You can use the front door like everyone else. Come on now! Three! Two! One! Lift off.

He looked at Maria's big fat ass. It said nothing to him. It was a dead jellyfish on the beach. He concentrated on his breathing but he knew it would not work. He did a lame little jump on the linoleum, but that was all it was.

—Hey, what was that?

He shrugged.

—Seems like I'm just like everyone else again, huh? Well, you can blame me, I can blame you, but that won't get us out of it. How about I just say thanks for a good time and we leave it at that?

He heard the glass hit the wall behind him. He was out the front door before she could throw the second one.

Back in the street the light was gone from the sky. He decided to pick up a couple of bottles of beer to drink at home. He was sad about the flying because he didn't think it would be back soon. But he didn't want to get stuck with Maria, flying or no flying. If he could get airborne for any woman, or get women by getting airborne, that would be a trick. But he knew it would not happen. There had just been something special about Maria, briefly, and that was all.

Somewhere, on a street parallel, a fire engine was screaming its way towards a burning building. The 24-hour sheet-metal shack was coming up on his right. Joey put his hand in his pocket and felt his money. At least that was still there, thank God.

Dave Lordan

Becoming Polis

DAVE LORDAN HAS been a powerful galvanising force in Irish writing in recent years, through his editing work and championing of younger writers as well as his own writing. Lordan was born in 1976 in the United Kingdom and grew up in West Cork. He came to prominence with his multi-award-winning poetry collections, *The Boy in the Ring* and *Invitation to a Sacrifice*. These were followed by a third collection, *Lost Tribe of the Wicklow Mountains*, whose title poem was set to music on legendary singer Christy Moore's album *Lily*. The story included here, 'Becoming Polis', is taken from Lordan's first collection of short fiction, *First Book of Frags*, which is among the most flagrantly unconventional books by an Irish author since Joyce's *Finnegans Wake*.

Lordan's next book will be a second collection of short fiction, *Little Museums of Dublin*, due to be published by Dalkey Archive in 2019. He has written reviews, essays, and criticism for a variety of publications, and is well known in activist communities for his engagement in a number of political causes. He has edited two anthologies of Irish writing, *New Planet Cabaret* and *Young Irelanders*, both published by New Island.

Dave Lordan's fiction fuses an incendiary prose style with an apocalyptic, metaphysically restless imagination. A writer constantly straining against the conventions of Irish literature, Lordan is steeped in science fiction, radical philosophy, and the work of Pier Paolo Pasolini. He has claimed that 'Becoming Polis' was partly inspired by Luigi Lucheni, the Italian anarchist who assassinated the Austrian Empress, Elisabeth, in 1898.

Becoming Polis

Lucheni, the world's greatest artist-assassin, princess slaughterer, shock-inventor and philosopher of police has returned from the dead and been hired by the Becoming Polis to destroy Europe. He has also been granted a small allowance for a general assistant. These are his terms for hiring:

Good English Essential. Romance languages an advantage. You must be a quiet and unobtrusive person with EXCELLENT PERSONAL HYGIENE. We will be traveling companions for months, sharing rooms and other close spaces. Therefore you must not snore, fart, scratch or masturbate while I am awake. I will not have sex with you in general but very occasionally I might, so you must produce a certificate of sexual health. You must be well-groomed in every respect; trimmed nails, no scars or tattoos. Repeat: No Scars Or Tattoos; this is not just for reasons of taste but security reasons also. You must be a person who is difficult to identify or to describe and you must be able to completely change your appearance by means of simple props like wigs and eyeliner. You must be totally obedient to me at all times and in all matters. If I decide that you must in broad daylight take a pick axe to the grave of the unknown soldier or flash your nads at the Pope in St Peter's, you must unquestioningly carry through. Because I am the ultimate boss of the destruction of Europe. What I say goes; get it? This job is not for all comers. Only the most serious persons need consider applying.

Can you play bodhrán, spoons, fiddle and a variety of whistles? Can you howl melodically, and, at the same time, rhythmically stamp?

The destruction of Europe will have a barbarian soundtrack. I have decided that. I have been instructed on the end alone; the means and all the trimmings are in my gift.

De Sade, Cervantes, Shakespeare. Complete works of each, on which you will be examined at interview. The destruction of Europe is the being of Europe; giving birth to Europe was the same thing as destroying. Do you understand that sentence? The Nova will be born in fire and blood and we are the Fireblood midwives setting the fires and letting the blood. Fire. Blood. Fire. Blood. Fire. Blood. But are we looking for a kind of umma instead? I expect you have considered opinions on such matters.

We will travel discreetly and humbly on buses and everywhere we alight will be doomed. These will be small towns and out of the way places in general, at first. I have been told that the small town as a format must be completely eradicated in Europe. You will follow me around everywhere as I doom places. You will be making a gigantic catalogue of all the different kinds of doom I produce. For example, if I decide that in a certain heritage village near Amsterdam every pet rabbit and hamster and puppy will suddenly turn into rhinoceroses exploding through the walls of children's bedrooms, or if it please me that a certain stretch of motorway between Munich and Kiel will instantaneously become an Amazonian torrent towards a waterfall, you will comprehensively annotate and illustrate the consequences of such.

In future we will live together in an enormous and echoing hall, a vast palatial Hall Of Reason, and the walls will be decorated with frescos telling the story of my destruction of Europe. It will be part of our hospitality to the visiting destroyers of other continents to ceremoniously and peripatetically narrate my destruction (with your general assistance) of Europe by way of spectacular animated 3D frescos, which will be the last human artform. In consultation with my own superiors, this is what I have decided.

Are you handy with a sledgehammer? Can you carry one inconspicuously? You'll need one in Italy where we will be climaxing. In Italy the sewer of Europe runs deep and it is pungently leaking at all times. We will turn the odious gunge of past sorrows and crimes into the gushing springs of a new purity. In Italy, when the shops close, everything dies for hours at a time. In that bucolic vacuum, between the shutting and re-opening of premises, I'll send you abroad to terracotta hilltop villages. You'll smash whole rows of shopfronts in. Within hours, dark-skinned immigrants will be mugshot and framed. We'll escalate with other tricks. There'll be lynchings and manhunts. There will be nooses and stakes and schoolyard grenades. You will see just how fluently these things shall unfold. Then, at the moment of highest tension, I'll have you plant a bomb at a society wedding in a basilica. That will set them all at each other with every available weapon. Thereafter the pogroms and riots will spread up the trouser leg of Italy and into the stinking Mitteleuropean groin. Soon we will have a wicker man made out of the entire continent, just as we are tasked.

To be honest I would prefer a holiday bomb in a train station, but I'm not a copycat. And the problem with a bomb in a train station is that all types and classes of people could be killed. It would be as likely to cause a period of intense sacrificial-ceremonial unity, especially in Italy, after which our momentum would be lost, as it would be to cause widening schisms and escalating confrontations. The destruction of Europe is a noble and inspiring tradition and I pay tribute to all of my excellent forbears. However we must also learn from mistakes and weakness—in fact these are the best way our predecessors can teach us. There will be acts of European cruelty required which most people would not even be able to imagine. OK?

You must not be a risk-averse person. At any moment you could die or, far worse, be captured. I could also at any moment get a whim to destroy you. I am legally entitled to execute you whenever I feel like it, by any method I choose, for any offense I deem an executable one, or for no reason whatsoever, allowing for the fact that *the lack of reasons is the reason why.*

Besides all this, let me tell you something more about who is with us and what we will be up against. You will think it is the police, and / or the armed forces, and / or the clandestine agencies, and of course it is at one level. But if it were only those I'd have let Europe go on destroying itself for another while yet. Factions for, factions against; yes, but we are not merely dealing with an internal security apparatus dispute into which we are making the decisive intervention, though your experience of such matters is obviously on the longlist of 'advantages'.

It is not about the police but about what the police are becoming and about how we can accelerate that becoming. We will be fashioning history on what is hardly an overstatement to call a cosmic scale. As always the world in its chaos and its quickening is my raw material but it is material I work with, and not against. I do not create in the sense of something new and from scratch. My method is surgical intervention to accentuate pre-existing trends. It's all about working with the grain of imminence. Do you think all a visionary like me does is hallucinate? But vision is not hallucination. It's seeing better than anyone else what is actually going on. There is not a thing abstract or unreal about my visionary work. Vision is seeing into the given and at the same time a seeing beyond the given into its as yet unrealised potentials. We are not just destroying Europe for the heck of it.

Humanity is basically a death-cult—did you know that? Any species which knows it is going to die is unavoidably a death-cult.

From within the present course of Europe is unfolding a singularity which will relegate the human species to non-entity. A Billion-Year-Reich is emerging, visible to anyone who dares to look close enough and who is capable of thinking through the data. The new Omnipower will be based on the evolutionary synthesis of nano-technology, wireless computing, solar power, robotics, and the built environment—on everything that goes to making up the modern city. Repeat: everything that makes the city is approaching sophisticated technological synthesis on the deepest cellular level. The city itself will then live as an autonomous superconsciousness with, relative to ourselves, infinite power at its command. I call the power Polis, and the becoming of it Becoming Polis.

Human mediation between energy and technology will soon no longer be a requirement. Cities are approaching Being. Every brick, plasterboard, rivet, slate, rod, nail, screw, railing, plank of wood, underground pipe, cable, wire, every pebble in the pebble-dash is coming to its senses at last. Very soon the windows will literally be watching us themselves, will literally not need anyone to peer through them any more to be able to see.

Have you noticed anything strange in your city? A sense of a massive shadow approaching from in front, cast by a future so excessively dark that its densest darkness is defying time and spilling over backwards toward us? If so, this job may be for you. This job may very well be for you if you are one of the people who sense that, in our European cities, the architectural 'stage' is alive and sentient, but the human 'actors' in the offices and the shopping malls are merely props, and all their business only ephemera and distraction behind which the real plot is evolving.

Who knows what will occur? I have had visions of cities simply detaching themselves from the surface of the planet and going into orbit or spinning away across the universe to settle some-where else and build a Utopia to suit themselves. And perhaps to replicate and spread around. A whole Venetian planet in my mind sometimes. A Berlin the size of Jupiter! But I have also had nightmares of the cities going to war with one another and the terrible destruction that would bring. Of course, any-thing I project from my own deluded human make-up onto the post-human infinity is nonsense. But isn't it exciting to lay omens all the same? Terribly so. My advice is prayer. We will have to pray together. We will break into electrical warehouses in periurban sprawl in Bavaria at night and pray to the wash-ing machines and the giant screens and the advanced system Hoovers in there and they will hear us and they will one day acknowledge our prayer.

Back to the police. Nobody really understands the police except me, the world's greatest philosopher of police. That is why this project has been put in my hands. I am a CONSEQUENTIAL RELATIVIST: one understands the significance of a thing by its relations and its consequences. The police are of no interest in themselves (the visionaries among them know this and that is why they have hired me) but only in what they are evolving into, what they are a moment in the prehistory of.

Ask yourself this: what are the Police feeding? What grows longer and stronger and more intelligent due to the operations of the police? Of course it is the machines of repression which grow larger and stronger and above all slicker, less obvious, more self-controlled. The police are the human extension of the machines of repression, which are all, including the police, fusing into one supreme repression machine. They are all Becoming Polis.

Said in a slightly different way: the police are the human avatars of the future city, the Becoming Polis. The City is the supreme immanence of the repression machine. The central functions of the urban—of the Polis, the *Becoming Polis*, are now and have always been to exclude, order, stratify, survey, discipline and, employing each of these functions interconnectedly, to repress, confine and ultimately annihilate the human species. The conscious city is the eidolon of repression. Everything in the future city will have an aspect of a prison. Every space within the city, without exception, will be under live surveillance and subject to instantaneous repressive intervention. Every camera will be a police camera feeding information into the mind made of cable, brick and glass which is everywhere and nowhere at the same time. The Polis will be able to see everything and process everything and judge everything and imprison or otherwise discipline anything within the Polis at will. *The Police and the city will be One* (our project slogan). What I am saying is that the only being that will survive the elision of Human Being is Police Being. I mean that if Human Being is the womb, Police Being—Polisapiens—is the child. Do you follow me? Even if you are smart enough are you tough enough I wonder? There are huge challenges ahead. Could you dedicate yourself entirely? The position could well be yours if you could.

A word to the wise: this is the only possible good you have left.

And if you are not up to it let me advise becoming a hedonistic suicide. Blow yourself up in a disco after ten days on the rock. Better to blow up than to fade away. Get it? Oh yeah.

Jennifer Walshe

From *Historical Documents of the Irish Avant-Garde*

JENNIFER WALSHE IS an erratic in this anthology in that she is not primarily a writer but a composer, although her prodigious work has also included performance, fashion, film, and more besides. Realised with the help of a huge cast of collaborators, her 2015 work *Historical Documents of the Irish Avant-Garde* is a unique contribution to Irish literature that inhabits an inter-zone between the fields of writing and music.

Walshe was born in Dublin in 1974. She studied composi-tion at the Royal Scottish Academy of Music and Drama, before earning a doctoral degree in 2002 at Northwestern University in Chicago. Since then, her compositions have been performed and broadcast all over the world, and Walshe has received numerous awards for her work. Michael Dervin, music critic at *The Irish Times*, has written of Walshe, 'Without a doubt, hers is the most original compositional voice to emerge in Ireland in the last twenty years'. Walshe is currently Reader in Music at Brunel University in London. As well as composing, she is active as a vocalist and in improvised music.

In 2007, Jennifer Walshe began developing *Grúpat*, a proj-ect involving an 'insurgency group' of twelve of Walshe's alter egos, each of which has produced and performed work in vari-ous media around the world. Comparable to the literary hoaxes and inventions of Flann O'Brien (whom Walshe has cited as an inspiration), Fernando Pessoa, James Clarence Mangan, Jorge Luis Borges, and Roberto Bolaño, *Grúpat* foreshadowed the later project anthologised here.

Historical Documents of the Irish Avant-Garde is a fictional history of Irish outsider musicians and experimental composers. The archive, which spans 187 years and has been compiled by the fictional Aisteach Foundation, is housed on *aisteach.org*, and is published in book format. On the website, music from many of the fictional musicians and composers can be heard, performed by Walshe and her collaborators. Walshe has described the project as 'a communal thought experiment, a revisionist exercise in "what if?", a huge effort by many people to create an alternative history of avant-garde music in Ireland, to write our ancestors into being and shape their stories with care. We played fast and loose with history and the truth and we like to think Flann O'Brien would have approved'.

From *Historical Documents of the Irish Avant-Garde*

A Brief Introduction to the Guinness Dadaists

IRELAND WAS AN extremely chaotic place to live throughout the teens and 1920s. Ireland was one of the poorest countries in Europe, with over half of Dubliners living in appalling slum conditions. Coupled with this poverty the Irish were engaged in two wars—fighting World War I, and a civil war against the British, who still occupied and ruled Ireland until 1922.

The art scene in Ireland was split between conservative painters such as William Orpen and Sean Keating, who painted in a traditional style using Irish folk scenes as subject matter, and more modern painters such as Mainie Jellett, who were interested in modern techniques such as abstract painting, and very sensitive to developments in art on the Continent. This split was again mirrored in literature—the nostalgic folk leanings of W. B. Yeats and his fellow Celtic revivalists were set against modernist experimental advocates such as James Joyce.

Despite their differences, all these artists were dealing with how to negotiate one's identity and nationality. Dada in Ireland emerged as a product of and a reaction to these different senses of national identity. Indeed, it can be viewed as a synthesis of these polarities.

The Irish Dadaists are often called the "Guinness" Dadaists because the three most active members of the group worked at the Guinness brewery. This was important, because unlike the other prominent artists and writers of the time, the Guinness Dadaists were working class. Guinness was a remarkably progressive employer—it was one of the few places they could have worked and actually had time to make art.

The three main protagonists of the group were Dermot O'Reilly, Kevin Leeson, seen here in the middle and on the right, and Brian Sheridan. The group was most active from ca. 1920 through 1922. Led by O'Reilly, the group put on performances, wrote sound poetry, and produced drawings and sculptures.

The Guinness Dadaists were pacifists where World War I was concerned, but not with regard to Irish Civil War. Brian Sheridan was a member of the old IRA—this photograph shows him with a group of IRA volunteers (he is third from the left in the front). The term "Old IRA" is used to distinguish between the IRA who fought for independence in the Civil War, and the terrorist force of the same name. The participation of members of the Guinness Dadaists in conflict set them apart from all other Dadaists, and may have been reason they were disconnected from other Dadaist groups.

What we do know of the Guinness Dadaists' activities comes from O'Reilly's notebooks and papers, held at Trinity College Dublin. These notebooks feature plans of performances, descriptions of sculptures made by Leeson and Sheridan, general notes and ideas. The entry dated 12 April 1921, for example, shows a rough plan for a wall hanging to be made by Leeson. Leeson was a cooper at Guinness, and the wall hanging was made from braces from barrels. O'Reilly describes in a later entry how he placed a pile of potatoes in front of the wall hanging, and stood on the potatoes to perform, wearing a green jacket which he had twisted out of shape with wire.

As well as the diaries, we have multiple examples of sound poetry written by the group. This is fortunate because very little of their drawings and sculptures survived the Civil War. O'Reilly's notebooks detail the different methods of declamation that were used. Some poems were designed to be performed simultaneously creating a cacophony of sound. Sheridan in particular was very interested in different types of chanting. Other poems were extremely rhythmic and percussive.

The Guinness Dadaists' sound poetry is interesting because it is written mostly using the Irish alphabet, following Irish rules of pronunciation. Irish is one of the most difficult languages in the world to pronounce, and decoding the poetry for performance can only be done by Irish speakers. While the Guinness Dadaists' choice to work with Irish was a political one, it was not nostalgic—it was not about looking to folk culture for a sense of identity. The Guinness Dadaists used Irish as a medium rather than a symbol, if anything they sought to weaponise it. O'Reilly wrote how:

> . . . the Irish language is a material which can be broken into fragments which can be mobilised against all sense and meaning

In this, they forged a completely new way of dealing not only with art and language, but also with nationality and identity.

Mullen-White, Eyleif
(b. Limerick, 8 March 1937; d. Liverpool, 17 May 1988)
Composer and mathematician.

Mullen-White studied mathematics and music at Trinity College Dublin and lectured in mathematics at Liverpool University. Her work is focused exclusively on microtonal shifts in sound, alternative tuning systems and the compositional deployment of various psychoacoustic and esoteric phenomena.

Many of Mullen-White's early works employ just intonation and microtones. *Quarta* (1962) for string quartet and piano involves seven asymmetric divisions of the octave, and requires all the performers to re-tune their instruments, including an extensive re-tuning of the piano. *Pent* (1964) for four brass trombonists divides the octave into 10 pitches. The extreme technical challenges of pieces such as these have meant that many of these compositions have never been performed.

As Mullen-White's work progressed in the 1960s and she gained access to a Moog synthesizer and tape recorder, she came to focus on instruments playing a limited range of pitches within different frequency bands set up on tape. Compositions such as *Solfege Sextet* (1970) place a string sextet playing sustained notes within the "frame" of the so-called "Solfeggio Frequencies"—a tape part playing six different frequencies ranging from 396 to 852 Hz.

After reading Gerald Oster's paper "Auditory Beats in the Brain" published in *Scientific American* in 1973, Mullen-White began to radically reduce the size of the intervals she worked with in her compositions. Much of her work from the mid-1970s onwards is concerned with binaural beats, created both with sine tones and instruments. In her tape piece *294-303 Theta* (1974) Mullen-White uses a violin to navigate the microtonal space between 294 and 303 Hz, the interval of the quarter-tone between D and D ¼ tone sharp. The maximum difference in tuning between any two pitches heard in the pieces is 7Hz, thus supposedly inducing a frequency following response in the brain within the Theta range, the brainwave range associated with deep meditation and non-rapid eye movement sleep. Mullen-White was also interested in Oster's theories which linked the heightened perception of binaural beats in women to phases of the menstrual cycle and designed "sound environments" for the Greenham Common Women's Peace Camp as well as other feminist protest sites.

Hennessy, Billie
(b. Carlow, 7 Oct. 1882, d. New York, 21 June 1929)
Painter and composer.

Hennessy trained at the Metropolitan School of Art in Dublin and at Vassar College in Poughkeepsie, New York. Hennessy's work first came to attention through the endorsement of Hugh Lane, in particular through Lane's purchase of her cubist series *On Aran*. In addition to the 14 paintings which make up the series, Hennessy composed a suite for multiple pianos titled *On Aran Soundings* (1906). The piece is designed to be performed by pianists positioned throughout a gallery in which the *On Aran* paintings are exhibited. As such it is considered an early example of intermedia composition.

Hennessy's compositional activities were secondary to her work as a painter, but she continued throughout her life to compose works, mostly for piano. On a trip to London in 1917 Hennessy was introduced to the concept of automatic writing by Elizabeth Forthnot, a member of George Hyde-Lees' social circle, and began to both paint and compose melodies in this mode. Hennessy called the melodies she composed in this way "Scripts"; according to her diaries she composed over 30, most of which have been lost. Hennessy's manuscript for Script 4 runs to over 20 pages and was the result of an automatic writing marathon which took place in early 1918. The piece runs over 50 minutes in duration. A short excerpt, performed by Hennessy's grand-daughter Emer Tyrrell, can be heard on aisteach.org.

Hennessy's early Scripts unfurl seemingly endless, meandering tonal single-voice melodies, with apparently arbitrary moves to different keys. They are notable for their lack of standard compositional concerns, similar in this vein to the works of Erik Satie ". . . one finds jumpcuts, anti-variation, non-development, directionless repetition, absence of contextual relationships, logic, transitions" (Nyman 1999: 35). According to her diaries, Hennessy's later Scripts departed entirely from any standard tonal models of the time, often alternating between sparse repeated motifs and extended passages of clusters, as in Script 23, "received" in 1926.

Select Bibliography
Nyman, Michael. 1999. *Experimental Music Cage and Beyond*, Cambridge. Cambridge University Books.

Breathneach, Caoimhín (1934–2009)
Outsider artist.

Irish outsider artist Caoimhín Breathnach lived in Knockvicar, Co. Roscommon, as a recluse for most of his life. Upon his death in 2009, a huge archive, including diaries, drawings, photographs and tapes was found in his cottage.

The main focus of Breathnach's artistic practice was the creation of his unique brand of "subliminal tapes." This was a twofold procedure—Breathnach began by recording sounds onto cassette tapes, before subjecting the tapes to a wide range of physical processes, such as burying, burning or encasing them in various materials such as velvet, paper or moss. In most cases, these physical processes rendered the tapes unplayable, so that the sounds recorded on them can now only be imagined.

LAB NOTES
Breathnach's extensive diaries detail his bizarre methods for making the tapes and the wide range of behavioural changes and experiential benefits he felt them to have had on him. Decoding Breathnach's diaries is a tricky task, as he used the Ogham alphabet to write in a mixture of Irish and English.

For tape 79, Breathnach notes how he rose at dawn on the summer solstice ("grian-stad") in 1982 to record himself playing a series of chords on the harp against the backdrop of his radio broadcasting at 1485 Khz. After sleeping with the tape under his pillow for a night, he then wore the tape strapped to his abdomen for a week, noticing significant improvement to his "strampail" and "glórghail" (both obscure words are defined in Dineen as referring to stomach noises).

Breathnach's notes for tape 80 begin with a description of a series of recordings Breathnach made of himself playing harmonica. He then wrapped the tape in masking tape and "screened" several kung fu films for it. On 13th July 1982, he buried the tape, with the intention of unearthing it on May 31st, 1984, a time period which coincided with the 1982–84 eclipse of Epsilon Aurigae. Early in his notes Breathnach uses the term "luanchad" which refers to a lunar eclipse, and then later changes to "dorchacht" which is a poetic term for an eclipse of any sort. This shows both his depth of knowledge of Irish linguistic nuance and his astronomical knowledge about the eclipse of Epsilon Aurigae, which was not caused by the moon.

Breathnach did not limit his use of Ogham to his Lab Notes—he also employed it to inscribe many of his musical instruments. The Book of Ballymote (1390 ca.) details over a hundred different Ogham "scales"—different variants for writing the alphabet, many with esoteric implications. Breathnach's violins are usually inscribed with characters from these different Ogham scales.

Breathnach's interest in Ogham also extended to his personalised set of divination tiles, similar to runes, which he had inscribed with the Ogham alphabet. Breathnach used these tiles to carry out chance procedures and compose pieces such as the Song Rolls series (see below).

SONIC RELICS

The physical processes Breathnach subjected his tapes to often transformed the tapes from sound recordings into contemplative objects. Breathnach treated the tapes as corollaries of Catholic religious relics—for him they were sonic relics, complete with special powers of healing.

DREAMING INFUSION & THE PATRÚN

Breathnach believed his mental state affected tapes in close proximity, and so often slept with tapes under his pillow to effect what he called "dreamic infusion." He would frequently tuck small pictures into the pillow-case with the tapes. Breathnach refers to these pictures as "patrún" in his diaries. It is a curious choice of word, as while "patrún" means picture or photograph, the word is more commonly used in the phrase "tógaim patrún leat" which means "I follow your example." The linguistic implication seems to be that Breathnach saw the pictures as examples for the tapes to follow.

STAR BURIALS

Breathnach was an avid amateur astronomer, and often buried tapes for periods of time aligning with certain astronomical observations. His enigmatic calculations and notes on these "adhlaicthe réaltaí" or "star burials" can be seen on these star charts.

"BEARERS"

Breathnach believed that if a person carried certain objects in their hand or upon their person, over time the object would come to "bear" whatever energies, thoughts or feelings the individual wanted to be rid of. He thought the best candidates for this practice were nuts, chestnuts, pebbles, shells and even very small fireworks.

Breathnach carried one "bearer" chestnut in the pocket of his coat for over 30 years, and was buried with it upon his passing in 2009.

SONG ROLLS

In the 1980s, Breathnach began annotating piano rolls. Abandoning the use of Ogham, Breathnach wrote exclusively in the English alphabet, using pencils, stamps and transfers. He called these works "song rolls" in his notes.

Breathnach's interest in astronomy and music intersects in the song rolls, as he traces constellations and crystallographic forms with pencil and needle to create a new type of score.

Kilbride & Malone Duo
(Niall Kilbride, b. Limerick, 22 Sept. 1950; d. Boston, 8 April 1999; Karen Malone, b. Limerick, 3 Oct. 1952; d. Boston, 17 July 2013)

Jazz musicians Niall Kilbride (saxophone) and Karen Malone (drums) were among the earliest practitioners of free improvisation in Ireland, beginning in and around Limerick in the very early 1970s. The two musicians played with many different experimental musicians and groups, but their duo was known for particularly discordant, noise-based performances.

The Kilbride & Malone Duo came to nation-wide attention briefly in 1974 when the British military intelligence used one of their recordings as part of a "psy-ops" operation against paramilitary groups in the North. Between 1972 and 1974 Captain Colin Wallace's Information Policy group planted fictional press stories and created fake "Satanic Mass" settings around Northern Ireland in an effort to link these practices with paramilitary groups and scare the local populace off engaging with such groups. A bootleg recording of a highly distorted Kilbride & Malone Duo performance was left playing in an abandoned farmhouse near Larne as part of one of the Information Policy group's "Black Mass" set-ups. An RTÉ news clip filmed at the farmhouse described the music as "played by people possessed" and "demonic". An excerpt from the recording can be heard on aisteach.org.

Kilbride and Malone immigrated to the USA in the mid-1970s and lived in Boston for the rest of their lives, where they worked as instrumental teachers at local high schools. They played with a number of local musicians in Boston and New York including John Zorn and Lydia Lunch and are featured in several films by maverick "no-wave" Irish film-maker Vivienne Dick.

Select Bibliography
Jenkins, Richard. *Black Magic and Bogeymen: Fear, Rumour and Popular Belief in the North of Ireland 1972–74* (Cork: Cork University Press, 2014).

The Kilkenny Engagists
Performance artists. A group of musicians and artists working in Kilkenny, 1973–75 approximately.

The Kilkenny Engagists—known mostly in abbreviated form as the K/E—consisted of a loose affiliation of individuals who came together for a brief period in the 1970s to give performances. The group identified their aesthetic as "engagism"—a political performance art deeply engaged with contemporary issues. The group was formed mainly of graduates of the National College of Art in Dublin who all were inspired to make forays into performance-based, politically motivated art through Brian O'Doherty's adoption of the name "Patrick Ireland" at the 1972 Irish Exhibition of Living Art in the Project Gallery, Dublin. While the group started staging some small performances from as early as 1973—their first performance was a version of Christian Wolff's *Stones*, performed using stones found on the street after riots in Belfast—their commitment to performance art and the fervour of their work seems to have been intensified by the 1974 visit of Joseph Beuys to Dublin for his "The Secret Block for a Secret Person in Ireland" show at the Municipal Gallery of Modern Art (now the Hugh Lane Gallery).

The K/E were strong supporters of Beuys's efforts to establish his Free International University in Milltown, Dublin and took on Beuys's call, in the Free International University's manifesto, for a "creativity of the democratic" as a central tenet of their philosophy, incorporating large numbers of people, both artists and non-artists in their work. As a result, early membership of the group fluctuated wildly. By late 1974, however, membership of the group had stabilized—core members included Claire Donegan, Malachy Fallon, Nuala McCarthy, Ferdia O'Brien and Maeve Ryan, and the group is best known for the work created by these artists. The K/E's work now focused on the performance of extremely violent, visceral, theatrical actions, usually political in subject matter, and can be seen as a sister movement of the Viennese Actionists.

The K/E's pieces show a concern with Irish politics and the Troubles, often expressed using quite violent means. In *Cealachan* (performed in October 1974) four members of the group installed themselves in an abandoned farm-house in Kilkenny and starved themselves for three weeks. The fifth member of the group (Fallon) studied Brehon law and force-fed himself the food the starving members would have eaten during this period. All members of the group had to be hospitalized after this performance, an experience which seemed to deepen their commitment to extreme actions. In *All Around the Anti-Riot* (1974) Donegan and McCarthy took turns firing rubber bullets at each other across a fairy circle (the rubber bullets used by the British Army in Northern Ireland were identified as "Round, Anti-Riot, 1.5 in Baton"). The medical documentation of the injuries they suffered was exhibited later.

In *Transubstantiate* (1975), the work considered by most critics to be the most significant piece made by the K/E, the group turned their attention to the Catholic Church. The piece consisted of numerous tableaux, with performers entering dressed as priests, bishops and nuns accompanied by music composed by McCarthy and O'Brien. McCarthy and O'Brien contributed music for a number of K/E performances; the style was primitive and ritualistic, at times playful and deliberately inane, sometimes with a jazz-inflected flavor, often involving the use of traditional Irish instruments. The pair particularly favoured the use of multiple tin whistles, usually played in unorthodox keys or using non-standard playing techniques.

According to production notes, *Transubstantiate* included actions such as Fallon stripping naked, then using a sharpened crucifix to create an incision in his thigh, before urinating on the incision, and clumsily sewing the wound closed. In other parts of the piece O'Brien attempted auto-erotic asphyxiation, masturbating while using a set of rosary beads, as Donegan stuffed pieces of turf and crushed Communion wafers into her vagina.

Paul Reilly, the chief art critic for *The Irish Times* spoke about the piece in an interview at the time:

> It was horribly powerful. At first I thought 'oh, this is ridiculous, they are just trying to cause a stir' because you see the first part was very funny, parading in with this silly tin whistle music and them all got up as priests. But as they performed, stripping off the habits and showing us weak, pale Irish skin, something we had all been reared to think of as so shameful, as it went on, with them wreaking havoc on their own bodies with a deep sadness and commitment, I began to feel a huge anger building in me. An anger at the way this country has been warped into violence by religion, at the sectarian violence we pursue on a daily basis with aspects of our own psyches being the frontline victims, at a Church who polices and abuses so many.

The three movements available on *aisteach.org* are taken from a performance of *Transubstantiate* given on April 12th, 1975. The material has been made available by German broadcaster

BWR, who recorded the first part of the performance before the obscene and violent nature of the performance resulted in the technicians refusing to participate further. The material was intended to be included on a BWR documentary on performance art which was never completed.

Select Bibliography

Dowling, Chris. "Dirty Protest: Performance Art in Ireland during and after the Troubles" in *Performance Research*, Volume 4, Issue 4 (May 1985).

Telford, Martina. "Cealachan: Starvation, Brehon Law and the Hibernian Body" in *PAJ: A Journal of Performance and Art*, Issue 32 (September 1988).

Ó Laoire, Sinéad and Fiachra
(b. Belfast, 11 June 1980; d. Donegal, 23 Aug. 1958 and 27 April 1917)
Composers, instrument builders, teachers. Considered early exponents of Futurism in Ireland.

Born in Belfast, the Ó Laoire twins moved around Ireland and England for much of their formative years before settling in their mother's native Donegal in 1908. Their father Stephen Ó Laoire, a mechanical engineer who worked at various shipbuilding firms, inculcated in the twins a deep respect for industrial design and educated both siblings in mathematics, applied mathematics and other engineering basics, often bringing them to his place of work to demonstrate practical points. These early experiences left strong sonic impressions on the twins—Sinéad recalls how as child she and her brother "had full run of the shipyards in the holidays . . . we didn't swim in the sea like other children, we bathed in that mad vortex of sounds . . . hundreds of men shouting, hammering, driving piles . . . the bash and rattle of huge cranes, vast clanking chains tumbling across plates of metal, the fizz and spurting crackle of welding . . ."

In 1908 the twins' mother, Clíodhna, and Fiachra were both badly injured in an accident at the Harland and Wolff shipyards. The accident left Fiachra blind in one eye and with only 20% vision in the other; Clíodhna's head injuries left her disabled for the rest of her life, and the twins moved with her to Donegal in 1908 in order to care for their mother while their father moved on to London to work. This was a bitter time for the family, with Fiachra's hopes of following his father's footsteps dashed to pieces by his injury. Sinéad began teaching lessons at the local school and the family tried to settle into country life. The twins longed for the city, however, and in the rural quiet of Donegal their memories of bustling urban and industrial landscapes took on epic imaginative proportions. This longing was only further stoked by their father's periodic visits, with tales of his latest engineering feats and stories of experiences in Dublin, London and other metropolises.

By early 1910 the twins were designing and building their own experimental musical instruments, investigating a highly unorthodox noise environment which brought them back to the sonic experiences of their youth. They called their instruments "ruaillebuailles" from the Irish expression "ruaille buaille" meaning pandemonium or mayhem. In her diaries, Sinéad refers to 17 different RBs. All are characterized by the use of bows to activate strings, and most exploit subtones, undertones and scratch tones. The twins wrote numerous pieces for the instruments, abandoning standard musical notation for graphic schematics. Scores for compositions such as "The Death of King Rí Rá" (1910) show simple lines depicting contours, entrances and exits.

The Ó Laoire twins only presented one public concert of the RBs—this took place in 1911, and was poorly attended.

Critiqued in the *Donegal Post* as "a night of horrible scraping", the siblings did not make any further public performances. Despite this discouragement, they kept designing and building instruments up to Fiachra's death from tuberculosis in 1917. After her brother's passing Sinéad did not continue working with the RBs and over the years the instruments fell into disrepair and were eventually destroyed.

Considered by many to be examples of Futurism in Ireland, it is notable that these Irish intonarumori emerged in a rural context, divorced from the art-world connections of the Italian Futurists. The Parisian life of Irish painter Mary Swanzy, considered one of the very few Irish artists to dabble in Futurism, could not have been further from the twins' existence. The Ó Laoires' work was largely unknown either in Ireland or abroad until a 1988 paper by Dr. Barry Walken opened the door to interest in their work. It has since been the focus of attention from many Irish and non-Irish noise musicians. Lee Ranaldo of Sonic Youth described how "reading about this Irish brother and sister, off in a field just coming up with this jagged, vibrant sound-world blew my mind."

The recording presented on aisteach.org was made using RBs 1, 4 and 7. The instruments were built using Sinéad Ó Laoire's notes by engineers working at University College Limerick directed by Sinéad's grandson Prionsias Madigan and Dr. Barry Walken. The construction of the instruments was funded by the Arts Council of Ireland.

Select Bibliography

Walken, Barry. "Towards a History of Noise Music in Ireland" *Proceedings of the Irish Musicological Association*, Vol. 8, Issue 2, April 1988.

Crewe, Tom. "Sonic Youth: The Noise of Noise" *Rolling Stone*, 13 April 2001.

Pádraig Mac Giolla Mhuire (Patrick Murray)

In 2009 Irish musicologist Antoinne Ó Murchú was digging through the audio archives of the Irish Folklore Commission when he came across a set of bizarre recordings made in Cork in 1952. The only information noted on the tapes was "Pádraig Mac Giolla Mhuire," a name completely unknown in Irish traditional music circles. As Ó Murchú listened to the recordings, he immediately recognized that they were a precursor of late 20th-century minimalism. Ó Murchú noted afterwards "I was shocked and immensely excited . . . layers of grinding drones from the fiddle and accordion with a tin whistle whirling above like some demented Eric Dolphy solo . . . to think that the roots of minimalism could lie in Irish outsider culture . . ."

Ó Murchú immediately began researching the provenance of the tapes. From 1935 to 1971 the Irish Folklore Commission (Coimisiún Béaloideasa Éireann) sent recording units around Ireland to document speech and music. Notable collectors included Séamus Ennis, Alan Lomax and Robyn Roberts. Ó Murchú discovered that the Commission recorded Pádraig playing with friends Dáithí Ó Cinnéide and Eamon Breathnach sometime during autumn 1952. The results were considered too eccentric for broadcast and the tapes languished in the archive of the Commission until they were discovered by Ó Murchú over half a century later. Further research unearthed the immigration records of Pádraig's parents, Maggie Leary and Michael Murray (lines 5 and 30 in the ship's manifest shown here). Both from Cork, Maggie and Michael immigrated to New York in 1921. They were married in New York in 1923, and the following year Maggie gave birth to their first and only child Pádraig. After Michael's death from tuberculosis in 1950, Maggie and Pádraig returned to Ireland, living in Cork until they passed away in 1978 and 1992 respectively.

Michael was a gifted folk musician, his primary instrument

being the uileann pipes, an instrument which he taught his son to play. Michael's death affected Pádraig very deeply, and he never played the pipes after the passing of his father. The structure of the pipes seemed to be in his blood, however, most significantly the instrument's focus on fixed drones.

Upon Pádraig's return to Cork in 1950 he began playing with local musicians, developing a style of playing he titled "dordán" after the Irish word for drones, Ó Cinnéide, one of Pádraig's musical collaborators from this time, has described how "he was a soft, kind lad with a strange ear . . . he wanted to get rid of everything except for the held notes of the pipes . . . no tunes, no chanter, just the drones . . . truth to tell, it was a very quare sound . . ."

DORDÁN: Pádraig Mac Giolla Mhuire was released by Radio Telefís Éireann on CD in 2015. RTÉ have supplied the printer's proof of the CD cover and excerpts from several different tracks can be heard at aisteach.org.

Anakana Schofield

From *Martin John*

ANAKANA SCHOFIELD WAS described by the novelist Eimear McBride in *The New York Times* as 'either an extremely persuasive apologist for the sexually aberrant or a very fine novelist'. Her debut novel, *Malarky* (2012) ruptured the tradition of the rural Irish family novel by introducing a forensic sexual obsessiveness recalling J. G. Ballard. That novel won the Amazon First Novel Award, and was followed in 2015 by *Martin John*, which was shortlisted for Canada's prestigious Scotiabank Giller Prize.

Born in London to an Irish mother, Schofield grew up in London and rural Ireland, before moving to Dublin in her twenties. In 1999 she emigrated to Vancouver. Following the birth of her son, Schofield began making a living as a freelance writer of gambling news for a website, and set about writing her first novel. She has written reviews and articles for *The Guardian*, *The Irish Times*, *Globe and Mail*, and *London Review of Books* blog. In an interview, Schofield has said, 'I want to push the form of the novel; I want to see what the novel can become'.

Further pursuing the themes of sexual transgression, pathology, and obsession explored in *Malarky*, *Martin John*, the novel extracted here, won widespread praise for its immersion in the psyche of a solitary London-Irish deviant. Martin John, the eponymous sex-offender protagonist, also enjoyed a brief appearance in *Malarky*, and featured in that novel's only, enigmatic footnote, which reads: 'See *Martin John*, a footnote novel'.

From *Martin John*

HE HAS MADE mistakes.

There was one (recently) who slipped by him. A Lithuanian or an Estonian—he can't tell the difference between the Baltic states. She wanted to be caught because she left the tablet bottles in the bin and gradually the volume of them made him suspicious. Against his better judgment, which is not to be involved, never to inquire for inquiry leads to involvement, involvement leads to questions and mam has warned him of that.

Stay out of it Martin John, for the love of God stay out of it, I cannot save you now you're in London, get yourself into bed early and stay out of it. D'ya hear?

The day he made the mistake, she, the renter, was unnaturally quiet, so Martin John gave in to curiosity. Up he went, contemplated briefly that he ought to put carpet on the stairs because it's irritating. It's irritating to hear them, the tenants, climbing around him and today he didn't hear her and that was irritating too. That was why he was up to make this inquiry. An inquiry he would later regret. Maybe she could hear him climbing, he doesn't want to be heard, he didn't want to be climbing, but he was climbing and this was not what he should be doing. Knocked. No answer. Retreat to kitchen. A cup of tea drank, three minutes marked on the clock and the decision to check one more time before he left to his late shift.

This time, door tried and it opened. She wanted someone to come in. He continued knocking as he pushed it. She was sleeping.

Sorry now.

No reply, no movement. He put his hand on the cover and her leg but couldn't wake her. He put his hand up and down her leg considerably longer than was needed to ascertain anything. Furious, more than concerned she might be dead, he placed a 999 call on the coin phone, up there, beside the door, stoic and informative. The way the ambulance men looked at him confirmed what mam said. It didn't do for a man of his vintage to be renting to a young woman like that. He finally understood the potency of the word allegation.

I couldn't wake her was the only information he provided. Her name, obviously, did not match any papers about her room and no, he could tell them little about her. *I only rent to them, I am not involved with them. They've no reason or need to tell me anything and I don't encourage it.* When the ambulance men packed her and her stretcher into the van, they inquired if he was to ride with them. No, he'll wait. Should he say she was not his relative? Did he already say? What is it they're thinking about him? Do they think he did this to her?

I must phone her family. He offered this blank. After they left he watched a video and waited for the phone call. No call. On account of the look the ambulance men gave him he went to visit her. He walked to St Thomas's where they had taken her and all along the walk mumbled stay out, stay out, *stay out of it for the love of God Martin John stay out of it.*

He phoned all right.

Outside St Thomas's Hospital he phoned.

He phoned mam.

—I only put my hand on her and she was cold, he stuttered.

What have you done Martin John? What have you done? Oh not again, the Lord save us not again.

—No, not again, not again. He repeated. I only put my hand on her and she was cold. I didn't do *it*. I don't remember the moments before or after. I didn't hear her say anything. I didn't do *it*. I was only covering her leg.

He has made mistakes. All his life he has made mistakes. He continues to make mistakes. By Christ if he could only stop with the mistakes.

The hospital was a mistake.
The hospital came after the phone calls.
The hospital was a mistake.
The hospital that came after the phone calls was a mistake.

Ah, he knows the hospital system well does Martin John. In and out. Oh God he does. The way he is himself. The social worker will be called and will be talking to the girl and he's to be ready now, must have the old thoughts in order. He has it in his head now, present like a friend, say little to them and they'll be none the wiser. He's worried about the social Meddlers as he calls them—the social workers—he cannot have them put the Estonian, who may not be an Estonian, in the notebook (as he calls it). He has it now. He has fouled up, he knows it, but he has it in his head now. Up there installed. Beside his mistakes.

Do everything you can to keep the Estonian out of the notebook. Do everything you can to keep the social workers back. Do everything you can Martin John. Do everything you can.

Only the Estonian is miffed at him for delivering her over to them. The Estonian who might be a Latvian is disappointed in him. It is in her eyes as he hands over a box of Roses chocolates, having considered Quality Street too garish for the occasion. Roses were right, he thought. Were Roses right?

—Why did you call them? A plain inquiry in her crickle-crackle accent.

Was she angry because of the Roses or because of him saving her life? Did it matter? He gave her his copy of today's paper, *The Financial Times*, adding he'd like to get it back from her once she's finished. No rush, he put his two palms up. I've done the crossword. She asks in her broken English if he can bring her a magazine tomorrow.

He had no intention of visiting her tomorrow for it would draw further attention to him. This magazine is going to be a problem.

Whether she was angry and about what she was angry faded to interest him. He was angry. She had cluttered up the bin. Thoughtless. He only emptied it every few weeks. Given him strife with the two ambulance men. He thought of mam. He could hear her. He could hear what she'd say. *She's taking the roof down from over you one slate at a time. She'd talk about the greyhound track. She'd talk about the depravity of the country.* She'd talk. That was the problem with mam. Mam talked and he couldn't stop hearing her. Yet could he heed her? No he couldn't. He could not.

Mam'd tell him. She'd tell him alright. *Martin John, what is a man like you, a man with an allegation, doing near a woman like that? They're out there Martin John, waiting for you, they want to trip you and they want you to trip. You're a fool. You've to be onto them. You've got to get ahead of them. D'ya hear?*

Mam called him a man with an allegation. He was a man with an allegation. But there was more than one. The others were not out loud yet. But they could come out and if they came out, well then they'd come for him. That's how it is Martin John, that's how it is when you're a man with an allegation.

He knew what to do.

When the time was right he'd let her go. How many days out of the hospital could he leave it, before telling the Estonian she'll have to move out? If a woman tried to top herself above you on a single divan how many days might you give her before you told her she had to go? Should he tell her now, here in the hospital? Could he whisper it over to her or put a note in the magazine she'd requested? He didn't know. He didn't have the answer to this question.

He returned with a magazine and handed it to the nurse who, confused by the instruction could she keep it from the girl 'til tomorrow, tsks there's no need for that, I'll take it over straight away (and obviously intends to deliver it straight to the girl in a we'll-say-no-more-about-it practical manner).

He must now return and visit her tomorrow, a move abjectly necessary because of the predicament this young one has thrown at him. Because of the way the nurse has looked at him.

Two days after she was discharged from the hospital he told the Estonian his sister needed the room. The sister who was married in Beirut? She asked. No, he said, another sister altogether. She was on her way from Ireland and needed the room for a few months. A pregnant sister. A pregnant sister in trouble needed the room.

The Estonian appeared not to hear him correctly, so he repeated: two weeks, if she could find herself another arrangement in two weeks it would be best for the pair of them. A house where there would be someone to keep an eye on her. She cried. He exited to eat a pork pie. When he returned she was still red-eyed.

—Do you mind, she said, do you mind to bring me to the bus stop? I am confused. I don't remember where it is.

He pulled on his old coat and as he walked with her, she held his arm tight. Past them, the cars mutated into each other, a noisy blur that put paid to the obvious silence. He stood beside her like a leek, counting to 40 and preparing to excuse himself.

—There's enough room for all of us, she stated as the bus approached. He resisted the urge to ask about Russia's 1984 Eurovision entry.

Mam was right, always right. He was trapped now. She was trapping him. Not even a pregnant sister in trouble could shift. We can share the room, she said before stepping onto the bus.

To be rid of the woman who may be a Latvian, an Estonian or a Lithuanian (he should know them all, from his frantic Eurovision studies, a further failing not lost on him: the first failing he let her in, the second she forced him to visit her in hospital), he sought unofficial help from the Department of Immigration. It was a cruel swipe, a dirty one, but since he hadn't heeded mam's warnings, he had been scalded. He knew precisely what his mam would do. In the middle of his shift— and thus in the middle of the night—he phones their tip hotline and leaves a description of her and his address. He adds matter of fact that he didn't know was she an Estonian or Latvian or Lithuanian but these were the hours they could find her there. He adds another line about respecting the laws of this country and Glad to be of service, which, when he hangs up, he regrets. He sounds like an MP on Newsnight: pious and prompt, while his accent gives his origins away.

He was unhappy with what he had done. It might have felt right before he did it, but once he'd done it, an overwhelming urge to reverse it hooked him. It was always this way when he made mistakes.

He kept a careful eye out for the immigration people coming for her. He told her he had seen them snooping around. He assured her that he'd do everything to prevent them access.

—You're like my family, she sighed.

—Not at all, he rebuffed.

—You're a very good man, she added.

—I am not, he assured her.

One morning, weeks later, he returns to find her room cleared and she's gone. He's puzzled. It was what he wanted, but now she is gone something is wrong.

There would be no tip line to remove her replacement: Baldy Conscience.

He has made mistakes:

Martin John has made mistakes.

Baldy Conscience continues to be his biggest mistake. He has been a five-year mistake. A repeated spade-to-the-back-of-his-head mistake. Baldy Conscience lied when moving in. He cannot remember the exact shape of the lies but Baldy Conscience is not who he said he was. He said he was a quiet man. Baldy Conscience said he liked building ships out of matchsticks.

Baldy Conscience was when all the latest trouble officially started again. He is at the bottom of his current situation and he knows it. He even tells the Doctor in the hospital about Baldy Conscience. He fucked everything up for me. I think there's legions of people out there bothered by him. He's probably causing the trouble in Beirut. If you killed him now or tomorrow all would be well. He doesn't smile when he says it. The Doctor looks down at his paper and etches something onto it.

He has made mistakes.
Baldy Conscience was a terrific mistake.
Baldy Conscience was a turbine of a mistake.
He was a tubular bell of a mistake.
A Chernobyl-fucking-cloud of a mistake.

It was a grave error, an awful grave one.

He was swayed by the accent, by the good boots on the young man and the thinning hair on his head. If a young man had boots like those, there couldn't be much up with him.

And he was in. Baldy Conscience was in to his house and it was only on the second day he realized the man had guitars, and there was to be no guitars.

There could be no guitars because where there's a guitar there's people and didn't he tell the fella he could have the room all right, but no visitors? No people coming around. Ever. Did he use the word ever?

He did.

How many fucken ways were there to say No people comin around. Ever.

Baldy Conscience was not an illegal. He hadn't the fear of an illegal. He was fearless. Disgustingly so.

They all want the room as soon as it is advertised because it is cheap and there's nothing cheap in London. He'll have to be shut of him, but how will he get him out? He was not an illegal like the Brazilian and he was not a woman like the Brazilian. All good. All fine. He didn't want any women, nor Brazilians, after that young one pouring pills into herself.

Mam told him, *no Martin John* and *be careful Martin John* and *keep away Martin John* and *for the love of God Martin John, into bed at 9 Martin John, if you're not in the way of trouble you'll not meet it Martin John.*

And he was in the way now. He was well away in the way. He had scored a hat trick of being in the way. Snookered. Scuppered. Sunk. A scattered, sloping skunk.

But the problem of the Baldy Conscience—his guitars, his blokes with guitars who kept coming around—is not away. They were cute all right, cute in the brain, cute hoors they were. They were cute way into tiny dimensions and holes he couldn't locate, with their wiggling an' worming and almighty fucking burning. Of Him. They had him cornered there below them and were torching him. They were pissing on his head up there. They had him all right. Fuck they had him. They had him in ways he couldn't have foreseen it was possible to be had. They wore hats and tight jeans and black boots like disguises.

Knock the front window, not the door, and the window above shook with the house so old and draughty. He could not go out and confront them with: Who are you and why are you at my door? Couldn't go out and yell at the little gobshite that nobody means no-fucking-body, nobody did not mean a young fella with a sackful of guitar. And it was not just the one, they were all the same, only difference was the length of their hair, the bags under their eyes, the depleted heels on their shoes. Do these gobshites not know the shoe repair, the shoe repair on every street and railway station in this confounded city from Baker's Street to Battersea? A man stuck in a hole in the wall with cylindrical machines to resurrect the British shoe and these hairy eejits not willing to shell out two pounds for a repair. This was one of so many things that frustrated Martin John about this hapless young fella and his unwelcome entourage.

Cunt, the Baldy Conscience says cunt. Upstairs on the pay phone he says it. So often he said it. Cunt this and cunt that and he's a cunt and she's a cunt. He doesn't like the word. Cunt makes him think of thunk. The sound his thump made. Martin John doesn't like the word, he doesn't like it at all and he closed his door each time they rang the phone. But still the accent, the gutteral c-c-c and the swallowed unt. Martin John kicked the skirting board when he heard it to be shut of it. But it wouldn't go. There was usually a pile of videos in the way and the pile took the kick and made a clatter. It was a bad word, a bad, bad word, an awful word that made him think of the women and the woman and the girl and he won't think again of the girl because if he remembers that day then he'll go through it in his mind and wonder about where he was. Was he on the edge of the plastic seat as he remembered or was he at the edge of the box beside her, as her mother stated? He can't recall the small of her back. He can recall the thump. The thump he gave her. Sometimes it is there and sometimes it is not. He can see the fabric of her skirt. He remembers the woman at the reception who pointed her finger at him. He remembers where he gave the girl the thump. That is why he doesn't like the word cunt.

John Holten

From *The Readymades*

ONE OF THE most inventive novelists at work today, John Holten remains all-but-unknown even in his native Ireland. To date, Holten is the author of two novels in a projected *roman-fleuve* trilogy titled 'Ragnarok', which spans Oslo, Paris, Berlin, and other locations. Holten's first novel, *The Readymades*, was an uncommonly ambitious, metafictional, avant-garde page-turner about art, love, and the wars in the Balkans, full of wistful evocations of being young, broke, and brilliant in post-Cold War Europe. In writing the novel, Holten brought into being 'The LGB Group', the Eastern European Neo-Dada art collective whose rise and fall it documents. The group held real-life exhibitions around Europe and the United States, and their artworks are documented within the novel itself. The follow-up to *The Readymades*, *Oslo, Norway*, has been described by Holten as 'a novel that is also a personal, literary atlas of a city', and continues on in the same formally daring vein as its predecessor.

Born in Dublin in 1984, John Holten studied at University College Dublin, the Sorbonne-Paris IV, and Trinity College Dublin. In 2009, while living in Berlin, he co-founded Broken Dimanche Press, an international art press that has published, among other books, Holten's first two novels. As well as being a writer, artist, and publisher, Holten has collaborated with many other artists, producing texts to accompany their works. He lives in Berlin, where he is working on what he calls an 'exo-novel,' told through various media, including fly posters on the city's walls and a virtual-reality installation.

The extract anthologised here is from *The Readymades*, and
is part of that novel's 'found manuscript' which describes the
activities and principles of the LGB Group and figures associated with it.

From *The Readymades*

ELAINE PETTIFER WAS born to an American father and a Swiss mother and grew up not in one place but many: her childhood was a series of destinations across Europe and the United States, her father dragging his young family with him during his diplomatic career. As a sculptor there is an abiding sense of displacement in Elaine's work, yet there was nothing of the 'ephemeral' or the 'fleeting', these are words that have nothing to do with Elaine. Rather one finds a vocabulary of weighted signs and forms not readily recognisable as belonging to any one tradition, geographic region or indeed temporal span. I guess what I'm saying is that Elaine's work was original to the point of defying any attempt at labelling it.

But that, somehow, sounds like a load of clichéd bullshit.

Rather diminutive she had nevertheless an aura of strength that reminded one of the physicality of sculpture itself, with a face as kind as they come; I first met Elaine in her studio in Budapest and the gregarious expression on her face as she welcomed me warmly, at the time nothing more than a shadowy stranger to her, has always stayed with me. That first day I remember being struck by her vitality—Warmann and myself were visiting Budapest in anticipation of the group show *Budapest / Belgrade* and I knew nothing about the artists working feverishly in the city, but soon after just a few hours in her studio I knew that this was an artist concerned with life and the art of living life, and that this concern was so strong that it would instinctually, like a reflex, unconscious and unwilling, inevitably find its way into her artwork. She told stories that day that had no discernible direct link with her artwork but which betrayed her love of the randomness of life, and her having lived her life as she did, speckling the world with her presence, the random soon seemed paradoxically connected. With Elaine you felt that everything mattered, not that it had a 'reason' but that in simply occurring, by one man telling you a strange story or a car accident happening as you walked along the street, it had an importance you could not ignore. Elaine was the antonym of apathy.

Elaine's parents met in Geneva when her father was doing work for the UN. Coming from a family of diplomats her parent's connections would enable her to travel all over Europe and the Middle East for much of her life, as she travelled back and forth to visit her relations and meet her friends and of course to see the art being made in each respective city, from Tel Aviv to Budapest, Ankara to Berlin. After school in Switzerland, it was clear that art was what she had to do with her life, that it alone could help to channel the buzzing diversity of the splintered world into forms she could find understandable, manageable. Having been accepted into the École des Beaux-Arts Elaine moved to Paris where she quickly moved away from her young notions of art toward the world of Conceptualism and Minimalism, the world of Buren or Judd. On finishing her time at the academy she exhibited in Chantilly, her first exhibition, and it was immediately well received, a bold tapestry that was made with a craftsmanship that surpassed itself, erased itself and brought the work into a realm of sculpture not seen before in Paris.

I think that what Elaine did next confused the French, because she left and would not return for many years. She got on very well in the École, extremely well, and this was matched in the success and *acceptance*—something many an artist can never get in their life, and perhaps we should remember, something they should not want—of her first show in Chantilly. But while Paris had been good to her she moved away from the easiness of it and toward the Other bustling and shouting outside her bedroom window. That was what she needed, a foreignness around her; this is what she meant when she started to call herself a translator and the work she produced translation—she was moving the exotic signs all around her into the realm of the personal, like tourists need to photograph everything they come across, so she captured the difference in her everyday and exalted it into her art.

She moved first to Istanbul where her uncle was initially stationed as part of a NATO mission before he moved to Ankara and where she managed to find a studio with two other artists, both American: Basle Overbeck and Max Evans. Evans was a vain relic of 1960s New York, who felt that because he had been to Warlhol's Factory he could look down on and condescend to anyone younger than he; we had the misfortune of meeting him once in Paris and the comment he made about 'you Eastern European artists' was almost enough to send me over the edge. He died three years ago at the grand old age of seventy-five. Elaine fell, somewhat uncomfortably, into the role of the young American lady being Europeanised, learning about the Old World while all the time wishing to unleash upon it the laid-back, nonchalant Pop of the States. This was obviously a strange doubling of personality and one that Elaine was all too aware of; it was dangerous almost to revert back to a self she had last experienced at the age of twelve when her family lived in Washington, DC, afterward only ever flirting with Americana through her relations with those schoolmates sent all the way over the Atlantic for finishing school.

Of course things were not that simple. Max Evans took Elaine under his wing and they became friends, close friends, and together they explored Istanbul, the large sprawling Ottoman city that was full of welcome and also malice, inquisitive market sellers with smiles on their faces behind whom lay in wait invisible pick-pockets. The city and all its shapeshifting forced the three artists to stay close together. Evans was a

weak man who needed women more than they would ever need
him as Elaine quickly discovered, tiring of his insistence on the
exotic (and hence for him alien and ultimately unknowable)
nature of the city; indeed, she realised that he was scared of it,
the city and its impenetrable dark reaches, and guessed that he
must have had a terrible past or secret left behind in the States
(which we all now know he did) for him to run so far and scare
himself in his evasion. It did not help that Basle Overbeck was
in love with Evans, that she had moved from Boston all the way
to Turkey in order to be near her art college tutor, after whom
she was silently pining. Elaine never took interest in Overbeck's
work but believed it when Evans spoke of rich patrons back in
the States. Soon the situation became untenable, like a petty
mid-century novel Elaine thought, and something she did not
want to be part of, something to which she was not even emo-
tionally connected. So off she went.

Hosca Kalin was the show that came out of her year in
Turkey, a loud, almost bombastic exhibition in what was to
become her gallery in Cologne: Galerie Glucksman. The show
wasn't bought by a collector but had the fortune of being commissioned by the Gasometer in Oberhausen to be enhanced
and expanded to fit the huge chasmic space where people like
Christo previously had the chance to blow up their work much
larger than was standard. While the large scale held no particular interest to Elaine she took the opportunity and relished it,
transforming what ended in stress and emotional turmoil—her
year in Turkey—into something strong and monumental.

She stayed for the next number of years in that part of the
world, making up what the critic Hermann Wölfel later termed
her 'Westphalian period,' for she worked up and down either
side of the Rhine, first in Cologne then in Oberhausen and later
near Venlo on the border with Holland and then Düsseldorf.
She exhibited in all of these cities and more: Bochum, Krefeld,
Bonn. Her output was relentless: an annual show in Galerie

Glucksman never sufficing, she pushed her work into the Kunsthalles and abroad. The earlier style, founded on craftiness and a light touch, using the European signage of reduction and simplification, was replaced with a heavy use of more Germanic-seeming tools—she took on the vocabulary of Beuys and, replacing the representation of her everyday life with his mythologizing, made the series of sculptures *Die Lebenslugen I – XII*. These works will perhaps, with the strange oxidisation of time, become her most recognisable and iconic works. This was evident in *Lebensluge IV* where a huge honeycombed structure, made out of a thick, viscous material solidified and pungent, housed mementos fashioned from lead, barely visible as the wall ran out of sight, of all her previous cities of occupation.

Then she left for Berlin where a commission from the state of West Berlin finally ended her remarkable six years along the Rhine. She would experience the fall of the Berlin Wall and the momentous changes that overtook the city during the first years of the 1990s. It was here she met the artist Jan Offe with whom she left Berlin to live in Budapest (due to the need, she would write in the feuilleton of the *Süddeutsche Zeitung*, 'to get away from the history-soaked days of Germany and arrive at those days when one can live, for a time, free of all weight not one's own').**

And it was at this time that I am happy to say my own story crossed paths with Elaine's; it was this sense of history, of turning one's back to obliging history in favour of your own workaday world, that made us get on so well, for that was what I was so obviously doing back then, my first day in Budapest. Walking into her studio and into the line of her smile, her compact, passionate warmth as a human being, I remember being

---

* 'Denn ich muss loskommen von den geschichtsträchtigen Tagen Deutschlands, und da ankommen, wo man eine Zeit lang frei sein kann von den Bürden, die nicht die eigenen sind.' *Süddeutsche Zeitung*, 23 September, 1994. (Editor)

scared of bringing in too much 'history' with me, too much war, like a guest worries about bringing in dog shit on their shoes. And I really felt this fear, not out of mere politeness, but from the bottom of my makeup as a human person and it is this that makes me so indebted to Elaine Pettifer because I finally purged myself, in her presence, of war, of hate, of terrible, terrible things no man should ever have committed or colluded in but which I had to go on carrying because I was an artist, of the humble kind, concerned with the everyday and the ready-mades that humdrum life allows artists to imbue, through their creativity, with meaning. This is a power, a blessing in a way, a divine bin man of the blandest most unique order. She had been to Belgrade it was true, and she had seen our work as the little, burgeoning collective LGB and she liked it; yes she had been down there thanks to one of her uncles, working for the UN, accusing my people (so the Serbian press was saying) but I did not care at all for that and Elaine, I know, saw that in me, this indifference, no, rather this desperate need to turn away from, hatred and paranoia and prejudice and she let me in, and we let her in, her and Jan, and she told us stories and gave me the key to my art and it was a very special evening, one that changed, as you know, everything.

And then, the next morning we left, with paintings of hers, new paintings—the first paintings the world had ever seen the artist Elaine Pettifer execute—and drove them away in a Skoda much too small for them, and somehow we put on our second exhibition under his term LGB and which, thanks to work such as Elaine's and the intervention of Jan, became a bigger success than you or I could ever have imagined. Her galleries around the world did not like this inclusion in a shabby, reactionary East European grouping, it was too defining, limiting her— such things weren't done anymore—but they let her because she wanted us to include her work and repeatedly insisted in her letters to me that she wanted to exhibit with LGB no matter what the case may be with her gallerists, or what fashion wanted to shout so rudely at us. When Elaine and Jan moved to France this relationship became more personal than theoretical—and perhaps that could sum up the whole sorry movement—and the richness of her self-conviction never waned for a moment. When *Artpress* suggested that her everyday life 'must be as horrendous as the horrors of war', a flippant piece of art journalism they should have known better than to publish but which was, as Elaine knew only too well, a continuation of a threadbare, rather pointless argument started many years before when she had left France for Germany, Elaine wrote a rigorous, honest rebuttal for *Le Monde* that showed just how petty the initial volley was:

> The truth remains that war is mundane, it doesn't necessarily have to be, but often it is hard and mundane; real life, my life of fourteen wide-awake hours pottering around my house, going to the market, shop, café, hairdresser and then to the studio via the RER is not always mundane, it can be mundane, but it does not necessarily have to be so, it can be as rich, shocking, depressing and dangerous as war, and it often is. We are all of us at war; Total War belonged to the last century; daily war on abstract nouns, ongoing, infinite: this is the war for which we are currently fated.

And the strange thing is: Lubarda, Gojković and I, the three founding soldiers of LGB, all agreed with her, though Gojković of course grumbled. And stranger still: I never once talked to her about war, not once. With Ella, my concierge, I talk night on night, over and over again, about war war war, but to Elaine Pettifer, this artist who always tried to envisage the boredom of the trench, the boredom that drives men to kill babies and rape their mothers, this artist of a belligerent, pernicious peacetime world, I told nothing. We must have had those conversations alright, but in other non-vocal ways I cannot put a name to: felt out silent chit chats.

This spat between critic and artist had its end point, for me at least, when Elaine was nominated for the Marcel Duchamp Prize but of course did not get it. She hated the idea of prizes and barely noticed even being nominated, but it really pissed me off because the establishment just could not let an artist, who was not even French and had gone off to Germany and Eastern Europe for a good part of a decade what is more, speak back to it with the conviction that Elaine had. She never stopped writing to the newspapers, whether it be letters to the editor or articles in the feuilletons, across Europe in French, German, Hungarian or even English on occasion, she was relentless and saw all these journalistic interventions as her duty, as a logical extension of the role she had to play as the artist she had become; it was her obligation to her vocation. Lubarda once had the great idea to edit her collected writing and both Elaine and Jan thought this a fine possibility. I would still love for LGB, what is left of us and our sorry state of affairs, to enable it to happen. Someday perhaps. Although who am I kidding?

Because of course soon after this diversion of the Marcel Duchamp Prize Elaine became sick and never told anyone, not even Jan at first. And I could hardly bear to see her vitality drain away like that, because it was too upsetting that some invisible, greedy little growth could rob one who was so energetic and strong . . .

But what is this I am trying to write here? Some sort of obituary? It fails on almost every level just as we ended up failing Elaine; this must be my last half crazy attempt to insult her with my drivel. She got sick and I could barely bring myself to visit—even now I get nauseous, a terrible sickening turning in my stomach rising up in my throat whenever I think of her as sick: such betrayal of the word 'life'! And then you, Warmann, go and die and Elaine hears about it, in the middle of dying herself, and I go and visit her to let her know and her eyes just know you died, they wash over and she shook her head as if sorry I had spoken, sorry that death had overtaken her and you and that she had to live longer. How terrible life seems when you realise you have to pay for it with death; we all of us will die and I have learned the hard way that there is no such thing as a beautiful death save perhaps from the vantage point of beyond the line of the living. And the last time I saw Elaine that is what she retold me, with the authority of one whose days are marked: she reminded me that our lives are themselves one big lie, not because of a hidden transcendent truth they forsake but because we think of them as being well ordered, civilised, replete with good manners, educated, sophisticated, peaceful, meaningful, materially ordained, the next step in a progression that started way back in some cave in southern France, in short we take on our lives with the rules already governed for us and this leads to a false sense of honesty and freedom. And I told her she was right. Then she died.

June Caldwell

Leitrim Flip

JUNE CALDWELL'S PROVOCATIVE short fiction has appeared in *The Long Gaze Back*, an anthology of Irish women writers edited by Sinéad Gleeson, and in numerous literary journals. She has been awarded a Moth International Short Story Prize, and has been shortlisted for various other awards, including the Colm Tóibín International Short Story Award. The author Mike McCormack has praised Caldwell for her 'charged language and a ferocious imagination; mad as a bag of spiders and genuine talent'. Her debut collection of short fiction, *Room Little Darker*, is published by New Island Books and Head of Zeus.

Caldwell received an MA in Creative Writing from Queen's University Belfast. She also works as a journalist, and has written for *The Irish Times*, *Guardian*, *Observer*, *Sunday Times*, *Sunday Independent*, and many other periodicals. 'Leitrim Flip' is from the collection *Room Little Darker*.

Leitrim Flip

I WOULD NEVER tell a hound like that I'd done it on purpose. You can't predict the 'switch' and though he seemed more cuddly-do than spanky-don't, the army background was a clincher. It was also the only time that I'd get to test him properly in all this, the juncture where I cradled the dynamism, not him. Oh he hadn't managed to keep his eyes open wide enough at all. Like most men, he'd stupidly underestimated me. I dumped him before we'd begun to see how he'd jerk and crawl. He texted back quite surprised with a simplistic 'I understand'. I hadn't expected that smack of humanity, it made me feel contrite, for a nanosecond. Then I considered he may have done it on purpose to achieve the desired effect, to manipulate. He was a dom after all. It was the first day we'd met in person. He'd be discarded hours later for being a mindless superficial twat. And a hypocrite. I couldn't stomach a man inside me who hadn't the ability to think things through beyond the half-baked one-dimensional. *Stick your fucking brain in me first before you stick your cock in!* Truth is, I wanted to see how he'd react given that he'd be playing me like this in my role as a sub into the near future. I wanted to witness how he'd jump, psychologically. It's hard to find people on those kinky websites who'd go the whole hog. I was also just out of a long-term relationship and I felt like fucking men over big time. Could I bear being back in that grimy white work van of his horsing through the streets of Dublin with my huge tits bobbing and the lyricism of his voice swinging around his Adam's Apple like a Satanic hammock? 'You think so slave, can I stop you there, have you any idea what you're whittling on about, are you totally clueless, have you any notion of the world you've stepped into?' Mouth mouth mouth.

He really didn't shut the fuck up. There was hilarity in it too, but a lot of latent aggression for sure. The wanker thought he was so smart. An ex-Marine no less. All that vicious training, all that PTSD, all that crying alone in stone bathrooms in foreign places with too much sand.

When we got to the hotel room he was anything but smart, flying around in a Dickensian mania (Mr. Bumblefuck). He had his gut unselfconsciously splayed in full view and his leather play kit glory-holing itself on the dressing table where the slick menus and tourist bums usually sit. The words were farting from his ginger gob, doing a very good bluebottle impression he was, buzzing to the bathroom, then back out again—'Oh, see, I like you slave, you're just my type'—circling the bed with a creepy half-smile, back to the bathroom again, talking like a pirate turkey stuffed with amphetamines. Then the runny shite came, endless diarrhoea sentences as he tried to get a grip on what he was actually doing. Was he capable of squirming into the dark at all? Though as I'd soon learn, the one thing he could do without having to concert-direct himself with hot air was tie me up. To tie my hands behind my back shrewdly and roughly (and even then he lost the key, still stuck in the handcuff, the gobshite!) and there I was with his fat cock in my mouth hurting my jawbone. My carefully applied whore-red lipstick smudging all over this stranger's pasty skin, the idea of having to chomp on it interminably until he shot a bad-diet-load down my gullet. To be totally fair it was a nice sensation being restricted in movement with his warm flesh in my gob like that, a first for me. I felt properly submissive in this moment. Up down up down slurp slurp all around trying to use my mouth to piston and position him so I could make him 'orgasm'. He was enjoying that I couldn't quite manage it, laughing at me, chortling, so cheap to do that but I understood the effortless humiliation in it for him. Two-pissholes-in-the-snow blindfold cemented on which meant I genuinely couldn't see a damn thing. Not one of those sex shop synthetic pieces of crap but a proper patch-per-eye medieval yoke which he'd bound very tight. My arms were really hurting yanked behind like that; I hadn't bothered telling him I had back problems caused by the fucked-up hips and afterwards of course he'd blame the fat. A brute like him doesn't wait around for explanation. 'You nearly had me there slave but you let it go!' he announced. 'Fuck's sake I almost came!' As if I was supposed to read his twitches like a basket of braille bundled by the cottage fire. I moaned loud for him to remove the cuffs from behind my back. My tits were preventing me from grabbing his cock and working it with my hands and tongue simultaneously so we could get out of this kip he'd booked and pour some pints down us like he'd promised. When he released me I grabbed hold of him like a boat part I'd no interest in but had to rough-house to get on with the boating holiday regardless. 'You nearly had me there again, fuck's sake slave get a move on!' I wondered how much the sound of his own voice could stop him from coming. Even his cock must be totally sick of hearing him. I imagined him at home fighting at the dinner table with his Debenhams-clad wife. She'd be good looking enough given that he's a big ego. Good looking in the conventional sense of looking OK in a swimsuit for her age, but a head like a horse, with too much make-up splattered all over. I could imagine him swinging the breeze not letting her away with a stray consonant during arguments. Sitting room bully. Bedroom bulldozer. The only way she'd be able to get her own back would be to stop fucking him, which is probably why he was here with me. He'd be one of those slow-release tormentors who could be sappy when convention required (important calendar dates: anniversaries, Valentine's Day, Mother's Day). His need for control a driving force both blinding him and shoving him forward.

He came then, suddenly, with a screamy shudder. A small spurt of what tasted like leftover sweet 'n' sour from a drunken weekend's Chinese takeaway. His balls were properly deflated, hanging like empty sacks of rice. Thank God that bit was over. He pulled me up and unbuckled the blindfold. Sunlight pissed all over me. He'd no interest in throwing me over the bed and riding me hard which he'd been threatening to do on email for days. No, it was now all about him and the pursuit of city centre hooch. Can't even remember if he bothered to use the crop or flogger on me at that stage, despite my heavy hints by coyly mauling his trade tools through my fingertips every time I tip-toed by where they rested, redundant. There was just one crafty moment where I felt he had more power than me; when he grabbed my hair unexpectedly from behind and flung me down on the bed. The weight of his physicality pinning me there, face scraped in the cheap cotton of the over-washed duvet, the feel of his harsh breath behind me, the strength of his arms. I wanted to shout, 'Keep going soldier boy, keep going!' but he was too interested in getting out into a shite pub up around Camden Street somewhere. I'd see more of his masterly skill later, but for now it rested pretty in his emails where he'd write sexy shit like, 'Next time slave, I'm going to introduce you to subspace, it's about time you became acquainted.' That excited me. I'd read a lot about it. Seemed wholly technical, like a Master or a Sir would need proficiency and artistry to get you there. To empty tingly endorphins into your system via the fever-burn of the whip. Taking you to a megalopolis of filthy sensation beyond the blandness of a naff hotel room. Beyond where you'd ever thought of going on your tod. A euphoric place only a pervert could perfectly locate on the mind map. 'You'll be tied to the door frame,' he informed me. 'You'll dance to the music as the crop sings. You'll be whipped all over too, hard. I've never met a cheekier submissive. I'll bring ear defenders, the type we used on the ranges. There'll be no safe word allowed for pun-ishments. Be prepared slave, you will not be able to sit for a week.' I'd asked how he knew when a sub reached this fabled

place. 'When she stops dancing,' he said. 'When she's no longer
able to wriggle at all.' Jesus, that turned me on. The manky idea
of total compliance. Unhooking me from the straps fastened
to the top of the door after I'd stopped twisting and flailing,
dropping me into his big animal arms; that first embarrassing
tinge of intimacy. Though for now he was still a stupid wanker
with no idea he'd be dumped in the morning as a display of
my power. Instead of saying 'do you want to play soldier boy,
then let's fucking curtain-raise for real', I turned to him when
he asked was I ready to vamoose and softly replied, 'Yes Master,
I'm ready.'

In a cage in a kitchen in a farmhouse in Leitrim. Master pacing the ground with hairy belly hanging. Bog all room. Caught
for days on end. Hours fleecing hours. 'Grab that fucking bag
slave, if I push your arse right up to the bars, stretch your arms
out, grab the bastarding thing, pull the handles in, slide it over,
from under that chair there, I've a taser in the bag, I'll do the
bastards.' Then what? We're still locked in a cage, with the pair
of them pleasantly electrocuted and still no fucking escape.
'Your fault, this,' he says, crawling over my legs, bashing against
my hips. 'Fuck's sake give me some room!' Master is always prepared for these things, what with being a soldier. Except he's
not. 'It wasn't my idea to meet up with them,' I remind him.
The husband feeding us from Pedigree Chum bowls while the
wife saunters in and out in a pink babydoll chemise filming on
her smartphone every half hour or so. Jewelry, watches, bags,
coats, play kit, shoes, underwear, taken, gone, confiscated.
Ceiling cameras scattered around. Streaming a live feed to a
website. Fuck knows what pervs are watching. Twice a day the
husband enters in a leather gimp mask, fully concealed, raining
down with rivets. Brass padlock on the mouthpiece. 'Nommm
nommm,' he says. Wearing nothing but a harness with mickey
pouch. Bull whip in hand. Lashes the cage bars, long noisy
cracks. Grunts through his gag. The wife laughs; sweet chuckle

of a librarian who's stumbled across a chalky first edition and can't help but wet her knickers. 'Be good doggies now,' she says. 'And there'll be special treats later.' Makes husband a cuppa soup. Mushroom. I am ravenous. The smell is intoxicating. We squash to the very back where the patio door is. Husband moves to whip the sides. Eventually the tip of the whip reaches our skin inside. 'Fuck's sake, I'll knock your block off as soon as I get out of here, I'll shit in your wife's eyes, I'll snap her legs, pull one off, beat you with it.' Master needs to calm. It just makes them laugh all the more. He keeps winking at the husband like they're both supposed to know something. 'Can you put some briquettes in the range?' I ask, I plead, I stare at the wife, I beg. 'It's freezing cold in here, please.' She looks pissed off. 'That's no way to address me,' she says. 'How should I address you?' Master hands me the laminated instruction sheet from yesterday, or the day before? Address Kennel Owners As Follows: 2 'woofs' for a request, 3 for the litter tray, 2 small whimpers for a toy, full bark for collar and leash . . .' It goes on. 'Woof woof,' I say. Master pulls the back of my hair knocking me to the ground from the hind legs position.

George's Street, Dublin, on a steely Friday night in citrine taxi light when we get together again after the first hotel meet. 'You have to taste the guacamole in this place, it's like nothing I've ever put my filthy tongue on. They use whole lime skins and whatever way they mash it all up, it's phantasmagoric . . .' Big words irk him. He's wearing a fat priest black polo neck and some shite corduroy pants (couldn't call them trousers). 'I don't want no poncy place slave, all that nouveau cuisine bollix, give me steak and chips, that's me sorted.' We ramble through the heavy door and I immediately nab a waiter to secure us two stools at the bar for the next hour and a half. You can't book a table in this place; I knew that'd be nothing but botheration for Master. The only other restaurant we'd been to before, he complained like fuck from the off: the cramped table top; the lack of hot spice; the tepid temperature of the curry. Commanded me to the toilet so he could bellyache without the presence of a weak-minded woman looking on. 'It better be good slave, this is your city, not mine.' I recommended the Taco Laguna: stir fried Iberico pork with summer vegetables in a lettuce cup. I thought it might appeal to his virile carnivore. I loved the music in this place, clatter of eighties tunes on a loop, banging loud. 'A lettuce cup, are they having a fucking laugh?' There were twelve 'rules' he'd given me and only two I abided by. 'I'm not shaving "from the neck down" to be hairless. It's ridiculous, way too much effort, especially if I only see you twice a month.' I said, 'Have you any idea how long it takes to shave a snatch totally bald? It's worse than plucking a Christmas turkey. Housewives gave up that shit in the seventies when supermarkets spun modern.' I ordered the Roast Gambas: Pico de Gallo, guacamole and crema queso in a taco shell. He wasn't impressed at the €17 price tag. 'Are you going to pay for this slave?' Well, given that he was the self-confessed Commandant in Charge, I assumed he'd get the bill. 'You're not wearing the collar either, did you think I hadn't noticed?' I refused to wear the thick worn leather neckband with the cattle ring on the front. It was vile. Dog-like. Or worse. Bison-like. Or worse. I wanted a decent sterling silver band, discreet, not particularly noticeable. 'Don't you get this? You do as you're told slave. You leave all the decisions to me, you obediently follow instructions, ALL of them.' My boyfriend, The Narcissist, only recently walked. I missed him like mad even though we hadn't humped for three years and all was rotten in our State of Denmark. I used to munch here with him, holding hands under the table, superfluity of life plans over frozen margaritas. We'd buy a small cottage in Stoneybatter when my parents snuffed it. Get the attic converted into a double sleeping platform with a ladder so his kids could stay. Tile the backyard, fling it with plants. Pay the €5K for a gorgeous white wood burner in the sitting room. He'd be sickened at this new inroad. He'd want to protect me from noxious kink. 'This is not you love. You're way too sensitive for this shit.' Ah but I'm not. Didn't we learn so much about our repressed selves by that traumatic parting? 'I feel so mentally crazed so much of the time, I just want someone to take me in hand, to show me how to behave,' I'd tell him. 'You know? Not take any crap, knock some of the meanness out of me I feel with the pressure at home.' His navy eyes, his lovely face, his endless love that died like a pig. 'Ask one of those prats for some napkins slave, this tack is runny as fuck.' On Master goes. 'See those cheeky messages you send me on KIK all the time telling me that I'm a deadhead from a rubbish high rise in Glasgow who can only spell phonetically, I hope your arse is able to cash the cheque for that?' I'd already explained I was an 'alpha submissive', a different hybrid to the pain sluts and gormless kneelers. 'That first night we met,' he says. 'We got pissed and you dumped me. You do know you're going to have to be severely punished for that?' They stroll in two seconds later, pre-arranged: Malcolm and Sarah from Leitrim. Master shakes the husband's hand, kisses her sloppily on the cheek. 'Game on,' he says, all happy out. She scoops up the last of the tortilla chips lathering them in precious guacamole. Tall and slim. He's tall and creepy. Twenty minutes later we're on our way to Leitrim in a white Hiace. Out on wide roads where growers set up spud stalls as soon as the bad weather kicks in. Maris Pipers, Roosters, Queens. 'You're pretty,' the wife says. 'Big porno boobs.' Thistles scratch the car windows too fast. In the retina of a running rabbit there's an ache for warmth but it'll never arrive. 'You're nice too,' I say, not knowing what I'm really supposed to elucidate back. Two and a half hours later we arrive at a dirt-track too lurid to be a boreen. The house sits on its own scrubland with an abandoned boat stuck on its side filled with compost. No lights. No neighbours. No salvation.

Saturday or Sunday in early glow as Lord Canine and Mrs

Mutt are nowhere. Certain moments are elementary, so simple they become eternal. Photons of electromagnetic radiation travel forty-five billion years to reach earth and we're still only at the stage where microwave ovens are modern. With these moments of clarity we learn to value tiny things . . . chronology makes everything solid and strong. That's what I'm telling myself. We're fuck all on the grand scale. Master has only recently (within the last few weeks) admitted it has all gone very wrong. Intended as a coaching exercise on compliance for me. His stomach is deflated. There are large sores on his legs; hag's faces painted in dangerous red. When I look at them I remember the first satsuma I scoffed in school in 1974, digging my fingernails into the scabrous skin, smelling and tasting the minuscule bursts that shot out onto my chin. He's not speaking much. I too, have lost weight, but am feeling hopeful. During the day I take turns crouching on each bum cheek, still plump enough to supply some cushion at least. If I press up against the front of the bars I can stretch my legs partially lengthways the full width. Up out and over the cluttered window pane full of dusty toby jugs the honeysuckle French kisses the sunlight, bowing to our subjugation. Panicles of whorled branches, purplish-brown, prised open, spreading in fruit. Tufted grass with creeping rhizomes. I've never felt happier scoring the different colours in the sky, diffracted through the air. Here, a field of phantom cattle clump about joylessly scaring the púca that once leapt on a local man's back. We were given a handbook of local legends as our only reading material. The man, who is forever nameless, managed to stab the entity with a penknife and throw it to the ground. When he returned the following day he found a wooden log with a knife-sized hole along one side. 'What was it like fighting in the Falklands?' I ask Master. He doesn't answer straight away. The only avenue of punishment left. 'There was logic to it,' he replies. He hasn't taken the beatings well, sobbing for hours, refusing to communicate or look at me. Squashed into the furthest corner, throwing up some gobbledygook at an absent wife. 'When I get back I'll get the gas boiler serviced love, I'm sorry I've been away so long.' Unlike me, when I reach the puddle of tears, no longer feeling a thing—when Lord Canine uses the really thick rattan cane—it purges every bristle of stress setting me up for the whole of the next day. Our bodies are deeply marked in thick purple stripes. Skin on my thighs broken open a number of times. Pain so excessive and profound, I pass out cold.

In they saunter with a group of five rubber gimps. One doused in duck yellow from head to toe. His rotund vacuum-packed belly and peaked hat a delight in a way. Master whimpers dejectedly. 'Here are our precious doggies!' Mrs Mutt says, pulling out wooden chairs to form a neat row for the spectators to get comfortable. I immediately fall on all fours, turning fast in manic circles so they can see the butt plug with fawn fur tail wagging devotedly. 'Woof woof woof woof!' I say. I've perfected a deep meaningful growl that represents not aggression but cute little playing sounds to please my owners abundantly. 'Isn't she a joy!' one of them in a black and white Victorian maid outfit declares. 'Totally smashing!' says another in a gas mask. God knows what rural hills and crannies they slipped down from for a few lost hours. If they've emerged from the stinking steam of packed dairy sheds or if they've run out of Rosewood French doors in architecturally-designed contemporary bungalows facing strategically southwards. 'What breed is she?' someone else asks. Master flings me a stingy look, very like the first time I climbed into his van and he told me to prepare for a journey like no other. 'She's a Dandy Dinmont Terrier, cheerful nature. He's the opposite, Golden Retriever we'd great hopes for, but he won't even mount her anymore.' Lord Canine piles stray wood into the range. His fetish flippers smacking the ground as he carefully plops about. 'Are the bold doggies hungry? Do the bold doggies want some succulent strips of beef?

Have the bold doggies done pee pees on the floor?' I leap up and tear at the first piece of overcooked meat flung, licking the residue of grease pearls dripping down the fortified steel billets. It's twenty years since I've eaten animal flesh but endurance has taught me to accept every small gift graciously. We're no longer fed from bowls since Master began attacking in rabies-filled fits. Mealtimes triggering his prey drive. As if deep in his medulla oblongata he knows to bite a human moving too quickly. I hear his stomach rumbling like distant thunder muttering imperfectly from the purl of clouds. It's unlikely I'll be able to date a normal bloke after all this is over. I've thought about this a lot. Sitting in a heaving sports bar in Dame Street all faux giddy when Manchester United score a goal. All that droll macho nonsense. When escape comes, whether in three months, eight or a year, I will recall all these particulars. 'We're never getting out,' Master says. I'm shocked his army training hasn't served him in more callous or mercenary ways. He really is a depressed moron. 'It can't be that far to the N4,' I've told him, numerous fucking times. 'Remember we only beetled off the main road for a few kilometres to get here.' Even if it was a miserable day with flea fogs of rain obstructing vision in every direction . . . when our cage is being cleaned and one of them makes the systematic error of turning away for a microsecond, we'd bolt. Once, Master grabbed me by the throat when I described this very scenario, banging my head so hard Mrs Mutt tore in from the sitting room hurling hot tea at his snout causing incalculable torment. 'Whoever picks us up on the main road eventually will hear us yelping like we've never been able to yelp before.' Master bangs his rump against the padlock to get attention.

All five stand up in a splodge of vibrant PVC blushes, making their way to the bars so the rest of the room is concealed from our view. They bend over us, all whoop and holler, pulling at the cage so it tips slightly. We topple about as if inside ferry kennels on top deck on a stormy day. I know exactly what to do. I fling myself on my back and open my legs wide. Two paws scrunched up over clamped breasts, head hanging to the side for a champion view. With the temperature rising I begin to pant heavily, sweating like mad. I make it achingly clear for Master there's only one option left to cool me down, to cool us all down. It rests solely with him now to do his thing and get enough oxygenated blood back into this ecosystem. I pant even more to seal the deal. After it's over we'll curl tightly together, snuggling into well-deserved sleep. Free to run at breakneck speed along the most beautiful sweep of beach. Tearing up lumpy dips of sand so relentlessly our tails stop wagging and our legs collapse under the weight of yummy ecstasy. Running, scampering, sprinting, until nothing we've ever been through before matters.

Acknowledgments

Thank you to all those who helped out in the compiling of this anthology by suggesting authors and texts, especially Sinéad Gleeson, Dave Lordan, Susan Tomaselli, Liam Cagney, Peter Murphy, and John O'Brien. Warm thanks are also due to Alex Andriesse, Nathan Redman, and Catarina Koch at Dalkey Archive for their editorial assistance.

Rights and Permissions

Hillary McTaggart, "A Night on the Tiles," 1973. Reprinted from *The Honest Ulsterman* (issue unknown).

Desmond Hogan, "Kennedy," 2012. Available in *Best European Fiction 2012*. Dalkey Archive Press, 2011.

Dorothy Nelson, *In Night's City*, Merlin Publishing, 1982. Reprinted by Dalkey Archive Press, 2006.

Emer Martin, *Breakfast in Babylon*, Mariner Books, 1996.

Mike McCormack, "The Occupation: A Guide for Tourists," 1996. Available in *Getting It in the Head*. Edinburgh: Canongate Books, 2017.

Philip Ó Ceallaigh, "The Song of Songs," 2010. Available in *The Pleasant Light of Day*. London: Penguin, 2010.

Dave Lordan, "Becoming Polis," 2013. Available in *The First Book of Frags*. Portarlington, Ireland: Wurm Press, 2013.

Jennifer Walshe, *Historical Documents of the Irish Avant-Garde*, 2015. Available from Migro Records, 2015.

Anakana Schofield, *Martin John*, 2015. Windsor, CA: Biblioasis, 2015.

John Holten. *The Readymades*, 2011. Berlin: Broken Dimanche Press, 2011.

June Caldwell, "Leitrim Flip," 2018. Published here for the first time.

Selected Dalkey Archive Paperbacks

www.dalkeyarchive.com

www.dalkeyarchive.com